# PRAISE FOR MARCUS SAKEY'S NOVELS

"Stunning."

*Publishers Weekly*

"Genius."

*Chicago Tribune*

"Brilliant."

*Huffington Post*

"Awesome."

*Kirkus Reviews*

"Gripping."

*io9*

"Surprising."

*Library Journal*

"Triumphant."

*Examiner*

"Compelling."

*Booklist*

"Tour-de-force."

*Cleveland Plain Dealer*

"It's depth and intelligence and passion and emotion that sets Sakey apart."
Lee Child

"Epic, compulsively readable, and thought-provoking to the very last sentence."
Blake Crouch

# AFTER LIFE

**OTHER TITLES BY MARCUS SAKEY**

# AFTER LIFE

## MARCUS SAKEY

THOMAS & MERCER

Text copyright © 2017 by Marcus Sakey
All rights reserved.

Published by Thomas & Mercer, Seattle

www.apub.com

Amazon, the Amazon logo, and Thomas & Mercer are trademarks of Amazon.com, Inc., or its affiliates.

ISBN-13: 9781477848470 (hardcover)
ISBN-10: 1477848479 (hardcover)
ISBN-13: 9781477848401 (paperback)
ISBN-10: 1477848401 (paperback)

Cover design by Shasti O'Leary Soudant

Printed in the United States of America

First edition

*It's a joy and a privilege to make my living spinning stories.*
*And so beloved reader, fellow dreamer:*
*This book is for you, with gratitude.*

# ONE

He was born into cramped alleys and foul air, fish-stink and garbage and the Bellman's call—*Remember the clocks, look well to your locks.* London, in the year of their Lord 1532. Father in the wind, mother barely remembered, he grew on the streets, working when there was work, begging and stealing and renting himself when not, and when he first saw *Persephone* bobbing in a halo of sun on a cloudy day, he thought her a promise someone should have made him.

He was thin and pale and restless of mind, unclear why some were born to silks and some to slavery, and unwilling to let things lie. Edmund watched the caravel unload, watched the sailors stagger to land. Amongst them he saw an apprentice no older than himself, and he followed as they laughed their way to a filthy alehouse with a sign in the shape of an anchor, where they drank watered beer by the gallon. When the boy went for a piss in the alley, Edmund buried a blade in the nape of his neck, sliding it up and twisting.

The next morning *Persephone* sailed with a new apprentice. Edmund worked himself raw and always had a joke, and the men liked him, taught him the ways of salt and sail. He slept on the deck, woke to kicks and curses, to clean air and sunshine, and for the first time knew what it meant to be happy. He learned his knots and took his lashes, ate salt beef and dry ship's biscuit infested with weevils, saw the New World and found it less than he had hoped, just land and trees and brown men.

The storm caught them two weeks into the return voyage. The sky was black and the sea was foam, and they journeyed not across the waves but up them, rising to the peaks of moving mountains, hanging for a heartbeat before plummeting into the canyons beyond. Edmund heard *Persephone* scream, watched the boatswain swept overboard along with the main mast, and as a wave high as London's Tower blotted out the world, he lashed himself to the foredeck and thought of praying but didn't see the point.

He woke to a world scoured clean. The sun burned fierce and the sea lay smooth, and the ship rode low and crippled, masts and sails and most of her crew stripped away. Of clean rainwater there was plenty, but the hold had been torn open and cargo and provisions lost.

The captain, his chest crushed in the storm, lingered in fever for two days, crying out to the Lord; and perhaps the Lord heard him, for on the morning of the third he was dead. The seven remaining men looked at one another, each harboring the same thought but unwilling to speak it.

The rats that had once fouled their food became their food. But soon the rats were gone.

After two more days of hunger, the barber and the cook broke down the captain's body. All of them ate, though no man looked at the others as he did so.

But Edmund, unwilling to let things lie, knew that with a split hull and no sails, any voyage to land would be a long one. A full belly made his mind sharp, and he saw that there was plenty of meat to be taken if a man had the will.

The barber was discovered in the hold, razor in his hand and throat open. A mortal sin, all agreed. This time there was no delay in eating, though still the men did not look at one another.

*Persephone* drifted, at the mercy of current and Christ.

When a sailor's drowned body was found tangled in lines over the port side, the men agreed he must have fallen overboard in the night. They said a rough prayer, and the cook went to work.

And still there was no land. The sun burned furious and the wind did not blow.

In accident and suicide, one by one the crew fell, until at last there were only two. The cook declared it was punishment from God, that they were to wander forever to pay for the crime of eating another man's flesh.

Edmund agreed, and together they prayed forgiveness.

He killed the man with the same blade he'd used to buy passage on *Persephone*. Edmund had watched as the cook had broken down the bodies of their companions, and though it was his first time, he thought he did well. He salted and smoked the meat, and ate his grisly rations staring at the horizon.

Weeks it had been since the storm broke them, and weeks more did Edmund drift.

And then one morning, long out of food, scorched delirious by the sun, he raised his head from the deck and saw land.

He wasn't more than a mile from it when he died.

———

It weren't really so different.

Edmund splashed to shore, wobbly on steady land. Stood looking. Waiting for judgment. Prepared, after weeks of naught but sun and sea and the twisting emptiness of his belly, for either angelic choir or wine-taloned demon.

Neither appeared, nor any other soul beside. Water lapped the coast. The breeze stirred trees grown freakish tall. A shallow creek trickled into the sand.

Red berries adorned the bushes.

Edmund threw himself on them, devoured fruit by the sticky handful. After, he lay on his belly to suckle the seep of icy water. When he'd had his fill he flopped on his back and reflected that the priests hadn't known so much. A hundred times he'd eaten on their charity, promising his soul for a crust of bread, and always considered himself to have gotten the better of the bargain. Here now was proof of it.

Eventually, he set to walking.

Salt on one side, forest the other, but the sea he knew and the trees he feared. A child of London, he'd never seen anything like it. Green grown so tall and tight that the space beneath was coolest shadow. Each breath of wind through the leaves seemed a whisper, a call to come lose himself, let dirt fill his mouth and roots grow through his chest.

The sky changed constantly yet stayed the same, the sun never more than a paler spot edging from horizon to horizon. No gulls soared the wind, no insects hummed in the long grasses. Alone, he wandered the dominion of death. At night thick clouds hid stars and moon, pouring down darkness so complete a man could hide from himself. He slept on shore, shivering in piles of needles and leaves.

After some days he came upon a broad river emptying slowly into the sea, and alongside it a circle of domed huts covered in brush. Neither smoke nor sound rose from the village. It were as if abandoned; as if some forgotten race had built this thing as a monument to their own vanishing. Edmund watched from behind a cluster of boulders the whole of the afternoon, but saw no others.

The huts were clever constructions of wood bent and lashed, of grasses woven into roofs. They were filled with the savages' possessions, clay pots and garments of animal hide and strange many-seeded plants. He imagined the hut alive, a woman preparing food, child slung at her breast. He could almost see her pause in the pounding of her grain; could imagine her squinting at the place he stood, wondering why her hands had grown clumsy and the nipple had tugged from a squalling mouth.

Edmund took dried fish from the rafters and sat in the doorway, watching the sky dim. Thinking of the stories he had heard of the world that came after life and pondering why any man believed them. For only one who had made the journey could speak; and even he could not be certain, for who knew if this pale and clouded place were the end? Them that claimed knowledge were fools or profiteers, and neither could be depended upon, for surely Edmund must be damned for all he had done, and yet this seemed no punishment.

He slept beneath a deerskin cloak on a mat of reeds, and knew he was not alone in the bed. Though he could not see them, could not feel or smell them, surely a man and woman rested there too. He wondered if their dreams were troubled.

He awoke in Hell.

A demon leered above him, man-shaped but for the quills and feathers sprouting from its head and the sounds that ushered from its mouth, guttural grunts and clicks of flashing teeth. Edmund lurched back and saw that behind the creature there was another, naked from the waist up with heavy brown dugs dangling. The man-demon raised a spear, and it were only luck that Edmund managed to get the deerskin onto it, the weight of the hide dragging down the shaft and allowing him space to leap forward and put his knife in the devil's chest.

Blood sprayed, and in that hot baptism, Edmund was reborn.

He lived as an Unalachtigo of the tortoise totem. Ran the forests with the other children, gaming and quarrelling, learning the ways of trap and net, fowl and fish.

As he grew, he watched the women plant maize and pumpkin, and yearned—and saw his stare returned.

By flickering firelight, he touched his new wife, the musk of her neck, the sweat of her belly, the clutch as he entered her.

In a swirl of cold clean snow, he held his tiny son in both hands, and wondered at the greatness of the Creator.

Reeking ferocious, the bear was hate and heat, a blow from one paw tearing open his woman even as he charged to her, claws and teeth and dank breath, a ripping of himself, like tearing the oily flesh from a bird's bone—

Edmund stood in the wigwam. Himself, again. The meat of the man he had been fell to the floor. The woman he'd known as wife stared in horror.

This time, when she spoke her strange clicking tongue, he understood it. She was cursing him.

A life, in an instant. A story gulped down like meat. Edmund was flush with it, filled with it, lit from within.

He looked at the woman and remembered sliding into the heat of her. And remembered the times stronger men had taken their pleasure of him, sometimes paying and others not.

The woman must have seen his thoughts. She bolted, bare brown feet flashing.

He smiled, and pursued her down the hunting trail toward the forest he no longer feared.

If this were Hell, he'd make a home of it.

# TWO

Chicago had gone strange.

Instead of blasting down the street with his foot to the floor, Brody should have been driving in jerking intervals, honking at taxis and cursing cyclists.

The sidewalks should have been packed with commuters and tourists and students. Crowds should have overspilled the corners, heads bobbing to earbuds. The nannies pushing strollers, the homeless rattling cups. Gaudy shopping bags and little dogs on leashes and *Do you have a minute for Greenpeace?*

But the sidewalks were forsaken. The crosswalks abandoned.

The few pedestrians moved erratically, heads up, trying to stare in every direction at once. When Brody's tires squealed, a woman in a business suit dropped prone on the concrete, her hands covering her head.

He blew past the Shell station on Jackson. Massive blue tarps enclosed the whole structure, the plastic rippling in the October wind. Most of the gas stations had done that, wrapped themselves like Christmas presents from mental patients.

Two blocks farther, an Orange Line train rattled into the platform above the avenue. No one got off. No one got on. The doors closed, and the El rumbled north.

As an elementary school blurred past, he spotted a military Humvee parked on the sidewalk. Men with buzz cuts and bulletproof vests stood guard, automatic rifles pointing downward. The playground equipment was abandoned. The swings stirred in the wind as though ridden by ghosts.

He held the accelerator down, the engine's roar counterpointing sirens screaming in from every direction. Chicago PD had been working to refine the roadblocks, dropping a net of concentric circles around any attack. It was a good idea in theory, but he hated the reactive nature of it, the implied surrender—

There.

The intersection was broad and generic: a bank, a Starbucks, a hotel. The northwest corner was a Mariano's, one of the grocery stores thrown up in the last few years to provide for all the new West Loop lofts.

Brody lived in one of the new West Loop lofts, and knew the store well. Three stories of glass and white brick, most of the street level given over to a parking lot, covered but open walled. The blue lights of a squad car parked in the middle of a lane cast garish shadows. He jerked to a stop behind it. A dozen people milled in a ring, skittish as cats. They kept swiveling their heads from the bright daylight to the shape at the center of the circle.

"Move!"

In the midst of the bystanders lay a woman. She was on her back, one leg awkwardly crumpled. Her chest was a mass of gore. A cop knelt astride her, trying to put pressure on the wound as he leaned in to blow air into her lungs. She'd dropped her bags, and her groceries were strewn around her, apples and bananas and coffee and a frozen pizza and a container of vanilla ice cream that had broken open on impact.

Number seventeen.

The shot had been precise. One moment she'd been walking from the grocery store, eco-conscious canvas bags on her shoulder, car keys in hand. Then her chest had exploded.

Had she been considering what to cook for dinner? Looking forward to seeing her husband or child? Remembering a favorite scene from a movie?

*She was probably thinking of the man about to kill her.*

Everyone knew that Chicago was a big city, and that the odds of being targeted were tiny. But on a gut level, everyone was certain that they were. That's what terror did. Terror shut down the higher impulses, love and thought and creativity, and supplanted them with brain-stem fear. It turned human beings into field mice skittering for cover, expecting the hawk's shadow and the pinch of talons.

The degradation made Brody almost as angry as the murders.

"Who are you?" The cop was a big guy, his belly straining below his bulletproof vest. His name badge read J. SOKOLOFSKY. He had his sidearm out.

"Will Brody, FBI." He fished for his ID with his left hand. "You the first on scene?"

"We'd just stopped for coffee." Sokolofsky started to gesture at the Starbucks with his gun. Brody caught it, said, "Whoa. Put that away."

"What?" The cop flushed, holstered the pistol. "Right."

"Did you see anything?"

"No. Just heard it, came running."

Brody turned to the city around him. Gauging sight lines, looking for bright flashes in dark windows. Not staring at any particular thing, just running his eyes over the world to see if anything stuck out. It was a way of seeing he'd developed on deployment, where everything had to be assessed in terms of potential threat. Minarets weren't graceful towers raised in praise of Allah; they were sniper nests. Winding streets weren't evidence of a picturesque history; they were death traps where bullets rode the walls and the barrel of an AK could jut from any window. As sirens screamed in and helicopter rotors whapped closer, Chicago felt more like Fallujah than like the home he'd known his whole life.

*It's amazing,* Brody thought, *what someone with a sense of theater and a rifle can do to civilization.*

———

On September 19th, four people were murdered in two hours.

Jerrie Simpson, a nurse and mother of three, had been playing Candy Crush and waiting for the El. She probably hadn't even heard the shot.

Michael Dillman, on the other hand, lived for almost ten minutes. The 911 tape of his wife begging for help had been replayed ceaselessly.

Larry Wong was pumping gas into his taxi when a bullet tore open his throat.

Dr. Riya Kumar was enjoying a few moments reading on a fine fall day. If a patient hadn't cancelled on her, she'd still be alive.

There was no connection between the victims. No connection between the thirteen killed since. The sniper had published no manifesto, issued no demands. He hadn't taunted the police or sent cryptic messages to the news. He—recovered DNA confirmed it was a man—had not been claimed by ISIS or al-Qaeda or white supremacists. If he was a terrorist, he didn't have a cause.

He just killed and vanished.

*Maybe the terror* is *the cause,* Brody thought. *If so, he's winning. He's remade my city in his image.*

"Everyone," he said, turning to the crowd, his credentials high. "I'm Agent Will Brody of the FBI. Did anyone see anything?"

The people looked at one another, looked at him, looked edgily at the skyline.

"Anything at all out of the ordinary. A car or a truck driving too fast. A window washer who didn't look right. A puff of smoke."

"I saw her fall," a woman said. Her fingers worked each other like prayer beads. "We got to the door at the same time." Her eyes suddenly wide. "Oh my god. Oh my *god.*"

"Ma'am?" Brody stepped toward her. "What did you see?"

"I . . . we got to the door at the same time, and I told her to go ahead." Her voice was manic, the words tumbling out almost atop one another. "She smiled at me, and I told her to go ahead. If I hadn't, would I . . . would she . . . I didn't know this was going to happen. I was just being polite. I didn't know—"

"It's not your fault." Brody touched her shoulder. "You didn't do this."

An ambulance screamed into the lot, the doors winging open. The cop astride the woman stood up. His trousers were soaked in blood, his hands dripping red. Two EMTs rushed over, one holding a resuscitator, the other pushing a gurney.

Brody knew they were too late. The woman was gone. Whatever hopes she'd cherished had been stolen. The little moments that made up a life were no longer hers. She would never finish the book she'd been reading. Never call her mother. Never enjoy the Sunday *Times,* eat sushi, check e-mail. Five minutes ago she had been a person. Now she was nothing.

"How is this happening?" Sokolofsky's face was pale.

"Start collecting names," Brody said. "No one leaves until they've been interviewed."

The pudgy cop nodded.

The air reeked of exhaust and the copper tang of blood. More police cars were squealing in. Helicopters hovered like dragonflies. The EMTs had transferred the woman to the gurney and were pulling a sheet over her.

Brody walked to where she'd fallen, scooped up her purse from the pile of groceries. The interior was a jumble of everyday objects, a life writ small: sunglasses and iPhone and keys and a Clif Bar and chapstick and gum and hand sanitizer and headphones. He took out her wallet. The driver's license had her name as Emily Watkins. In the photograph, she wore a coy smile, equal parts mischief and warmth. It looked practiced, a stock expression she probably pulled out whenever a camera was pointed her way. Her phone was locked, but he'd bet if he were to scroll through the photos, she'd wear the same smile in most of them. The address was on Aberdeen, two blocks from Morgan. They'd been neighbors.

In the five minutes since the shot, the parking lot had become a riot of activity. Officers spoke to witnesses, hoping that this time, someone, anyone, had seen something. A ring of cops held back a crowd of spectators, most of whom had their phones out, recording Emily's body being loaded into the ambulance. Brody never ceased to be baffled, bemused, and frustrated by people's appetite for ugly. *Hey, look, her blood is running into the melting ice cream! Quick, Instagram it.*

He shook his head and went to the ambulance. One of the EMTs was inside, maneuvering the head of the gurney. The other was pushing from the back end, but as he leaned in to lock it in place, the stethoscope slipped from his neck. The tech bent to snatch it before it hit the ground.

When he did, the brake light of the ambulance shattered. Which was weird, because the guy hadn't been anywhere near it—

Brody grabbed the medic's shoulders and hurled him sideways, the man's face contorting in surprise just as the sound waves of the sniper's shot caught up to the bullet. The tech stumbled, tripped, and sprawled to the ground. Brody followed in an awkward dive. Something whipped through the air behind him, a screaming hum like a furious bee, the second bullet missing by inches, the crack arriving a fraction of a second afterward, a distant echoing report. He hit gracelessly and hard, but the pain was far away. Someone started screaming, and the gawkers began to shove and jostle and drop. Police knelt behind their squad cars, pulling weapons and staring in different directions.

The medic was scrambling like a crab, his back to the tire, good, he was out of the line, which freed Brody to wriggle forward on elbows and knees, head low as he stared beneath the ambulance—

Rapid flashes of bright light in the distance, onetwothreefourfive, and by the time he'd counted the fifth the first had already slammed into the side of the ambulance with a metal *thunk* followed by four more. The shots had come from an alley tucked between two squat buildings three or four blocks away.

*There you are.*

Brody stood and took off at a sprint, grabbing the edge of the ambulance to slingshot himself around it. He circled one police car, leapt onto the hood of another and ran across it, his shoes bonging on the steel. Jumped off that and dashed into the street, the traffic already at a standstill, everyone locked down by the checkpoints, and as he ran between the lanes of cars he caught peripheral flashes of the people within, men huddling beneath steering wheels, a mom in the back of an SUV struggling to unbuckle her daughter's car seat. It was only now, sprinting down the street, that it occurred to him how exposed he was.

Brody leaned into the run.

A block before the alley he darted between parked cars, leapt onto the sidewalk, then put his back to the building and drew his sidearm, holding it low in two hands. He moved fast, eyes glued to the mouth of the alley. His pulse was racing and he could hear his breath over the sirens and helicopters. Thirty steps, twenty, ten.

Brody blew two fast exhales and spun around the corner, leading with the Glock. A typical Chicago alley, telephone poles and the sweet stink of trash, the ground pitted and pebbled. No one in sight. Three dumpsters, two of them locked shut.

The chain for the third lay in a heap. The lid was open.

Brody checked the angle of the late-afternoon sun, sidestepped so his shadow wouldn't give him away. Stalked forward, weapon up, finger on the trigger. The dumpster revealed itself inch by inch. The garbage had been shoved to one side, leaving an area big enough for a man to kneel. A collection of ejected brass cartridges shone dull against the rusted metal.

Abandoned amidst them was half a cigarette, the tip still glowing.

A trail of smoke rose, twisting, ephemeral, to vanish into the air.

# THREE

Two hours later, Brody stared through the windshield at a five-story building. Once a factory of some sort, it had been converted to condos. New balconies attached to old brick, wide windows with bright curtains. A rack for bicycles. A boutique coffeehouse across the street. He'd never really noticed it, but knew it in a peripheral sort of way. It was on Aberdeen, two blocks from his own loft on Morgan.

He had a headache, and his suit was stained and torn. He wanted to go home and sit in the shower for an hour and not think.

Instead he got out of the car, walked to the front of the building, and pressed the button marked #411. After a moment, a man's voice crackled back through. "Yes?"

"Mr. Watkins?"

"Yes, who is this?"

"Sir, my name is Will Brody. I'm an agent with the Federal Bureau of Investigation."

"Ummm . . . okay. What can I do for you?"

He hesitated. There were a few moments in a life when everything changed. Intractable moments that divided time into before and after. Chad Watkins didn't know it, but he was on the cusp of one. Wasn't there a certain kindness in delaying that, even by a few seconds?

"Hello?"

"Buzz me in please, sir. We need to talk."

———

"I don't understand." Chad Watkins sat on a vibrant red sofa in the center of his bright living room. Feet on the rug, elbows on knees, hands clasped together. Leaning in with his head slightly cocked. "What do you mean Emily is . . . I don't understand."

"I'm sorry. Emily is dead." Brody forced himself to speak in a level, clear voice. He hated the way the words came out, wanted to say "passed away" or "expired," but one was misleading and the other insulting. Emily Watkins hadn't drifted off after a long illness. And she wasn't a carton of milk. Pretty lies weren't going to shield Chad from anything. "She was shot and killed this afternoon."

"That can't be. She has a dentist's appointment tomorrow."

"I'm very sorry."

"Wait. This is a joke, right? One of Emily's pranks. You're from the troupe—"

"No," Brody said more sharply than he intended. He took a breath. Fought the urge to look away. What was he doing here? Normally CPD informed the next of kin. But they'd been neighbors, and it had seemed like something he should do. "No jokes."

"What . . . was it him?" Chad's eyes went wide. "I got a news alert on my phone that there had been another victim. Was that her? Was that Emily?"

Jesus. Brody sometimes wondered if the reason there seemed to be so many more crazies in the world these days was that they all had a platform. "I'm afraid so."

Chad stared at him. His hands trembled. He opened his mouth, but no words came out. Suddenly he lurched upward, his feet almost tangling in his hurry to stand. Brody rose too, reached out to steady him, but Chad jerked away. He pressed his fingers into his forehead until the tips turned white.

Brody studied him for a moment. Then turned and walked past the sofa toward the kitchen. His eyes cataloged details automatically. A banquet table with artfully arranged knickknacks and a stack of mail. A framed 8 x 10 of Chad and Emily on their wedding day, goofing around downtown, him in a tux, tight-roping on the railing of a bridge while Emily threw her head back in laughter, a bouquet clutched to her chest. The exercise bike in the corner had dust on the pedals. An open-frame bookcase was stacked with novels and photography books. An orange-and-white cat dozed on a sunny windowsill, oblivious.

The kitchen opened off the living room, and Brody went to the cabinets by the sink. Opened doors, seeing plates, liquor, spices, finally the glasses. He took out a tumbler and filled it with water.

He returned and held the glass out. After a moment, Chad took it. Lifted it to his lips and drank tentatively, then again. When he set the glass on the coffee table, Brody noticed he used a coaster. "What happened?"

"We're still investigating. She had just come out of Mariano's and was on the way to her car." He hesitated. "It was very quick. She wouldn't have felt any pain."

"Why?"

"She was shot in the heart and—"

"Why?" Chad repeated, and Brody realized what he meant.

It wasn't really "why?"; it was "how?"

How was it possible that when he kissed his wife this morning, he hadn't known it was the last time? How could something so important pass unnoticed?

How could you spend decades trying to be decent and good, finding someone to love, building a life together, only to have it all taken in an instant?

How could there be no reason?

How could this be the way it worked?

How?

"I don't know," Brody said.

They sat in silence for a moment. The clock on the banquet table ticked softly. Brody wondered which had been Emily's favorite spot. If she preferred the sofa, or if she liked to curl up in the chair where he now sat.

"I don't believe it," Chad said. He glanced at his phone. "It's after six. She should be getting home soon. I'm making Bolognese. We're re-watching *The Wire*."

Brody nodded. He didn't know what else to do.

"Is there something I . . ." Chad picked up the water glass, then set it down again. "Emily's body, should I . . ."

"There's no rush."

"Why did he choose her?"

"I don't know."

"She never hurt anybody. She's a graphic designer." Chad rubbed at his eyes. "God, why haven't you caught him?"

"We will. This is one of the biggest law enforcement task forces in history. There are literally thousands of people working to catch him—"

"Who cares?"

"We're doing everything—"

"*Who cares.*" The man turned to him. "What good does it do if you catch him tomorrow? I don't care about tomorrow." His voice was harsh, a wounded boxer throwing punches at random. "Why didn't you catch him yesterday?"

Brody held his gaze. Thought of a dozen answers. Pictured the shattered brake light on the ambulance. Remembered the mother he'd seen trying to unbuckle her daughter from a car seat as he sprinted toward the alley.

"Before I joined the FBI," he said slowly, "I was a Marine. This was right after 9/11. I wanted to help, most of us did. We had the idea that we could take care of a few bad guys and then everything would work out." He shook his head. "I knew a lot of people who died. Good people and bad. There's no logic to it. Or at least, no rules that I understand. Maybe God does, but I don't."

Brody set a business card on the glass coffee table and then rose slowly. "I'm sorry, Mr. Watkins. I'm really sorry I couldn't save her."

He had reached the door when he heard the man say, "Agent Brody?"

"Yes?"

"Will you promise me something?"

"What?"

"Catch the man that did this. Whatever it takes. You catch him."

He turned. Chad was staring at his shoes, and Brody waited until the man looked up at him, until their eyes were locked. Tried to put into the gaze all his sympathy and all his regret and all his rage.

Then he said, "Count on it."

# FOUR

Claire McCoy sat in her desk chair and watched a press conference featuring Claire McCoy.

It was now 11:02 p.m., according to the clock in the corner of her laptop. She'd gone in front of the cameras more than three hours ago, but the sniper had the attention of the nation, and given the lack of compelling visuals—footage of the bodies was restricted for privacy reasons—CNN kept running the short clip like it was news. It wasn't; it was just Claire standing in front of a podium and saying that they were doing everything they could, that the investigation was massive, and asking for calm.

Her phone rang. She stared at it. Lately she'd been developing an unreasonable fear of it ringing. Every time it did, it might be someone calling to tell her that the sniper had killed again.

*No,* she thought, *he's already had his sacrifice today.*

And on the heels of that, *Past patterns are not accurate predictors of future behavior. After all, he changed his methods when he hung around to shoot at a medic.*

And finally, *Stop being an idiot and answer your phone.*

"McCoy."

"ASAC McCoy, please hold for Director Mikkelson."

"Sure." Claire leaned back in her chair. Out the windows, the sky was as dark as it ever got, October clouds lit the color of fading bruises.

On television, murders were solved with brilliant intuitive leaps. Reality was about grinding it out. Investigating every reasonable clue, every flagged tip, every profiler's hunch. Managing the team, interfacing with other agencies, securing resources, coordinating with local law enforcement, feeding the media enough to keep them from airing wild theories but not so much they overshared. It was the job, and it worked, eventually, but in the meantime—

"Claire."

"Director, good evening."

"Nice job on the press conference. Just the right tone, sympathetic, determined."

"To be honest, for once I wish CNN would say, 'Folks, this is terrible, but we literally have nothing new to tell you, so just, I don't know, be good to one another.'"

Mikkelson gave a one-syllable laugh that was all nose. "What's the interpretation of his attempting a second victim?"

"We suspect he's losing control. Today's escalation was a bigger risk than he's taken before. It also supports the likeliest profile, that he's former military. Terrorists have been using that method for years: one attack to draw first responders, the second to target them directly."

"Wouldn't that also support the theory that he's a foreign radical?"

"Behavioral Science says no. The feeling is that if there were any group affiliation, he would have been claimed by now."

"Hmm. Anything else to report?"

"Nothing of note. ERT is still analyzing the rifling, but the bullet is a .223, consistent with previous victims. No prints. We recovered DNA from a cigarette, but of course we already had DNA, just no database match. No witnesses or closed-circuit footage of use . . ."

She laid out the technical details, but the shorthand was that from an investigative standpoint, the murder of Emily Watkins had been meaningless. In the Wikipedia page that would one day exist, the future entry chronicling this crisis, Emily's name would appear in a table between Luis Orlando and whoever came tomorrow. Her name would not be bolded, would not have a side note saying that this was where the sniper made a mistake, where law enforcement found the clue that let them end this madness.

*It's a bad habit,* Claire thought, *thinking of the present in terms of future Wikipedia. Especially while talking to the director of the FBI.*

Mikkelson said, "What's this I hear about an agent running down the street?"

Claire grimaced. "Special Agent William Brody spotted muzzle flashes during the second attack, and pursued."

"A hot shot?"

"A good agent with impulse control issues. He also saved the life of the EMT."

"Alright. How's morale?"

"It's . . . everyone is feeling it."

"If you need more resources, just ask."

"It's not that." She blew a breath. "The sniper is different from anything I've ever seen. It's almost like . . ."

"Yes?"

"Never mind. Just thinking out loud."

"Claire, there's a reason I promoted you. Tell me what's on your mind."

"Well, it's like he's being guided. He seems to know exactly what not to do. Exactly where our blind spots are. Like he's working with someone, maybe even someone in law enforcement."

"Hmm." The director paused. "Okay. Check it out."

"Yes, sir."

"And Claire. We—the FBI, the city of Chicago, the nation—we need this to end. You have my full faith and confidence. But get it done."

"Yes, sir."

After they hung up, Claire stood, put her palms on her sacrum, bent backward. Didn't get a pop, but it still felt good.

She wanted to sit down and get back to work. To push her way through this on sheer will and effort, as she'd done at Georgetown, at Quantico, in every posting since. But there was nothing to do. Sitting at her desk wouldn't change that.

11:21 p.m.

She picked up the phone, dialed. "This is Claire McCoy. I'm heading out. Call my cell with anything."

"Yes, ma'am. Have a good evening."

There was a cold inch of coffee in her mug, and she drank it. Her eyes felt like they'd been dipped in sand. She closed her computer, tucked it in her bag.

*Get it done,* she thought. *Yeah.*

---

The streets were abandoned. The YES, WE'RE OPEN signs in bar windows had a whiff of desperation. A CPD squad car turned from a light and pulled in behind her. Claire could see a cop typing her license plate into the system and flashed the spinners to save them all time. The officer nodded and threw a half salute.

Longevity in law enforcement demanded compartmentalization. It was an intense job with demanding hours and high stakes, but still a job. You had to be able to work a case for months or even years, to stare at brutalized victims and burned bodies, and still be able to go home and have a life.

At least, that's what everyone told her.

At her building, she parked in the deck, walked to the elevator, and slumped against the wall. When they caught this guy she was going to sleep for a week and get every spa service known to woman. Soft chimes marked each floor, and for a second she might have drifted off, because it didn't seem like there had been nearly enough to reach the twenty-first.

Claire unlocked the door to her apartment, switched on the lights, dropped her bag. She wandered to the kitchen, opened the fridge, discovered leftover Thai. That was a happiness. Squeeze on half a bottle of Sriracha, eat it straight from the container, maybe take a shower, maybe not, then go to bed and get a full seven hours—

"Hey."

The voice came from behind her. Claire dropped the noodles and spun, hand flying to her hip, the Glock coming out smooth as she aimed—

At Will Brody, who sat in the chair by the window, a couple of empty beer bottles on the table beside. "Whoa," he said, putting up his hands.

"Jesus Christ. What the hell, Brody?" She lowered her sidearm. "What are you doing sitting in my apartment in the dark?"

He snapped on a light, then stood up. "Waiting for you." He stepped forward, his eyes intense.

"I've had a long day."

"Me too, ma'am." Brody squared up in front of her, uncomfortably close. She held her ground. He reached out, touched her shoulder. Her adrenaline was still up, and she could smell his aftershave and a whiff of soap. His eyes never left hers as he slid his fingers down, barely touching her, skimming the outside curve of her breast, down her side, tracing the lines of her stomach, then her hips. "So I decided to go home."

"This is my apartment."

"This is your apartment," Brody agreed. He stepped closer still, so she could feel the warmth of him, see the gold flecks in his eyes. One hand slipped around her back, the other cupping her neck, tangling in her hair. "And *this* is home."

The kiss started soft, but his hand drifted lower and pulled her pelvis against him. She could feel the muscles of his chest, the heat of him, and she holstered her gun and put her arms around his head, gripping handfuls of hair, the kiss turning bruising, the rough skin of his face scraping at her lips and chin. When he moaned she could feel it against her whole body, and she tugged harder on his hair until the moan became a gasp. His right hand pushed her skirt up to bunch around her waist and with his left he fumbled to undo his belt, metal clinking, the buckle cold and hard, and then he pushed his pants down and jerked her panties aside and hoisted her into the air to press against the hardness of him.

She gasped, the sensation too strong, too sudden, too sharp, but in the best possible way, her body responding even as she pulled away. He held her tighter, not letting her retreat as he stumbled to the wall, the pants around his legs giving him a convict's stumble, her holster clip coming free and the Glock falling to the floor with a thump, and she laughed, giddy with the moment. The wall was cool against her shoulders as he pressed against her and she was ready, Jesus, what was it about him that she could be ready so fast and of course now he decided to tease, sliding against her, between her. She arched her pelvis to capture him, but he wouldn't let her, the friction delicious but not enough. Claire took a hand from his hair and gripped his left nipple and pinched like she was popping Bubble Wrap, so hard his knees wobbled. He pulled her off the wall just far enough to slam her back into it, the picture frames shaking, and eased into her, as gentle there as he'd been rough with the rest, short strokes taking him into her an inch, and then two, holding there until she clawed at his back and jammed herself down the length of him and they both shuddered.

The nearest picture vibrated and bounced against the wall. Not long after it finally fell, he gripped her hard, thrust deep enough to hurt, and exploded inside her.

She blew her bangs out of her eyes and looked at him and said, "I win."

"You win." Without withdrawing he slid a hand between them, thumb finding her clit and rubbing delicate swirls that made her lean in and bite his shoulder, the taste of cotton in her mouth as wave after wave shook her, took her, wrung her out.

When she finally stopped shaking, they were both panting and slick with sweat. Her skirt twisted halfway around. Gun on the floor, handcuffs jamming into the small of her back. The picture, a landscape she'd bought at a DC art festival, was half-obscured by a jagged lightning bolt of shattered glass. It was ridiculous, and she started laughing. Will buried his face in her neck and laughed with her.

When they could breathe again, she said, "That was some serious Nicholas Sparks crap, your line about this being home."

"Hey, it worked." He leaned back, lifted her off him, both of them shivering at the separation. "You hungry?"

"Starving."

———

She pulled a beer from the fridge, then changed into a robe and returned to the kitchen. The leftover Thai was all over the cabinets. While she cleaned it up, he banged around in her kitchen, putting a pan on the stove and staring into the fridge.

"You have no food."

"You say that every night."

"Because you have no food." He took out a container of eggs, a sad lemon, half an onion in a Ziploc bag. He was shirtless now, the tiny silver cross his mom had given him nestled in his chest hair.

She said, "So what the *hell* were you thinking?"

"Huh?"

"Charging down the street like that. Cops on scene said that you didn't even use cover. Just ran your big dumb head off. You know you were running toward a *sniper*, right?"

He laughed. "Yeah, that occurred to me too."

"The city's going crazy already, the last thing we need is footage of a dead FBI agent. I had the director asking me about it. Seriously, Will, what were you thinking?"

"Honestly?" Brody leaned the knife on its point and sighed. "I was thinking, 'That's him, right there, the guy who just killed an innocent woman, and he's *right there*.'" He shrugged and resumed chopping onions. "Maybe it wasn't smart, but I couldn't not."

A few months ago, if someone had told Claire that just after taking a leadership position, she would start sleeping with another agent—one who reported to her—she would have told them to adjust their meds. No chance, zero, that she would make such a stupid mistake. The Bureau was more progressive than a lot of law enforcement, but only about 20 percent of agents were women, and that percentage plummeted with rank. Female agents couldn't afford impropriety. Especially if they had her ambition.

Then she'd met Will, and he'd given her that smile. It was hard to say why it made her feel the way it did. He was good-looking, but it wasn't like he sported a shock-and-awe George Clooney grin. It wasn't even an aesthetic thing, really. It was more like a sense of recognition. Like they were old friends pretending to meet for the first time in order to pull everybody else's leg.

And since then, despite the fact that it was a terrible idea wrapped in terrible timing, they'd been doing this. Retreating to her apartment every night and pulling the world closed behind them. When it came to routine, schedule, and rest, girl meeting boy had been akin to trailer park meeting tornado. And yet she knew what he meant about home. They had become each other's calm.

Of course, there were reasons why cross-rank relationships were a bad idea. Claire couldn't say for sure that she'd be reacting the same way to another agent right now. Was she annoyed because he'd broken protocol, or because she cared about him?

*And then there's the other question—would you want to be with a man who'd played it safe while a killer escaped?*

Tricky. Claire decided she was too tired to deal with it now. "You're a moron."

"See, that just calls your taste into question." Brody looked up and winked. "Find anything on the scene?"

She shook her head. "Nothing useful."

"So we're still waiting."

"No. We're investigating every credible theory, running down tip line—"

"Yeah."

"You know the frustrating part?" Claire gestured with her beer. "Eventually we're going to catch this guy, and he's going to turn out to be a loser who watched *Batman* too many times and got turned on by the wrong character."

"You blame Heath Ledger?"

"Hell no. I wouldn't be an agent if it weren't for Jodie Foster."

"A census taker once tried to test me," Brody replied. "I ate his liver with some fava beans and a nice Chianti." The onions sizzled as he dropped them in butter, stirred them around. "Chips?"

"Pantry. I'm just saying there won't be an explanation, and that bugs me."

"Because you want everything to mean something." Brody crushed handfuls of corn chips into the eggs. He had nice forearms, muscular, enough hair to mark him as a man without crossing over to gorilla. "I get it. You're anal."

"Ha-ha. I can't help it if I think. One of us has to."

"Ouch."

"I'm not crazy, though, am I? Things have gotten weirder. More surreal. Kids walking into schools with automatic weapons. Assholes in costume opening fire in movie theaters. That guy in Michigan, the Uber driver, who picked up fares between killing strangers." Claire leaned forward to prop her chin on her elbow. "I miss Ted Kaczynski."

He laughed. "The Unabomber?"

"It must have been so good to catch him. Genius IQ, Harvard at sixteen, messed up by CIA mind-control experiments. Moves to the woods and mails bombs to engineers to provoke an anti-industrialist revolution. Nuts. But at least he had a goal. Whereas our bad guy is going to be like that Uber driver. No good reason. No reason at all."

Putting the pan into the oven, Brody said, "White blood cells. That's what I tell myself when everything starts to seem a little too crazy. We're white blood cells. Something harmful gets into the body, we take it out. There doesn't have to be a reason."

"Wouldn't it be better to cure the actual disease?"

"Sure." He wiped his hands, leaned back against the stove. "Any idea how?"

A few minutes later Brody took the pan from the oven, having somehow turned random ingredients into a fluffy circle of deliciousness. He squeezed lemon over the top and set out the hot sauce, and they stood in the kitchen eating it by the slice like pizza until there was nothing left but grease stains.

"That," she said, "was amazing."

"When this is over, I'll take you out for a proper meal. I know this steakhouse down by the river. We'll drop a week's salary on dry-aged beef and pinot noir."

"It's a date." Claire stacked the plates in the sink. Caught a yawn in her hand. She considered bringing up the thing they had tacitly agreed to leave unspoken. Decided against it.

Then was surprised to hear herself say, "When this is over, we're going to have to talk."

There was a pause. "Yeah?"

She looked over to where he leaned against the fridge. "Well. I mean. We can't go on this way. There's my career—both our careers—I'm just saying, if we want to make this work, we'll need to figure out how."

Brody nodded. It wasn't agreement. More to indicate he'd heard. Confirmation of message received. He crossed his arms.

"I'm not proposing to you," she said, feeling herself go hot. "I'm not asking for anything, I know it hasn't been that long. I just mean we'll have to talk."

"Listen. Claire." He looked away. "You know I care about you."

It was like ice poured over her head. Claire stood with a dirty plate in one hand and the dish scrubber in the other and stared at him. He met her gaze, his expression impassive.

Until he burst out laughing.

Her fingers tingled. "I'm going to kill you."

"You should see your face." Still chuckling, he walked over, took the plate from her hand and set it down. "We don't have to wait until it's over. Are you kidding? I know it hasn't been long. I know there's a whole world to Claire McCoy I haven't seen. I know it's ridiculous to feel like I've been waiting for you to come along. And I don't care. I *have* been waiting for you." He shrugged. "We'll figure it out. I'll quit the Bureau and write traffic tickets if that's what it takes to be with you."

She realized her mouth was open, and closed it. There was a helium feeling in her chest, and her smile hurt. She took a breath, glanced at the clock. 1:29 a.m. "Well, shit."

"What?"

Claire undid the sash, slipped the robe off her shoulders. "I was really looking forward to getting some sleep tonight."

# FIVE

Simon Tucks was two people.

Most of his life he had been a sad, pointless little man. Stormy days. Long bleak black.

But something fearsome had grown inside him. Bloomed like cancer. His True Self. With each sacrifice, he grew closer to it. Like a baby ten pounds too heavy clawing free, ripping its mother apart in the hurry to be born.

The labor had begun a month ago.

That morning he'd awakened from a dream he could not remember and yet was sad to leave. Sunlight burned through his blinds. He thought of getting out of bed but did not get out of bed. Why? What for?

Everyone else seemed to know. Like there had been a meeting no one had told him about, where a secret was shared. Those who knew the secret did not wonder why they should get out of bed.

He had lain there hating the sunlight and thinking of the chef's knife in the chopping block. The way the edge of it shone. Thinking of a warm bath and a fast, deep cut up the length of each forearm.

It was a game Simon had played all his life. Walking downtown, he imagined stepping out on the ledge of a skyscraper, pictured a clench and a leap and a howling plunge to nothing. At the hardware store, he fingered lengths of rope, thought about nooses.

The double handful of pills washed down with cold vodka.

The dive into the lake and eastward swim until his limbs failed.

The Toyota in the garage with windows down and engine idling.

It was just a game. A way to pass the time when he sat in his cubicle, when he rode the train home, when he ate cereal for dinner. But that particular morning, he realized he needed a gun.

He needed one *now*.

An hour later he passed beneath a sign welcoming him to Indiana, Crossroads of America. He drove without purpose or plan, and yet steered directly to a shithole town called Kokomo, where in a flat brown field a squat grey building hosted a gun show.

Simon had intended to buy a pistol. Something machined and heavy that would taste of metal as it clicked against his teeth. Yet for some reason, he allowed a long-haired man with a grizzled face to sell him an assault rifle. A Smith & Wesson M&P15 OR. Then he let a pretty blonde convince him to buy a Burris MTAC 1.5-6x42mm illuminated scope. She even mounted it for him, and he stared at her fingers moving fast and fluid, at the creamy skin of her neck, at the shadow of her cleavage revealed by her tank top—

It wasn't until he got back home and laid the rifle on the bed that Simon asked himself why he had bought it. Perhaps he could brace the stock against the floor, put the barrel in his mouth, then lean forward to press the trigger? He supposed that would work.

But why the scope? A rifle and a scope were for hunting, and he didn't hunt.

It was then a voice had whispered to him. The voice was clear and firm and not his own. It spoke in his head, and it said just one word: *yet*.

With that word, his birth began.

He embraced it. Each day he heard the voice more often, and louder. Each day he spent longer as the man he wanted to be. The voice was remaking him into something new, something stronger and in control. The voice was his friend, his partner, his master. Like horse and jockey. The two existed together, depended on one another. Without the horse, the jockey could not ride; without the jockey, the horse would not race.

And his True Self wanted to race.

But the transformation wasn't complete. There were moments when he was alone. Just the horse. Dark moments like this one, spent staring at the ceiling as the city slept around him. Moments when he pondered planting the rifle stock against the floor, and wondered whether he would hear the shot.

How many of them had? Perhaps the woman today. He'd been in position for half an hour. Rifle braced on the edge of the dumpster, only an inch of the barrel protruding. The sweet smell of rot surrounding him. Horse and jockey together, unified. Calm and potent.

Savoring.

An elderly couple walked with the comfort of decades, her arm in his as they tried, comically, to hurry. He centered the crosshairs on her heart and imagined taking her from her husband. Leaving the old man to stare down at his life's chest blown out.

Moments later, he'd traced the skipping body of a little girl. She had a ponytail and a worn bunny clenched in one fist. Her mother was tugging her along, and the girl was trying to keep up. A squeeze of his finger, and the mother would be pulling meat. For the rest of her days, the woman would know that she had spent the last second of her child's life frustrated and impatient.

The feeling thrilled him. Filled him. Once, he'd overheard a man on the train talking about how after he had sex with some girl he felt like a god. It was like that, only better. When the jockey was in him, guiding his hands, steadying his aim, he didn't just feel like a god—he was God. The fate of all those people in his hands. They even prayed to him. Their darting eyes, their quick steps, their nervous looks at the horizon, these were all rough dedications offered up to him. Entreaties to God: not now, not yet, not me.

That's what the woman today had been thinking. According to the news, her name was Emily Watkins, but when he'd looked at her through the glass of the scope he had seen only a supplicant, powerless and praying, and he had rejected her pleas and exercised his divine right with one squeeze of a finger.

She'd wobbled when the bullet struck. Light had sparkled off her wedding ring. The bags had fallen from her shoulder, contents spilling out, ice cream tub breaking open on the concrete.

The moment had given him a thrill electric as orgasm. He had lingered, watched the police arrive, the ambulance. He'd decided to try for a second sacrifice, and almost succeeded. If only that detective hadn't thrown the EMT, he would have—

*What have you done?*

He wasn't the jockey now. He was just his sad, pointless self, and the memory filled him with horror. As though it hadn't been him that went to the dumpster, that set up the rifle, that stared down the scope—

*What are you doing?*

Simon lurched out of bed. His feet tangled in the covers, and he hit the ground hard. His palms burned and pain rang up his knees. He crawled frantically to the corner. In the darkness the rifle was insect-perfect. The barrel tasted of oil. Simon fumbled for the trigger.

*Do it, do it now, now while you see clearly, while the jockey isn't looking, do it, do it, do it—*

Emily had fallen backward, crumpling to the ground. Through the scope he'd been able to look right up her dress. The toned thighs framing white cotton underwear. A little tuft of brown hair escaping one side.

Thinking about it, he felt a tingle in his groin. And then came the jockey's voice, and with it, calm, and certainty.

Emily Watkins was just a sacrifice. He was a god.

Simon took his mouth from the gun. Rose, carefully wiped the barrel, and leaned the rifle in the corner. The taste of metal lingered on his tongue, and he went to the bathroom, got his toothbrush from the medicine cabinet.

When he closed it, he saw himself in the mirror. Not the old one, droopy and small. His True Self. The one from his dreams. The jockey that rode the horse.

In the mirror he was himself, but taller, broader, stronger. His cheekbones were sharp diagonals. His eyes blazed.

In the mirror, he wasn't in a dingy bathroom. He was on a throne beside a massive pyre, the flames leaping twenty feet into the night sky. Flickering light painting his face in oranges and shadows. Around the fire men and women writhed, danced, groped. Sweating demons ecstatic in their debauched worship. Simon sat above them, expressionless and impassive as a woman serviced him with her mouth, her bare breasts glistening, his hand twisted in her hair to push her down farther, farther, to hold her there—

He ran his fingers down his chest and took himself in hand.

Just a moment of weakness. Resistance from the old self he was cutting away. How could he think of ending it?

Tomorrow was going to be special.

# SIX

Through the open window Claire could hear the mutter of traffic, the beep of a truck in reverse. She floated toward consciousness, wallowing in the warm bed and the languid glow of satisfaction. Even freshly shaven, Brody's face had rubbed her chin and lips raw, and she was sore—the way they'd been going at it she'd have to be made of boot leather not to be—but the pain was sweet.

When there was no pretending to be asleep any longer, she yawned and opened her eyes. The curtains fluttered in the October breeze, parting to splash sunlight on her still-bare walls. *Need to do something about that someday.*

She'd moved from DC to Chicago in July, spent a weekend assembling furniture and buying towels, and then thrown herself into her new job. As a woman who had hurtled up the ranks of what remained a man's organization, she'd found that efficiency, competence, and intelligence were only part of the equation. As important was flawless presentation. It wasn't a matter of sexism, exactly. It was genetics. Below the surface, both genders were wired to expect strength from men and support from women. Which of course was nonsense, but arguing it didn't help, and neither did overcompensating. An attitude considered tough in a man tended to get a woman written off as shrill.

The best solution she'd found so far was simply to focus on the job and demand others do likewise. And the best way to express that was to embody it. Doubly true for a woman who had parachuted in to lead the office; though the org chart said she was number two, the Special Agent in Charge was months away from mandatory retirement. Whereas she was a rising star, one of the director's anointed.

All of which added up to her having to hustle her butt off. Fine. She'd never really learned to unplug anyway; Dad often teased that her tombstone would read WORKED HARD. July and August had been a blur. Then, just as she was starting to feel established, Brody had happened.

God, that thing he'd said last night. Over the last weeks they had traded histories, not the way she was used to, where both people presented the version of themselves they wanted the other to believe, like a relationship CV. With Brody it had felt like exploring a marvelous new city, wandering the main thoroughfares and twisting back alleys with equal fervor, trying to capture it all. Lying in the dark, his voice soft and disembodied, he had painted pictures of a suburban childhood, sprinklers and summer shrieks, tree forts, a blue-and-silver BMX Mongoose. Of teenage alienation, train rides into the city to see bands she'd never heard of. The crunch of autumn leaves as he strolled campus. Where he'd been on 9/11—a coffee shop, hungover—and his horror at the helplessness of the people trapped, and how that had driven him to enlist the next day.

So Claire understood how genuine was his need to aid, to protect, to be the guy who did the thing. And of course she'd read his file, and knew that he was an exceptional agent. Not destined for upper echelon—his leap-then-look approach wouldn't fit, and he couldn't smile while chewing a shit sandwich—but his FBI career would last as long as he wanted.

So for him to say that if need be, he would put it aside . . . well. There had been plenty of guys in her life, but mostly they had felt like boys. Even the ones in thousand-dollar suits. It took a man to say the things Brody had. To put his partner's ambition before his own.

No, that wasn't it—to make *her* his ambition. Thinking of it made her stomach float and her chest fluttery. She'd never been a princess, never fantasized about her wedding, but here she was, mooning like a schoolgirl. And more than that, not caring.

"What are you grinning about?"

She turned, saw him staring, his head on the pillow just inches away. Habit tempted her to say something flip. Instead she rolled on her side to face him. "Us."

"Us, huh?" He smiled, and again she felt a stab of familiarity that outstripped their time together. Like they'd been trading secret smiles for decades instead of a couple of weeks.

"Us," she repeated, staring into his eyes and thinking that people spent most of the time not quite looking at each other. That even when two individuals managed to lock eyes, one or both of them were thinking about that fact, concentrating on not looking away.

Not here. Not now.

Her phone rang.

Claire groaned.

Brody snorted a laugh. "Tough to be king."

She rolled away, sat up. Took the phone off the charger, registered the number, the Chicago office switchboard. *A new victim?* She cleared her throat and put on her professional voice. "Claire McCoy."

"Good morning, ma'am. I hope it's not too early—"

"Of course not. What is it?"

"Yellow flags."

As soon as it became clear that the killings weren't an isolated incident, Claire had implemented a tip line. The phone number was in constant rotation on the media, and the number of calls grew daily, with more than eight thousand in the last twenty-four hours, according to the agent.

That was the thing about terror: it made rational people act irrationally. From a certain perspective, the fear was more destructive than the actual killing. Fear had brought the city to a standstill. Fear had closed schools and flatlined the economy. And fear made normal people pick up the phone to accuse cranky neighbors and creepy brothers-in-law, recount odd behavior and partially overheard conversations. Every call was logged, recorded, cross-referenced, and prioritized. Red flags were followed immediately, but they were rare. Analysts generated a daily list of yellow flags, leads worth pursuing but not considered hot.

Eight thousand calls. It was at once an exercise in frustration and an important tool.

She said, "Go ahead."

Brody rolled out of bed, cracked his neck, then padded away naked, scratching his belly.

By the time she hung up, he was out of the shower, toweling his hair like it had done him wrong. Billows of steam filled the bathroom. Claire brushed her teeth, then climbed in the shower, turning it from the flesh-melting temperature he preferred to merely scalding. She sighed as the water ran down her back.

"Yellow flags?" Through the steamed glass door, Brody was a ghostly shape, his edges amorphous.

"Yeah. You know we got eight thousand calls yesterday?"

He whistled. "Any worth anything?"

"An Iraq veteran gone off radar. Caller was his sister, claimed he wasn't returning her texts. His VA therapist confirms he's missed his last three sessions."

"That's not good."

"No." Given the skill involved in the killings, the leading psych profile suggested the sniper was ex-military. They'd been reviewing lists of discharged soldiers for weeks. "Guy was a helicopter mechanic, though, not exactly special forces."

"Army teaches mechanics to shoot too."

"What else. Two reports of neighbors that own assault rifles. Some calls about a storefront religious group named the Sword of God preaching violence to hasten the Second Coming. A couple of overheard conversations, people admiring the sniper."

Brody groaned.

"I know." Her shampoo filled the shower with the scent of mint tea. "An abandoned church on the West Side, three calls about someone coming and going, one of which said they saw a gun. And two claims of responsibility, both unlikely."

"Those flags are a very pale yellow. Practically beige."

"Yeah." Claire tipped her head, let the water sluice down her hair and back. They had a morning status meeting in an hour, and she was already working a grid, mentally divvying up assignments. Then a call to the director, check in with CPD, do pregame for today's press conference. God, she was tired. "You worked the West Side, didn't you?"

"Yeah," Brody said. "The cartels use West Side gangs to distribute. Want me to take the church?"

"Would you? Have CPD back you up."

"Yes, ma'am," he said.

"Hold on." She slid the door open. "Come here."

The kiss started sweet but got hot almost immediately, her hands around his neck, her body leaning into his. He pulled away, said, "Hey, you're getting me wet."

"You'll dry."

"Lady, if it were up to me, I'd climb in there with you. But my boss is a hard-ass."

She laughed. "Fine. Good luck catching bad guys."

# SEVEN

*Someone's going to die today.*

The mantra was a slap of cold water. It had become a ritual of Brody's, a way to remind himself that his life spanned two worlds.

One was Claire's place, the universe pulled shut behind them. Going at each other until they were raw, and then spending half the night talking. Waking up to stare into each other's eyes with childish wonder.

The other world was this one. Where someone was going to die. Today. Unless he could stop it.

Chicago's West Side was row on row of sagging bungalows and gang-tagged apartment buildings. The church fit right in; the doors were secured with thick chain, weeds stood three feet high, and at some point a fire had shattered the windows and blackened the stonework. The plywood covering the holes seemed to be holding the building together. A group of teenaged boys in puffy coats eyed them from the stoop of a house.

"That place?" Sergeant Morgan shook his head. "I hope not. It'd lower my already poor opinion of the sniper." Morgan was weightlifter-big and as comfortable in his ballistic vest as a golfer in a polo shirt. Brody liked tactical cops; they tended to combine proficient ass kicking with amiable cheerfulness.

"Probably nothing." Brody took his own vest from the backseat, began strapping it on. "Your guys ready?"

Morgan nodded, spoke into his radio, issuing orders to the rest of the team, five tacticals jammed in an SUV a block north. Brody tucked in an earpiece. "Ops, gear check."

"Confirmed, Agent Brody," said a man's voice. "Signal is strong, and we're watching via surveillance cam."

"We?"

"ASAC McCoy has joined me."

Brody failed to keep the smile off his face. "Good morning, ma'am."

"Agent Brody," came Claire's voice, cool and professional. "What's the situation?"

"The church looks abandoned. I'm supported by CPD Sergeant Ryan Morgan and his merry band of door kickers. We're ready to roll."

"Understood. Good luck."

"Thank you." Brody shook out his hands. Took a deep inhale through his nose, blew it out through his mouth. Then put the car in drive and hit the accelerator. Morgan called go on his radio.

They arrived in a squeal of brakes and were out the door in an instant, weapons low. It felt good to be in motion. Training took over, and Brody stepped swiftly and carefully, eyes swiveling everywhere. The young drug dealers scattered like seagulls. On a balcony fifty yards away, a man smoked and watched the show. No sign of motion from the church itself.

The front doors were tall and heavy, a chain threaded between the handles. Brody took up position on one side. Morgan had the bolt cutters out, but when he closed the jaw on a link, the chain came free of its own accord.

Softly, Brody said, "Ops, the chain on the front door was previously cut."

"Roger. Do you want backup?"

"Negative. Probably just squatters."

Even so, he felt his hopes rise. He allowed himself to imagine catching the sniper inside, the man asleep on a cot, a .223 rifle on the floor beside him. Maybe no one needed to die today after all.

The iron handle of the door was cold. Brody yanked it open and spun to one side, weapon up and pointing.

The foyer—*the entrance to a church is called a narthex*, his brain informed him, a stupid pet trick it enjoyed in moments of tension—was strewn with trash. Brody moved quickly, and Morgan followed, spiking the door open for light. Graffiti had been Sharpied on the walls, gang tags and genitalia. The doors leading to the nave had been torn off their hinges, but the interior was dim. Brody clicked on his flashlight, holding it with his left hand and bracing the Glock above. Morgan did the same, their beams sweeping back and forth. They went in together, splitting to opposite sides to check corners. The resonant hammer-bang of a ram taking down a door echoed, the rest of the team piling in the back.

The chapel reeked of ash and ammonia. Shards of broken glass sparkled amidst rags and faded newspapers and broken hypodermics. White streaks of bird droppings slathered everything. The plywood covering one of the windows had fallen, and a parallelogram of dusty sunlight stabbed through it. A smoke-stained Jesus stared down with a long-suffering expression, half his torso burned away.

The room was empty.

They took a minute to be sure, sweeping flashlights beneath pews and banging in adjoining doors—bathrooms, a small classroom, an office, storage. The team was good, kept their movements coordinated, called out as they cleared rooms.

Two pews had been pushed face-to-face into a makeshift bed. The reek coming off the blankets was pure homeless.

*Well, shit.* Brody holstered his weapon. "Ops, there's no one here. Looks like somebody was crashing, but I doubt it was our target."

"Understood," Claire said. "One of the calls mentioned a weapon. See if you can find it."

"Roger."

The tacticals drifted back in teams of two. They'd come in hard and professional, but now relaxed. One of them pulled a pack of cigarettes, lit up. "You mind? Always wanted to smoke in church."

Brody shrugged. As his eyes adjusted, the shaft of sunlight cast plenty of illumination. There was trash everywhere, old newspapers and Popeyes bags. Someone had bothered to heap up a pile of glass three feet high, multicolored shards that must have been stained glass. Sergeant Morgan stepped on an empty Pabst, crushing the beer can flat. "What do you want to do?"

"Someone sliced the chain. Let's do a search. If we find something, groovy; if not, I'll buy lunch."

"Hey," said the cop with the cigarette. "I've got something." He clicked his flashlight on a pew; in the center of the beam a used condom lay like a beached jellyfish. "Want to collect DNA?"

In spite of himself, Brody snorted a laugh.

"Kurtz, you asshole," Morgan said. "Alright, you all heard the man. Get to work. Grid search, outward from center."

The team split up. Brody left them to it, wandered over to the beam of sunlight, his eyes cataloging the junk on the floor. Somebody could shoot an art exhibit on the depth and variety of detritus in abandoned squats. There were always broken bottles and broken needles, but he'd seen doll's heads, chess pieces, snow globes, stethoscopes, paperweights, bicycle tires, underwear. His foot nudged a coverless paperback, water-fat and faded. He picked it up, read the first line—*The man in black fled across the desert, and the gunslinger followed*—smiled, tossed the book back in the corner.

Out the busted plywood the sky was pale blue. The smoker on the fire escape was still there. Thinning hair and sloped shoulders, a melting-wax sort of face, his cell phone out to take a picture. People and their conflict videos.

A ring sounded behind him. Brody turned, annoyed. Tactical units should know better. The sound was coming from Kurtz, the comedian with the cigarette. Brody was about to tear him a new one when he registered the cop's expression. It wasn't *oops, I forgot to turn off my phone*; it was *what the hell is that?*

Which made sense, because the ring was coming from the pile of broken glass.

*Oh. Oh no.*

"Down, down!" Brody charged, slamming into Kurtz and sending him sprawling as the phone rang a second time.

The church filled with parti-colored light, like a rainbow sun had been born in the center. For a fraction of a second Brody was staring into it, a blast of furious illumination blooming beneath the stained glass, and then the shattered pieces leapt up from the ground and the shock wave hit and everything went loose, he was flying, swept up in a blast of heat and a hundred shimmering razors and if he hadn't been in the midst it might have been beautiful and then—

# EIGHT

Patterns of swirling dust. Skirling dust, twirling rust.

Skirling was a funny word.

Something wrong.

Wrong, gong, bong song, swirling song . . .

Was it a word? Skirling? Couldn't remember.

He blinked, coughed. Where . . .

Brody sat up, and in the process realized he'd been lying down.

His chest felt heavy, and he fumbled at the straps of the ballistic vest, releasing the Velcro with a rip. He sloughed it off and lurched up. Wobbly. The world was sparkling dust, and standing made it worse, cut his sight to inches. He took a breath. It felt like inhaling needles.

Claustrophobia struck, animal panic. Lips tight, Brody dropped low and launched into a frantic crawl. The floor was covered in rainbows. His leg hit something, inertia driving it forward.

His knee exploded in brilliant blinding agony.

A dagger of glass stuck out of his leg. It was a vicious inch wide and jammed deep. Blood bubbled up around it, staining his pants.

The pain was revelatory. It cut the fog, and he realized that the rainbows on the ground were pieces of stained glass. The ones heaped up to cover the bomb. The dust sparkled because it was powdered glass. Which explained why it hurt to breathe.

Panic beckoned, but he forced it down. If he lost control he might pass out. Still holding his breath, he took the glass between thumb and forefinger and pulled. Inch after sickening inch slid out. The edge was jagged and slick with blood. He tossed it aside. It shattered on the floor.

Locking his leg straight, Brody rose, took the edge of a pew in one hand, then hopped to the next.

His lungs were burning by the time he shouldered out of the ruined church and collapsed amidst the weeds growing through cracked concrete. His first desperate breath set fire to a hundred tiny cuts in his mouth and throat. The knee throbbed, and his pant leg was soaked with hot blood.

Gritting his teeth, he forced his leg to bend. It did. The glass knife hadn't cut whatever tendon ran there.

He patted for his other injuries, found none. Incredible luck; he'd been next to the bomb when it blew. But then, he'd been low, tackling the cop, so maybe the shards had passed above—

Where were the others?

Brody looked around, saw his car parked where he'd left it. No sign of the tactical team, though. He remembered the earpiece, said, "Ops?" He toggled the power button. "Claire?"

Not even static. The explosion must have damaged it. And his phone, when he pulled it from his pocket, was blank, the screen cracked.

Brody looked around. A meh block in a crap neighborhood, frame houses sagging under the weight of grey skies. Leafless trees, faded fire hydrants. There were people in the street. Three, running this way. They must have heard the explosion.

*The sniper is nearby.*

Adrenaline slammed through him, muting the pain in his knee, making the pulse pound in his forehead. He forced himself to his feet. "Get down!"

The Good Samaritans kept coming, moving at a sprint. Brody waved his arms above his head. "Stop! Stop, the . . ."

There was something odd about them.

When disaster struck, some people cowered, while others hurried to help. But even the helpful ones did it cautiously. Eyes darting. These three weren't even looking around. They were just racing at him.

*My god they're fast. How are they . . .*

The woman wore jeans and a sweatshirt, turquoise running shoes, and a Bowie knife. As she drifted to a stop, she drew the blade, ten inches of sharpened steel with sawback serrations down the spine. The men were armed too; the big guy in the expensive leather jacket carried an aluminum baseball bat, and the pale scarecrow slashed the air with a machete.

Samaritans they were not.

Brody drew the Glock, aimed with both hands. "FBI. Drop the weapons."

The woman stalked forward. She was maybe twenty. There was something feral to her expression, a wild grin on a dirty face.

*The psych profiles are wrong.* There wasn't a single sniper operating alone. It was a team, some sort of cult, and these three were members. "Down. Do it now!"

They kept moving.

Fine. Brody aimed at the girl's thigh, squeezed the trigger.

The pin clicked. Misfire. Almost unheard of with a Glock. He racked the weapon to clear it, aimed and squeezed again.

Another click.

The gun wasn't working. It was three on one, and the sniper was out there somewhere, maybe sighting in on him now.

Brody turned to run.

First step, he knew he was in trouble. The moment he put pressure on the knee it nearly buckled. Standing, he could lean on the other. But there was no way to run with one leg.

*No way to fight either. Suck it up, Marine.* He staggered forward, clenching his fists. Adrenaline pushed the pain far enough that he could keep hobbling along. Not very fast, and not for long. But he didn't need long. Backup was on the way.

The tactical team must have been wounded in the explosion, but he'd had an open line to the FBI operations center. They'd been watching the raid on surveillance cameras. The strong arm of the law was racing here now. Squad cars, helicopters, SWAT team. All he had to do was survive until they arrived.

The street was empty, no traffic in either direction. Brody cut across a parked Jeep. Pounded the pavement. Every footfall an explosion. There must still be some glass inside the knee socket. Jesus that was an awful image.

A glance over his shoulder showed the three giving chase, their faces twisted into snarls. They weren't more than thirty feet behind him. He could hear their footfalls, thought he could smell them, a whiff of sweaty body odor. Every time his right foot hit the pain wiped away the world. If the glass worked deeper, his knee would crumple. He'd go down and never get up again.

There was a liquor store on the corner, the sign burned out, security screens over every window. He angled for it, pushing through each starburst of agony. Behind him, the woman wolf-howled and the others laughed and Brody remembered their speed. They could run him down in a heartbeat.

They were playing with him. They were dogs and he was the chew toy.

The thought infuriated and terrified in equal measures.

He stumbled to the store and yanked the metal door of the security cage. An open padlock dangled from the loops, and he snatched it, slammed the gate shut with a clang, then fumbled with the lock. His hands were slippery and the holes were rusty and the shackle caught on the edge, they were closing, the baseball player winding up, and then the padlock slid home and snapped shut. Brody leapt backward as the aluminum bat slammed into the thick metal bars with a sound like a car crash. He'd made it.

The other two joined the baseball player, the three staring through the thick metal bars. The scarecrow with the machete smiled, revealing a horror show of tweaker's dentition. There was something about them, some side effect of fear hormones or trick of the light that made them seem hyper-real, as if they were in sharper focus than the rest of the world. He could smell the sweet foulness of their breath, though Brody noticed that where he was panting and soaked in pain-sweat, they weren't even winded.

"Feeling safe?" The baseball player rested his hands on the bars, gave them a test rattle.

"About a thousand cops are on their way," Brody said.

"That right?" The scarecrow's laugh was high-pitched and manic. He slapped the baseball player on the back. "You hear that?"

"Very frightening." The men exchanged looks, then set their weapons on the concrete. They moved languidly, like they had all the time in the world, as they took hold of neighboring bars and began to pull.

Brody almost laughed. This was a lousy neighborhood, and one thing shop owners invested in was security. The bars were an inch thick. It'd take a tow truck's winch to make them wobble.

The veins stood out on the men's arms. Their teeth grit tight. Feet braced against the cage for leverage.

With a slow scream, the bars began to bend.

The panic that drenched Brody then was unlike anything he'd known. There had been moments in his life when death seemed imminent, and every single one of them had shaken him to the core. But this.

"See, little bunny?" The girl smiled. "No one can save you."

He turned, banged through the door into the shop. There were no customers, and the fluorescents were out, leaving the air soupy with screened daylight. He limped to the counter, encased in inch-thick Plexi. No one behind it. The door to the office was locked. Over the shriek of yielding metal he heard the woman's crystalline laugh.

A weapon. He needed a weapon.

The Glock could probably be fixed, but not in time. He had his cuffs, but no pepper spray or backup gun, extra weight eschewed by most agents.

The liquor bottles were all behind the Plexi. There was a rack of candy bars, another of chips.

"A little more. Just a little more!"

Neon signs hanging in the window. A display of magazines.

The girl pushed her head through the hole in the bars, wriggled her hips, and slid inside.

A fire extinguisher on the wall.

Brody yanked it free. It weighed about fifteen pounds, and he held it with two hands, one top and one bottom. The woman slowed when she saw it, a flicker of amusement crossing her face. Her eyes darted to his wounded knee, the pant leg sodden with blood. "Oh, sweetie."

When she lunged, it was just a blur of motion. Like a train speeding past. He barely got the canister up in time. The steel took the blow with a bong. The impact rang up his arms and numbed his fingers and nearly tore the extinguisher from his hands. Somehow this slender girl could hit like George Foreman. Brody reeled back wrong footed, and a blast of pain from his knee almost dropped him. The girl rebounded and lunged again, too fast to see. He didn't even try to block. Just threw himself backward like reverse diving into a swimming pool.

Midair the edge of her knife parted his shirt and cut a line of fire across his belly, and then he crashed into the rack behind him, the gaudy colors of candy wrappers flying in all directions as he tried and failed to break his fall.

His back hit the floor square and the breath blew out of him and he lost his grip on the canister. The world wobbled in and out of focus.

Brody told himself to move. To get up. All he could manage was rolling to his side and sucking desperately for air. Everything hurt. Spots danced in his vision.

A pair of turquoise running shoes stepped in front of his face.

*Move. Move or you're going to die right here, on the floor of this liquor store. Gutted by a sorority girl with a Bowie knife.*

"Don't worry, bunny." Her voice drifted down. "I'll make it quick."

Air, he needed air, his lungs wouldn't accept it and his belly burned every time he tried and something had gone very wrong with his knee.

"Finish him, Raquel." A man's voice growled from far away. "Take him."

Brody stared at her shoes, and at the ankles that protruded from them, the calves. He saw the ripple of muscle in them as her weight shifted. She would be stooping down with her knife, the edge already slick with blood, but he just stared at her shoes.

When the heel rocked off the floor he grabbed the trigger of the fire extinguisher with one hand and the nozzle with the other and pointed it up and fired a blast of pressurized potassium bicarbonate where he imagined her face to be.

The girl shrieked and toppled back on her butt. Her legs splayed out and flailed, the rubber squeaking on the linoleum floor. She dropped the knife and clawed at her eyes, her face frosted with powder. Brody forced himself to sit. He gripped the base of the canister in both hands and tightened his core, ignoring the agony from the slash in his stomach as he unwound a full-strength backhand swing to the side of her head.

He felt her skull crack. Her hands dropped from her face. Her eyes went glassy.

And Brody found himself outdoors.

# NINE

He was in a suburban backyard. Though he'd never seen it before he knew that it was his. The air was thick with the smell of lilacs. Daddy had his arm around Mom. On the wrought iron table there was a cake with HAPPY 5TH BIRTHDAY RAQUEL!!! in pink icing. Beside it was a wrapped present, big enough that it might contain an American Girl—

Before he touched the box, he was in Kara's house. They'd been inseparable in sixth grade, BFFs, and Kara's room, with its slanted ceiling covered in pictures of Fall Out Boy and My Chemical Romance and shirtless David Beckham, had been home-away-from since Dad bailed. They'd already played at makeovers and now were watching a video of a stoned cat and laughing so hard they couldn't breathe, like, literally, it was hurting—

The world was chlorine smell and the roar of the crowd. Arms spinning in a butterfly stroke, the water turned to foam by the force of the motion. Neck and neck with that Lahser High bitch, the stuck-up chick who always won. Blasting through the pool, goggles too tight, hair tugged back in the swim cap, dragging himself through the water, two of them almost in sync, the end of the lane in sight, both of them pushing, reaching for the wall, and he got there first, he knew he had, but the judge called it for the other girl, took away the victory that belonged to—

The dorm ceiling was only three feet above the upper bunk, and between the ceiling and his body was Aaron Rutgers, he of the bangs and the dimples. Aaron's hands were on Brody's breasts and he was fumbling around down there, trying to get it in, and then he sort of lunged and something tore in Brody's vagina, it hurt, a lot, actually, but way behind the pain there was something else, something almost nice—

Sunset over the quad, the sky glowing gold, the trees bursting with buds. Walking across campus and already beginning to disconnect from this place. The whole world out there; the chance to build a career, get married, have beautiful children. Or be repeatedly fired, date a string of losers, have abortions. Either way, life was about to—

Smeary and loose, muscles not right. Throbbing that was too big for his head to hold. Face on dirty concrete, and blood starting to pool, his blood. Above, voices. Someone said, *shit, why'd you hit her so hard?* and another replied, *get her purse, come on.* The strap snapped as someone yanked at it. Footsteps running away. Black spots growing. It wasn't fair, it just wasn't fair, he'd been waiting so long to begin and everything had been taken over thirteen bucks and a cell phone—

Brody gasped, jerked like he'd fallen asleep in the bathtub. He reeled backward and up, standing fast, wanting to get away from the woman with the caved-in skull. That had been her. Raquel.

*He* had been her. Impossible. But he knew it, could still feel it.

"No!" Metal screamed against metal. The Scarecrow jerked the security gate hard enough the whole store seemed to shake.

Brody went automatic. Dropped the fire extinguisher and picked up the knife, holding it with a hammer grip and assuming a triangle stance like he'd been trained, his shield hand up. Knowing it was pointless, but unwilling not to fight.

The tweaker stopped yanking on the gate. His eyes narrowed as if in calculation. Beside him, the baseball player sucked air through his teeth.

*What are they waiting for?*

The tweaker looked at the woman on the floor, then back to Brody. "We can take him."

"Nah."

"But he killed Raquel."

"Look at him." The Baller shook his head. "I'm out."

The thin man rocked from foot to foot like he needed a bathroom. His lips twisted in a snarl. Finally, he shouldered his machete. "See you around, maybe."

The two turned and walked away.

Brody lowered the knife. Took a deep breath that smelled of dust and urine. Raquel's bladder had cut loose when she died.

He stared down at her. It was all impossible. The men bending the bars, the speed and power of Raquel's attack. But most of all, what had just happened. He possessed two sets of certainties. Both were absolutely true. And completely contradictory.

He'd never seen the woman before; he'd felt her grow up. She was a complete stranger; he knew her most intimate thoughts. He was Will Brody; he had just been Raquel Adams.

What the hell was going on?

He'd been Raquel Adams.

Ridiculous, but true.

He'd *been* her. He'd smelled the lilacs, felt hands on his breasts, watched the blood pool. That had been her birthday, her virginity, her death. But of course it couldn't have been her death, because if it was she wouldn't have been running around the streets of Chicago with a knife—

Shock. He was in shock, and hallucinating. Okay then. Help was on the way. In the meantime, he should sit down, take deep breaths. Improvise a bandage to minimize blood loss.

He lowered himself to the ground. Setting the knife down, he pulled up his pant leg, gritting his teeth as he eased it over—

Over his perfect, unblemished knee.

# TEN

Claire stood very straight and very still. Her only motion was the slow rhythm of breath and the slight yielding of her skin as she dug a thumbnail into her palm. The pain felt like it belonged to someone else. She kept pushing.

The table in front of her was spotless metal, cold and brilliantly lit. High-wattage bulbs glared down from multiple angles, erasing shadows, casting everything into surreal clarity. The chemical tang of formaldehyde stung her nose, almost strong enough to mask the smell of burned meat.

The corpse on the table didn't look much like Will. It bore only a passing resemblance to a man.

The Evidence Response Team was still analyzing fragments, but the device had been smokeless gunpowder in galvanized steel piping, triggered by a cellular signal. Classic pipe bomb, crude by the standards of even a middle-of-the-road terrorist, but effective. Especially when buried in a pile of broken glass. As the gunpowder ignited, the pressure had built until the steel pipe shredded from the inside out, the shock wave turning the glass into a tornado of whirling razors.

Like a blender twenty feet across.

Claire had seen plenty of bodies, people cut nearly in half by shotgun blasts, victims of torture, the burned remnants of murdered children. You did get used to it, strange and horrible as that sounded. It was the disconnect. The thing that had made them a person was gone. Call it a soul or a spirit or a consciousness, bring in religion or see it as pure biology, it didn't matter. In the dead, something was missing, some ineffable person-ness. See it a few times, and bodies became things. But it was different when it was someone you knew. Someone you might have loved.

Loved. Love-d. Past tense. Will Brody had become past tense.

"Ma'am—oh god." Agent Huang jammed the back of his wrist against his mouth and turned away. "Oh god."

Claire stood very straight and very still and drove her thumbnail into her palm.

She'd been watching. The leader of an FBI task force observing a routine raid had been a bit out of character, but one of the nice things about being the boss was not having to explain yourself. She hadn't been worried—okay, sure, maybe a little, which was why office romances were not a good idea—but she'd still been pleased to hear Brody radio the all clear. Claire had removed her earpiece, thanked the team for their work, and headed for the exit.

Then came his yell, and that boom, not a seat-rumbling cinematic explosion but just a sort of dull pop, and a moment later dust was pouring out the doors.

When she arrived at the church twenty minutes later, it looked very different. Hundreds of cops locked down the neighborhood. Blue lights strobed off every faded frame house. A line of officers held back a crowd out for disaster porn, half of them shooting video on their phones. Three of the tactical cops were on the way to the hospital, all expected to survive; none of them had been as close as Will. An officer named Kurtz had actually been closer, but Brody had knocked him aside, his body absorbing the glass meant for the cop.

Kurtz himself told her that. Sitting on the curb, a dazed expression and blood running down his cheek. "I didn't even know the guy." He held an unlit cigarette. "I didn't even know him."

In that instant, she had hated Kurtz with furious intensity. Then hated herself for wishing him dead and Will alive.

Claire stared at the ruins on the autopsy table. This was what was left of the man who had teased her about having no food while managing to cook something amazing for her every night. Those shredded mittens and limp sleeves had been the hands that traced her body, the forearms that caught her eye. That ruined face and shattered skull—

"Ma'am?"

They hadn't known each other long but they had known each other well, had clicked on some deep level, and now he was gone. Her chest felt too frail to contain the rage and grief. They twisted like saw blades. But she made herself stare, and stand very straight and very still.

"Ma'am?"

Agent Huang had arrived moments ago. Unbidden, her memory supplied relevant details from his file: HUANG, EDWARD "EDDIE," law degree from Wharton, married no children, good reports from supervisors . . .

Without turning, she said, "Did you find the phone?"

"Yes. The nearest tower shows seven calls to cellular numbers within that area in a ten-second window. Six have been accounted for. The seventh belonged to a pay-as-you-go, and the pings are coming back negative."

"The detonator."

"There's more."

Something in his tone caught her. She tore her eyes from the table, met his gaze.

"The call that triggered it relayed off the same cell tower. Also a prepaid phone, and neither had GPS, so we can't pinpoint it. But towers are everywhere these days. Which means—"

"He was there." Three words. But Claire didn't think she'd ever said three words more loaded with hatred. "He was watching."

Huang nodded.

On one level it didn't matter. Killing from up close wasn't really any different than killing from half a world away. Except . . . it was.

It wasn't just that the sniper had claimed an eighteenth victim. It wasn't just that the victim was a cop. It wasn't just that the cop had been a man she might have loved. It wasn't just that Brody was there on her orders. It wasn't just that he was dead because he'd saved someone else.

The man who had killed Will Brody had wanted to watch him die.

Careful to keep the fury out of her voice, she said, "Purchase data on the phones?"

"Both bought nine days ago, from a convenience store on Elston. Buyer paid cash, and the store security system is multiple cameras sharing one hard drive, new files overwriting old ones. It only goes back about three days."

Like every other piece of physical evidence so far. They had rifle casings, footprints, even DNA from hair follicles and cigarettes, and none of it was worth a thing. Again she had that feeling that he couldn't be working alone. The sniper was being protected, guided in some way.

"Ma'am, we can't be certain this was the sniper. The other attacks have all been with a rifle. It could be a copycat, someone—"

"It was him." Claire knew it with perfect certainty.

"Behavioral Science says maybe, maybe not. They're waiting for DNA—"

"And when we find it, it will match. This was him."

"Okay," Huang said. "Well, if you're right, it supports the profile of a veteran. Making an IED would be in the skill set of a soldier who had seen action."

"Except that this was obviously a trap aimed at killing cops. And if he's an angry vet wanting to stick it to authority figures, he would have been killing cops from . . ." Claire trailed off. There was something there. Some connection she had missed.

It only took a second. "Wait. This was a trap."

Huang said, "Yes, but the point—"

"No, you're not getting me. It was a trap."

"So?"

"You have to *bait* a trap."

Huang hesitated, following her thinking. Then his eyes widened. "Oh."

Claire whirled and took off at a run.

# ELEVEN

Brody sat and stared at his knee for a long time. Remembered pulling a dagger of glass out of it, the slippery sick pain of that. He hadn't imagined it—his pants were soaked with drying blood. And yet the skin was unbroken, and he could move his leg through the whole range of motion without a twinge.

Stomach too. His shirt was slit edge to edge, but though Raquel's knife had parted his belly like a scalpel, there wasn't a mark on his flesh.

Come to think of it, he could breathe easily, and the razor-fine cuts on his lips and tongue weren't bothering him. In fact, physically he felt kind of . . . well, kind of great. Like ten hours of dreamless sleep followed by eggs Benedict and a blow job. His body was limber, muscles strong and ready. He wanted to move, stretch, go for a run.

He started with standing up.

Raquel's body lay where it had fallen, splayed out in an awkward position. Brody stood looking down at her for a long moment. He'd killed before, he was pretty sure, but that had been in war; chaos, smoke, insurgents ducking out from alleys and the roofs of mosques, the crack of his M4 making his ears ring. It had been different. He thought about saying something, couldn't think what.

Instead he turned and walked to the security cage. The way the thick metal was bent looked like a cartoon, the bars bowed sideways in the center. Brody stuck his head and shoulders through, then wriggled the rest of the way out.

The neighborhood was silent. It wasn't just that there weren't police; there was no one at all. No gawkers, no corner kids, no older folks chatting. No traffic. No distant honking. No rattle of the train. No buzz of electricity. No hip-hop anthems blaring from houses, no television voices drifting through an open window.

A shiver ripped through him, one of those that came from nowhere and made his whole body twitch. Brody took a deep breath, and another.

The clouds were low and thick. Wind ruffled leafless trees, stirred trash on the street. Windows were black eyes peering at him. A swing wobbled in the breeze, the chain creaking.

A silver Honda Civic was stopped at a stop sign, and for a moment he let himself hope, but the car was empty. It sat in the right-hand lane, bumper just past the line. As if the owner had parked in the middle of the street, turned off the engine, and climbed out. When he tented his hands over his eyes against the window, Brody could see keys in the ignition. The seat belt was locked across an empty chair.

A block north, a weatherworn F-150 was similarly abandoned. To the south, he could see a line of three cars, all in the correct lane, all frozen. The bodegas and fried fish places and barbershops were empty and lost to shadow. The world had stopped and everyone in it had vanished.

He'd had dreams in his life that felt truly real. In them he'd been able to see the stitching of his jeans, the hair on the back of his hands. He could feel emotions and frame thoughts. Everyone had dreams like that occasionally.

But he couldn't remember a dream where he'd felt real pain; it was more like the idea of pain, a notional counterfeit his mind treated as currency. Slamming three inches of glass into his knee had fucking *hurt*. Besides, he was positive that he'd never had a dream where he asked himself if he was dreaming and then stood around debating it.

*Okay. You know what's happening. You haven't wanted to admit it, but there's an explanation.*

It went like this: he'd been beside the bomb when it blew, yet he'd woken without a scratch.

Which meant he hadn't actually woken up. Instead, he'd suffered serious wounds and been rushed to the nearest hospital. He wasn't wandering an empty version of Chicago; he was undergoing emergency surgery.

This was an anesthetic-induced fantasy. A lucid dream spun by his own mind.

He'd have preferred something in the Arabian harem style, fluttering silks and girls feeding him grapes. Or better yet, Claire's bed on a Saturday morning with nothing to do but make love and breakfast. But his subconscious had the wheel, and it employed the materials at hand: a city gone empty and strange, people killing each other for no reason. Nightmares tended to be rooted in reality. That was what made them frightening.

*Nonetheless, note to subconscious: Go fuck your hat.*

———

Brody couldn't say how long he'd been walking, but it had to have been an hour or more. Past gas stations and grocery stores, bars and restaurants, offices and El stops. As he drew closer to downtown, there were more cars stopped in the middle of the street. Empty, they waited at stoplights that did not shine, beneath grey skies in which no planes flew.

He had no destination. He was walking because he couldn't think what else to do.

The skyline grew closer, the Willis Tower, the Chase, Franklin Center, scores of others huddled together like children's blocks. The offices and homes of a million people. Not one light in one window.

After crossing beneath the eerily silent Dan Ryan Expressway—packed with unmoving cars, a traffic jam from hell—he reached the southbound leg of the Chicago River. The Cermak Bridge was an industrial expanse of metal gridwork painted the color of rust. To camouflage the actual rust, he supposed. The sound of his footfalls changed as he stepped onto the bridge. Lines of empty cars in both directions. He walked to the halfway point and leaned against the railing. The murky water looked cold, and the air smelled faintly septic. A cluster of branches speckled with sodden leaves drifted lazily. Had to give it to the subconscious; what it lacked in taste it made up in detail.

Brody didn't like his theory, but he liked having one. A significant part of him wanted to freak out and start screaming. Having a theory helped keep that tamped down, even if it didn't change anything. Lots of prevailing theories didn't. Take the Big Bang:

*So there's literally nothing, not empty space but not-space, and then poof!, a singularity of infinite density just sort of happens, an unquantifiably small point that contains every scrap of everything that will ever be, every mote of dust and every sprawling galaxy, every piece of matter that will burn in the heart of a star, even time itself, and it explodes outward in all directions and 13,800,000,000 years later a boy is born to Sue and Glenn Brody, and they name him William.* Pretty neat, but not useful when it came to making decisions.

When he looked up from the river he saw a cluster of figures at the far end of the bridge. Relief washed over Brody. He wasn't alone.

Then he saw that they were armed. Knives and bats and hammers, the same makeshift melee stuff as the strangers who had attacked him. Only this time there were ten of them—

No. Not just ten.

On the roof of a squat brick building, a line of armed men and women stood silhouetted against grey skies.

More watched from the balconies overlooking the river.

One even rose atop the bridge operator's tower, a teenaged boy with long hair and a faded canvas duster. He had a bow in one hand, a quiver of arrows slung over his shoulder.

Brody turned, knowing what he'd see.

Another group stood at the other end of the bridge.

*Idiot.* He'd been caught up in his thoughts and let himself get surrounded. The moment had a cinematic surreality to it. Like an ambush in an old Western, the hero riding a dusty canyon with silent enemies lining the rim.

*There have to be twenty of them. Maybe more.*

They weren't real. He was on an operating table. Doctors were working feverishly to save his life. There were machines humming and fluids in IV bags and anesthetic. He didn't have to be afraid. These people were no more dangerous than daydreams.

*Of course, it would suck to find out you're wrong when one of them buries a claw hammer in your skull.*

Brody spun in a slow circle, tried to think through the pounding of his heart. They all stared at him. Their clothes were dirty, their faces smudged. He still had the knife, the grip sweaty in his fingers, but what good would it do? He glanced over the railing, considered the drop to the river.

A man at the east end of the bridge raised a hand. Slowly, palm out, like a student in a classroom. The others waited.

Whatever was going on, the rules had shifted seismically. *When the rules shift, you shift with them, or you lose.* Brody returned the wave.

Through cupped hands, the man shouted, "Come say hi."

"How about you come here?" Brody paused. "Just you."

That caused a ripple, people muttering and shaking their heads. The man said, "Yeah, that's not gonna happen, not the way you shine. How about a couple of us?"

*The way I shine?*

He supposed it didn't make much difference; it was in-or-out time. Brody nodded.

The man gestured at two companions and the three of them started walking. Brody split his attention between them and the others, especially the kid with the bow. He knew nothing about archery, and had to imagine that fifty yards was a difficult shot, but it seemed like a doable one. The moment he saw the kid nock an arrow was the moment he went over the side.

It struck him how very odd a thing that was to be worried about, someone shooting him with an arrow on a bridge in downtown Chicago, but he packed it away.

The man he'd been speaking with was broad shouldered and athletic, and carried a fireman's axe lightly in one hand, the head of it swaying an inch above the ground. He was flanked by a middle-aged man with a cop moustache and a police baton. A woman with the face of a soccer mom and the body of a yoga instructor came last, carrying, sure, a samurai sword. Brody eased closer to the railing.

When they reached him, the man glanced at the river below. "Water's cold, man."

Brody said nothing.

"Name's Kyle. This is Antoine and Lucy."

"Will Brody."

"Nice to." Kyle's eyes flicked over him appraisingly, stopping on the holstered Glock. "Police?"

"FBI."

"Wow, never met one before. You guys?"

Lucy shook her head. Antoine spat over the railing.

"Wanna see a trick, Will Brody? I'm going to read your mind." Kyle put his free hand to his temple and mimed concentration. "You're thinking this is the weirdest dream you've ever had. Right?"

Brody said nothing.

"Kyle, why are you messing around?" Lucy held the sword in a way that made Brody believe she knew how to use it. "Look at him. He's an Eater."

"He's fed. That's not the same thing," Kyle said. "We felt someone arrive."

"You saying a new arrival took an Eater alone?"

"I don't know yet," Kyle said. "So let's hear from our man here. What's your story, Will Brody?"

Brody said, "What's an Eater?"

"Well, we're not the first new friends you made today, right?"

It was a test, he realized. All of this. Some sort of interview. He didn't know what these people were talking about, or what they stood for, but they were measuring him. "I was attacked by three strangers. Two men and a woman. They had weapons, a machete, a knife. And they were . . . fast. Strong." He hesitated, shrugged. "They did impossible things. I hit one, and the others backed off."

"You hit him, and they just went away?"

"Her," Brody said. "It was the woman. And I cracked her skull with a fire extinguisher." He held the gaze, shoulders back.

After a moment Kyle nodded. He glanced over his shoulder at Lucy. "Self-defense."

"If it's true. He could be trying to bluff his way out."

"A desperate Eater might try that, one with no gas in the tank. But he's shiny. If he didn't want to fight, he could have run. Not like we could catch him."

That gave Lucy pause. Kyle turned back to him. "Sorry about all this, Brody. If you are what you say you are, I'm sure you're confused. But we have to be certain. This far out, newbies mostly end up dinner. But"—he gave the axe a little swing, like a one-handed golf putt—"somehow, you took three."

That might have been the most dramatic understatement Brody had ever heard. But he was very aware of the sway of Kyle's axe, the comfort with which Lucy held the sword, the way Antoine had slowly been circling. If this was a test, he hadn't passed yet. "I made it into a liquor store, locked the security gate. Two of the men, the, ah, Eaters, they bent the bars. The woman came through alone. It took her all of a second and a half to beat me down. I'm only here because she got cocky and I got lucky. After I killed her, the others backed off. Now can I ask a question?"

"Shoot."

"I'm a special agent with the FBI. Why are you all acting like I'm a security risk?"

Antoine snorted a laugh. "I think he's okay."

Kyle turned to Lucy. "You?"

The woman bit her lip, studied him carefully. Then nodded and lowered her sword. Brody exhaled.

"Sorry about that," Kyle said, slinging the axe on his back. "It's just that it's rare for new arrivals to make it unless we get to them first. I've never met a flush newbie."

"Flush?"

"Minty fresh. Sparkly. Full tank."

Brody just stared at him.

"Right. How to explain." Kyle scratched at his chin. "Okay. Do me a favor and remember that we're the good guys."

The man lunged at him, left hand flickering out in a fast jab. On instinct, Brody started to put up a block.

Everything changed.

Kyle's punch turned from a lightning strike to a gentle crawl, his fist creeping through the air as if punching underwater. Brody dipped his shoulder, conscious of the ease and play and power of his muscles as he planted his foot to spring forward, closing his left hand around Kyle's wrist and twisting, locking the elbow and tugging the shoulder. He could see Kyle's expression change, one micromuscle at a time, the pain tightening his lips and widening his eyes. Brody maintained the grip on Kyle's wrist as he stepped forward and put the blade of the Bowie knife to the carotid artery.

No one else had moved more than a couple of inches.

"Shit!" Kyle yelped. "Easy, easy, you'll break my arm!"

Lucy cursed, and Antoine cocked his baton. At a distance, the others yelled, raised their weapons. Time seemed to have returned to normal. Brody maneuvered Kyle between him and the archer kid. "What the hell?"

"I thought it'd be easier to show you than—Jesus, man, seriously, lighten up on my arm, you don't know your own strength right now."

He eased back, though he didn't release the hold. "Start talking. What's going on?"

"You're not dreaming. You know that, right?"

Brody could feel the warmth of Kyle's breath, could smell the slightly sour odor of all three of them. Could see every detail of the buildings beyond the bridge, hear the murmur of the river. His feet were tired from the walk, and his hands were sweaty. He nodded.

"Okay, so you're not dreaming, but everything has changed." A bead of sweat ran down Kyle's temple. "You already know the truth. I'm sure you've got theories to explain it away, but in your heart you know."

"What do you mean?"

"Come on. The whole city has taken a powder. A couple of strangers tried to murder you with machetes. What's the last thing you remember before it all got weird?"

*A rainbow sun born in a dark church, and a wave of shimmering razors riding a shock wave that hurled you into the air—*

"That's it," Kyle said. "I can see it on your face, man. You got it."

It couldn't be. It was impossible. There was no way, no *way*, that this was . . . he was on an operating table, Claire was in the waiting room, this was a hallucination . . .

"Brody. Listen to me. I know what you're going through. We've all been there. Stop messing around and say it." There was honest sympathy in Kyle's voice. "Say what you know is true."

The air smelled of river rot and rusted metal. Cloud shadows reflected in ten thousand windows. Funny, the sky had been bright blue when he went into the church.

Brody let go of the man's wrist. Lowered the knife and stepped back. "I'm . . ." He knew the next word, felt the truth of it, but still, it caught on his tongue. He took a breath and tried again. "I'm dead."

"You're dead," Kyle agreed, rubbing at his elbow. "Welcome to the afterlife."

# TWELVE

There was little in the way of sunrise or set but there was day and night, and by that measure Edmund passed months and years and decades and more.

Afoot and alone he wandered, startled by land that seemed to sprawl forever. In the beginning he stayed near the sea, but as he encountered others like himself and fed on their spirits as he had fed on the bodies of his crewmates, he took from them the things they knew, and grew confident. Grew hungry to wander the breadth of this new world, his kingdom.

Edmund saw many things.

Forests so dense he stood where man might never have. Trees ten people couldn't have encircled, wet brown bark carpeted in moss. Ridges of broken stone spires like fingers grasping for heaven. Crystalline caverns stretching into intractable darkness. Swamps of treacherous mud spanning the horizon. On nights he'd eaten the soul of another, sometimes the clouds broke enough to reveal pinpoint stars circling the firmament.

The world changed around him. The huts of savages gave way to buildings of sawn lumber and churches of stone. Trading posts grew to towns and then to cities. Many of the things he saw in them were unfathomable; and yet it was in cities he most found others, though never one so fast or strong as he had grown, and so he came to understand pendulum clocks and pocket watches, sextants of brass and pianos of wood.

He fed when he chose, from hunger or desire. He dabbled in pleasures and he dabbled in cruelties.

From a fierce nigger whipped until his skin hung in ribbons and blood sluiced down his legs and his heart exploded, Edmund saw another land, and on it a golden cat the size of a calf. A predator that fed without fear and lived lazily between meals, and he liked the image.

Edmund watched battles in their aftermath, men rising from the ground only to see their enemies rise also, and as the bloody slaughter began again he laughed, for surely he was no longer of man.

On the muddy flats of a muddy river, in a city named Nouvelle-Orléans, he took a girl with skin like polished mahogany, and she cried out names of gods he had never heard of until he tasted her life and learned of Legba and Agwé and Samedi, not gods at all, but powerful spirits, capricious and wild, who rode their believers like horses.

No longer thin or weak, he remained restless of mind, and the idea that seized him seemed so obvious he could scarce believe it hadn't before.

Flush with the girl's energy, he stalked the city, looking for living ghosts. Pale people whose hold on their world was so slender they were almost in his. For centuries he had seen them, faint and flickering spirits, but still on the other side of the boundary. Beyond a gulf he could not cross, no matter how many souls he consumed. They were alive, and so not his to feed upon.

But perhaps to ride.

He found a woman ragged from poverty and mourning a husband gone. She drifted through her days like a shadow, picking through garbage and begging on the street, her squalling son beside her crowned in flies. At night Edmund crouched beside her rags and whispered, nourishing the blackest parts of her, tending her despair like a garden, and on the third morning she took her infant boy to the river and held his body beneath the muddy water until the splashing ceased.

And Edmund, plucking the reborn child up into his own arms, looked down at the wailing animal and knew that he had found a greater truth than any penitent or priest.

When God unleashed the flood, he had done it not to cleanse, but to grow.

It was in that rush of water that he became divine; in the slaughter that he fed. Not for hunger or pleasure but for power, harvesting the tiny energies of a million souls.

People, who glow like candle flames; faint and small alone, but in quantity enough, brighter than the sun.

# THIRTEEN

*Thank you for calling the Federal Bureau of Investigation tip line. All calls are recorded. Do you have something to report?*

*-Umm, yes, hello. I live in West Chicago, and there's a church. It's shut down, but I keep seeing a man going into it. He looks very suspicious.*

Claire skipped to the next.

*-Thank you for calling the Federal Bureau of Investigation tip line. All calls are recorded, do you have something to report?*

*-I, I think so. I keep seeing a man in a hoodie going into this church off Kedzie—*

To the final clip.

*-Thanks for calling the FBI tip line. All calls are recorded.*

*-Yeah, I just saw a man go into this abandoned church. It's been closed up for a while. It looked like he was carrying a gun.*

*-A gun? What kind of—*

Claire slumped against the counter and rubbed at her eyes.

That it was a trap had been immediately obvious. An abandoned building was a pointless target if you were hoping for casualties. But in the crush of the investigation—half the city descending on the church, securing the perimeter, going house to house in the neighborhood, attending to the wounded, communicating with the media—the obvious corollary had taken a few hours to realize.

If the sniper wanted his bomb to kill cops, he had to get them there. And the easiest way to do that was to call the tip line and report himself. She was listening to the voice of the man who had killed Will Brody—and seventeen other people.

From one perspective, it was sloppy that headquarters hadn't caught this. But they were dealing with thousands of calls a day. Each had to be transcribed, collated, and analyzed. And the lead had been pretty small; if there hadn't been the mention of the gun, it wouldn't even have been yellow flagged.

She'd heard the conversations a hundred times already, but even so, she set her phone to loop, let the words echo around her kitchen. 1:22 a.m., and the last place she wanted to be was home. But there was nothing else to do right now.

The sniper's voice was bland, calm. Probably white, probably Midwestern. The team had spent the whole afternoon working the calls. All came from separate burner phones. All were made in public places, none of which had closed-circuit cameras. Voice analysis specialists had pored over every word, looking at nuances of pronunciation and diction, ethnographic hints, idiom, word choice. Audio engineers had magnified the background noises and filtered the sound fifty different ways.

She supposed she should take some consolation in knowing that she'd been right when she'd told Agent Huang that this was the sniper. They'd used the data from the cell tower to pinpoint a handful of likely vantage points. On one of them, the fire escape of a neighboring building, they'd found cigarette butts. Camel Blues, the same brand the sniper favored. Formal DNA results would be available tomorrow, but the techs had already given her unofficial confirmation.

Yet like every other piece of evidence they'd collected, it offered them no leads. They already had the sniper's DNA—they just didn't have a match for it.

Several hours ago, Claire had called the director and asked permission to release the tapes to the media. He'd refused. The voice wasn't distinctive enough. All it would do was cause more panic, more useless tips they'd have to wade through.

He was right, she knew that, but it was driving her crazy to be so entirely on defense. To not have a single useful lead. Eighteen murders, and the man hadn't left one piece of evidence they could use to catch him—

*Stop,* she thought. *Stop pretending this is casework. Stop pretending you're not about to fall apart.*

She straightened, paced the length of the counter. Went to the windows and drew the curtains, then felt claustrophobic and reopened them. The plates from last night were still in the sink, bits of egg floating in a thin slick of water. Claire flashed on Brody teasing her last night, pretending to go cold, and then saying that thing, the most romantic thing she'd ever heard. She thought of Brody's hands in her hair as she undid the sash of her robe. When she'd looked at the clock it had mostly been to set up her joke, but she'd noted the time anyway, 1:29 a.m., and now the same clock read 1:23, which meant that less than twenty-four hours separated then and now.

Amazing. Impossible.

Twenty-four hours ago, she and Will had the door locked and the universe to themselves. Most people would call it foolish to discuss a future based on a few weeks of illicit romance. Neither of them cared. What had he said? *I know there's a whole world to Claire McCoy I haven't seen. I know it's ridiculous to feel like I've been waiting for you to come along. And I don't care. I have been waiting for you.*

She had felt exactly the same. Had imagined a life unspooling in front of them. When in fact he'd been hours from the end of everything.

Maybe it was the modern era, digital music and pictures in the cloud, hard drives and off-site backup, but it was impossible to believe she couldn't get back to that moment. The sheer strength of her desire to should have made it so. But there was no pressing CTRL+Z on a day, no loading a previous copy. She knew that time only flowed one direction, but it was one thing to know it and another to be standing on the opposite side of the divide, where every passing second pushed her farther away. Tomorrow at 1:29 it would be forty-eight hours. Some day it would be ten years.

*-Umm, yes, hello. I live in West Chicago, and there's a church. It's shut down, but I keep seeing a man going into it. He looks very suspicious.*

Claire went to the bathroom and splashed cold water on her face. As she was drying herself with the towel, she saw Will's ratty old toiletry kit. Robbed now of purpose. No one would shave with his razor, use his hair gel. Through the shower glass this morning billowing steam had made Brody a ghost, far away gone already. And he had in fact been hours from dying. How was it that she could not have known, not have sensed it?

*-I keep seeing a man in a hoodie going into this church off Kedzie—*

In the bedroom closet, two of his suits hung amidst her own clothes, along with a couple of shirts in dry cleaner plastic. She'd let him stake that claim in the first week, and it had felt weird not because she was scared but because she wasn't. Making room for him made perfect and uncomplicated sense.

*-I just saw a man go into this abandoned church. It's been closed up for a while. It looked like he was carrying a gun.*

Slowly, she turned and confronted the bed.

Told herself not to do it. Then crawled up onto it and collapsed with her face in the pillows on his side and buried her nose in them and breathed deep, and a fit of trembling swept her, sudden as an earthquake, her hands shaking and the tears so close, but god if she started crying—

The bedside clock changed to 1:28 a.m.

Claire leapt up and ran down the hall. Snatched her coat and purse and cell phone, then hurried out and let the door slam behind her.

# FOURTEEN

"Okay, listen," Kyle said. "I know how you're feeling. I went through it too, we all did. I know you've got a million questions. But we want to be home before dark. Safer that way. So." The man put a hand on his shoulder. "Are you okay?"

"Am I *okay*?"

"Are you okay enough? We got miles to cover."

Brody took a deep breath. "Yeah."

"Good man." Kyle turned away, cupped his hands over his mouth and shouted. "Everybody, this is Will Brody. He's coming with us. We'll do the get-to-know-you stuff back home, okay? Ready up, let's keep it fluid."

They cut east on Cermak to State, moving as a loose group past bland buildings and uncertain trees. The cars in the street were still. The shop windows were dark. The only things moving were the clouds and the thirty of them.

There were curious glances thrown his direction, but the bulk of everyone's attention was directed outward. They had an air of vigilant readiness to them, like soldiers moving through potentially hostile terrain. Brody was surprised how very glad he was to see other people. He drank in the details of them, the way a Hispanic dude in a Carhartt jacket favored his left leg as though it had been injured long ago, the quick smile of an older woman whose long hair was the color of cigarette smoke, the hushed joking of a pudgy boy with a snapped pool cue and an ebony girl carrying a length of rebar. It was comforting to be near them.

How quickly he'd come to fear wandering eternity alone.

Kyle had been right; Brody had known all along. He'd rebelled against it—he still rebelled against it—but some essential piece of his being knew. A metaphysical sensor light had blinked on. He was dead.

This was the afterlife.

He had so many questions they all seemed to collide, tangling in an intractable jumble of how's and why's and what next's. He opened his mouth, not sure what was going to come out. "So," he began. "This isn't Heaven."

"I sure hope not," Kyle said.

"Is it Purgatory?"

"Shit no. It's Chicago."

"Is this a redemption thing, we're here to atone for our sins?"

"I don't think so, but it might be." Kyle sighed. "Look, I'm not trying to be unhelpful, I'm really not. But we all got here the same way you did. We died, we woke up. If God is involved, he hasn't introduced himself. The echo didn't come with an instruction manual."

"The echo?"

"What we call it. Idea being, life is the sound, this is an echo. It's the world, but faded. So right now we're walking up State Street, the real State Street. That's why there are cars stopped at the lights, and keys in the cars. Everything that's in the real world is here except the people. Look, see that trash can?" Kyle pointed to a bin overflowing with newspapers and takeout containers and coffee cups. "It's full because the one in the world is full. If you swung back here tomorrow morning, it'd be empty, because Streets and San will have come by."

"So why can't we see people?"

"Because they're there, and we're here. They're creating the sound, we're living in the echo. There are drivers in the cars and clerks in the stores and ladies walking dogs. Living people, doing their thing. Totally unaware that at the same moment, us dead folks are walking through an echo of their world."

Brody tried to picture it, an overlap of the real and the invisible. If Kyle was right, it meant that throughout his life, everywhere he'd been, he might have been surrounded by the dead. When he went into Starbucks for his morning coffee, murdered men and women had pressed against the glass. When he jogged down the street, he'd been running through people he couldn't see. Last night, when he and Claire made love, a dead child might have been sitting on her couch.

The thought made him shiver. It was repellent, horrifying, to imagine worlds overlaying each other that way. The dead existing in a world at a right angle to reality. What right did they have?

Then he remembered that now he was one of the dead, and shivered again. He would never do any of those things again. Never have a hot cup of coffee, or enjoy a morning jog.

*Or see Claire.*

The thought was a gut punch. Too big to grasp. He wouldn't see her again. Wouldn't touch her, wouldn't talk to her, wouldn't get to enjoy the pyrotechnics of her mind at work. And not just her. His parents, his sister, his friends, his—

With an effort, he forced the thoughts down. There were questions that needed answering. He had to understand. "So why aren't the cars moving? I get that we can't see the people, or I'll accept it, but if this is an echo—"

"No instruction manual, remember? But my guess is that it's because we're not quite dead. Or, really, we're not quite *gone*. We're dead, yeah, but here we are, walking and talking. There's something left to react to." Kyle looked sideways, read the bafflement on Brody's face. "Okay, like this. Those cars are frozen in the place they were when we came along. But when we leave, the echo will go back to reflecting the living world."

"So if we went around the block—"

"We'd come back to different cars in different places. But if we set up camp here tonight, everything would stay the same. Something about us holds this world in place. But when we leave, it refreshes like a web browser."

They'd reached the southern edge of downtown, the rust-fenced parking lots and bland academic buildings of Columbia College to the east, the gargoyled grandeur of the Harold Washington Library ahead of them. An unlit sign on an empty bar offered Coronas by the bucket. They walked down the middle of the street, threading their way between cars. The quiet was startling. Brody had never realized just how loud the city was until all the sound went away, air conditioners and El trains and the buzz of neon.

He was dizzy with the effort of trying to observe and evaluate and understand, to parse and place and sort. Everything here felt real, and yet everything had seismically shifted. It reminded him of his first deployment. In Afghanistan, he'd realized that the rules he'd assumed to be foundational were actually just affectations Americans enjoyed. The revelation had shaken him, but there was something brilliant in a hard slap to the cheek too. It woke you up. Reminded you that everyone had their own reality, and yours was just one version.

*So do now what you learned to do then. Accept that the new rules are the only rules, and learn them, fast.*

"The way I moved when you tried to hit me. That's what you meant when you said I was flush and shiny and all that."

"Yup."

"And I can do that because I just died?"

"Because you just killed."

"Huh?"

"How did it feel?"

The question put him back there, the cool painted metal of the canister, the visceral yielding of the woman's skull. "What's that got to do with anything?"

"I'm answering your question. How did you feel?"

"She and her friends attacked me. They'd have gutted me if I hadn't—"

"Shit, Brody, I don't mean 'Boo-hoo you killed someone how do you feel about it you monster,' I mean: How. Did. You feel."

"I felt . . ." He realized now what the man was getting at. "Good. I felt good."

"You felt great," Kyle said. "Win the lottery great. Weekend in Cabo with bisexual lingerie models great. Right?"

*Right.* There had been the healed wounds, of course, but it had been more than that. A loose-limbed power, and a sense that everything had grown more vivid. Like a drug, only clean. No intoxication, no blurriness. He still felt it, like he could run for days.

*Or bend steel bars. Or move so fast everyone else seems to be standing still.*

"Kill here, you get stronger," Kyle continued. "Dunno why. But bottom line, it lets you do some pretty incredible stuff."

"And you can tell by looking at me?"

"Yeah, you sort of glow."

Brody held up his hands and squinted at them. No light he could see. But he remembered his feeling at the liquor store, huddled behind the security cage. A sensation that the three were more in focus than the rest of the world.

"So the Eaters hunt people for a rush. What, were they serial killers when they were alive?"

"Nah," Kyle said. "Most of them were just people. I mean, you know that, you lived her."

Brody felt a rush of shame, like he'd been caught digging through the girl's underwear drawer. True, the violation had happened through no intention of his own, but it had been a violation nonetheless. And a far more personal one than looking at lacy underthings. He'd snooped on Raquel's most intimate moments, experienced her secret thoughts. She hadn't been a bad person. There'd been baggage, sure, but it hadn't been excessively weighty.

"What happened to her?"

"Word is you smashed her skull with a fire extinguisher."

"No, I mean." Brody paused. "We're already dead, right? So what happens when you die here?"

"You die," Kyle said. "Maybe there's an echo after this one. But nobody's come back to tell us about it. So don't get any ideas of jumping off a building like you're going to wake up."

"But . . . what's the point? It has to mean *something*. Why are we here?"

Kyle hesitated. He dug in his pocket for a tin of Kodiak and placed a fat wad behind his lip. "Did you have the answer to that question when you were alive?"

"I . . ." Brody blew a breath. "I guess not."

"There you go." Without slowing down, Kyle turned in a circle, scanning the whole group, his lips moving as he counted them. Satisfied, he faced forward again. "Doesn't need to be any more complicated here."

It was an interesting notion. Brody hadn't spent a lot of time demanding an explanation from the cosmos. He'd just lived. Tried to be a good friend, a good person. To enjoy the moment. But didn't knowing this truth change things? Surely there was some purpose, some meaning.

Kyle looked over, then clapped him on the shoulder. "Listen, man. It's a lot. Don't try to get it all at once, okay?"

"Take death one day at a time."

"You got it."

Downtown Chicago. Buildings scratching the bellies of swirling grey clouds. Dark stairs to the Red Line, dull stoplights swaying in the breeze.

Construction scaffolding without workers. Mannequins in the windows of American Apparel and Forever 21, coquettish guards for racks of clothing fading into gloom. *And you thought the city had gone strange before.*

As they passed Macy's, Brody caught a flicker of movement. A man's face in the third-floor window, a crossbow in one hand. Beside him stood a boy carrying a claw hammer.

"They with us?" He nodded to the third floor.

Kyle tracked the gesture. "No." He put his thumb and forefinger in his mouth and blasted a whistle that would have made a drill sergeant proud. "Vamps, up top!" Hands flew to weapons, and postures stiffened. The archer nocked an arrow to his bow. Behind the glass, the two stared, faces twisted like hungry predators eyeing a meal they knew they couldn't bring down.

"If we're going to fight—" Brody started.

"We're not." Without glancing from the figures, Kyle waved a lasso gesture and shouted, "Keep it moving, keep it tight. I know we're close to home, but we ain't safe till we're safe. And how come the newbie spotted them first?"

The troop continued north, leaving the Eaters behind. The last Brody saw was the boy's hands shielding his eyes so he could press his face to the glass.

"You didn't go after them."

"No."

"Thirty of us, two of them."

"Yeah."

"Why?"

"Because I don't kill unless I have to." Kyle's voice was hard. "Do you?"

"How'd you die?"

Kyle glanced sideways. "Why?"

"Just making conversation. Trying to wrap my head around things."

The other man spat a stream of black juice on the ground. "I was a fireman. We were on a warehouse call. Smoke pouring out the windows, but no flame, and situation like that you gotta find the heart of the fire, so we're knocking in doors." He shrugged. "I didn't notice a hole in the floor. Woke up in the basement. Fell four stories with fifty pounds of gear on, but I'm fine. Not a scratch. It's a miracle! Until I realize the whole world has taken a hike."

His tone was acrid. Brody thought again of Claire, and his family. All the things he'd lost. He let the subject drop. They walked in silence up State to Wacker, the multileveled thoroughfare hugging the river.

"Home." Kyle gave an offhand point.

Brody followed the look to a clean black obelisk of Mies van der Rohe modernism standing fifty stories tall. A grid of mottled clouds reflected in the windows. "The Langham Hotel. That's home?"

"Pricey for the living, but free for us dead folk. I like the suites. Gotta climb a bunch of stairs, but when I bed down, I can pretend there's some society hottie getting nailed beside me."

Despite himself, despite everything, Brody smiled. "There's something very wrong with you."

As they neared the river, a whistle blew from the other side, not Kyle's thumb-and-finger version, but the old-fashioned metal sort favored by coaches and cops. The sequence was picked up and repeated by others farther away, the shrill notes bouncing discordantly off dark high-rises. The mood of the group eased notably, hands leaving weapons, people pairing off or hurrying across the bridge.

The hotel was nestled into a curve with limited avenues of approach. Anyone swimming the river or crossing the bridge would be an easy target for the sentries who watched out broken windows. And the streets running north, Brody knew, were broad and exposed, with few good hiding places. The choice of location began to make sense. Solid defensive ground.

The east side of the hotel was a curved driveway bounded by a curved sidewalk, and seemed to be the informal common area. Brody heard a guitar, and the sound of laughter. People lounged in chairs and expensive sofas, sharpening weapons and passing bottles. Their clothes tended to utility rather than fashion, the informal uniform being Levi's or Dickies, sweatshirts layered under work jackets, and good boots. The men ranged from scruffy to bearded, the women wore short hair or ponytails.

"Jesus, how many people are here?"

"About two hundred disciples of the Gospel According to Ray."

"The what?"

"Come on."

Everyone knew Kyle, and he nodded and smiled and shouted yo. When they saw Brody, their expressions changed, sometimes to curiosity, sometimes to something more brittle. It wasn't hostility, exactly, but a heightened awareness. The way people might look at a large dog wandering without a leash. He fixed a mild smile on his face and kept his posture relaxed.

A crash of breaking glass followed by high-pitched laughter made him jump. He turned to see a gang of children stomping on a parked cab. One of them wound up a Louisville Slugger and knocked the windshield the rest of the way in while the others danced and cheered.

Kyle followed his gaze, shrugged.

Brody said, "They're . . ."

"Dead? Sure. Get a lot of kids. Dylan there," pointing to the one with the bat, "chased his ball into the street. Got creamed by a delivery truck. Dragged his body thirty yards. But," Kyle smiled wolfishly, "he did get his ball back."

Before Brody could reply, a woman stepped out of the hotel, letting the door drift shut behind. Medium height, brown hair, a pretty face running to elfin. He recognized her immediately. Even after everything he'd already seen, after his existential certainty and his grudging acceptance, that was the moment he knew.

*A carton of vanilla ice cream melting onto pavement.*

Emily Watkins. The seventeenth victim. He'd stood over her body yesterday. He'd looked through her purse and visited her house. He had a flash of sitting opposite her husband, trying to think of anything to say. Noticing all the details of a life, the photographs and bookshelves, the bills and the furniture, and thinking how Emily would never again see them. Would never again curl up in a favorite chair, or cook a meal, or reach out for her husband after a nightmare.

Yet here she was, walking toward the river. In-turned shoulders and a haunted look in her eyes, yes, but walking.

*Oh my god. Oh my god.*

It was so huge and horrifying it was almost funny. Everything he had once thought about Emily Watkins now applied to him.

Just this morning he'd awakened next to Claire. Her eyes had been open, and she'd been radiant, smiling. When he asked what she had been thinking about, she'd said, "Us," and rolled over to face him, and they'd lain there grinning and staring like kids. Silently imagining forty or fifty more years of waking up like this.

Instead, he had been hours from losing everything forever.

"Brody? You okay?"

A ribbon of vomit had leapt to the back of his mouth. He forced himself to swallow. "Sure."

"I want you to meet some new friends."

# FIFTEEN

Kyle picked a path between the couches and chairs, the clustered groups. The mood was jovial, people laughing and flirting, drinking from plastic cups. It put Brody in mind of a heavily armed block party.

Near the river, Kyle found the person he was looking for, a handsome teenaged boy playing an acoustic guitar. There was something familiar about him, though Brody couldn't place what. He was pretty good, playing what sounded like an acoustic cover of a Lil Wayne song as kids, none older than six or so, danced with spastic unself-consciousness.

Kyle waited until the teenager finished, then said, "Hey DeAndre, want you to meet somebody. New arrival. This is Will Brody."

The teenager held the guitar by its neck and stuck out his right hand, then looked at Brody and made a double take. "Whoa. You did an Eater?"

It was going to need some getting used to, the idea that people could see on him a physical manifestation of something that had happened hours ago. "Yes."

"Damn, man. New to the show and you faced off a vamp. That's something."

"Three," Kyle said. "My man here got jumped by three Eaters, and came out on top."

"Shit." DeAndre stretched the word out. "That's something," he repeated.

"It was luck," Brody said. "I mostly got my butt kicked." As he spoke, he saw that the boy's eyes had dropped to the Glock on his hip.

DeAndre's posture had stiffened. In a colder tone, he said, "You police?"

"FBI."

"He's one of the good guys," Kyle said. "But he's had a long day. We need to fill him in on things. Lucy's grabbing Sonny; could you do me a favor and find the Professor, send him up to the lounge?"

"Sure."

"Thanks, man." Kyle bumped fists with the boy and then gestured for Brody to follow. When they were out of earshot, the man said, "Sorry about that. He's not a big fan of cops."

"Why?"

"One of them killed him."

"Huh?"

"Chi-raq, right? That's what DeAndre tells me people are calling it now."

"He was a gangbanger?"

"Nope. Just black at the wrong moment."

Suddenly Brody remembered why the kid had looked familiar. DeAndre Williams had been shot and killed by police officers in June. The cops' claim that he had fired first had withered under scrutiny—he'd been an honors student with no history of violence, no weapon was found, and their body cams had mysteriously failed. Brody sighed, rubbed his eyes. "Crap."

"Yeah. Speaking of, unless you've got a sentimental attachment, you may as well toss that." Kyle gestured at the Glock.

"Guns don't work here?"

"Not much does. Come on."

They'd gone through the lobby and up a set of stairs to the lounge. Brody imagined the space was normally seductive; dim lights and glowing candles, wall-to-wall glass showcasing the river and the sparkling city beyond. But seductive wasn't the word he'd choose now. The only illumination was muddy daylight. The river looked cold and the city beyond was dark. Kyle flopped on a couch. "You a bourbon man?"

"Sure."

"In the other room, behind the bar, top shelf, there's a bottle of Pappy. Wanna grab it?"

Brody nodded, then headed off in the direction of Kyle's wave. The floors were pale polished hardwood, and the light fixtures funky discs of bronze, the bulbs unlit. As he rounded the corner, he saw a massive glass-fronted wine cellar, hundreds of bottles presented like holy artifacts. At the top of the tiered bar, he found a three-quarters-full bottle of Pappy Van Winkle 23. He'd never tried the stuff—it was way above his pay grade—and couldn't resist pulling the top to inhale the rich caramel heat.

He returned, bottle in one hand and two rocks glasses in the other, and set them on the table. Before he could sit down, Kyle said, "Thanks, man. But we've got friends joining. Could you grab a couple more glasses?"

Annoyance spiked him. He'd died, and somehow he was a gopher? He grunted, said, "Sure."

When he was five steps away, Kyle said, "Oh, while you're there, grab the Pappy, would you?"

He stopped. Spun on a heel. Looked at Kyle splayed on the couch, already pouring from the bottle of bourbon. The man winked at him, a small smile on his face.

Brody turned, walked back around to the bar. Took in the wine cellar. The tiered bar. The bottle of Pappy Van Winkle 23, right exactly where it had been when he grabbed it a minute ago. It appeared to be identical: it faced the same direction, had the exact same amount of bourbon in it.

*No. Not identical.*

*The same.*

He took it and a couple more glasses, then walked back. "So that was a teachable moment, then?"

Kyle smiled. "Better to show than tell, right?"

"Does your elbow agree?"

The fireman, halfway through a slug of bourbon, cough-laughed amber liquid across the expensive couches. "Hey, don't make me waste it. People are crazy for this stuff, drop a couple grand a bottle."

"Lemme ask you. What would happen if I went back to that wine cellar and smashed everything?"

"You'd make a helluva mess."

"But only here."

Kyle nodded. "Echo only goes one direction. There were probably plenty of moments in your life when some dead dude was having a screaming hissy fit right next to you, smashing up the place and crying his eyes out, and you never knew it."

"Or maybe," a man said, "you sensed it even if you couldn't see it."

Brody turned to see a short, paunchy man standing at the entrance to the lounge. There was something almost grey about him, like in the right light he might be translucent. "Maybe we affect the world of the living all the time. Did you ever have a moment when—for no reason at all—you were suddenly melancholy, or angry? Nothing to do with you. As though the mood had been floating around like weather."

"Sure."

"Well, maybe that was a dead man having a 'hissy fit.' Maybe you felt his pain and loss. Maybe the connection between life and death is more porous than we think."

"Brody—I assume everybody calls you Brody, I'm sure going to—this is Arthur Johnson. We call him Professor."

"Kyle does, at least."

"You *were* a professor."

"I taught high school science. I was a babysitter." Arthur stepped forward, held out a hand. "Nice to meet you. So you killed an Eater?"

Brody sighed. "Yes. Barely."

Kyle grinned. "My man Brody here took on five Eaters—"

"Three."

"And came out on top."

"And got lucky."

"I assume," Arthur gestured at the sidearm, "you were in law enforcement?"

"I am—was—an FBI agent."

Arthur lit up. "That's wonderful! Just wonderful."

"It is?"

Kyle nodded. "You're going to be a very popular boy, Brody."

"What he means to say," Arthur said, taking the glass Kyle handed him, "is that trained fighters are always welcome. You're going to make this a safer place."

"I . . ." Brody raised his arms, lowered them. It was nice to know he was welcome, but somehow he wasn't in the mental space to take on responsibility for other people right now. "Can I have one of those?"

Kyle slid a drink across the table, the liquid sploshing over the side. Brody caught it just before it fell. He raised it, took a moment to bask in the glow of the scent, then sipped. Autumn sunlight slipped down his throat and radiated through his body.

"Good?"

"Yeah."

"Enjoy it. It won't always taste so sweet."

"Huh? Why?"

"You boys started without us." Apart from the katana jutting up from her hip, Lucy looked like a soccer mom, the sexy new breed that did CrossFit and wore yoga pants. She was of average height, but the guy beside her made her look like a miniature. Brody put him at six four and 240. His shaggy hair and biker leathers gave him the aspect of a Viking. There was something odd about him. At first Brody thought he'd turned the lights on, but nothing else was brighter. It was just that the dim illumination of the lounge seemed to fall more strongly on him.

*Like Raquel and her friends.*

*Like you.*

Brody set down the glass and stood. There were knives slung on the biker's belt and patches on the leathers. They marked him as an Outlaw, a one-percenter motorcycle club that trafficked meth in significant quantities. For a moment everyone stopped.

"Sonny," the biker said.

"Brody."

"You killed. Recently."

"You too."

"Self-defense."

"Me too."

Sonny paused, nodded, then came around the side of the chairs and lowered himself onto a loveseat. Lucy unbuckled her sword, leaned it against the table, and sat down beside him. Brody noticed their thighs touched.

"You get that we're dead, right?" Sonny's voice was surprisingly mellifluous.

"Yeah."

"So the things between us don't much matter anymore."

There was a part of Brody that wanted to argue. The choices made in life had to count for something, even in death, or what was the point? But he reminded himself that he was in a new world with new rules. Not like he was going to flash his badge. He made a noncommittal shrug and kept his gaze steady.

Meanwhile, Kyle had poured two more bourbons and passed them out. He threw the now empty bottle of Pappy against a mirrored wall, where it exploded. With a grin, he raised his own glass. "To our newest arrival."

Brody hesitated, then leaned in. The five of them clinked glasses.

"Mr. Brody—" Arthur started.

"Just Brody is fine."

"You must have questions."

Not an hour ago Kyle had delivered the most dramatic understatement of Brody's life. *What are the odds another would top it in the same day?* He wanted to know so many things it was hard to figure out where to start. He paused, tried to organize his thoughts, then just picked one at random. "The math doesn't work."

The others exchanged glances. Arthur said, "Which math?"

"Kyle says this is where we go when we die. But if that's true, it should be elbow to elbow. Like fifty people should've popped in while you poured drinks."

"Not everyone ends up here," Lucy said. "Just people who died too soon."

"No," Arthur cut in. "That suggests destiny. We don't know that predestination is involved. It's more accurate to say those who die *abruptly*. Especially those who were vital and strong. Murders, fatal accidents, tragedies."

"Why?"

"Are you religious?"

Brody held up a hand, rocked it back and forth.

"Religions are rooted in explaining what happens after death. Live by certain tenets, and afterward you float on clouds playing a harp, or lie in gardens with virgins, or join the mind of God. Maybe that's true, but it's not where we are. And unfortunately all any of us know about this world is what we've been able to figure out for ourselves."

"Kinda like life," Kyle said.

Arthur continued as if undisturbed. "I was stabbed trying to fight off a mugger. Stupid. Kyle fell fighting a fire. Sonny was executed by the cartels. Lucy—well, she'll tell you if she wants. Drive-bys, car accidents, house fires, domestic violence. That's the start to everyone's story here. How did you die?"

"In an explosion," Brody said. "I was chasing a terrorist. He's killed seventeen people in the last two weeks."

"We know," Lucy said. "Where do you think they went?"

Brody flashed back to Emily Watkins, staring out at the river. Holy shit. If the victims were here, he could talk to them, see what they remembered. Maybe they'd seen something useful, something that could—

*What? Help you arrest the man who killed you?*

Brody said, "Why just people who die that way?"

"Are you familiar with the term 'potential energy'?"

"More or less."

"Watch." Arthur scooped up a glass with an unlit votive candle and held it above the table. "Mass, height, and gravity combine to give this potential energy measured in joules. The candle itself hasn't changed. But." He opened his fingers, and the glass and votive clattered to the polished wood surface of the table. They bounced apart, then rolled to a stop. "Simple physics. Now, a thought experiment. Imagine two people die. One is an old man riddled with cancer. And the other is a little girl hit by a car."

Brody shrugged. "One's typical and the other's a tragedy."

"Yes, but imagine the potential energy that child possesses. How many decades might she have lived? How many children and grandchildren and great-grandchildren died along with her? Think of the weight of that, the energy, the *mass* of the future gathered in a child."

"You're talking about fate," Brody said. "I don't believe in fate."

"No, I'm talking about undiscovered science. A thousand years ago, people believed the earth was flat. Five hundred years ago, doctors thought diseases were caused by an imbalance in the humors. A century ago, visiting the moon was the stuff of fantasists. There are always things we don't know yet, and they always look like superstition until we understand." Arthur paused, leaned forward. The light played strangely on his skin, and for a moment Brody almost thought he could see through him to the window beyond. "Is it really so hard to imagine there's energy to life we don't know how to measure? Some vital, quantifiable connection between ourselves and the universe that doesn't appear under a microscope?"

"So this is a behind-the-scenes dimension." Brody stared at the amber reflections on his fingers. "A filing cabinet for people that slip through the existential colander."

"For people who died with too much potential energy to move on to whatever comes next. Yes."

"How long?"

"How long what?"

"How long do I stay here?"

The four exchanged glances. Finally, Arthur said, "I've been here twenty years."

Brody laughed, once. The sound hung awkwardly in the air. The others just looked at him. After a moment he stood and walked to the window. The ghost of his reflection overlaid the city. Even with all the lights out and darkness falling, it was a tremendous view, the skyline a graphite cliff. On the sidewalk below, he could see shadowy figures lounging on couches. Laughter carried up, and the sound of DeAndre's guitar. Brody took a sip of bourbon. It reminded him of something. "What did you mean before, Kyle? About this not always tasting good."

"Remember how I told you to think of this as an echo? I didn't just mean the city. I meant us too."

"So?"

"So, what happens to echoes?"

It all clicked. Brody had an almost physical sensation of understanding, an intuitive leap that he knew to be true. A clean, cold, ruthless logic underpinning all he'd seen. He walked back and dropped on the couch. The leather was very soft. He felt a sudden urge to lie down, to use his forearm for a pillow and stretch his legs and close his eyes. "They fade. Echoes fade."

"Exactly."

"That's why there are no lights on, or fires going. Why my gun doesn't work."

"Those things either require or create energy."

"And that's the real reason the Eaters do what they do. Because echoes fade. They never get stronger. So the only energy here"—he paused—"is us. What we bring."

Arthur nodded. "And we're fading too."

"But you can take the energy from others," Sonny said. "Kill here, the sky gets brighter, food tastes better. Do it enough and maybe you live forever."

"Not to mention being able to punch through a wall," Kyle added.

"My god." Brody rested his hands on the table and took deep breaths. It was as though he'd been studying blueprints, only to realize they were for a concentration camp. People cut down in their prime, cast into a bleak middle space, hunting each other for the scraps of remaining life. "My god."

"There have always been people willing to crush others for their own benefit." Arthur shrugged. "It's just more literal here."

From outside came the sound of glass shattering. The bourbon's glow had turned into fiery heartburn, and he had an urge to vomit right on this expensive table. This morning he'd woken in a warm bed with the woman he loved. "No," Brody said. "This can't be it. This can't be what happens."

"It is." Sonny's voice was calm and steady.

"No." He rose fast. The motion felt right, vital. Brody stood looking at them. Four armed strangers sprawled across the darkening lounge of a luxury hotel in an abandoned city in a dead world.

"Brody—" Kyle started to say.

But he was already heading for the door.

# SIXTEEN

Walking turned to jogging turned to running turned to sprinting.

Down the steps and through the lobby, blowing past two people coming in, their startled exclamations left behind as he hit the curved driveway. Night was falling, and the people arrayed on couches were dodgy shadows and eye glints, their voices rising to him, some jovial, some alarmed, but Brody ignored it all, just chose left at random and pushed into the sprint. His muscles reveled in it, the motions easy and strong, leaning into the run and bounding on his toes, each stride longer than the one before. Running like he'd never run before, running faster than it was possible to run, the wind whipping his face and the world almost blurring. He gave it everything, wanting his lungs to burn and his heart to rage and his guts to tremble. The physical sensations would overwhelm anything else, and though they wouldn't last, for a brief time the world would narrow to nothing but screaming muscles and a gasping for breath.

It occurred to him to wonder if being out alone would make him a target for Eaters, and he felt a flash of savage joy at the prospect. Bring them on.

Blocks flowed beneath his feet, became a mile. Then two. Five. All at an impossible, inhuman sprint.

And yet the pain wouldn't come.

When he finally realized he wasn't going to be able to punish the world away, he let the run fade. He drifted to a stop, the sound of his footfalls bouncing off the walls of empty buildings. His breath came as easily as if he'd been sitting still.

While he'd been sprinting, he'd paid no attention to where he was going, taking turns at random, focusing on nothing but trying to find the pain. Now, as he looked up and saw where his feet and subconscious had brought him, he realized he'd been successful after all.

He'd found the pain.

———

"Lunch. Kind of a get-to-know-you thing." The new boss wore a tailored black suit with a white blouse, top two buttons open, revealing a delicate silver pendant. Her hair was down, and her perfume was clean and citrusy. Word was she'd been handpicked by the director. Hard to know what that meant, but no one had been happy to hear the ASAC job had gone to someone from DC. "You pick the place."

It wasn't passive aggression, the restaurant he chose. So what that he'd applied for the ASAC position himself, and thought he had a good shot? That didn't mean that he was trying to make her uncomfortable. Okay, sure, she'd probably meant something a little more formal. A restaurant with silverware, for example.

She parked in front of a check-cashing place and they stepped out into a sweltering afternoon, the air gritty and filled with the rumble of trucks. The block was aggressively ugly, carpet wholesalers and chain stores and cracked concrete with weeds growing through it. He gestured to a taco joint painted a shade best described as Kermit. "Hope you don't mind eating with your fingers."

She'd smiled like she knew what he was doing, and okay, maybe it had been passive aggression. "L'Patron, huh? Smells good."

They waited in line and talked small. Fans whirred in the tiny kitchen, fighting a losing battle against the smoking grease. The radio blared '90s power pop. When they finally reached the counter, he made the *you first* gesture. But instead of ordering, she paused, looked right at him. "Can I trust you?"

There was something in it, a swagger that he dug. Brody turned to the cashier, said, "Four carne asada and two tilapia tacos, please. Elotes. Oh, and pickled veggies."

———

Under swirling grey skies, in a dead city, Brody stood opposite the dark restaurant. Hands in his pockets, then out again. Arms crossed.

It was the same, but not. The same hangover color scheme, the same cracked sidewalk, the same payday loan place. But no people, no smell of grilling meat or rumble of trucks.

Just silence like he'd never heard before.

———

"Oh, merciful god," ASAC McCoy said, around a mouthful of food. She held the taco in both hands like she was afraid someone would take it away. "I want this for lunch every day forever."

"Right?" He was halfway done with his first carne asada, hadn't meant to be, but goddamn did these guys know what they were doing, a serious char on steak still pink in the center wrapped in homemade corn tortillas.

"Nice pick, man." She sucked juice off her fingers. "Everybody else is choosing these boring places. Eddie Huang took us to a hotel restaurant, for god's sake."

"Fail."

"Yeah," she said. "Big fail."

His teeth had just sunk in, and he kept going, took the bite, chewed it slowly. Thought. "It's a sort of test, isn't it? 'Get to know you' means more than one thing."

Her smile came and went fast, but it was made of moonlight.

"Huh," he said, and wondered if there was a reason he hadn't gotten her job.

———

Brody stared. The memories gnawing sharp as rats in his gut. He forced himself to take a breath, then another. Some part of him wondering what he was breathing. He was dead. Did he need air? Was this air, or just a pale reflection of it?

The brutal logic of the echo kept running in his head. He supposed he'd gotten lucky with the fire extinguisher. It was a simple mechanical device, just gas under pressure. If there had been an electronic or chemical component, he'd be dead now.

*Dead. Ha.*

He couldn't stop cataloging the things that were no longer. A dead world with no energy of its own. No fire, no heat, no computers or cell phones. No steaming showers or hot meals.

But really all that meant a thing to him was, no Claire.

———

"After that I worked gangs, posing as a money man for Sinaloa. Funny," he wiped his mouth with his fourth napkin, "I thought undercover, I thought, you know, *Serpico*. Long hair, no showers. But instead I had a budget to buy Ermenegildo Zegna suits, Barker Alderney shoes."

She laughed. "I liked it better when the bad guys dressed disco. With snakeskin boots."

"Not me. Those suits were *nice*." He shook the ice in his cup. "What about you?"

"What about me?"

"Ever work undercover?"

"You're asking, bean counter or cop."

"No." He paused. Shrugged. "Okay, yeah."

"Bit of both," she said. "I got my law degree at Georgetown, fifth in my class, *and* I shot 97 percent on my last firearms quarterly. What'd you shoot?"

"Um. Less."

She barely registered his words, just leaned in, fire made form. "Do I have my eye on the big chair? Yes. Did the director give me this job? Sure. Was it because I earned his respect? What do you think?"

He dropped his napkin, leaned back, hands up. "Whoa. I didn't mean—"

"Yes, you did."

Brody opened his mouth, closed it. "You're right. Sorry."

She'd been about to say something else, he could see it in the way she aimed the taco at him. For a moment she hung on the edge, ready to engage. Then, when he added nothing else, she pulled back slowly. "Huh."

"What?"

"Just not what . . . nothing."

———

When Brody tugged the door, it opened. The squeak was familiar, a detail his brain had collated and stored. But instead of being hit with a blast of smoky air and the smell of grilling meat, the place smelled faintly dusty. The interior was dark, the tiny kitchen past the counter falling into shadow.

Even in the dim light, he could see that the chalkboard listed today's special. Napkin dispensers stood beside squeeze bottles of salsa. The trash was full of balled-up waxed paper and aluminum foil. Chairs were pulled out from the tables, cocked at angles. Like he'd wandered into some sort of practical joke, everyone told to hide a minute before his arrival.

Then he realized the truth. The chairs held people. It was the dinner rush. He was surrounded by people. The chairs were pulled out because people sat in them right now. The place was probably packed, a line out the door. That two-top might hold college students on a date. A mother might be offering a spoonful of corn to her son, telling him to try it, you don't know if you like something until you try. Hell. Claire could be here.

*If anyone is hiding, it's you.*

Brody wanted to grab a chair and toss it through the window. To topple the trash bin and hurl the salsa bottles and rage that he was here, he was right here, for the love of Christ, he existed, he was among them.

*When a dead man screams, does anyone hear?*

———

"My dad," Claire said.

"Cop?"

"Hmm? No. He was in the lighting business. Custom stuff, restaurants, cars. But my mom was sort of . . ." She shrugged. "I don't know. Checked out. She was an okay mom and all, but just not really present, you know? I don't think she had the life she'd imagined."

"What was that?"

"You know, I've got no idea. Princess of Monaco?"

"Good work if you can get it."

"My dad, though, he and I always understood each other."

"Example."

"Okay." Her eyes on him but far away. "He bought this old sailboat on a whim. A 1978 Beneteau he'd spotted rotting behind a gas station. Thing was a wreck. We patched the fiberglass and rebuilt the engine and put in new teak. Took like a year, every weekend we were out there."

"How old were you?"

"Ten? No, eleven."

"So were you just passing tools and stuff?"

She shook her head. "Some dads with daughters wish they had sons, so they try to make them into boys. Mine was more like, 'Why wouldn't I teach them both the same things?' He was fine with me getting my ears pierced and wearing skirts, but he also had me using a circular saw when I was seven. I did most of the engine work because I could wriggle back there. I think about it sometimes, the way it felt to be crammed in. Sweat in my eyes, the smell of diesel and oil, something digging into my back."

"He teach you to sail too?"

"That's the best part." Her laugh was great, full throated and unabashed. "Day we launched was the first time it occurred to me to ask. We're at the marina, the crane is lowering it into the water, we're both petrified it's going to sink right to the bottom. But it floats, just bobs there pretty as anything. We cheered and hugged and slapped hands. And then I asked him if we could take it for a sail. He looked at me funny, and said, 'Monkey, I don't know how yet.'"

"You're kidding."

"Hand to God."

"Then why'd he buy a sailboat?"

"Well, the 'yet,' right?"

———

Brody paced the empty restaurant. Trying to control his breathing. Hand tracing chair backs. Out the window, the buildings were just dark shapes against dark clouds. His ghostly silhouette trailed in the windows.

This was where they'd sat. These two seats at the window counter. The wood stained and scarred, the stools uncomfortable.

Brody pulled his out and sat down.

———

Claire glanced at her watch. He took the cue, said, "Time to go?"

"Yeah."

He piled their baskets on the tray, then started to stand. Halfway through, he realized she'd made no motion to leave. Brody looked up, questioning, and their eyes met.

They'd been looking at each other the whole time, but this was different. It was like something stuck. She didn't blink, and neither did he. They just looked at each other. Openly. Honestly. Too long.

He felt something shift inside him. Like the hesitant instant when an airplane first took to the sky, the wheels only a bare breath above ground. And he could see that she felt it too. A vertiginous moment, a galvanic shiver of recognition.

*Oh,* he'd thought. *Oh. Hello.*

———

Brody laid a hand on her stool. The vinyl was cool and worn. He spun it to face him, just as it had been. Only weeks ago. Only a lifetime ago.

The sob tore through him, a physical thing yanked free. He clenched his fists until his hands shook.

And sat, alone, in an empty restaurant in an abandoned world, trying not to remember.

# SEVENTEEN

By the time the sun broke the edge of the lake, the sky was bright blue from horizon to horizon. With no clouds to dance on, the sunrise felt explosive, molten metal pouring across the waves. The water lapped gently, and from the harbor came the steady metallic ping of a halyard against a mast.

Claire thought, *The first sunrise of a world without him in it,* and something in her tore like tissue.

After fleeing her apartment she'd ended up driving aimlessly, cruising the streets of this city gone strange. Around four, dangerously tired, she realized she had to stop. The parking lot of Montrose Harbor had seemed as good a place as any. She lay in the front seat of her car for two hours, exhausted and restless and unsleeping, then gave up and wandered out to watch the day begin.

*It's time to go to work. Pack it away and go do your job.*

She watched the waves and thought about Will's ruined body. Remembered that smile of his, how it always made her feel like they'd been together forever, like they were meant for each other. Was it only yesterday morning that she'd indulged in the ludicrous, luxurious fantasy that maybe they were?

*Don't cry. Don't you dare cry.*

Claire dug out her phone, thinking she'd call Dad. She wanted to hear that delighted tone of his, the one he always had when her name came up on his screen. The one that reminded her what it felt like to be four years old and safe in strong arms. She could smell his aftershave, imagine the scratchy stubble on his chin.

But it was early. He'd answer, but he'd answer worried. He'd ask what was wrong, and she might tell him. And if she did that, she'd start crying, and she wasn't sure she'd be able to stop.

She forced herself to stand up, her body stiff and joints creaking. She took one last look at the water, and had a desperate desire to be out on it, gliding over pewter waves and leaving everything behind.

Instead she walked back across the withered grass to her car. The dash clock read 6:57. Her apartment wasn't more than a ten-minute drive from here, and on the way to the office. There would be time to shower.

Then she remembered the dirty dishes in the kitchen sink.

Claire stepped back into cool morning air, walked to the trunk. Long hours were part of the job, and she'd learned to stash clothes everywhere. She changed right there in the parking lot, too weary to care if a morning jogger caught a glimpse of skin.

Back in the car, she set the heat to blasting, then flipped down the visor. Did what she could with her hair. She'd have to stop at a drugstore on the way in to grab a toothbrush.

"Okay," she said, staring into her own eyes. "Get it together. Everyone is counting on you."

Her grief would have to be her own, and walled away. There was a killer out there. A city of millions living in terror. She couldn't afford to be distracted. If she got distracted, someone else would die.

*It wasn't a lover you lost yesterday. It was an agent under your command. Got that?*

*Do you?*

———

The room was quiet, none of the usual joking and theory trading. Around the table agents sat with expressions ranging from shell-shocked to furious. They all looked exhausted, and plenty looked like they'd been crying. Somehow she hadn't imagined their grief. But of course they felt it; they'd known Brody far longer than she had.

Claire took her chair and a deep breath. Everyone looked at her.

She put her hands on the table. Picked up her pen, uncapped it, recapped it, suddenly remembering that it was Brody's. The day before yesterday she'd been trying to sign some routine documentation, she couldn't remember what, overtime, maybe. Her pen had left only scratches on the paper, and he'd slid his across the table. It wasn't fancy, just a drugstore Uniball, but it had been his, and she'd forgotten to give it back.

Suddenly Claire realized that she'd been sitting silently gazing at the pen, and she wasn't really sure for how long. She looked up. "You all know what happened yesterday."

Agents around the table and lining the walls stared at her. Wanting her to give them what they needed. Strength, inspiration, focus. A reason this all made sense.

"Will Brody was one of us. He was—"

*Warm. Impulsive. Impossible. Beautiful. Mine.*

"—an exceptional agent. An exceptional person. He literally gave his life to protect someone else."

*And why? Damn it, Will, why couldn't you just have yelled and thrown yourself at the ground like a normal person? Why did you have to tackle a stranger and take the death meant for him?*

"We'll all mourn the loss. I'm not a religious person, but today I believe in Heaven."

*None of you know what we were. What we could have been.*

"Because Will Brody deserves one. And I know he's there."

She paused. There was a scream building, and she wouldn't let it out. Claire took a breath, and folded her hands across the pen. Waited until she was sure she could speak without a tremble. "I'm not going to give you a rah-rah speech. I know you're already doing everything you can.

"I'm just going to say this: Officially, every murder is the same. Inside this room, we know the truth. Will Brody was ours. It's personal." She took a moment to pan the room, making eye contact with every agent there. "And we're going to crucify the fucker who killed him."

There were somber nods and vicious smiles and, in her breast, a wind howling across a barren and frigid plain.

"Now. Status?"

---

Morning briefing.

Psych profile revisions.

Yellow flags.

Coordination with CPD.

Update call to the director.

Confirmation of DNA match from the cigarette butts.

Budget allocation for overtime hours.

Review of preliminary report from the Evidence Response Team.

Media management in preparation for the press conference.

Press conference.

Update call to the director.

Coordination with citizens' groups.

Phone meeting with the mayor.

Fifteen hours.

Two hundred thirty-eight e-mails.

Fifty-four phone calls.

Eleven cups of coffee.

Three distinct moments she almost lost control.

One tuna sandwich choked down at her desk, then thrown up in the ladies' room.

No new victims.

# EIGHTEEN

Brody had returned to the hotel last night—where else to go?—but the others had read his expression and kept their distance. Kyle broke the unspoken barrier just long enough to help him "check in" to the hotel; the locks were electronic, so the process involved a crowbar. The room was stylish and elegant and painted in shadow. Brody had wondered if there was someone in the bed right now. Flipping channels in their underwear, or reading a book. He wondered if they'd feel him crawl in next to them.

"Don't leave, or you'll have to smash the door again." Kyle gave him a bottle of lukewarm water and a weary smile. "Try and sleep. We'll talk more tomorrow."

To his surprise, Brody had passed out almost immediately. There had been dreams, a woman with white hair and something about a boy alone on a ship, but he couldn't recall any details and suspected that was a kindness.

After he'd risen, used the toilet that didn't flush, and brushed his teeth with his finger, he headed down. There were plenty of curious looks thrown his way as he moved across the lobby, and he'd done his best to ignore them. Lucy and Sonny had been sitting together, and something the biker said made her laugh with her head tilted back. Outside, the morning was cloudy and cool. Though everyone was armed, no one seemed anxious. They mingled, chatting and eating cold breakfast. Arthur sat cross-legged in the street, surrounded by a ring of children. The teacher seemed fainter in the light of day, a biology textbook held in one grey hand, but his voice was animated and the kids were paying attention. On the bridge, the sentries played poker, only occasionally glancing up to scan the street.

Brody wandered away, found a bench by the river. He sat down and stared at the water, not really seeing it. His attention was inward, trying to tally the things he'd lost. Evaluating the scope of the wound to see if it was survivable.

First to mind was Claire. Speaking of potential energy. It was excessively cruel that he had only just met her. He'd been in something like love before, but nothing close to their bare-wire voltage.

But of course it wasn't just her. He'd never again smoke cigars and play chess with Dad, never shake the man's hand or smell his particular scent or feel that neck-cracking hug. Never have lunch with Mom, bathe in the expression she wore when she looked at him; never talk about books they'd read, or hear her laughing protestations when he said something intended to shock her.

The breath caught in his throat.

There was his sister, Samantha, three years younger and weirdly conservative these days, especially for the girl he remembered dancing to pop music in their basement. Her four-year-old twins, Ashley and Amy, the three of them a mutual adoration society based on wrestling and tickling and songs about farts.

There was every friend he'd ever had. High school boys he'd stolen beer with. Marines he'd gone to war with. The other agents in the Chicago office, whip-smart and sardonic in their government suits.

He'd never see any of them again. Not unless they died. Violently. Abruptly. Badly. The contradiction between wanting to see the people he loved and the price they would have to pay for that to happen—

*Too much. Too big.*

Understanding was impossible. It was too big even to grasp the shape of it.

He tried to start smaller. Considered his fourth-grade teacher. The cashier at the grocery store. The UPS driver who whistled Christmas songs all year. The neighbors he traded restaurant recommendations with. The woman he saw sometimes at the pool, with that tattoo on her hip.

Nope. Nothing. He hadn't really known them, and like most people, he was just solipsistic enough to not truly believe they existed when he wasn't there. We're all background characters in someone else's movie.

Maybe people weren't the way to grasp this. Their loss was either too huge to bear or too small to matter. He decided to try things, the places and facts of life he was no longer privy to.

No restaurants, flickering candlelight and sexy music, waiters presenting dishes elaborate as jewelry.

No technology. No cell phone. No longer would the answer to any question, from an actor's sexual orientation to schematics for an A-bomb, reside in the pocket of his jeans.

No morning runs to the gym, cold air rasping in his lungs. No swimming a mile of tiresome laps, then sinking into the Jacuzzi to let the hot water soothe his muscles.

No movies. He would never again see the screen light up and lose himself in a story and the roar of speakers.

Shit. For some reason, that one got him. No more movies. Ever.

"Don't do it, Brody! You have so much to not-live for!"

Without turning, he said, "Kyle, you're kind of an asshole. You know that, right?"

"Hey, you aren't all blow jobs and candy yourself." The man dropped on the bench beside him. "You eat? Kitchen's full. One thing you got to give the echo, no matter how many times we raid the fridge, there's always more."

"Not hungry."

Kyle pulled out a tin of Kodiak, offered it, shrugged at Brody's look of disgust. "Yeah, I know. Not as good as cigarettes, but at least I don't have to worry about cancer here. One upside of the echo, no diseases." He tucked a wad in his lip, then put the tin away. A sudden breeze stirred ripples on the river.

Brody said, "You have family?"

"Everybody has family."

"How do you—"

"I don't. I don't let myself." Kyle stared out at the skyline. "You know the stages of grief? Denial, anger, all that."

"Sure."

"When you're alive, if you lose someone, it sucks. There's a hole in your world. But we didn't lose someone. We lost *everyone*. There're no stages of grief for losing everything. You just have to pack it away. Like it happened to somebody else. Somebody you used to be. Just . . . pack it away."

"Pack it away. That's your advice." Brody shook his head. "So that I can stay here? Never have a shower or a hot meal. Never see the people I love."

"Yeah. Because here is what you've got." Kyle brushed off his knees and stood up. "Let's go for a walk."

"Where?"

"Come have some fun."

———

The three sentries didn't like it.

Their table was littered with playing cards and poker chips. Brody presumed the table itself had been carted out of the hotel; it looked like it cost two weeks' salary. The guard with the cowboy wrinkles set down his hand. "What do you mean, alone?"

"Alone," Kyle said. "The two of us. *Solamente a dos.*"

"You know better than that."

"My man here needs to see his kingdom."

"Kyle—"

"We'll be fine. Didn't you hear? Yesterday he faced down seven Eaters all by himself."

Brody started to argue, figured what was the point. "I'm flush."

"No vamps are going to take us on, not with him like that." Kyle slapped the sentry on the shoulder. "Watch out for Laquan there, I think he might actually have the inside straight he's representing."

"Oh, come *on*," another man said, and then they were walking across the bridge.

Brody touched the knife at his belt, the handle reassuring. "We need permission to leave?"

"Permission? No. Nobody's in charge here. We're what you'd call an egalitarian society. Really only got two rules."

Brody walked three steps, four, five. Finally, he said, "Okay, I'll bite. What are they?"

"First, pull your weight. Second," Kyle said, and glanced over with a smile, "don't eat other people."

"Seems simple enough."

"Mostly it is." Kyle went left, and Brody followed. There were cars on the street, stopped in that same ghostly ballet, though fewer than yesterday. It was early. People were just getting up. Showering, thinking about work. Taking for granted the miracle of their existence.

"Your Spanish sucks," Brody said. "*Solamente a dos* means 'Only at two.'"

"So how do—"

"*Solamente nosotros dos.*"

"*Muchas gracias.*"

"What do they play for?"

"Huh?"

"The poker guys. They were too intense for it to just be chips."

"Oh," Kyle said. "Chores. Patrol shifts, keeping an eye on the kiddies, graveyard sentry duty. That last one's du-ull."

They cut onto Michigan, strolling down the middle of the street. There was a brighter spot on the clouds to the east, but nothing that Brody would call a sunrise. The same heavy pall of swirling clouds hung above.

"So here's the deal." Kyle stepped up onto the hood of a sleek Jaguar XJ, walked the length of it, then dropped to the other side. "You can focus on all you've lost, and decide to throw yourself off something tall. But remember, you didn't know the echo was here, and you don't know what comes next. Big gamble."

"I sense an 'or.'"

"*Or* see it as new and exciting. This is our city. Our kingdom. You can do whatever you want."

Millennium Park was empty. Brody didn't think he'd ever seen it literally and completely empty before. Even in the middle of the night there were cops, drunks on the benches, couples holding hands on their way home. Kyle quick-stepped up the stairs, headed for a giant sculpture. It was named Cloud Gate, but Brody had never heard anyone call it anything but the Bean. A slab of curves sixty feet long and shaped like, well, a bean, the surface was a highly reflective chrome, mirror-like in finish. When he'd first seen it, his analysis had been shiny tourist junk. But there was something hypnotic about it. The first visit, you enjoyed the funhouse mirror aspect, the way the shape distorted everything. The second, you noticed the way it took in the whole skyline—the whole sky—as if it were subsuming it, rather than simply reflecting it. After a while, you half expected to see a previous version of yourself staring out.

He'd never been there when there weren't others around, though. In a minor way it was, he suspected, like Machu Picchu, or the Great Pyramid—a place you always forgot you'd never have to yourself. People imagined visiting them alone, climbing the steps in quiet contemplation of the past. They forgot about the stalls selling T-shirts and kebabs, forgot the tour buses of sunburned Americans, forgot velvet ropes and security guards.

But now it was just Kyle and him. The surface shone so cleanly it was hard to tell what was cloud and what was cloud reflection. Kyle walked under the central curve and flopped on the ground. Brody followed suit. Warped versions of themselves stared back.

"Admit it," Kyle said. "This is cool."

"I feel like a tourist."

"Still cool."

Brody nodded. For a moment he just let his gaze roam the mirrored surface, the bent versions of themselves, the hints of swirling sky and staring city. "So if I pack it away. What would I do here?"

"Whatever you want. You're free now. Freer than you ever were in life." Kyle pointed upward at the chrome, his reflected finger pointing back down at the two of them. "Groove on somebody, and they groove on you? Bang like bunnies. You're not cheating on anyone, and you don't even need a condom, no babies here, and no disease. See something you wish you could have afforded? Take it. Pissed off? Visit the Art Institute and slice a van Gogh to ribbons. You don't even have to feel guilty, because the moment you leave, it'll stitch itself back together."

"If it's so free, how come everyone is hiding out at the hotel?"

"Well, the Eaters are always out there. But so long as you can pull your weight and only kill in self-defense, you're good with us. And as long as you're with us, you don't have to worry about them. They're like jackals. Jackals are vicious bastards. If one finds you alone, you're in for a bad afternoon. But against a group, they've got no chance."

Brody remembered the bending bars, the speed. "Looked to me like they had more than a chance."

"Oh, a single Eater can mess up a single person, or even a couple. But if there's twenty of us, they won't even try."

"Unless there are twenty of them."

Kyle shook his head. "Doesn't happen. Biggest Eater group I've ever seen is five, and I saw that exactly once. They can't trust each other. You're talking about a group who chooses—not has to, chooses to—kill others for a fix. How would you sleep next to somebody like that?"

"What if I wanted to just leave? Head out of town."

"Go for it. Me, I didn't go to the suburbs when I was alive, not planning to start now. But if you feel like finding a white picket fence, knock yourself out. Sounds lonely, though." Kyle slapped the ground, then rolled up to standing. "Come on. I'm hungry."

He led Brody down Michigan Avenue another couple of blocks, then cut in front of a bus. The way he did it was jarring, and Brody had an impulse to put an arm up, keep him from walking into the street and getting creamed. But of course, the bus was as still as the rest of the traffic. He wondered how many people were on it. Imagined climbing aboard; would there be purses and bags?

Kyle paused in front of a broad window. "You like sushi?"

"I could be buried in it."

The other man unslung his axe. He spun it around with the ease of a man who knew his tools, wound up, and slammed the back end into the window. The glass splintered like ice, but didn't break; the second hit smashed it in, shards raining everywhere. He scraped the bottom of the frame to clear the last fragments, then climbed in.

Brody followed. The restaurant was dark, chairs on tables. Kyle wound his way to the counter, turned and lifted himself onto and then over it. He stooped to the refrigerators below, came out with a plastic-wrapped tuna loin. Set it on a cutting board and began to slice.

Brody hadn't thought he was hungry, but the fish was fresh and cool, odorless but possessed of a faint briny tang. The flesh almost melted in his mouth. He found himself wanting sake, wishing he could hail a waiter. Then he remembered where he was, and walked to the bar, helped himself to a bottle of Akita Homare. They ate with gusto, each bite of rich tuna washed down with bright and floral rice wine.

"We're actually kind of lucky," Kyle said. "At least we died in Chicago. Imagine the echo in Mosul, or Mogadishu."

"My god." Brody paused. "Imagine dying in a shooting war. You'd wake up—"

"And find some of the other side waiting for you. None of you knowing what was happening. Probably go right back to killing each other." Kyle skewered a piece of tuna on his knife. "While you're at it, imagine the echo in Manhattan on 9/11."

Suddenly Brody wasn't hungry anymore.

The next stop on the tour was an alley behind the Hilton. Kyle went to an unmarked door, pulled a credit card from his pocket. "These things still have uses."

Two minutes later, they were climbing a three-hundred-foot metal ladder. The fire escape rungs were thin and cold, not built for comfort. Up and up and up they went, Brody feeling a tug in his belly that part of him found funny. What was he worried about—dying?

Thirty stories later, Kyle strutted the thin ledge of the Hilton's rooftop. He walked to the corner and sat down. Brody followed, tamping down the vertigo, his arms and legs quivering from exertion. He put a hand on Kyle's shoulder and lowered himself to sitting. Their legs dangled off the edge, heels tapping the glass. Far below, the abandoned cars looked like toys. The architecture was rendered strange by angle and shadow. The clouds seemed almost close enough to touch.

"I shouldn't be here," Brody said.

"No cops to stop you."

"No. I mean, I shouldn't be *here*." He turned to face the fireman. "I spent my life fighting for people. I died saving someone."

"You expected the pearly gates, Saint Peter waiting with brandy and a blonde?"

"No. Maybe. Who knows about Heaven. But I was a good guy. I tried to make the right choices, to be kind—"

"Helping little old ladies across the street and such."

"—and I get the same afterlife as a meth-dealing biker?"

"Careful." Kyle's voice was suddenly hard. "Sonny's a friend."

"I'm sure he's wonderful. Fun to hang out with, good with the ladies. But how many people you think he cut with those knives? How many tweakers picked their faces raw on his supply?"

"That's over now. Same as you being an FBI agent is over. We all start fresh here."

"Well whoopie-de-goddamn-do," Brody said. "So the choices we made didn't matter. Being a good person didn't matter. Rape, rob, murder, who cares? Everybody gets the same as a firefighter died in the line. Lucky Sonny."

Kyle grimaced, then rubbed at his head with his hands, the bristles of his short hair riffing. "What do you want? I didn't design this place. You want to mope about how unfair it all is? Fine. But you got a second chance. Maybe it's not what you expected, and yeah, you lost a lot along the way. But if you can get over yourself, you can make a life. And not for nothing, but people here could use your help."

"Doing what?"

"Being human, man." Kyle sighed. "Look, yesterday I told you we lived by the Gospel According to Ray. It's a bit of a joke, and it's not too. Ray was actually Raylene. I never met her, she was gone before I got here."

"Where'd she go?"

"Faded."

Brody started to respond, caught himself. Thinking of the way Arthur had appeared almost translucent. "Like the Professor?"

"Yeah, like the Professor. Arthur won't kill, even in self-defense. Neither would she. You stay here long enough and don't take energy from somebody else, you fade. One morning we'll wake up, Arthur will just be gone."

"Where?"

"How would I know? On to new adventures. Maybe there's another echo after this one. And fading happened in life too, we just called it getting old. At least here you don't fall apart."

"We don't age?"

"Nope. Bit of a kick in the crotch for the kiddies, but a nice benny for you and me."

Brody rubbed at his cheek, the stubble rubbing back. "If we don't age, how come our beards grow?"

"I dunno."

"If you're hurt, do you heal?"

"Yeah."

"That doesn't make sense. If we heal and our hair grows, then we should—"

"Brody," Kyle cut in, "don't try to lawyer the afterlife. You're not going to catch it in a technicality and suddenly be alive again. It is what it is. Can I finish my story?"

"Sorry."

"Anyway, Ray, she organized people. Until she came along, there was no safe zone. No place we could be okay. Arthur told me—remember, he's been here two decades—he told me he spent the first *year* hiding in a storage room. Because it was kill or be killed, and those were the only choices. Ray came along, she started getting people together. She reminded us there was no reason we had to live that way. So long as we could trust each other, we could be safe. Because that's the thing the Eaters can't do."

Brody thought about that. The three who'd come for him had worked together, and the Scarecrow with the machete had been upset about Raquel. Even so, they'd just walked away. Turned their backs on the man who killed their supposed friend.

"So the question is, who are you when the rules change?" Kyle turned to look at him. "You say your choices didn't matter, I say they still do. You can be them, or you can be us. Jackals or men."

The clouds reflected off a thousand windows. It was so quiet Brody could hear himself breathing. He closed his eyes. Remembered Claire in her kitchen, talking while he cooked. The knowing tilt of her smile. The curve of her neck. The smell of onions sweating in butter. He took a breath, and tried to let her go. "Okay."

"Okay?"

"Okay."

They stayed for a while. Sometimes talking, sometimes not. Eventually, they stood, and stretched, and went back to the ladder, and headed for home.

They were almost there when the screaming started.

———

The voice was high-pitched and frantic. Brody thought it was a woman, though he couldn't be sure. The sound shredded the silence and echoed off the buildings.

They exchanged a glance, and then started to run.

They'd made no more than a dozen strides when Brody remembered the difference between them.

Kyle ran with everything he had. He was fast. But Brody had gone three times as far.

*I'm flush,* he thought to himself, and now really came to understand what that might mean. Then he stopped thinking and just pushed.

He left Kyle behind, the world blurring around him. Feeling like a demigod, or an avenging angel. The woman screamed again. Brody blasted around the corner of Randolph and Michigan, leaping up onto a nearby taxi, his steps crunching divots in the steel, trunk-roof-hood, then a leap to the SUV in front of it. The height gave him a vantage point to the intersection ahead. Two figures. One on the ground, one standing. A meat cleaver in his right hand.

The figure on the ground was Emily Watkins.

*You were too late to save her once. Not again.* Brody leapt off the cars to the street.

The man straightened, turned. He was wiry and tattered looking, his clothes dirty. There was something about the way the light hit him that was strange, and yet faint. Like he'd fed some time ago. Then Brody was there, a hundred yards covered in heartbeats, bowling into the guy, one arm up to block his downward swipe. The blow had force, it smacked against Brody's arm, might have broken it if he weren't so full of power. He maintained his momentum, took the man off his feet and drove him into the girder of the El platform. The metal bent around the shape of the man's back, and the cleaver went flying end over end to shatter the window of a frozen yogurt shop.

This close he could see the hairs sprouting from the man's neck, and smell him, a sour sweat odor. Brody cocked an arm and unleashed an elbow strike that snapped the guy's head sideways. The man swayed, leaned, slumped. Rode the girder down. Brody raised a foot—

"No!"

He froze, his foot in the air, about to stomp down on the Eater's temple and drive it into the concrete. Risked a glance over his shoulder.

Kyle was rounding the corner a block back. "Brody! Don't!"

Why not? It wasn't a man, it was an Eater who had tried to kill a woman. Besides, the energy Brody had used in the sprint, in the blow he'd absorbed and the blows he'd dished out, had sapped some of his power. It was only right that he replenish it. The Eater was weak, desperate, he still had strength, not a feast but a meal—

Brody froze with his foot above the man's skull. What had he been about to do?

*Feed,* a voice inside him said, both an answer and a request. *Feed.*

He stumbled back, lost his footing, landed hard. The impact rang up his spine, slammed his teeth together.

Kyle slowed as he got closer. He took in the scene, Emily bleeding on the ground, Brody on his ass. "Good, man. You did good." He unslung his axe. "You don't want to do it twice, not so fast."

Brody was about to ask why, but realized he knew the answer. Felt it in his marrow, in the itch he had to stand up and stomp the Eater to death. "Emily?"

She coughed, rolled on her side. Her shirt was soaked in crimson. Brody rose, hurried over to her. Though her eyes were wide with panic and pain, the wound was superficial. Ugly but not deadly, a raking blow that the ribs had stopped.

He thought about carrying her, extended a hand instead. "It's okay. I've got you."

After a moment, Emily took his hand, and he pulled her to her feet. She moaned, put an arm around his shoulder. Together they staggered over to where Kyle stood.

The Eater was pushing himself off the ground. His breath whistled over broken teeth. "You bitch oh you bitch."

They stood above him for a moment.

From his belt, Brody pulled the knife he'd taken from Raquel. Offered it to Emily handle first. For a moment, he thought she was going to refuse. Then her eyes focused, and she extended a hand.

As she bent over the Eater, Brody saw something happen to her. Before the knife plunged down, before the Eater buckled, before her chest knit itself back together.

Something like ownership, or birth.

Something that told the jackals and the savages to beware.

Emily was done being a victim.

# NINETEEN

Claire spun into the church, weapon in one hand, flashlight in the other. The beam made the world, the circle of white creating graffiti and garbage, a tableau of urban ruin. Pews spattered white by birds. A heap of broken glass three feet high.

There was no one waiting.

As the other cops searched, she drifted away. Stooped to pick up a discarded paperback and read the first line—*The man in black fled across the desert, and the gunslinger followed.*

Out a panel of broken plywood, she could see the sky, and part of a building. A man stood on the fire escape, smoking and using his phone.

Claire knew what happened next. She turned and ran for the nearest cop, sending him sprawling as a sun flared beneath the glass, and she was lifted by rainbow razors—

She jerked awake, flailing. One hand hit something it wasn't expecting, and the thing moved. She was just conscious enough to realize it was a lamp. It toppled sideways, the shade bouncing off the bedside table as the bulb burst with a pop.

A dream. It had just been a dream. She drew a shuddering breath through cupped hands.

Whose lamp was that?

She sat up. A strange room. A hotel. She'd checked into a hotel. Couldn't bear going home.

Claire sat, calming her breath and rebuilding herself. Remembering Will's ruined body. The bland voice of the man who'd murdered him. The dishes still in her sink.

Through the gap in the curtains, the sky was softening. She pushed out of the blankets, stumbled to the bathroom. Peed, then brushed her teeth. She looked half-dead in the bathroom fluorescents.

That dream.

The detail had been incredible: the streaked bird droppings, the texture of the light, the grip of the Glock against her palm. Nothing impressionistic or symbolic about it. Her subconscious had really pulled out all the stops.

Strangest of all had been seeing the man on the fire escape. Usually dream monsters lurked unseen, always just behind you. But he'd been so . . . physical. Cigarette in one hand, phone in the other. Pale skin and droopy features. The whole thing didn't feel like an invention so much as a reliving of Will's last minutes.

Shower. Coffee. Bagel. Then head in, see if there had been any progress overnight.

As she stood under the steaming water, she pondered the dream. Everyone liked to believe they were in charge of their thoughts, but it just wasn't so. If the mind was a factory, then the machinery that did the real work was a closed system, and the finished products rarely resembled the raw materials. We don't build our thoughts any more than the CEO of Ford builds cars.

Obviously, she hadn't lived Will's last minutes. The man on the fire escape was a figment, a stand-in. His face belonged to a forgotten teacher, or someone who had served her coffee. But the intensity of the dream made her wonder if her subconscious, grinding away in the dark factory of her being, had discovered something. Sometimes small details unnoticed by the conscious mind were caught by the machinery beneath.

She got out of the shower, checked her watch. There was time.

The church was in a drab zone of slumping frame houses, discount cell phone shops, fried fish joints. It wasn't yet seven in the morning, and she'd crossed the city without the usual snarl of delays. The corner kids were out even at this hour, and she felt their eyes tracking her, noting the municipal license plates on the sedan.

The church had been sealed off, and yellow tape fluttered around the perimeter. Down the street she saw a liquor store, the only thing open at this hour. A CPD squad car was parked on the street to discourage disaster tourists. She pulled alongside and they both rolled down their windows. The cop had black hair and that Chicago build. "Help you?"

"Yeah." She flashed ID. "You have a key?"

They walked up the path together, weeds growing through the sidewalk. The officer unlocked the door. "Need a flashlight?"

"Thanks."

The cut of its beam through darkness gave her a shiver of déjà vu, but only for a moment. The inside of the church looked different than her dream. She'd imagined it as Brody had found it, before the explosion and the investigation. Now there were footprints everywhere, and yellow evidence flags. A fine layer of sparkling dust blanketed the interior. Slender tracks marked where a gurney had been pushed through it.

For a moment she stood in the center, spinning in slow arcs. Examining both the scene and her emotions.

A shaft of light fell through the single busted window. Claire moved to it, her footsteps mirroring the ones in her dream. Through it she could see the apartment building, and the fire escape where they had found cigarette butts. The sniper's vantage point, where he'd stood to murder Will Brody. The same place she'd dreamed of, and from the same angle.

There was no sad-faced man smoking a cigarette and holding a cell phone. Obviously.

She felt suddenly foolish. This was not the time to humor the preposterous. Hundreds of cops and techs had scoured the area. If there were clues, they'd have found them. She was just tired and sad and furious, and it was affecting her judgment.

No harm done, but no point wasting more time.

Claire turned to leave, and as she did, her flashlight played across something white tucked into a mound of trash. Her first thought was, *bone,* but it wasn't. It was paper. Stained and faded, rain soaked and dried fat. A book. Just one more piece of trash left by a squatter. Nothing at all to do with the sniper.

There was no cover. She opened it. As her mind processed the first line a tremor ran from her chest to her fingers. The book slipped from her shaking hands. But not before she'd taken in the words.

*The man in black fled across the desert, and the gunslinger followed.*

# TWENTY

*I'm losing it.*

That was the only explanation.

Too much stress, too little sleep.

She was the head of an FBI task force that was failing to catch a terrorist. The man she loved—*admit it*—had been murdered. They had no leads, none. Someone was going to die today. And now she was looking for clues in her dreams. Claire McCoy, Psychic Detective.

It was funny in a way that did not make her laugh.

Was it time to call the director and step down? She wouldn't have to mention the emotional entanglements. Her ride in the fast lane would come to an abrupt end, but it wouldn't destroy her career.

Thing was, she didn't believe anyone else could do a better job. They weren't failing, they were getting beaten. Somehow.

Someone knocked on her office door, and she jumped, knocking over her mug. Tepid coffee spilled across her desk.

"Shit." She yanked open a drawer, dug for napkins. Snapped, "What?"

"Umm. Want anything to eat?" Her assistant, through the door.

"No." She said it sharply and didn't add *thanks*.

Okay, yes, it was very weird that she had dreamed the book. But she could have noticed it yesterday when she was on the scene—

*The cover was torn off. Even if you'd spotted it, you wouldn't have known what book it was. According to Google, that's the first line of Stephen King's* The Gunslinger, *which you've never read. So how did you know it?*

Alright, fine, but—

*And how did you dream the church the way Will experienced it, when you only saw it* after *the explosion?*

Well, visualization is an important part of the job, and it's not like—

*And how is it that you can still remember the man's face so clearly? Usually dreams melt before you're out of bed.*

She would stand up, leave her office and go do one of the thousand things people were depending on her for. Yes. That's what she would do.

Claire leaned forward, logged in to her laptop, and then to the FBI database. Navigated to records, then facial recognition. Opened a blank search, and clicked on the physical description section. She paused for a moment, focusing on her dream. Confirming the memory.

The face lingered in front of her eyes so clearly she could almost touch him.

Claire twisted a curl of hair into her mouth and started typing. Entering gender, race, age range, estimated weight and height, hair color.

The search returned 72,904 results.

She presumed no gang affiliation, US citizen. Voice analysis suggested that the target had been born in the Midwest and lived in Chicago for at least five years.

11,062 results.

Claire clicked to apply linear discriminant analysis, scanned through the classes of facial structure, selected the four that seemed closest.

962 results.

She displayed them as tiles, four photos to a row, eight rows to a page. Thirty-two mug shots appeared. None of them were him.

Claire clicked for the next set.

And the next.

And the next.

Like a late-night slot machine addict. The sheep who stared and spun and stared and spun, each time believing that this was the one that would pay off.

And the next.

And the next.

*This is ridiculous. Stop.*

And the next.

And the next.

*Seriously. Stop. You're losing perspective. Maybe you* should *call the director—*

The man from her dream stared from her computer screen.

Claire closed her eyes, rubbed at them, looked again.

The man from her dream stared from her computer screen.

Pale skin, drooping face, aura of sadness. A little bit younger, but that was him. She clicked up his sheet.

Simon Tucks, currently 41, arrested five years ago for solicitation. Probation and a fine. Last known address, 1739 N. Orleans. No other arrests. No prison time. No military record.

He was white and male, but other than that he didn't match their profile in any way. There was nothing to suggest that he could be the man who had killed eighteen people.

Except her dream.

This was ridiculous. The sniper pulled off single-shot kills on moving targets from blocks away. He'd wired an IED and laid a trap for the FBI and evaded capture despite an unprecedented effort.

Simon Tucks, on the other hand, had been busted trying to get a hand job.

Claire had a press conference at one. A call with the director. A meeting that included the mayor and the governor. She'd averaged four hours of sleep a night for weeks. The man she loved had been brutally killed and she hadn't cried about it and no one even knew what they'd meant to each other. She was exhausted. This was clearly an attempt to exert control over a situation spinning away from her.

*But how did you know the first line of that book?*

Claire took another look at the address, then stood up and walked out.

# TWENTY-ONE

Brody's sleep was a troubled and fractious thing. Dream fragments like pieces from different puzzles. A rainbow sun in a darkened church. Emily's face as she leaned in with the knife. The view through a bay window of a sad-faced man, somehow familiar, pacing a dark living room. Claire in her car on a tree-lined street, staring out the windshield, her gun in her lap. A woman with impossibly white hair and ancient eyes, talking to him calmly, telling him secrets. A boy alone on a broken ship, chewing smoked meat.

He woke tangled and sweaty, still in his clothes. Grey daylight poured through the windows. He staggered to the bathroom, dumped half a bottle of water over his head. Splashed the rest on his face. Jesus, those dreams. They'd had a clarity, a simplicity, that made them hard to shake.

*Claire in her car on a tree-lined street, her gun in her lap.* He planted his fists on the counter and leaned in, closing his eyes, straining to remember.

He knew that street. It was in Old Town, an area where he jogged all the time; it was pretty and largely untrafficked. The street—Willow? Orleans? Menomonee?—was in the heart of the neighborhood, a tangle of one-ways and dead ends near St. Michael's.

The thing that made it odd, though, was that in the dream he hadn't known she was in Old Town, or what street she was on. It was only in hindsight that he could put it together. His conscious mind was analyzing the imagery.

*So keep going.*

The more he focused, the more detail he could remember. The image was like a still from a film. Claire with eyes ringed in black and hair mussed, fingers tracing the grip of her Glock as she stared out the windshield. It had the tenor of a suicide, but he couldn't imagine her eating her gun.

Then why the drawn weapon? Hell, Claire had outshot him; she wasn't the type to pull her sidearm to play with it. Which meant there was a reason.

Maybe she hadn't been staring blankly. Maybe she'd been looking at something.

He was surprised to realize that he could remember what, as though seeing it through her eyes. A brick townhouse choked in ivy, with a large bay window.

A bay window like the one he'd dreamed a sad-faced man pacing behind.

No. A window like the one he'd dreamed *the sniper* pacing behind.

The man had seemed familiar because he was the man Brody had seen on the balcony, cell phone in hand, detonating the bomb that had sent him to this pale place. Which meant that he'd dreamed Claire sitting outside the sniper's house. Without backup. No SWAT team, no support. She was walking in alone.

*Just a dream. It doesn't mean—*

Brody bolted for the door. Took the stairs two at a time, and burst into the lobby. A handful of people were scattered, dirty and clad in leathers and sweats that assaulted the elegant décor. They tensed when they saw him, hands going to weapons.

"Kyle?" he asked the room at large. No one said anything. "Kyle, where is he?"

A woman he didn't recognize pointed outside.

A gloomy day, but still bright after the hotel lobby. A group of kids were fighting with broomsticks. Lucy paced around them, coaching and correcting. The archer kid, Finn, had dragged a two-thousand-dollar leather chair out to the street and was firing arrow after arrow into it, *twang thunk, twang thunk.* Two men stood on the bridge, one scanning the city with binoculars, the other leaning on a vicious spear. A post-apocalyptic world without an apocalypse.

"Brody." Kyle sat atop a mailbox, eating potato chips and slurping Coke. "'Sup, man. How'd you—"

"I need your help."

# TWENTY-TWO

She'd driven here in a kind of daze, the city outside her strange and silent and draped in fear. The tarps hiding gas stations, the blue-and-white presence of CPD on every block, the held-breath feeling of empty streets and empty stores. Claire wouldn't have thought it was possible for the city to grow more frightened, but the news had been filled with the bomb, talking heads speculating about the sniper moving from individual targets to public ones, about poison gas in ventilation systems and explosions in the subway. Maybe there was no bottom to fear. Maybe that was what made it fear.

Her cell had vibrated a dozen times in the twenty-minute drive, and she had ignored it each time. What could she have said, that she'd dreamed a man, and a book?

The neighborhood was one of the prettier in the city, all red brick and money. The grey steeple of St. Michael's was edged by brilliant blue sky. Somewhere she'd heard that the borders of Old Town had been decided based on how far the sound of the church's bells carried. Orleans was a one-way south, shaded by broad trees with leaves colored in fire. 1739 was a two-story brick townhouse. A soft blanket of ivy framed the windows, and a faded wooden fence hid the view of a small side yard.

Claire drove past, then circled around again and parked in a tow zone half a block up. Killed the engine and sat there listening to it tick. No church bells today, but the faint *bing-bong* of the Brown Line at Sedgwick. Idly, she unsnapped her Glock and set the weapon in her lap.

Maybe this was the rabbit hole. Maybe she was tumbling down. She was tired of trying to formulate theories to explain what she was doing.

The best way out of this strange recursion was forward. She would knock on the door and introduce herself. Explain it away as a routine canvass. Civilians loved to help the FBI. It made them feel like they were in a movie. Simon Tucks would look just like the man she had dreamed—obviously, since that was how she'd found him—but he'd be a nobody. A stand-in her brain had decided to use in a starring role. He'd offer her coffee, she'd accept. Spin five minutes of BS about how she was following up a lead about someone else in the neighborhood, nod her way through his replies, and hopefully remember where she knew him from. Regardless, she'd leave free of this nonsense and ready to do her job.

Claire thumbed the magazine release of the pistol, checked the load—she knew it was full, but habits were habits for a reason—slapped it into place, racked the slide, and holstered it on her hip. She stepped out into autumn, a cool breeze with a thrilling hint of woodsmoke, then put her jacket on and adjusted it to cover the weapon.

There was an elementary school on the opposite side of the street, a two-story building behind a wrought iron fence. The playground was empty, and all the windows had been covered with bright construction paper. She pictured the children inside, the teachers jumping at every loud sound. She wondered how many kids had been held back from school today, how many families huddled in their houses with the curtains drawn. Strange how swiftly the illusions of safety and civilization shredded. The things that we take as a given are not given. They're imagined and implemented and maintained and protected one day at a time, and they are delicate.

Claire walked beneath blowing leaves and blue skies to Simon Tucks's door, and rang the bell.

# TWENTY-THREE

"I'm telling you, it was real. That was Claire, and it was happening *now*. Or it's about to." Brody's skin had shrunk tight enough to split, and he couldn't stop pacing, talking with his hands. "It was real."

"No offense, man," Kyle said, "but you've had a rough couple of days. You might be putting too much stock in a dream."

"This wasn't a dream. It was something else. A vision, or a message."

"So you can see the future now?"

"No, I." He ground at his forehead with the tips of his fingers. He didn't blame the man for his skepticism. But then, two days ago he would have been skeptical about a whole lot of things. "I don't know, okay? This is all new."

"Yeah," Kyle said. "That's what I'm saying. Plus, you fed."

"What does that have to do with—"

"I've fed before. We only kill in self-defense, but, you know, that happens. Each time I have, for weeks afterward, I'll have these flickers. They last until the power fades. It drains away, you know. That's why the Eaters are always hunting. You must be starting to feel it weaken some, after your fight the other day."

"Yeah, I have, but I don't care about that right—"

"Anyway, the flickers. I'll be, say, sitting in the bar, and suddenly the room will be full of people. Real people, alive. I can hear them, that jumble of too many voices talking at once. Smell the perfume of the woman at the stool next to me. See the cat hair on the back of the host's jacket. A second later, they'll be gone, but it's real. I'm seeing through to life."

"Okay! So then—"

"But," Kyle said, "it doesn't matter."

"Doesn't *matter*?" Brody spun. "What do you mean, it doesn't matter? She's alone, and—"

"Who?" Lucy must have seen the energy developing between him and Kyle. She'd ambled behind them and stood with her hip cocked, the hilt of the katana jutting from her waist. Behind her, Sonny loomed, his face carved out of stone.

"Claire," Brody said. "My. The woman I love." The words fell off his tongue so naturally he almost didn't realize he'd never said them before.

The biker said, "She's dead too?"

"No," Brody snapped. "That's the point. She's alive, but she's in danger."

"How do you know?"

"He had a dream," Kyle said.

"I had—yeah, okay, fine, it happened while I was sleeping. But it wasn't a dream." The words sounded ridiculous, and he was briefly embarrassed to be saying them, especially in front of Sonny. "She's about to face the man who killed me."

Mildly, Kyle said, "So what?"

Brody fought down an urge to knock him right off the mailbox. "So we help her."

"I'm not saying I don't care about your girl. But you're dead, and she's not." Kyle shrugged. "Sorry, but that's the situation. She could be standing right there with a gun to her head, you wouldn't know until the trigger gets pulled."

"Kyle's an asshole," Lucy said, "but he's right. You can't reach her. Look around." She gestured at the street, the city. They stood in the heart of the tourist district. Half a block from the Magnificent Mile. In the middle of a street full of abandoned cars. Wearing weapons.

He wanted to scream.

When he'd been chased by Raquel and her friends, he'd been as scared as he'd ever been, in a life lived loud. When Arthur and the others had filled him in on the echo, he'd been confronted with the bleak horror of things, and the existential dread had been unlike anything he'd known.

Helplessness was worse.

Claire was in trouble. He knew it. And they were saying there was nothing he could do about it.

No. He wouldn't accept that. Brody paused, took a breath.

He'd only worked undercover for a couple of months, but they'd been instructive. When you were trying to game the Mexican cartels, assessing personality and playing to it wasn't just part of the job. It could keep you alive. Maybe it could help here.

*Kyle died a firefighter.*

*Sonny ripped off his employers, and was murdered by them.*

*You don't know Lucy's story. But the sword, the swagger, the biker boyfriend; she prides herself on being tough.*

*Start there.*

Staring into Lucy's eyes, he said, "Claire is not a damsel in distress. She's the most capable person I've ever met." He shifted his gaze to Sonny. "But she doesn't know what she's walking into. If she did, she wouldn't be doing it alone." Finally, to Kyle. "She needs help."

He let the words hang for a moment, then, slowly and carefully, spoke again. "I understand what you're saying. But the woman I love is in trouble. Maybe I can't do anything about it—but I will goddamn well try. And I could use your help."

# TWENTY-FOUR

*ZZZZZZZZZ*

Claire took her finger off the bell. The door had a window at head height, and a ghost of herself was reflected in it. She looked lousy.

She didn't care.

*Get this done. Whatever nonsense this is, do this to clear it. Then get on with saving lives.*

She waited. A breeze ruffled the trees above. The sky was that perfect shade of October, like a child's dream of blue.

The standard twenty seconds or so passed, and she pressed the button again.

*ZZZZZZZZZ*

If he wasn't home, that would mess up her plan. She glanced at her watch, 9:21. Whoops. Hadn't thought about that. 9:21, people were at work. As she was supposed to be, instead of aggressively looking for rabbit holes—

Footsteps.

Funny how even from outside the house she could sense the inside. There was a metaphor there, but for what she couldn't quite say. Something about the way we do and don't know each other.

A face appeared in the window, and she almost jumped. It was the face from her dream.

*Of course it is, moron,* she thought. *That's why you're here.*

Once that cold-shower shock passed, she was able to notice how very normal he looked. Weakish chin, shortish hair, slightish ownership of his space. But perfectly everyday.

Good. That's what she needed. To be reminded of reality.

The door started to open, then stopped abruptly three inches wide. A chain.

"Hi," she said, and flashed a corn-fed smile she'd practiced in the mirror for just this sort of moment. It was sweet and warm and innocent of intelligence or intent. "I'm Agent Claire McCoy." She held up her credentials, offhanded. "I'm with the FBI. Are you Simon Tucks?"

He looked at her ID, just a quick glance, verifying she was holding something. He nodded.

"I was wondering if I could have a moment of your time. It's probably nothing, but we've had several calls to the tip line regarding one of your neighbors. In conjunction with the sniper, obviously."

"Oh," he said. "Which neighbor?"

Two words. Three if you counted "Oh." Not even particularly interesting words.

But they changed everything. The world fell from beneath her feet.

The voice.

Conservatively, Claire would estimate she'd heard it a thousand times.

It had played on loop while the techs analyzed every syllable, every scrap of background sound.

Played on loop as she wandered her condo, touching the things that had been Will's and now were nothing.

Played on loop while she drove aimlessly through three a.m. dark.

This was the man who had—

"James McIntosh," she said. "He's on Menomonee."

"Sorry, I don't know him."

"Well, like I said, probably nothing, but still, it would be very helpful if we could—"

"Sure," he said. And shut the door.

One second. Two.

*Shit.*

She'd tried to cover her reaction, but to a man who had murdered this many people, there was no accidental visit from the FBI.

Claire took a step back, planted her left foot and lashed out with her right, a wicked kick at the handle. The frame gave, the door ripping open, then hitting the chain and bouncing back.

She drew the Glock, aimed it at the chain, and fired.

A blast of sparks and the chain split in two.

The door drifted open, revealing a spare living room. Bland couch, bland table, TV. No pictures, no décor. No one there.

Claire aimed with her right, snatched her radio with her left, identified herself, gave an all-points emergency call saying that she was entering the sniper's house at 1739 N. Orleans. She hadn't even finished speaking before she heard sirens.

*Got you.*

A sound from further in. A crunchy-sliding sort of sound.

He was running.

She didn't bother reclipping her radio, just dropped it, double-handed her weapon and swept in. A staircase traced the wall, but instinct told her that was wrong, she hadn't heard the sounds of panic-running up it, and besides, it was harder to flee from the second floor. An arch led through to a kitchen, clear, one bowl in the sink with one spoon inside it, a box of cereal on the counter, speaker wires running along the floor, another arch beyond. Training took over, and Claire cleared it like she'd cleared Hogan's Alley a million times back at Quantico. A hallway, door to the left, open, a spare room, but the sounds were ahead, and she hustled, careful not to trip in the wires, spinning round the door frame into a den with a window half open and the man, Simon Tucks, hands on either side of the frame.

"Freeze!"

Everything about him went rigid. There was something stuck in the back of his pants, a weapon.

"Put your hands on your head and turn around! Do it, do it now!" Using the command voice.

Simon Tucks lingered for a moment. Then he put his fingers on his head and turned, slowly.

The sirens were louder, much, drawing close. The whole city was on high alert.

"Keep your hands on your head and get on your knees and cross your ankles."

Simon stared at her, a sad expression, no menace in it. Hard to believe, at a glance, that this was the man who had killed eighteen people, including a twelve-year-old girl.

*Including Will Brody.*

Claire put her back to the wall, the gun never wavering. Simon lowered himself slowly. He looked up at her with liquid eyes. Scared eyes. The sirens grew louder.

She had him. This was it, this was him. The man who had brought a whole city to its knees.

*And how, exactly, will you explain that?*

Claire had no doubt, none, that his DNA would match with the cigarettes and soda bottles they'd found. That in a search of the house, they'd find the assault rifle he'd used. Bomb-making materials. Schematics. Notes on future targets.

But the law she served was a strange master. By the letter, she had no reason to be here. No reason to have kicked in his door.

Under the circumstances, it was unlikely to matter. Eighteen dead, including a child and an FBI agent.

*But it could.*

Obviously, she couldn't say that she'd seen him in a dream. But she could . . . well, she could make something up. He was a mass murderer. Lying about how she'd found him was not a sin.

*No. But this will be the highest profile case in America. You've got maybe twenty seconds to come up with a lie that you have to stick to forever. You'll be questioned over and over. If you get it wrong, once, if you leave room for doubt . . .*

Everyone knew O. J. Simpson was guilty. But he went free mostly because the cops screwed it up.

*This man killed mothers and fathers. He killed a child.*

*He killed Will Brody.*

*It doesn't matter how you found him.*

*He has to die.*

The sirens were screaming now, not one or two but dozens, from all directions. They'd be here in seconds.

Could she just execute him? No judge or jury, no proof, just her certainty? Yeah. She thought she could.

Maybe he saw something in her eyes. Because with surprising speed, he released his hands from one another, reaching behind his back and sparing her the decision.

Claire put three bullets in his chest in half a second.

He shuddered. Froze. The thing that had made him a person fleeing fast. His body slumped. His hands fell.

And she saw, an instant before it hit the ground, the thing he'd been going for.

It wasn't a gun after all. It was a small box, maybe three inches by one by one. Aluminum. Simple looking. A button on one side, about the size of a key on a computer.

As it fell, Claire remembered the speaker wires. In the kitchen. The living room. The hall. Here.

*Those weren't speaker wires.*

Then the detonator hit, and everything vanished in a flare of white and a blast that—

# TWENTY-FIVE

The sky was grey.

Swirling.

Why was she looking at the sky? And why was it grey, instead of bright blue?

Claire coughed.

*The sniper,* she thought. *You shot him, and . . .*

Right. She tried to sit, and was surprised to realize she could. She was dazed, dizzy. Confused. She patted herself, expecting agony. But everything felt okay.

How the hell was she okay?

She pulled herself to her feet. She stood in front of the townhouse, or what had been a townhouse, a moment ago. Now it was a shattered ruin of broken brick and smoke. A bland couch lay in front of her, upside down, the fabric ripped half off.

Claire swayed, caught herself. Blinked against the dust in the air.

It wasn't that everything came back to her; it was that it had never left. Reality had just experienced a hiccup. A second ago she'd seen the detonator falling, seen it landing, felt a blast that turned her inside out.

Something caught her eye, a dozen feet away. Her Glock. Scooping the gun up helped. The smooth, machined weight of it made her feel grounded. Like gravity applied, when she'd never expected it not to.

Claire took a deep breath, then another. Looked around.

Somehow, she'd been thrown clear of the explosion. She'd landed on the sidewalk, probably thirty linear feet from where she'd been standing. Amazingly, she didn't seem to have suffered so much as a sprained ankle.

Stupid of her to miss the wires. She'd been in too much of a hurry. Simon Tucks must have known that sooner or later they'd find him, and wanted to be ready to go out with a bang.

Looking around, she could see that he had succeeded.

The two-story townhouse was now a one-story pile of rubble. Bricks and broken glass and bits of furniture. The houses on either side slumped and leaned. The school across the street was still standing, though many of the windows had been blown in, the construction paper hanging in tatters.

*Even at the end, he had to hurt people.*

She couldn't imagine how she'd survived, but somehow, she had. And without a mark on her.

It was over. The single man who had turned a city of millions into prisoners was dead. Brody was avenged. She was alive. It was over.

Claire hobbled out to the street. At the end, she could see a squad car rounding the corner. She leaned against the broken stump of a tree, fishing out her identification. A miracle she'd made it. But it was over. The others would be here any . . .

The squad car hadn't moved.

There were no sirens.

No bystanders. No teachers rushing out from the school. No neighbors screaming and bleeding.

Just her . . . and something moving inside the house.

A shape uncoiling itself from a pile of rubble. Rocks and dust slid off it like it had burrowed out of the center of the earth. She imagined a monster, some pale tentacled thing.

But it was a man. A bit shy of six feet, lithe and strong. He coughed. Looked around.

*No, no, no, that's impossible, it can't—*

Simon Tucks. The sniper.

It was him, and not him. She saw in him the man whose mug shot she had looked at earlier, the man who had opened the door, the man she had shot three times through the chest.

And yet, he didn't look the same. He was leaner. Taller. His cheekbones were sharp lines, and his eyes blazed. The rest of the world seemed blurry behind him.

He noticed Claire. "You?"

Panic tore her. It was the distillation of four-year-old fear of the monster in the closet, the one beneath the bed, the certainty that the moment her parents left the world changed into something darker and more dangerous, something that was waiting for her, something that knew her and was excited by her fear.

She snapped the Glock up and fired.

*Click.*

Misfire. She racked and aimed again.

*Click.*

The thing that looked like Simon Tucks leapt.

From forty feet away it leapt, and at the height of its arc it had to be twenty feet in the air, and then it landed in front of her, and it smiled.

One arm moved in an impossible blur, a backhanded slap, and she was the one flying.

The world was fuzzy, everything too fast, too much, too loud, the ground lurching up too hard, and she hit with a scrape that took the skin off her palms and one cheek. The gun was gone, lost somewhere. She pushed herself to her knees and then burning agony seized her skull, every inch of it on fire and the world shifted and she realized that she was being hoisted up by her hair, Jesus God that hurt, she kicked, flailed, screamed, reached for his arm and got it, pulled up enough to take some of the pain off, and realized she hung two feet off the ground, and this new Simon that could lift her with one arm stared at her with eyes that had in them a thousand deaths, that had lived for centuries, and a mouth that was beautiful and cruel, and he said, "I'm not scared." There was something like awe in his voice. "I'm not scared anymore."

The blow hit her stomach like a machine-driven piston, a force beyond human strength, and her breath fled and her consciousness nearly followed, and her grip failed so that she hung by her hair, and the thing shook her like a cat with a toy, there was the ripping of scalp coming loose, and then it threw her, by her hair, and again the world lost focus and this time she welcomed it, anything to end this, the concrete racing to embrace her, and when she landed the blur took everything.

*Stand up,* she told herself, *stand up and run run run do it now*

The thing, this new Simon, stalked toward her. "I'll never be scared again. It doesn't hurt anymore." He leaned over to pluck a chunk of masonry from the ground with the same effort it would have taken her to lift a fallen dinner fork.

Claire had never really prayed before. She'd wished for things. Wanted things. Had occasionally asked a vague and nameless force for them. But never truly prayed. Never poured all her thoughts and desires and hopes and fears into a single desperate cry to something bigger than her. *Please. Please, I need help.*

The sniper stopped. Fifteen feet away and victorious. Staring at something.

She needed to know what. Managed to turn her head to look where he was looking. Expecting Jesus, or an angel, or love incarnate come to save her. Something a thousand feet tall and blasting light.

But all she could see were four figures. Shadowy, her vision or the dust, she couldn't say. A woman raising a sword. A man clutching a fireman's axe. A biker with a knife in each hand. And . . .

Will Brody.

The darkness rushed toward her, and Claire welcomed it.

# TWENTY-SIX

Edmund flourished.

For centuries he had subsisted on the souls of the dead. He had wandered his new country from one end to the other. Watched cities rise with no one to build them. Hunted for hunger and hunted for power. He had believed himself at the limits of strength, and been content to live that way. Like the lions he had seen in a dead slave's memories.

Now that he rode the living, drove them to madness and murder, he discovered he had only reached the threshold. No longer was his sustenance a matter of chance encounter. Now he could make the living deliver themselves to him.

Restless of mind, he began to experiment. To toy with mortals like a child tearing apart dolls. He stalked the cities, seeking the desperate and the lost, the lonely, the broken. Whispering to them. Spinning webs of darkness. Tending misery like a farmer in his fields.

At his urging, the brokenhearted threw themselves from cliffs, the bereft cut veins in warm water, the desolate stood above sleeping family members with hammer in hand.

Power flowed like rain, and he came to understand that power was all. The intricate arrangements of people—personality, friendship, love, law, order— were nothing but trappings to disguise that fact.

Life was power, and it could be collected. He stockpiled like a sultan, until his treasury overflowed with glittering wealth.

Soon he saw that there were worlds beyond life and its pale echo. Worlds beyond counting, growing ever darker. Like a rope left too long in the water; tight-knit at one end, it softened and unraveled and gave way to rot.

As he had once walked America, now he walked between those worlds, from end to end. From the shining edge of life, bright and noisy, to the faded fields where shades stood aimless and drained. Waiting for nothingness. He could tear them like old paper, the essence of them crumbling away in his hands.

For his own amusement, he chose a living woman and rode her through the worlds, haunting her like the Furies. At his urging she lit her house aflame with her children inside. When she dropped from the gallows, he was waiting on the other side, and after he had fed upon her, he pursued her into the next world, and the next. He ate her soul in small bites, careful to leave just enough of her to continue. When he had hollowed her out, and she stood on the edge of the merciful abyss, he bled some of his power into her, returning color to her world and strength to her body, only to abandon her with the knowledge of all she had done and all that had been done to her. There had been a perfection to her screams.

Edmund flourished. And when his power had grown beyond what he'd ever believed possible, he began to see the others.

First at a distance. Manifestations of energy he could barely comprehend, like hurricanes on the horizon. For centuries he had thought himself unique, the apex predator of a great plain dotted with prey.

Now he understood that he had never been alone. Nor was he the strongest.

They were few and fearsome, older than he. In steaming jungles, Axayacatl had stood astride temples and cut the throats of babes. The tattooed sailor Magnus had begun to tack through the tides of power a thousand years ago. The Comanche had been a war leader, ferocious astride his mount, terrible in his retribution. On the other side of the veil he had skinned prisoners alive and raped children before their parents' eyes. When they met on a windswept plain near the end of the worlds, the man's gaze had glowed like red coal, and for the first time in centuries, Edmund remembered fear.

They moved as he did, traversing the worlds, spreading the tendrils of their power from the wellspring of life to the brink of nothingness. They cultivated horrors in the living world and reaped the benefit in the afterlife. They had walked the same path and gathered their strength the same way, and he could feel their hunger. They sensed his power, knew it less than their own, and licked their lips.

It was Isabella who made him understand why they did not fall upon him and plunder what he had spent centuries building.

In appearance she was of middling age, white haired and handsome. But that meant nothing, just as the teenaged body he inhabited was no measure of him. She crackled like a summer storm. He who had fancied himself at the limits of power now felt a pale boy again, thin and weak. She could wipe him from all the worlds.

But, he realized, not without risk. Like animals battling for dominance, even a victory could be too costly. Any wound he dealt—and he would not go quiet—would weaken her. Which would make her prey for the others.

Thus the risen gods existed in a state of constant wariness. Never a risk. Never a rash move. Ready always to feed upon their kin. Trust was weakness. Time meant nothing. Only power mattered.

But Isabella had ideas.

As her dress slipped from her milky shoulders, she told him she had been watching him. He was young, and his perspective was fresh. The restlessness of his mind shone against the complacency of the others. Perhaps, she said, as she straddled him, engulfed him in her searing heat, they could complement each other. Grow together into something beyond all the others.

It wasn't bodies coupling, not really. They transcended the physical. They manifested their own realities. Their will became their world. They were gods, and their sex was lightning across bleak skies, the rumblings of waking volcanoes.

Together they danced in disaster. They seeded madness and destruction. Fed bloody ideas to those who made bloody reality. Raised up monsters and fed on their offerings, and when the monsters fell, they fed upon them too.

And Edmund flourished.

# TWENTY-SEVEN

Someone was moaning, very softly.

It was a moment before she realized it was her.

She wasn't awake and she wasn't asleep. Something wet and soft brushed at her face. It was gentle but insistent, moving methodically. Claire tried to open her eyes. They seemed stuck, the only thing coming through a trickle of hazy grey light.

"Shhh," came a voice. She knew it. Trusted it.

Tired, so tired—

There was a feeling almost like falling.

———

Brody wrung out the washcloth. The water in the steel mixing bowl was pale pink. He poured another splash from the bottle and went back to work, scrubbing as softly as he could at the crusted blood around her eye. The damage was superficial, though it must have hurt like hell. Her knees looked like she'd fallen off a motorcycle. There were clumps of hair and scalp missing, the remnants bloody and raw. He'd had to pack her nose with gauze to staunch the bleeding.

He worked carefully, cleaning the wounds, dabbing away the dirt and dried blood, the touch of the cloth making her unconscious body twitch. On the way home they'd raided a Walgreens, Lucy keeping watch as Kyle grabbed bandages and bottled water, and Sonny clambered over the pharmacy counter for Tylenol-3. Brody had stood in the dim store holding Claire like a child, her weight nothing against the new power of his muscles, his mind whirling.

Claire was here.

Claire was dead.

———

The next time she opened her eyes, they seemed to work better. The light was still grey and hazy, and one eye felt thick and swollen.

Her brain was in a compression device squeezing from all sides at once. Like a blood pressure cuff inside her skull. Her mouth was gummy.

Claire blinked. A surface swam into focus, eight feet above. Ceiling. She was lying down. Somewhere soft, a bed, blankets pulled to her chin.

She tried to turn and immediately regretted it. Her neck was so sore it seemed frozen in place, and the movement spilled agony through her head, like the pain was an overfilled glass.

"Easy."

It was impossible. But she knew that voice. "Will?"

Abruptly he was in her sight, leaning down, his features carved with worry. He must have been sitting in a chair beside her. Jeans and a sweatshirt, a scruff on his cheeks, a ripe smell like he'd been working out. "I'm here."

"What—where—"

"Easy, okay? Take it easy. I promise I'll explain." He made a sound that wasn't a laugh. "Or do my best. But first I want to make sure you're alright. Can you focus on my finger?"

He ran her through basic triage, checking for a concussion, squeezing her arms, her legs, her ribs, asking if they hurt.

She thought, *Your dead lover is touching your body to see if you've broken anything.*

He pressed some pills in her palm. "Take these."

Claire struggled to sit. Brody put a hand behind her back to help, then held a bottle of water to her lips. The pills stuck to her tongue, but the water, oh sweet Jesus, the water. She swallowed the pills and kept going, deep gulps, rivulets spilling down her chin. When she was done she coughed, then wiped at her mouth with tender fingers.

Finally, she said, "Are you real?"

"Yes."

"This isn't a dream."

"No," he said. There were dark circles under his eyes, and an air of sadness. "I'm sorry. I let you down."

"Huh?"

"You shouldn't be here. I tried to . . ." He made an open gesture with his hands and trailed off.

She planted her hands, scooched back against the headboard. Pain splashed over her like scalding water. She closed her eyes and waited for it to ebb. Then blinked and took in the room. Stylish, impersonal. A hotel. "I don't know what you're talking about. Can you please . . . what's happening?"

"I knew you'd be there, and I wanted to help. They said I couldn't, that I wouldn't be able to reach you, but I had to try. I felt you both get here, and somehow he'd already become an Eater. I guess he kind've was already; eighteen murders, all that pain, all that panic. Anyway, it's good we were there. He saw us, and maybe it was that there were four of us, or that Sonny and I have both fed, but he bolted."

She blinked at him. "What?"

Brody rubbed at his temples and gave a wry laugh. "That probably didn't make a lot of sense. Okay." He took a deep breath. "I'll explain. It's not easy to hear."

He did.

It wasn't.

For the last two days, behind the rage and frustration, behind the fear of failing to prevent another murder, behind the howling grief she didn't dare acknowledge, there had been something else. The feeling she got watching a magic show, or a round of three-card monte. A sense—no, a certainty—that she was being played.

It was as though her life had become part of the spectacle, a confrontational comedy prank to catch her off guard. *Ah-ha!* she imagined the host saying. *Gotcha! Claire McCoy, FBI agent, lawyer, rational woman, you have begun to listen to voices from beyond!*

How else to say it? Everything, beginning with the dream that wasn't a dream, all the way through finding Tucks in the database, had felt like the setup to a scam. A trick. It felt that way still.

But she had killed Simon Tucks, only to see him reborn. She had watched him leap forty feet to hoist her one armed. And as tired and funky as Will was right now, he looked a great deal better than he had the last time she'd seen him, on the table at the morgue.

Could you still call it a trick when the magic turned out to be real?

———

"I think I've got it," she said. "It makes sense, sort of. Entropy always increases, but not like flipping a switch. And this is *life* we're talking about. We don't really understand life at all. What it means, what it is, even how it began. 'Umm, well, there were amino acids and then maybe . . . lightning?' Physics tells us things fall apart, but life is the opposite of that. Life grows, spreads, changes. It's like the reverse of entropy. So if life is the alpha, and nothingness is the omega, then why shouldn't there be stages in between? I bet there are more stages than this one. Other echoes, growing fainter."

Brody gaped.

He'd been blown up, been hunted, had witnessed impossible feats, killed a woman and then lived her story, wandered an abandoned city, joined a group of post-apocalyptic humanitarians living out of a luxury hotel, dreamed true events, and arrived just in time to see the man who had murdered him attacking the woman he loved. He'd have thought that he was beyond surprise.

And yet. Claire's face was bruised, her hair matted with blood, gauze up her nostrils. He'd just told her that she was dead. And instead of going to pieces, instead of doubting and arguing, she'd simply begun to rebuild her worldview.

*What a woman.*

It struck him that he was sitting here with her, and all the things that meant. He'd only just begun to mourn the loss of her. As hard as the last days had been, they had been only a down payment on the pain. He was still in a sort of emotional shock. Ahead of him he'd seen the looming immensity of suffering to come. The unfairness of it, the ridiculous, horrifying randomness of having lived thirty-seven years and only finding Claire at the very end. Falling in love with her just in time to lose her.

Now it seemed he hadn't lost her after all. The realization brought a complicated mix of emotions. There was part of him, a big part, that was just so glad to see her, to be spared the agony of losing her forever. But what a selfish, childish, way to look at it. He hadn't lost her—because she had lost everything.

There was a family in the hotel, a father and two daughters, that Kyle had told him had been killed in a car crash. The mother had been in the car too, but she must have survived, because only the three of them had awakened in the wreckage. Brody wondered how they felt. Surely the man would prefer his children had lived. But was some part of him happy that at least they were together? Did he secretly wish for the death of his wife, so they could all be reunited—and did he hate himself for it?

"Claire . . ."

She'd been leaning back against the headboard, idly tracing the bruise on her face as she spoke. Looking at the city but clearly not seeing it. Now focus swam into her face. They stared at one another. That same unblinking stare they'd shared the other morning, when their heads were on the pillow and their future was taking shape in front of them. Whatever it was he'd been about to say slipped away. There was a communication in their gaze that made words clumsy things.

Slowly he reached out a hand. Cupped her cheek, the heat of the bruise burning off it.

———

"I'm sorry."

"For what?"

"That I couldn't help."

"How could you?"

"I don't know. I just."

"I was alive. You were dead. Pretty much by definition, you couldn't help."

"Yeah."

"You couldn't."

"Yeah."

"Sometimes things can't be helped, Brody. Sometimes people can't be saved. It's not your fault. It's the world."

———

They lay together, spooning, their bodies fitting like Velcro. Like they would have to be pulled apart.

Out the windows, the sky was a cauldron of swirling grey.

The light through the window was pale and hollow.

"I thought I'd lost you."

"Shhh."

———

There were tears, and touching. Not sex; touching. The comfort given in the middle of the night after a particularly vicious dream. Touching meant to calm and to claim. To say, wordlessly, that you are where you belong, and the nightmare was only that.

But had it been?

Or was it just beginning?

———

Late in the afternoon, Brody went downstairs, ignored the questioning gazes and knowing smirks, and found the kitchen. The industrial fridges were packed with beautifully marbled rib eyes and quivering pork belly and plump Cornish hens, but there was no fire to cook with. Instead he loaded a tray with fruits and nuts and bread and cheese. Bottles of water. A two-hundred-dollar pinot noir and two glasses.

They spread the feast on a café table in their room and ate ravenously. Through the window and six stories down people milled in front of the hotel. Practicing with their weapons. Keeping watch. Talking and drinking and flirting. A group of children played chase, sprinting over cars and through buildings, their laughter arriving late and muted by the glass.

"I'm hungry," she said, spreading triple cream on crusty bread.

"Me too."

"Funny that we're hungry here."

"Arthur says it's a residual thing. We don't actually need to eat, but our minds don't get that. He says that we adjust after a while, only eat if we feel like it. Twenty years he's been here, I guess he'd know."

"He's in charge?"

"No. No one is. There was a woman, years ago, named Ray. The way they talk about her, you'd think there would be a shrine somewhere, candles and offerings. Of course, it would vanish the moment they wandered away. Anyway, Ray, she got them together, made a safe space."

"Because everybody else was . . . eating each other." She spoke in that testing tone, not quite doubting, just hitting the weak spot in a story to see if it gave.

"Not literally eating, but near enough." He paused. "You remember Emily Watkins?"

"The seventeenth victim. The one before you."

"I ever tell you I visited her husband? CPD was going to inform him, I said I'd do it." He could picture their loft perfectly, the dusty exercise bike, the drowsy cat, and the framed 8 x 10 of them goofing on their wedding day, her husband tightrope-walking the bridge railing. "I told myself I was doing it because we were neighbors, but it was more than that. We want to save everybody, the good ones at least, and sometimes we can't. That's the thing I hated about being a cop. But the reason I bring it up, Emily is here."

"Here, here? The echo?"

He nodded. "Yesterday she got attacked by an Eater. I don't know why she was out wandering alone. Anyway, this time I made it."

A slow smile bloomed on Claire's face. "You saved her."

"The second time. Better than nothing, I guess."

She reached across the table, took his hand. "I'm proud of you."

"Don't be. I almost killed the Eater. I'd taken him down by then, he was helpless, no threat. But I wanted to kill him anyway. I mean, I *wanted* to. It wasn't just anger. It was." He paused, looked at her. Ashamed to say it. "I had the taste for it."

Claire met his gaze. He could see her thinking, but there was no judgment in her eyes. "But you didn't."

"No. Emily did. She was hurt, and feeding fixed her. In more than one way."

"'Feeding.' You make them sound like vampires."

He laughed. "People here call them that. Vamps. It occurred to me, I wonder if maybe the whole myth of the vampire came from here. From some living person seeing into the echo."

"I thought the dead and the living—"

"Yeah, I know, but maybe certain people. Maybe artists, or prophets, or madmen." He shrugged. "Just an idea."

"Maybe," Claire said, "it's seeing across that boundary that makes them artists or prophets or madmen."

"Darn."

"What?"

"Well, if I'd known that the street corner crazies were actually seeing dead people hunting each other with machetes . . ." Brody paused, timing it. "Well, I'd definitely have given more dollars."

Claire had just taken a swallow of wine, and tried to catch a laugh-cough in her hand, but didn't quite make it. Red dripped from her fingers, and that got him going, first a cackle, and then when she grabbed her glass and spit the rest of the wine into it, a howl, and for a moment she hesitated and then she joined him in it, the laughter growing into hysterical *can't stop* proportions, each of them prompting the other. Finally Claire caught her breath, wiped at her eyes. "You're bad."

He smiled. "It's nice to hear your laugh."

"You too. Even if it's your fault I'm dead." She nudged his leg under the table with the tip of her foot.

"Ha-ha. What happened, anyway? How did you find him?"

"That dream you sent."

"Huh?"

Claire cocked her head. "The dream of you in the church. Finding the Stephen King paperback, seeing the sniper out the window?"

Brody felt like he was on a call with bad reception. Like he could understand most of what she was saying, but that certain crucial words weren't coming through. "You dreamed that?"

"Yeah, like you meant for me . . ." She trailed off. "You didn't send me a dream?"

"How would I?"

"I don't know. I figured it was an echo thing."

"Not that I know of. I mean, I did find that book. *The Gunslinger*. And I did see him. He was dialing his phone, and when I heard the pile of glass ringing I figured it out. Too late."

"Not entirely. That cop you tackled? You saved his life." She bit at her thumb and turned her grey eyes out the window. "I was mad at you for that. Is that terrible?"

"Yes."

She snorted, then kicked him again, harder this time. "Anyway, after the dream, I went to the church and found the book. I couldn't believe it, I didn't. But I remembered his face so clearly that I searched the database for it. I thought I was going crazy, but there he was. Simon Tucks."

"Simon Tucks? That's the name of the guy we've been chasing, the one who terrified a whole city? Simon Tucks?"

"Turns out." Claire told him the rest of the story, driving to Old Town, knocking on the door, recognizing the voice. Tucks's flight and her pursuit, the three rounds she'd put in his chest, the wires throughout the house she'd missed. At the end, she looked at his face and said, "What?"

"Before you went in, did you sit in your car with your weapon in your lap?"

She nodded. "Making up my mind. Why?"

"Because I dreamed that." Brody stared at her. "That's how I knew you were in trouble."

"So we both had dreams—"

"—that weren't dreams. Yeah."

They sat in silence for a minute, chewing on that. Brody felt certain it meant something. He just didn't have the faintest idea what.

On the bridge below, a gang of kids had lined up alongside a Jeep and were rocking it back and forth. Timing their jumps, getting the thing bouncing, bouncing, higher each time, until the wheels began to leave the road. They hooted, kept going, getting it high enough that they could put their backs to it, the truck hanging on the diagonal a long moment before toppling sideways to teeter on the railing. The kids charged, and then the Jeep wobbled, hung, and fell over the side to plunge into the river below. Water geysered. Screeches of laughter and cheers floated up. Brody found himself smiling.

"He's still out there, isn't he?"

"Tucks?" He thought for a moment, nodded. "Doesn't seem like Eaters want to take each other on. They like easy prey."

"Meaning he'll keep going."

Brody stiffened. All of his attention had been on Claire—on trying to save her, caring for her, filling her in. He hadn't really had much time to ponder the fact that the man who had murdered them both was now a neighbor. "Yeah."

"Only now, he'll be murdering the poor confused people who just got here. People who have already lost everything. Terrified, helpless people."

"Yeah," Brody said, slowly.

She looked at him across the table. Her face swollen and purpling. Scalp torn where clumps of hair had been ripped out. Her posture was perfect, her voice commanding. Brody suddenly remembered that in addition to being his lover, she'd been his boss. "We okay with that?"

# TWENTY-EIGHT

"Brody! Come introduce the missus." Kyle waved from the edge of a couch, a bottle of bourbon in his hand. It was early evening, the sky still bright enough to carve the buildings into stark relief. There were probably a hundred people hanging out, cross-legged on the hoods of cars or splayed on couches. In a fancy leather chair, Lucy knelt astride Sonny, grinding into him, her arms around his neck, locked in a tongue-heavy kiss that showed no sign of either ending or accelerating. Finn, the archer kid, sat talking to an older woman knitting a scarf. DeAndre and Antoine tossed dice with a handful of men. The Hispanic guy in the Carhartt lay on the hood of a hundred-thousand-dollar Mercedes, reading a Punisher comic book. Somehow they'd hauled the piano out from the lobby, and Arthur played a rollicking version of The Beatles' "Lucy In the Sky with Diamonds." Everyone had weapons close at hand, although Brody had realized that was less about fear of an attack and more so they didn't simply disappear, vanish into wherever things went.

*O brave new people, to have such a world in you.*

Once Claire had raised the question back in the room, the answer had been obvious. No, they most definitely were not okay with it. Simon Tucks had to die again.

"Problem is," he'd said, "how? Even setting aside how to find him, our guns don't work here, and it's not like we can call in SWAT. And you saw what Tucks can do."

"Yeah." Claire fingered the bruises on her face. "Okay. So we need help. Maybe your buddy, what's his name, Kyle. And that biker you mentioned?"

"There's a woman seems like she knows how to use a sword too." Brody had stopped. "I wonder, though. We didn't know this world was here. The echo. What if there's another after it? We might just be passing the buck."

"Then someone like us will have to kill him there too," Claire said. "We can only do what we can do."

He nodded. "These people, the Disciples of Ray. They have rules. They only kill in self-defense."

"Good rule," Claire had said, "I like it. I live by it. But we're talking about a terrorist. Nobody can want this guy running around."

"I don't know," he'd said. "You just got here. Things are different."

"They can't be that different," she'd said, and he'd recognized the tone, knew better than to keep arguing.

Which had led to them getting dressed and heading downstairs to join the party.

Brody wasn't an introvert, but big groups had never been his scene. He liked close teams and real conversation. This kind of thing, trying to make small talk on a grand scale, people wandering in and out of a group, all those names to remember, it wore on him.

Claire, though, shone.

He'd known she was far more outgoing than he, the ready politician. She'd confessed early on that she planned to become the first female director of the FBI, saying it as if daring him to laugh. He hadn't. Putting aside the way they felt about each other, she was easily the best boss he'd ever had, tireless in her work, relentless in her thinking, and effortless in her socializing. Despite the bruises and the bandages, she charmed everyone. Learned each name the first time it was said. Asked personal questions and listened to the answers, her gaze cool and level. When Kyle passed her the bourbon, she didn't hesitate, just tilted it up in a long swallow, and then another.

Brody followed in her wake, content to be there. To be standing near her, watching her do her thing. He knew it was selfish. He didn't care.

He was glad she was here.

Arthur had moved through "Love Me Do," "Yellow Submarine," "Paperback Writer," others Brody didn't recognize, and was now onto "Hey Jude." It was the hour the fire pit would have been lit, if fire burned here, and he and Claire had joined a group of people on a couch near the piano. His arm was around her shoulders, her body warm and the smell of her in his nostrils, and he could have stayed like that forever, had almost forgotten they were working an angle when Claire said, "You guys want to hear a story?"

She told them about a morning in September when four people were shot in two hours. About a little girl killed in front of her father. About a woman gunned down in a grocery store parking lot—Brody looked around, relieved that Emily wasn't nearby—and an FBI agent who died in an explosion. About two dreams, and a second explosion. Everyone sat rapt; no television, no Internet, and Brody imagined stories had special currency.

"This is the guy we saw?" Lucy was fidgeting with her sword, sliding the blade out an inch, then back in, the metal whispering softly. "The one who, umm . . ."

"Kicked my butt?" Claire nodded. "That's him."

"Something weird about that," Kyle said. "He'd just gotten here, right?"

"About two seconds before me."

"But he was mad flush. We only caught the end of the show, but the way he held you with one hand?" Kyle shook his head. "Only Eaters have that kind of strength."

"He killed eighteen people in the last two weeks," Brody said.

"Yeah, but living people, when he was alive. We didn't think that crossed over."

Claire shrugged, spread her hands. "Maybe he's a special case. He's certainly a special kind of crazy."

The piano stopped abruptly. The sudden silence was sharp as a gavel's bang. Arthur said, "You want to go after him."

"It's not revenge. This guy is a monster. He won't stop killing."

"No," Arthur agreed. "He'll probably get worse."

"I'm glad you understand," she said. "Because we could really use some help."

Glances flew around the circle, bouncing like Super Balls. The mood shift was palpable. Kyle said, "Claire, you're new. We've got two rules, just two. First, pull your weight—"

"Second, only kill in self-defense. I'm an FBI agent, I get it," Claire said. "And this *is* how I pull my weight. Trust me, this guy is different from what you're used to. I head one of the largest joint law enforcement task forces in . . ." She paused. "I did, I mean. And this guy—"

Arthur asked, "How's the pay?"

"Pardon?"

"In the FBI. You work for money, right?"

"I get a paycheck. I wouldn't say that's what I work for."

"And vacation days. Direct deposit. An IRA. A mortgage. Maybe a pet. Furniture from IKEA. A gym membership."

"Where are you going with this?"

Arthur started fingering the piano keys again. The melody was immediately familiar, but it took Brody a moment to recognize the song as "Yesterday." Without ceasing to play, Arthur looked up. "None of that is true now. No mortgage, no IRA, no cat. Everyone starts over. Sonny doesn't ride with the Outlaws. Kyle doesn't fight fires. And you're not an FBI agent."

"That doesn't change the fact that Tucks is a monster."

"No. It just means that it's not your place to hunt him."

Brody said, "Look, everybody, we understand the reasons for the rules. But we're not talking about an average Eater. This guy is—"

"A psycho," Kyle said. "We get it. How's that different from the woman you killed the other day?"

"Raquel was just a regular person who . . ." Brody trailed off. Who what? Who died, and took that rage out on the first person she saw? Who had probably killed many times since? The easy mockery in her tone as she stood over him hadn't come from a tortured conscience.

Arthur took advantage of the pause to segue songs, his fingers going from delicate tinkling to more pronounced chords. Brody recognized it after a minute—"Live and Let Die." He couldn't help but snort.

"Half the people in the echo are serial killers," Lucy said. "Maybe not before, but now. It's the way of it."

Claire didn't respond immediately. He could see her analyzing, that ferocious mind of hers recognizing a dead end and changing course. "How many children end up here?"

Again, there were glances. Kyle said, "Plenty."

"One a day?"

"Could be."

"So how many children do you think Tucks will murder while you sit here playing the fucking piano?"

Arthur sighed, and took his fingers from the keys. "When you were alive, there must have been people you knew were evil, but you didn't just kill them. Why?"

"We're a little past courts of law, don't you think? This isn't about abstract morality. It's about protecting ourselves. About protecting children."

"The rules," Arthur said. "That's why you didn't just execute people. Well, there are rules here too. *We do not kill unless we are forced to.* And you're right, it's not about abstract morality. It's about practical reality. The rules allow us to live together. To have a community."

Lucy leaned forward, put a hand on Claire's knee. "I know you mean well. And this guy sounds like he deserves to die. But it's not about them. It's about us. It's about being able to sleep at night without worrying our friends are going to feed on us."

"It's more than that," Sonny said softly. He'd been silent throughout the exchange, sitting stone-faced with his palms resting on the pommels of his knives. "It's wrong."

Despite himself, Brody broke out laughing. "Really? The meth-dealing biker is lecturing us about violence?"

"I did some things when I was alive," Sonny said. "Didn't bother me then. Fought plenty of times I didn't have to. Cut on people I wanted to scare. Killed some of them. A lot of it I was high, but really, I just didn't care."

Brody shot a glance at Kyle. *Remember when I called BS that you and he are in the same place?*

"When I got here, I thought shit, turns out God is an Outlaw. This place seemed like heaven. No cops, no cartels. Take anything I want, do anything I want.

"I went on thinking that until the first Eater. I've been fighting strong, fast assholes my whole life, I know how to do it. I cut his Achilles with one blade and his throat with the other. And then." Sonny's usual poker face seemed to waver a little. "Then I lived him."

Brody remembered being Raquel. Her backyard birthday party. Makeovers with her friend. Her swim meet, her virginity, her murder. He hadn't been watching, he'd *been* her. Felt the things she'd felt, thought the things she'd thought. It was beyond empathy. Some part of him almost loved her.

"It's funny," Sonny said. "Wasn't till I died that I really understood killing." He shrugged, turned to Claire. "Yeah, we got rules, and they're good. But it's not really about the rules. It's about knowing killing is wrong. Echo just makes it clearer."

Brody found he couldn't speak.

"I've lost friends to Eaters," Sonny continued, "and I've lost friends because they became Eaters. I see 'em sometimes, people we all knew. I don't mean memories, I mean out there." He gestured at the dark city. "But they had to go, because we couldn't trust them. They'd started to get a taste for it."

Sonny's words mirrored the confession Brody had made to Claire only hours before, and the fact unnerved him. He looked at her, saw her looking back.

For a moment, he pondered what it would be like if they went it alone. The empty city. The sound of wind. The lonely shadows of an absent world, and the howls of the people hunting them.

Could they survive? Probably. They were very capable people. They'd have to be on guard. Maybe leave the city, find a cabin somewhere quiet. Only each other for company or conversation, and no "me time"; it would be too big a risk to ever separate.

Still, some day an Eater would try for them. Lose that fight, and one or both of them were gone. Win, and there would be another. And another. Each time would get easier. Each time it would mean less.

One day, they'd decide to attack instead of defend.

Claire was looking at him. If she asked, he'd go. Take her side, and abandon the others.

If she asked. But he stared back, trying to communicate that he really hoped she wouldn't.

Arthur stood. "Your old life is over. You can pretend that's not true, or you can join us. Make the hard choice, not once, but over and over. Be a human being. Perhaps," he shrugged. "Perhaps even learn to play the fucking piano."

# TWENTY-NINE

They lay in the morning dim, legs tangled, sheets like whipped egg whites, heads on their pillows and eyes locked. Too much to say to bother trying. Claire had her hands tucked angel style under her cheek. With the tips of his fingers, Brody traced the bruise across her face. He could smell her breath, and their bodies, the scents mingling, a little sour but warm and homey.

*Boom boom boom.*

Someone thumping at the door. A muffled voice yelled, "Yo. Wakey-wakey."

Brody sighed, rolled to sitting. He shrugged into a hotel bathrobe before opening the door. "Eggs and bakey?"

"I wish," Kyle said. "But I got a smushed Clif Bar if you like. The missus up?"

"Claire's awake."

"Good. She hasn't seen the world yet, time to pop that cherry. Meet you in the ballroom." Kyle turned, started down the hall, whistling what sounded like the Looney Tunes theme song.

"What's going on?"

Over his shoulder, Kyle said, "Patrol."

----

They found the ballroom by the burble of voices, the overlapping cacophony of a hundred conversations. The room was broad and pretty in a corporate way, high ceilings, unlit chandeliers, white curtains swept aside to show the city. Brody was getting used to seeing the skyline dark, and to the clouds hanging low.

The room could have held several times the hundred or so milling around the center of it. Brody cataloged weapons: lots of knives, lots of baseball bats. A few bows and crossbows. Pool cues. Lengths of pipe, lengths of chain, cans of pepper spray.

An earsplitting whistle shattered the noise. Everyone turned to look at Kyle. "Alright, folks. First off, we've got a couple of newbies. If you haven't met them, that's Will Brody, that's Claire McCoy. They're doing a little *Romeo and Juliet the Sequel* thing, the lucky kids."

A hundred people turned to look, muttering hellos, smiling. Brody threw a casual salute back.

"They'll be going out with me this morning." He pointed at a map of Chicago taped to the window. Bright red lines broke the city into four roughly equal quadrants, spanning as far north as Devon and as far south as 87th. "We're gonna break them in easy, take the North Side. Rhonda's team is northwest, Sonny and Lucy, you guys have the hot spots, southwest and south. As always, if you get an arrival, hustle, but don't take foolish risks."

The whole thing wasn't much different from roll call for law enforcement, or the prepatrol briefings in the Marines, and Brody fell into habit, listening while also looking around. Everyone seemed calm.

"—and no skylarking, okay? Everybody back by late afternoon at the outside. Gets dark earlier these days, and we've been cutting the daylight a little fine. Any questions?"

Twenty minutes later, Kyle was doing a head count of his squad, and then they were moving out, north down the middle of the street. They fell into loose conversational groups, pairs and trios, but everyone was alert, hands near weapons. Kyle gestured for them to join him at the front. "Sorry for the wakeup call," he said to Claire. "You still hurting?"

"I'm okay."

"So we're clear, if we happen to come across your boy, leave him be."

"What if my 'boy' feels differently?"

"Hey, if he attacks, you can defend yourself," Kyle said, "and we'll all have your back. But don't get any ideas of trying to make it happen. Stick to the spirit of the rules. Meanwhile, you need to see what it's like. Hanging in the hotel is the reward, not the life. We patrol every day, rotating so everybody gets a weekend."

Brody said, "Trying to keep the Eaters back?"

"Nah." Kyle tucked a wad of tobacco in his lip. "Our job is to get to new arrivals before they become an amuse-bouche. We swing by likely places, dangerous intersections, hospitals. Lotta customers in hospitals. South Side teams haunt gang territory. Everybody keeps an eye on the freeways. But mostly we just walk around, stay ready."

"Big as Chicago is," Claire said, "the odds against stumbling on someone must be huge."

"Would be, only it's not luck. You can feel when someone arrives here. Sort of a pull in the gut. Professor thinks it's about how scarce life is. We're the only energy around, and there aren't many of us. So when someone new lands, it changes things."

"Like adding a cup of water to a bowl," Claire mused in her *I'm thinking* voice. "Versus pouring it in the lake. How often do we find someone?"

"People arrive most every day, but the Eaters tend to get to them first. Wider net."

"We could split up," she suggested. "Break into smaller groups, cover more terrain."

Kyle smiled. "Lady, once you've seen a vamp punch through a brick wall, you might feel different."

They walked a few blocks north, then cut east. The city right and real in every detail, apart from all the things that made it vital. They passed a darkened Starbucks, and Brody felt a palpable urge for a coffee. Large Americano with an extra shot, and a splash of cream, just enough to round it out.

"Italian beef," Finn said loudly. The boy—Brody guessed he was seventeen—wore sunglasses with red lenses and a ridiculous leather duster, his compound bow slung over one shoulder. "Dipped, with hot peppers."

Without missing a beat, the Latino dude in the Carhartt jacket said, "Movies. Tub of popcorn with extra butter." He turned to Brody. "Love those superhero movies. My luck, I died a week before the new *Captain America* came out. You see it?"

"Yeah," Brody said. "A lot of things blew up."

"Shit," the man said, mournfully. "Wish I'd seen that."

A woman carrying a baseball bat said, "Facebook." Half the group groaned. "What? I liked the pictures. And people complaining about things. Don't know why I liked that, but I did."

"The fire pit in my backyard."

"Video games."

"Girls in bikinis."

"Warm barbecue and cold beer."

"Jesus Christ, Finn," Kyle said, "do we have to do this every time?"

The boy looked hurt. "What?"

"Every time it's the same. Food, the sun, and then somebody says hot showers and we all get sad."

"Hot showers," said a pudgy girl.

"Fuck."

They turned onto Michigan Avenue, the Magnificent Mile. Always a misnomer in Brody's opinion; a mall stretched down a street was still a mall. Jarring, though, to stroll down the middle of the sidewalk without dodging tourists or bumping into performers. No cops, no kids snapping selfies. Unmoving cars stopped at dark traffic lights. He glanced at Claire, saw her in-turned shoulders and darting eyes. "You okay?"

She nodded. "It's so strange. I was expecting something out of a movie about nuclear war. The buildings crumbling, vines everywhere. But it's like we're walking through a photograph of the city. Like somebody took the batteries out of the world."

"Other way around." Kyle scooped up a soda can, crushed it, then hurled it absently to bounce off a shop window. "The world is fine. We're the ones got taken out."

Claire said, "Is that supposed to make me feel better?"

"Why not? Plenty of life was bullshit. Here, there's real freedom. No need to do a job you hate. No point saving for a rainy day. No need to mow your lawn or get your hair cut or pay your taxes. No Facebook," he said, loudly, and the woman shot him the bird.

They passed glittering storefronts with dark windows, double buses with empty seats. Up the length of the Mile, past the ominous looming black of the Hancock. Farther north, they reached Lake Shore Drive. Beyond it, Lake Michigan rolled in, water and sky the same cold color.

Division Street looked pretty much the same alive or dead, an odd blend of parking lots and unfrequented stores. On the El tracks at Sedgwick, a train stood unmoving. Stopped for maintenance? Or just frozen by their presence, locked in a pocket universe that would continue once they were past, the same way broken windows regenerated and smashed doorframes healed?

Several blocks farther north, they stopped in front of a huge REI, the outdoor sports store in a multistory building fronted in glass. Brody said, "We going camping?"

"Shopping. Your attire doesn't sync with our corporate culture." Kyle gestured at Brody's slacks, Claire's stylish pumps. "We're a sweatshirt-and-jeans organization. Plus, another upside to the afterlife?" He smiled wolfishly. "No wallets."

———

They left half the group to watch the street. The rest tromped inside, and, after a quick check to be sure the store was clear, started pulling things off the racks. The shop was two stories with an open center and glass fronting the whole thing, which allowed just enough light to navigate the darker aisles. Tents were open on the floor, kayaks hung from the ceiling like strange fish. There was something deliciously illicit about it, like sneaking into the library after dark.

Claire shopped with startling focus. No browsing, no chitchat, just hard target search. They picked heavy jeans, thermal undershirts, and moisture-wicking hoodies. Windbreakers, a small backpack each. Underwear—"It's not exactly Victoria's Secret, but clean beats lace, right?"—and wool socks. Leather hiking boots that cost four hundred dollars a pair. The others seemed to have favorite items, and often changed on the spot, dropping their old clothes on the floor and stepping into new ones, flashes of pale flesh dimpling in the cold. Brody supposed modesty came to seem rather silly here, but it was still startling, and when Claire followed suit he stared openly. When she caught him, she put a hand beneath each breast and mashed them together, laughing at him.

The new clothes were warm and soft, and the boots felt like pillows. Kyle nodded approvingly. "That's better. Now. What kind of weapon says 'Claire McCoy'?"

"A Glock 23 with a Talon grip and Trijicon iridium sights."

"And your second choice? Most of us carry knives, but you'll probably also want something else with a little more heft." He unslung the fireman's axe from his back. "Like Bessie here."

"Bessie? Seriously?"

"Hey. Don't mock a man's weapon."

They selected expensive Benchmade knives with scabbards, strung them through their belts. Claire picked up a wicked throwing hatchet, took a couple of practice swings. "I feel ridiculous."

Half an hour after they'd entered, the group of them left. Piles of clothing on the floor. Display cases smashed. Wearing twenty-five thousand dollars' worth of new gear between them.

Brody had to admit, it was a kick.

They continued north, in a meandering course determined by whim and interest. Hector, the movie buff, wanted to walk past a theater to look at the posters. He paced the row, pausing here and there to stare reverently. A woman called Adina wanted to visit her old church. After clearing it, they left her alone, kneeling in the third pew. At the door Brody paused, staring at the woman and the pews and the figure on the wall. Conscious of the cross around his neck, the one Mom had given him before he deployed the first time.

Claire touched his arm. "Do you want to join her?"

"No," Brody said harder than he intended. He gestured at the world around them. "With all this . . . it just seems kind of silly. I mean, what's the point?"

"What was the point before?" Claire shrugged. "So you're dead and it's not what you expected. Doesn't mean you have all the answers."

"Yeah, but what would I be praying to, the architect of the echo?"

"That's what faith is, right? Belief in things you don't understand. Belief that there is something behind it that does. Maybe now is exactly the time to pray."

Brody found he had no reply.

Around noon they raided a Whole Foods, plundering the prepared food counter for Tuscan chicken breasts and couscous salad and grilled salmon filets. Finn filled a basket with bottles of wine and a sleeve of cups. They ate in a playground two blocks away, sprawled across jungle gyms and benches. The clouds seemed thinner today, like the sun was on the verge of burning through. The swings swayed gently, which was odd, because the branches of the trees were still.

When he glanced back at the swings, there were children in them.

Two little girls, sisters by their features, bundled in sweaters and laughing as they arced higher and higher, their hair unfurling like flags. Behind them a rumpled man in his forties stared at his phone while he absently alternated pushing them.

In the grass two boys kicked a soccer ball.

Near the water fountain, a young mother bent over a stroller, adjusting a blanket.

Across the street, a hipster in tight jeans walked a bulldog.

A car pulled to the corner, and the back door swung—

Then they were gone. The echo was exactly as it had been. Just the crew of them sprawled across the equipment, eating chicken legs and sipping wine in Solo cups.

"You okay?"

"What?" He blinked, rubbed his eyes, looked at Claire. "Yeah. I just . . . for a second I saw people. Living people."

"In the park?"

"In the park, on the sidewalk, in cars. Everywhere."

"A daydream?"

He shook his head. "Kyle said it would happen. Something to do with having fed. Little flashes of the real world."

"I wonder if they could see you."

"Huh. I don't know. Maybe that's the explanation for people seeing ghosts."

"Not to split hairs," she said drily, "but you are dead."

He laughed, and was about to respond when a wobbly sensation ran through him. It was mild but distinct, an inner ear feeling. Something like the way a small boat tilts when someone climbs out.

At first he presumed it had to do with what he'd seen, but then he noticed that everyone else had felt it too. People were reaching for weapons, rising to their feet. Kyle lowered his sandwich. Claire pulled the hatchet from her pack.

For a moment, no one spoke. Then Finn said, "Strong one."

Kyle nodded, then went back to eating.

Brody looked back and forth. "Why aren't we—wasn't that a new arrival?"

"No," Finn said. "With arrivals the world seems more, I don't know, full. And you kinda know where they came from. That's how we found you."

"So then, what was—"

"Departure," Kyle said. "Not a newbie. That was an Eater dying. A powerful one."

"What does that mean?" Claire still held the hatchet.

"Nothing." Kyle tossed his sandwich. "Risks of the lifestyle."

"I thought they don't fight each other."

"Mostly. But it's like overpopulation. Just because lions mostly eat zebras doesn't mean they're above a mouthful of cat." He stood, dusted his hands. "Come on, let's move along. I want to swing by Wrigley Field, see if they're flying the W."

The group wound up, leaving their garbage where it lay. There was something shocking in that. A lifetime habit of putting trash in the can made the notion of just dropping your junk almost obscene, even with the knowledge that it would vanish, that if they returned here in ten minutes there would be no sign of their presence.

Kyle took the lead, and the rest fell in. None of them said much of anything. Brody and Claire locked eyes, and he could practically hear her voice.

*A powerful Eater?*

*Like Simon Tucks?*

# THIRTY

A day passed, two, then three. The patrols became routine, almost pleasant. Each trip they saw Eaters, but always at a distance, the men and women staring with naked hunger held in check by fear. The second day, one of the other squads brought in a new arrival, and when Brody introduced himself, her searching gaze reminded him of the way soldiers arriving for their first deployment looked at the veterans.

He and Claire made love, gently because of her bruises and laughing about it, joking about her being an old woman. On patrol, he reached out and took her hand as they walked, and she jumped, surprised, and it occurred to both of them that this was something they'd never been able to do before, hold hands on a walk in public. At work they'd had to keep their relationship secret, and there hadn't been the time—

There hadn't been the time.

They met most of the people, learned some of their stories. Hector, who had fallen off a construction ladder a week before the release of his beloved superhero movie. Antoine, a corrections officer shivved on a routine court transfer by a teenaged Latin King. Madeleine, who knit gorgeous scarves that she purposefully abandoned in the echo, some cross between prayer and art project. Finn, who had learned to use a bow hunting deer with his stepfather, and died when the man, smashed, drove their pickup into a bridge support.

"If he was drunk, why weren't you driving?"

"I was drunker."

One evening Emily Watkins made a point of coming over to the couch he and Claire sat on. Previously, there had been something ghostly about her, a sense of sadness worn like a shawl. Now she seemed vital, her cheeks pink with cool air and her skin glowing with that hyper-focus, the feeling that invisible spotlights shone only on her. "I want to thank you."

Mildly embarrassed, he said, "No need."

Emily turned to Claire. "He saved me. And not just from the Eater." To Brody, she added, "I was about to make a terrible mistake."

It clicked for him then, why she had been alone out beyond the bridges. "I'm glad you didn't."

"Me too."

Brody considered telling her the rest of it. How he'd stood over her body in a parking lot, how he'd visited her husband to inform him of her death. But why remind her of the things she'd lost, just when she was starting to notice the things she'd gained?

Over three days, they felt the weird tilting sensation five more times. Five more Eaters gone, and one of them so powerful that Brody stumbled, had to hold the wall for balance. Though it set everyone on edge, no one seemed to have answers, or feel the need to investigate.

Each day Claire mentioned the idea of pursuing Simon Tucks less frequently, but he could see she was wrestling with the notion that it was no longer her responsibility. That that Claire McCoy was dead. He got it, felt the same.

There were moments when grief gutted him. Stilettos of loss and regret that made him reel, close his eyes, take deep breaths. Partly for the people he had lost; partly for the fact that he knew they were suffering, mourning for him.

Yet there was something about being on the flip side of disaster that changed everything. Sure, it hurt to know that the people he loved were suffering, but there was comfort in knowing they were alive. That whatever pain they felt, it was part of a larger life. It turned out that there was a difference between knowing you'd never see someone again and knowing they were dead.

Especially when you were the one in the brave new world.

And he had to admit that there were moments of adventure and play. Yesterday, exploring the hotel, he and Claire had discovered the swimming pool. A broad, gorgeous space of pale polished stone, white deck chairs, and sheer curtains glowing twilight shades. The chemical smell was vivid, exciting. Claire had whooped and stripped her sweatshirt off without hesitation, dumped her bra, then started hopping on one foot to yank off the boots. A minute later they were swimming.

It felt wonderful to knife through the water in a clean crawl, the way he'd done most mornings of his old life. On his tenth lap he'd bumped into Claire drifting on her back, and they both swallowed water and came up laughing and coughing. She'd wrapped her arms around his neck and pressed her body against him, cool water and warm skin, her chlorine lips like a memory of summer. They'd made it to the side without breaking the embrace, and then he'd hoisted her up onto the pool's edge and kissed his way down her shivering thighs to the warmth between them. As he worked her with tongue and mouth her cries echoed and rebounded off the stone and her feet churned the water.

When they left, they found five people waiting in the hallway with towels slung over their shoulders and grins plastered on their faces. They burst into applause. Claire flushed so red she looked boiled.

Now, sitting atop the concrete wall of the parking deck neighboring the hotel, watching an impromptu soccer game, Brody smiled to remember the wolf whistles, the good-natured teasing. He loosened his boots and kicked them off, rubbed at road-sore feet.

Today's patrol had been simple enough. He'd grown accustomed to the twenty-pound sledgehammer slung across his back—when he'd told Kyle he wanted a baseball bat, the man had said, "Son, right now you could lift a car. Think bigger"—and when they'd spotted two Eaters a block away, part of him hoped they'd attack. No one seemed to have a fixed answer on the half-life of his new power; it depended on the strength of the Eater. Kyle said to think in terms of weeks, and less the more he used it. Though he still felt flush from Raquel, a voice inside whispered that he could always have more.

So perhaps it was for the good that the two Eaters had retreated, their hollow eyes staring.

The team had raided stores, broken out the windows and half the wall of Katsu to let in enough light for them to eat sashimi and rice by the handful. Stopped in a sports store for Brody's new swim goggles, and a jewelry shop where Claire, with an expression of delight that bordered on the fetishistic, had smashed the case and withdrawn a twenty-thousand-dollar Rolex.

The soccer game was casual at best, the goals marked by discarded jackets, the teams oversized and in constant flux. It was mostly kids, the youngest a four-year-old cutie with her hair bound up in silly bun twists. They scrambled after the ball, yelling and laughing, no one particularly worried about scoring. The top floor of the parking deck was walled on all sides and open to the sky, making a safe play space in an unsafe world. The effect on everyone was palpable. True, every few minutes the ball went too far and ended up rolling down the ramp, but the kids had even integrated that, everyone sprinting to be the first to touch it. Adults were in the game too, Kyle and Hector and a handful of others, with Antoine acting as ref. On the outskirts dozens of people loitered, cheering on the players or talking in small groups, drinking beer, eating chips.

The door to the stairwell was propped open, and he saw Claire reach the top, panting only slightly. One thing with the echo, you got your cardio in. She put a hand over her eyes to scan the field, and he waved. She approached, gave him a theatrical look, then flipped her left wrist up to glance at the watch. "It is now 5:22 p.m."

"It was killing you not to know, wasn't it?"

"Totally."

"The battery works?"

"Battery?" She scoffed. "This is a fully mechanical automatic watch, constantly wound by my motion, and waterproof to a thousand feet."

"Thank god. I was wondering how we'd tell time at the bottom of the ocean. How'd you set it?"

He lowered a hand to her, but she waved it away, grabbed the lip of the wall, and pulled herself up. The hatchet on her belt clattered against the concrete. She'd been practicing throwing it, spending an hour a day hurling it into the rich wood of the lobby desk, the same way she had once spent that time down at the firing range. "Walked down to Macy's on State, the one with the big clock out front."

"Alone?"

"Lucy came along, Madeleine, Rosario, Patricia."

"Was there girl talk?"

"Of course."

"Should I be worried?"

"Why is it," Claire said, twisting a piece of hair in her mouth, "that when women talk, men think it's about them?"

"We just assume everything is."

A cry went up from the soccer game. The little girl was racing downfield, kicking the ball with great determination and slightly less accuracy, pursued by teenagers who could have caught her with ease. Kyle stood in the goal, knees bent, arms out. She ran straight at him, more pushing the ball than controlling it, and gave a last mighty kick that almost sent her flying. The ball took to the air, and Kyle somehow managed not to stop it. Her team exploded, yelling, "Goal!" and hoisting her onto their shoulders.

"It's not bad here," Claire said.

He turned to her. The bruises on her face had moved from purple to yellow-green, and her scalp had scabbed up. But the changes went deeper than that. There was, he realized, a calm about her. Something akin to the way people relaxed on vacation, how it became normal to wave to strangers, to smile good morning at everyone. "No," he said. "No, it's not."

"I keep thinking that I should resist it more. That I should be fighting this. But who would I fight against? Where would I file a complaint? We're here. That's that. I guess I won't become the first female director of the FBI. Do I hold on to that?"

"Look at it this way," he said. "You're the highest ranking FBI agent in the world right now."

They sat watching the game, their thighs touching. She fiddled with her watch. "It's all a matter of perspective, isn't it? Like, from one perspective, we got a terrible deal. Simon Tucks took everything from us, everything we'd built, all the people we loved. And that's unbelievably awful. You could say that we had terrible luck.

"Or," she shrugged. "Or, you could say that after we both carelessly lost our lives, we discovered there was something that came afterward. A strange place, yeah, but one with warmth and community, with people trying to help each other. And not only that, but we have each other. Lots of people here are fooling around, and some are in relationships. But not like us." She paused.

"So do we have the most hideous luck on the planet? Or are we the most fortunate people in history?"

"Yes," Brody said. He smiled at her, and after a moment she smiled back. They kissed, soft and slow but with heat behind it, and right out in the open.

A whistle blew, two long blasts. All of the guards on the bridges and nearby buildings carried them, and there was a system of signals. One long note meant the squad from sector one returning, two for two, three for three. Continuing blasts meant danger, everybody up. Brody had made a *Game of Thrones* joke to Arthur about it, and received a blank stare in return. Twenty years in the echo meant missing a few cultural touchstones.

"They're late," Claire said, glancing at her new toy. Before he could respond, another sound came.

A loud, shrill whistle—that didn't stop.

# THIRTY-ONE

"You're sure about this?"

DeAndre slid a toothpick from one side of his mouth to the other. Claire put him at about seventeen, tall and handsome, his scalp shaved but a sculpted goatee framing his features. He had some South Side swagger, but not the dead-eyed stare corner kids learned early. He'd died before she moved to Chicago, but she'd followed the story of his shooting with the same queasy horror as the killings of Freddie Gray and Eric Garner. DeAndre said, "Saw what I saw. They was setting up for the night."

Brody said, "They might have sentries."

"Might," Kyle agreed. "Not their SOP, but neither is this."

"We could wait for daylight." Claire still couldn't get used to how very dark the city was with nothing on, how cold and quiet. She remembered Kyle's description the other day, of the echo as a dead world, and it seemed more apt than ever. A dead rock spinning through space with the remnants of a world left behind on it, and a few stragglers clinging. She fought a shiver at the image.

"No," Sonny said. The biker's voice was surprisingly honeyed, not the gravelly snarl she would have expected. Like he'd done voiceover work instead of running meth. "Come morning they'll be rolling."

"How do you know?"

"Because they don't hold meetings. If the boy's right—"

"Don't call me boy—"

"—they're on the move."

There had been a moment, as the panic whistle lilted into the sky, when everyone on the rooftop stopped. Frozen, staring at one another. Good humor and certainty of action evaporating. Claire had seen it happen before. It was the reaction people had when things that weren't supposed to happen, did. A lightning strike change in the landscape. It was what had made Simon Tucks so terrifying. A gunshot in a war zone was commonplace. A gunshot on a clear blue Chicago day tore the underpinnings out of reality. No one knew what to do in those moments, and everyone stared at one another, desperate for answers. Pack mentality: *someone tell me how to act now.*

Then Kyle was bolting for the stairs, she and Brody right behind.

By the time they made it to the street, scores of others had joined, their weapons out and eyes wild, trying to look in all directions at once.

The squad that had just come in from patrol were pale and gasping, many of them collapsed on the ground outside the hotel. They looked like they'd sprinted miles with wolves at their heels. Which turned out to be true, more or less.

The squad was led by a woman named Rhonda, a former cop from Atlanta, who three years ago had slipped on an icy El platform just as the train came in. *Thing musta tore me in pieces,* she'd told Claire yesterday. *Y'all live in a dumb climate.* She was panting too hard to speak, and she'd gestured to DeAndre to explain.

The kid told them what he'd seen. How he'd split from the group to do a little recon, climbing the stairs of a mid-rise university building that offered a broad view. "Not many tall buildings over there," he'd said. "I keep track. Don't mind climbing, and plenty of times I can spot trouble."

What had followed DeAndre's story had been an hour of disbelief and argument, of two hundred people trying to talk at the same time. Of frantic orders to get the children inside the hotel and triple the guard on the bridge. The sounds of breaking glass from all around as cars were pushed to block the road and vantage points in the hotel were opened.

She had been the one to suggest a small group investigate. Brody had backed her, and Kyle and a few of the more aggressive members had quickly joined in. Arthur had been opposed to the idea, but while he was clearly respected, he didn't seem to be in charge, and so shortly after dark, a team of six—she and Brody, DeAndre, Kyle, Sonny, and Lucy—had set off to the southwest. They'd moved carefully, darting from alley to alley. The empty city had unspooled around them, the river a slick dark ribbon, the trendy restaurants on Randolph lonely in the quiet. At the concrete spaghetti of the Circle Interchange, where three highways met, they'd left the road and hiked the grass beneath vaulting ramps. Smells of rot and wet grass. They held their weapons in hand, and didn't speak. All around them buildings stared in mute judgment. It had taken almost three hours to cover four miles.

Now, standing amidst the tree-lined order of the UIC campus, she could make out the building DeAndre had been talking about. An ugly concrete tower, pale against the dark clouds, the windows like slit eyes, narrow and tall. It looked more like a fortress than a science office. Probably built in the '60s, when students were occupying universities. From the south she could hear a faint hum and crackle, impossible to interpret but definitely not the wind. Brody stood beside her, a huge sledgehammer dangling from his hand as lightly as a stick he'd snagged to swat leaves.

"Okay," Kyle said. "We're here. Now what?"

It took Claire a moment to realize he was looking at her. The others too. Partly, she suspected, because this had been her idea, but more because she and Will had been FBI agents. Funny; these people had found a way to survive here, had faced more danger on a daily level than many agents did in a career, and yet they were still responding to an authority pattern.

"Where did you get in the building, DeAndre?"

He pointed at the north entrance.

"Right. Well, let's hope it stays open late." She paused, considering. "Okay. We keep the building between us and the field. Weapons out, no talking, stay close. If anyone spots us, we run." Claire had a flash of Simon Tucks hauling her into the air one-handed, and her scalp ached at the memory. *And pray they don't follow.*

They crossed the street to the sidewalk. A wrought iron fence separated them from the grounds, a bent bicycle frame still U-locked to it. Sonny took two quick steps, planted a foot, and leapt. He cleared the five-foot fence with two to spare, landed soft as a cat, and turned back to shoot them a grin. Brody, who had already reached out a hand to the railing, paused, then stepped back and did likewise.

Watching the man she loved leap ten vertical feet like it was nothing, she felt a sudden pang. What power came with abandoning the rules. They could sprint for hours, swing a sledgehammer one-handed, move like superheroes. Brody had told her that there were moments when he could almost see the sun, whereas for her, the sky had been a relentless mass of swirling grey. In this dead world, life force was power, purely translated. How addictive a feeling that must be. What a hunger it must breed.

*No wonder they all live according to the Gospel of Ray. Dive off that wagon, you're never crawling back on.*

Claire and the others got over the fence the old-fashioned way, making a little more noise than she would have liked. With Brody at the front and Sonny watching the rear, the six of them skulked through the campus, bike racks and lounge space, posters for bands and plays, all of it belonging to a world they were no longer part of. She imagined drunk frat boys crossing the quad, teenaged lovers holding hands, all of it right here, separated by a thin but uncrossable membrane.

*Not uncrossable. One way.*

As they drew nearer the university tower, the noise they'd been hearing grew louder. The ugly bulk of the building hid the source and distorted the sound, but she thought it was overlapping voices. After the silence of the last hours, it seemed reckless, swaggering.

The north entrance was a row of metal doors in metal frames with small inset windows. Claire tried one, found it locked.

"I can open it," Sonny said.

"Does that mean tear it off the hinges?" She shook her head. "Too noisy."

"Look." Lucy pointed.

Three stories up, a window was cocked open. The narrow horizontal kind that opened outward and never let in a breeze. It looked wide enough for someone to squeeze through, but unless they doubled back, found a grappling hook and some rope—

Something blurred past her and hit the wall.

Months ago, before she moved to Chicago or met Brody, she'd gone to Los Angeles for a conference. Worn out by the flight and a series of boring conversations, she'd spent the night in her hotel room flipping channels, and had happened on something called *American Ninja Warrior*, a competition show with a ridiculous obstacle course. She'd found herself entranced by it, and by the competitors with their sweetly toned physiques and lithe grace.

The final challenge was a curved wall fourteen feet high that they had to run up. It had seemed ridiculous. Impossible.

But now she watched Brody hit the side of the building, plant a foot and push, hurtling himself upward to grab the frame of a window on the second story, then snap a fast pull-up that somehow launched him a full story into the air. He caught the inner rim of the open window—thirty feet off the ground, easy—and wriggled through. All in maybe two seconds.

A moment later, one of the doors swung open. Brody stood on the other side wearing a broad grin. The others smiled and golf clapped.

She said, "Enjoying yourself?"

"Huh?"

"Being a superhero looks like fun."

"Claire—"

"Just saying, heroin is fun too. Until you run out."

For a moment he looked like he was going to snap at her, and she wondered if they were about to have their first fight, right here in front of four near strangers and god knew what lay on the other side of this hideous university high-rise. But he bit his tongue, sighed slightly, and nodded. "Yeah. Roger that."

The simple mindfulness of him surprised her, again. How many men would have gotten pissed on principle, would have resented a woman for telling them what to do? She stepped forward, put a hand behind his neck and another around his waist. "I love you."

"I love you too." He cocked his head. "Huh."

"What?"

"First time we've said it to each other." The smile he wore was the same as when they'd lain in her apartment, staring into one another's eyes, hours from events that would change everything. She leaned in and they kissed, hard, tongues sliding against one another.

"Jesus, you two," Kyle said. "A little sympathy for the single, huh?" He pushed past them, squinted into the blackness. "D-Money. Where are the stairs?"

The city had been dark, but the stairwell, a shaft of cinderblocks unbroken by windows, was something else entirely. Blackness like blindness. She literally couldn't see her own hand waving in front of her face. There was the stale smell of cigarettes, and echoes from every scuffed foot, every indrawn breath. DeAndre went first, the others following. The only connection to the world was the pressure of her feet on the treads and the cool metal of the handrail. In seconds she'd lost all other frame of reference. Up, and up, and up they went, breath coming shorter, thighs starting to tingle. Finally, after what seemed a very long time, DeAndre's disembodied whisper drifted back. "Careful. Last one."

Then they were stepping through the door into an academic hallway. After the pitch black of the staircase, what little light trickled in seemed enough to read by. Bulletin boards and glass cases, benches and worn industrial carpet. DeAndre put a finger to his lips and led them down the hall to a closed door. He tried the handle, and it turned. The sounds were louder now, definitely voices, raucous and overlapping, and something else. A crackling.

She stepped through the door into a small lounge, and gasped.

"Holy *shit*."

# THIRTY-TWO

The windows were slender and tall, and ten in this room alone, making the walls seem like bars. They could see easily now, reflected light bouncing through the glass to flicker and dance.

Eleven stories below a huge bonfire roared. Tables and chairs and stacks of books, all heaped together and lit ablaze. A sloppy, wild pyre twenty feet across, the flames leaping into the air, cracking and roaring. Claire could feel the heat through the window. A ropy column of choking smoke twisted upward against darker skies.

Surrounding the fire were people. Some stood hypnotized, staring and swaying in time to the shimmering waves playing across the embers. Near the edge, a woman danced topless, her breasts glistening, belly slick with sweat. A stylish black man with a baseball bat and a skinny white scarecrow shared a bottle and watched. Teenagers sprinted around the blaze, leaping through the fringes, whooping like matinee Indians.

Farther out, others talked tensely. Their body language was rigid, all tightened shoulders and loosened knees, but there was something habitual to the pose. None of them were fingering weapons, no one was squaring off. It was more like they were predators unaccustomed to the company of anything but prey.

Staring at the figures was oddly difficult. They all seemed more in focus than the world in a way that competed with the bonfire. The flames caught in their eyes, carved monstrous shadow mouths.

Eaters.

Scores, hundreds of them. All together.

"My god," Kyle whispered, his voice filled with wonder and terror. "Fire."

In the brilliant heart of the inferno something cracked, the leg of a table or the arm of a mannequin yielding to destruction and sending a cascade of sparks toward heaven. Claire looked at the others, Lucy and Sonny and DeAndre. They were pressed to their individual columns of glass, hands and foreheads pushing in. Their faces were contorted with something akin to lust. Teenagers pressing against the glass of a sex show.

*Right,* she thought. *Nothing burns.* She'd only been here a few days, and had barely begun to miss things like warmth. The magical, world-conquering power of fire. No wonder the Eaters were all together.

"Claire," Brody said, the word humming with thin lethal tension, like wire strung at neck height. She turned, saw him pointing, followed his eyes and finger.

Beside the fire stood a broad table of polished wood. A shapeless bundle rested beneath it. Atop the table was a chair. The man sitting in it was tall and lean, his cheekbones razors. All the Eaters looked sharper than the world, but this one bent light like a black hole. Looking at him made her eyes ache.

She knew him. She'd killed him—just before he'd killed her.

Simon Tucks was not the drooping-faced loser he had been in their world. Though some essential detail of him was the same, he'd grown taller, leaner, harder. He gazed out over the assembled monsters—murderers all, eaters of souls—as though they were his subjects. Atop a chair beside a bonfire in a world where nothing burned, he seemed a dark prince or a fallen angel.

*Not a chair,* Claire corrected herself. *A throne.*

"W-w-w—" DeAndre paused, took a breath. "We oughta go. Right now."

None of them moved. None of them spoke. Claire could hear the wet sounds of their breathing. Down below, the bare-breasted woman danced to the rhythm of the fire, her skin glistening as if striped in lava. In leathers and beards and weapons, facing a bonfire of burning trash, the Eaters cut ghastly silhouettes, something out of a Bosch nightmare. A hot acid terror bubbled in her belly. It wasn't about being caught. It was the scene itself. There was something so fundamentally wrong about it, so inherently evil. Like stumbling upon the second hour of a gang rape.

*DeAndre is right,* she thought. *We should go. If they spot us, we won't make it out.*

But before she could voice the thought, a hush fell over the crowd, spreading in fast ripples. Conversations ended, bottles froze halfway to mouths. The dancing woman froze.

Simon Tucks had risen. He stood atop the table radiating haughty insouciance, and every eye turned to him.

For a long moment, he said nothing at all. Just stared. When he finally spoke, his words were clear even from here, eleven stories up and a hundred yards away.

"I am come."

Claire had listened to the messages Simon had used to bait his trap a thousand times. That voice had been nondescript; Midwestern, slightly nasal. Now he thundered like James Earl Jones.

"I am the gladiator of a fearsome god, and I am come." Simon spread his arms wide. He let the moment linger before continuing. "Some of you have sensed my master. He's moved in your dreams. Revealed himself when you take a life. You have felt the truth. There are worlds beyond this one, and gods dwell in them.

"Now my master comes to you through me, and you will obey."

The Eaters shifted uneasily, exchanging glances. It was easy to forget, the way everyone here talked about them, that they weren't mindless zombies. They were human beings; corrupted, perhaps, but still human. Simon Tucks was making them nervous as newborns.

"Some have tried to resist me. I have feasted on their stories."

Claire glanced at Brody, saw the same thought on his mind. All the "departures" of the last days hadn't been coincidence. They had been Simon, killing other Eaters.

"On the other side of the veil, I harvested eighteen souls for my master. Eighteen innocents. Men, women, children, taken at his whim and with his guidance. He taught me to kill, and guided my hands to the work. It was he who aimed the rifle, he who built the bombs. He told me of the traps that had been set for me and steered me through them. In his name, I held a city of millions in terrified thrall.

"Now I have crossed beyond, and I have become my True Self. My master changed me, shaped me. Filled me with his essence.

"I have given you proof of his power." He gestured to the bonfire, his face lit manic by its fevered light. A pendant around his neck caught her eye, though she couldn't make it out at this distance. "In this world without flame, I have come to burn. I have shown you something you did not think possible. Now I will show you something else."

Simon dropped from the table, flexing his knees as he landed. The nearby Eaters backed away. He laughed, then reached beneath the table and hauled out the cloth-wrapped bundle. It was large and awkward, heavy looking, but he lifted it with ease.

Then the bundle began to writhe, and Claire realized what they were looking at.

"Oh god," Lucy said. "That's—"

With a flourish, Simon yanked off the sheet.

The woman was middle-aged and pale. Crusted blood ran down her face. She was bound with yards and yards of duct tape, arms strapped to her sides, rolled up like a rug. Tape covered her mouth, and she made muffled gagging sounds and tried to wrest free, hurling herself forward, twitching and flopping. Simon's grip on her arm didn't even wobble.

"You fight each other for scraps," Simon said. "Never enough to grow stronger. Until now."

He kept his left hand on the woman's bicep, and used his right to remove the tape covering her mouth.

"Ohgodplease, please, I don't know what's happening I'll do anything please I must be dreaming I'm dreaming oh god please god, *please.*"

"Shh," Simon said, stroking her cheek. "Shh."

She stared at him with horror and hope, her face pale, her trembling clear even from here. Simon smiled at her, then turned to the Eaters.

"We will take this dead city for our own. We will slaughter all who are not with us. We will harvest all who arrive. And as we do, we will grow strong enough to see across the veil. We will find others amongst the living, and ride them as my god rode me. We will seed destruction and fear among men, and we will feed upon it. More than that—we will *share* in it."

Simon spun the woman to face the fire. Orange light played across the cocoon of duct tape. She began to scream, her words running together.

"Ohgodno ohpleaseno don't Ihavechildren Ihave*children* I'msoscared please-*god please* god!"

"Yes," Simon said. "It is time for you to please god."

With no more effort than it would take to toss balled-up paper at a trash can, he lifted the woman and hurled her into the center of the bonfire.

"No!" Brody lunged for the door. Claire had anticipated it and threw herself in the way, wrapping her arms around him and bracing. But she'd forgotten the strength of him now. His arms moved with hydraulic power, peeling her off and pushing her aside so hard she tripped and fell. She yelped as she did, a stupid helpless sound of surprise, but it got the others' attention. Kyle moved first, hitting Brody from behind and wrapping him in a bear hug. With an outward flex of his arms Brody sent the other man flying.

From outside, the woman began to shriek. A terrible, high-pitched sound, like an engine spinning out of control. It was the sound of madness, of agony unimaginable.

Brody's face twisted. He went for the door.

A blur of motion struck him just before the frame and drove him sideways. Drywall shattered and dust flew everywhere, dancing in the orange light. The noise was drowned by the lunatic shrieks of agony from below. Sonny's tackle had taken Brody at waist height, a clean hit that slammed them both down, and then the biker wrapped his arms around Brody and squeezed. "You can't."

"She's going to burn—"

"Bitch is barbecue," Sonny said. "Nothing you can do about that."

Claire stumbled over. "Will, he's right, you can't save her. There are too many."

"I can—"

"No." She knelt, put her hands on Brody's cheeks. "She's dead already. And if you go, we are too."

Brody stared up at her, his eyes manic, but no longer fighting Sonny. The biker held his arms and Claire held his gaze and together they kept him from doing the thing that was most sacred to him.

Outside, the woman screamed.

For a long, long time.

# THIRTY-THREE

Edmund moved, and reality bent.

A scant scattering of years he had been alive. For centuries after, he had wandered the primal echoes that border mortality. Feeding, growing, learning, until he could abandon those realms for the chain of worlds beyond. The endless spectrum of decaying existence stalked by risen gods. Like Isabella. Like himself.

Together, they had transcended. Ascended.

Like a whirlpool their power grew. Each sucking current harnessing the next even as it was subsumed. Each minor obliteration magnifying the fury of the whole. For decades they danced.

They gave birth to new realities, realms that could not exist. Realms where their will was their world; pocket universes built entirely of themselves. From them, they stretched out to the mortal world that was the source of all. They haunted and manipulated and whispered, planting rotten seeds and raising them up in darkness.

And when it was time, they harvested.

Edmund thought it an amusement to stand on real ground, in an echo of the world. To walk streets laid by the living, between skyscrapers built by human hands. There was no need. They could have fed from their own world. But there was pleasure in the crudity of it.

Beside him, Isabella glowed white, her skin flawless and fair, her true self burning ravenous through, a beast of a thousand mouths. Her hunger a coiling thing, a twisting worm of ceaseless lust, never sated, never shrinking. She reached for him, took his hand, digging her fingers into the raw stump where he had hacked away part of himself, her nails driving deep, playing pain like an instrument.

They had taught each other much.

When their puppet arrived, he did it in pain and panic, clutching his chest, feeling for wounds that were no longer there. So small, people. Pale as daydreams.

Like so many others, this one had been lost when they found him. Wandering without hope or purpose. They had spilled poison into his dark hours, nursed his fear into terror, his loneliness into hatred, his shame into rage. And then they had unleashed him and fed upon the pain that flowed in his wake. The lives he had taken and the lives he had destroyed. It was a pattern they had repeated many times.

But Edmund remained restless of mind, and with this they had tried something new. An idea rooted in the changing mortal world. A singular notion that had succeeded.

The man stared, gibbered, spoke. Edmund could see that he recognized them, knew them for the architects of his fate. And too he could see that the creature imagined reward, or redemption. Alive, he had done monstrous things. He had made himself into a specter to haunt the world. More powerful even than the death he delivered was the fear. And yet in his last living moments he had come to fear all he had done, to wonder if he had been misled. All puppets dream of being players.

Isabella smiled. Beatific. Radiant. An angel.

Hope bloomed across the animal's face. His fears melted. He knew that he was saved. Divine. A tool of gods, and beloved by them.

Then Isabella's bloodied nails pushed through the skin of his chest, slick fingers penetrating the clutch of ribs to slip inside. The animal screamed, writhed in an ecstasy of agony. The kill was an inch deeper, but she held short of it, her fist gripping his ribs, fingers stroking the secret inner parts of the animal. She leaned in to lock her teeth on his lips, blood running down her pale chin.

Then, instead of finishing the beast, she paused, and offered the creature to Edmund.

And Edmund knew confusion. They did not share. This one was hers. For what reason would she freely offer that which belonged to her?

Gratitude, she explained. Once she had been the teacher. Now they were the same.

Edmund hesitated for only an instant. Then he tore the heart out of the thing and crushed it between his fingers and rode the rush of energy, transfixed.

But it wasn't the animal in front of him he was savoring. It was an idea.

Gratitude?

Could it be that she, who had lived centuries longer, who had as much power as any elder god wandering the shadows of the world, had forgotten their rules? Their very nature?

Interesting.

They turned from the limp thing and left this little echo, soaring out into darker realms. Her fingers sought his hand, and the wound there, pushing into him, the cruelty a connection. As her nails squirmed into his flesh, Edmund was conscious of the finger he had torn from himself, now hanging against the muscles of his chest like a necklace. Another new idea.

Perhaps that one would wait, though. Perhaps there was a richer opportunity.

A monster who had forgotten the nature of monsters.

Life was so beautiful. So many ways to feast upon it.

# THIRTY-FOUR

Brody felt filthy.

He knew they'd been right. Even if he'd somehow been able to get past the sniper and a hundred Eaters and pluck the woman from the flames, even if by some miracle they'd escaped, so what? The poor woman had been trapped in the heart of an inferno. There was no burn ward here. No skin grafts. All he would have bought her was more agony. The best he might have done was end it for her. Spare her some pain. But that would have meant death for the others, including Claire. Nonnegotiable.

Still. He had chosen not to help an innocent person in desperate need. Sure, at first Sonny had him. But while the biker had the same supercharged strength, Brody had been a Marine and an FBI agent. He could have freed himself.

He'd just chosen not to.

*Live with that.*

When the screaming had finally stopped, the party below had really started. By burning his victim alive the sniper had somehow shared her with all of his followers. Instead of one Eater gaining strength, all of them had. And drunk on power and fire, and having broken new boundaries of depravity, the only thing was for the evening to become an orgy in all meanings of the word. Drums laid a heavy tribal beat, and many had stripped down and danced and screwed right beside the flame.

The sniper had sat on his throne, laughing as the flames shot higher. The dancing woman had climbed onto the table and knelt before him, and he'd used her mouth without seeming to notice, his attention everywhere else, a small, cruel smile on his face.

Brody had wanted to leave immediately. They all did. But it would have been reckless. They'd been lucky to get in without being noticed. The Eaters might be distracted, but they were also freshly fed and amped up. Better to wait for booze and bloodlust to take their toll.

So they sat avoiding each other's eyes while outside the Eaters celebrated the end of worlds.

It was after four in the morning that they finally risked it. The fire was down to a dance of embers, the revelers at the mad ball strewn amidst discarded clothing and broken glass from smashed bottles. Simon Tucks strolled as if keeping watch, or standing judgment.

In silence, the six of them fumbled their blind way back down the stairs and out the north side of the building. The sky had lightened just enough that they could make out the column of smoke rising against the ever-present clouds. They took a moment to scan for motion and set off.

With each step there was an urge to turn a walk into a run. The scene was seared on all of their eyes, brighter every time they blinked. Night and fire and figures dancing to the rhythm of screams. Brody may have been raised Catholic, but he'd never believed in Hell. He'd studied history, understood the importance of the church as a political and economic force over the last two thousand years. Much of that power had come through promising salvation from eternal suffering. And so what had begun as metaphor became dictum, and begat everything from coffer-swelling indulgence scams to fevered Renaissance images. The notion of a real Hell, a world of fire and demons and torture, had always seemed silly. Especially in light of the actual statements attributed to Jesus.

It didn't seem silly anymore. Not after their voyeur's view.

Perhaps the truth was that Hell wasn't a physical location; it was an idea that could be summoned into being. Hell had been created countless times before, from the Crusaders' massacre of Jerusalem to Stalin's "hunger-extermination" of seven million Ukrainians; from reeking, disease-ridden slave ships bound for New Orleans to the systemized horror of Auschwitz; from Lieutenant Calley to the Khmer Rouge. There was almost an equation to it. Hell was born when some decided others weren't people.

If they weren't people, then you could do anything you wanted to them. Rape, torture, murder. Feed.

"I'm sorry," Claire said. She looked as exhausted as he felt, her skin pale, dark circles beneath her eyes.

"I know."

"I had to."

"I know."

"Are you okay?"

"No."

She nodded, her lips set in a thin line. "Do you believe what Tucks said? About his god?"

"I believe he believes it."

"It would explain a lot."

He cocked his head. "It would?"

"I used to wonder if the sniper was working with someone in law enforcement. He always seemed to know where no one was looking, knew how to shoot like he'd been trained, knew how to vanish without a trace. Like he was being informed. Or guided."

"You're saying it would make sense to you that Simon Tucks was possessed by a god who demanded sacrifices."

"Well. Yeah." She shrugged. "I guess I am."

Brody sighed. A few more blocks and they'd be home. Or what passed for home these days. "You know what? I'm all full up on strange right now. I can accept this place as undiscovered science. An echo generated by the force and energy of life, like another dimension. If you believe string theory and the multiverse, it's not even that big a step. But start adding gods into the equation, I'm out." He shook his head. "Tucks is just a psycho. A guy who gets off on power over others. There's no god controlling everything. And there's certainly not more than one of them."

"So how did he make fire?"

Damn it. It was one of the things he loved about her, the ferocious precision with which her mind worked. She immediately found the weakness in a line of thinking and hit it hard, even if that ended up bringing the whole notion toppling down. He used to love watching her run a meeting: Claire sitting at a table of men who had all applied for the job she'd taken, disassembling poor thinking with such facility that it made her place at the head of the table self-evident.

*Do you love it less when it's your poor thinking being disassembled?* No. But that didn't mean he enjoyed the wreckage. "I don't know."

"I know it sounds crazy, but what if it's true? That there are . . . things out here. Maybe not gods, exactly, I'm not saying Zeus is wandering around. But beings of some kind that can reach out to our world. Maybe communicate with people who are already a little unbalanced." She sucked her lips between her teeth, her thinking tell. "It could explain a lot. Tucks didn't fit the profile. Not military, no evidence of training, but he was building bombs and nailing head shots. Maybe he had homicidal impulses, but no skills. Think of all the mythology behind deals with the devil, or possession. Think of the serial killers everyone said were so nice."

Suddenly he understood. "You're still doing it."

"What?"

"Still looking for reasons. Remember, your rant about the Unabomber? You wanted to believe that the sniper had a reason. That he wasn't just a broken guy who'd been abused by his uncle or whatever. Wanting to believe that there's a logic behind insanity. More things in heaven and earth."

Claire shrugged. "Look around you, Horatio."

Despite everything, despite his failure and his fear, Brody laughed. Just once. But still. There were worse definitions of love than someone who could make you laugh as the world fell apart. Even once.

The sentries spotted them as they rounded Clark onto Wacker, walking in the middle of the street between high-rises with spires lost in cloud. Brassy whistle blasts had split the morning air, echoing off stone and glass. He and Claire had drifted apart from the others as they talked, and hurried to rejoin them.

It was early yet, barely five, but there were dozens of people milling around, eating breakfast or sharpening weapons or staring at the southwestern sky, where the smoldering column of ash still rose.

"What the hell is going on?" Finn yelled from atop the bridge tower, his bow slung on his shoulder, hands cupped around his mouth. "Is that . . . smoke?"

"Get them up," Kyle yelled back.

"Who?"

"Everyone."

# THIRTY-FIVE

Two hundred and nine. Counting Claire and himself, that was how many people lived in the Langham, how many followed the Gospel According to Ray. Two hundred and nine men, women, and children.

They sat in Vietnam Veterans Memorial park, just the other side of the river. Tiered stone benches had been carved into the hillside, and the names of several thousand native sons killed in the war were etched in a long slab of black granite behind a reflecting pool. Brody had never been down here before—the Riverwalk was a tourist thing, and this park was more often used to scarf down Chipotle than to remember the dead—but it made a perfect amphitheater. They'd taken a seat on the third bench, near the end. It felt good to sit down, way, way too good, and so Brody had started counting as a focus exercise.

People looked at once exhausted and keyed up. A dangerous combination. Everyone was asking everyone else what was going on. Since none of them knew, the conversation was all fearful speculation. Voices overlapped and jostled, the tone tense. The only mercy was that in the hour it had taken to gather everyone, the column of smoke had finally faded, first to a dark smear and then altogether.

Arthur was among the last to arrive, shooing forward a mob of children, some as young as four or five. He must have been a good teacher; he was a natural with them, cajoling some, comforting others, keeping them all moving together. He got them settled a short distance away, the younger ones tossing things in the river, the older ones climbing up on statues or flirting awkwardly.

Brody watched them play, and thought about the woman wrapped in duct tape.

A piercing thumb-finger whistle split the morning, shutting off conversations like a tap. Kyle stood on the lip of the fountain, his axe slung over his shoulder. He let the silence settle, then said, "There's probably a way to do this better, but I was never in Toastmasters, so I'm just gonna say it. The Eaters are working together."

Brody watched the news hit. A fit man leaning on a spear seemed to droop. Madeleine's knitting needles stopped clicking. Antoine sucked air through his teeth. They looked surprised, disconcerted, but not terrified. *They don't get it.*

"They've got a leader. It was the guy that killed Brody, and who Claire wanted us to hunt down when she got here." Kyle's nod wasn't regret, but there was at least an acknowledgment that she'd had a point. "The sniper, the guy who's been wasting people the last few weeks. Somehow the dude is more powerful than your typical vamp. Next level shit. He made fire."

The sound that rose was a strange mix of shock and desire. They must all have known what was coming; though it had finally faded away, the column of smoke had risen to the clouds. Yet despite the proof, they'd ceased to believe in the possibility of it. *What a powerful thing fire is.* People joked about the wheel, but it was fire that had been the first civilizing tool of humanity. Fire changed everything. Every culture had myths about it, tricksters and heroes who stole flame from the gods and brought it to earth. *And now Simon Tucks joins their ranks. Prometheus recast as a serial killer.*

"That's not possible," Arthur said. "I've been here twenty years, and nothing burns, not ever."

"Sniper's changed things," Kyle said. "Last night we snuck into the building DeAndre spotted them from. There were more than he'd seen, a lot more, so I guess they kept coming. Maybe the fire drew them. Sure as hell drew us. The thing took up half the quad, a huge bonfire. The heat coming off it . . ." Kyle's tone had become almost loving, and he caught himself. "Anyway, it's real, we all saw it."

Finn said, "How?"

"Simon says he's an angel."

"Gladiator," Sonny said, in rich, rounded tones. "The gladiator of a dark god."

"Right. Gladiator. Dark god. Anyway, his plan is to kill all of us, and take over the echo. Then eat everyone who arrives. He's got a way for them to share the power somehow. To prove it, he . . ." The light, *I-mess-with-life* tone faltered, and Kyle drew a deep breath. "He had a woman with him. A new arrival. He . . . he threw her into the fire. She burned to death."

A hundred exclamations at once, gasps and half-formed questions and muffled cries.

"She was a sacrifice," Lucy said. "A human sacrifice. They burned her alive, and instead of one of them getting fed, they all did. Do you understand? It's not zero-sum anymore. The Eaters can work together. They're an army now."

And finally they got it. That this wasn't a joke or a prank. That there was no good news to offset the bad. That the relative measure of safety they'd enjoyed had faded like last night's smoke.

People stood, yelled, shouting questions, *how many* and *where* and *what are we going to do*. Madeleine began to cry, her back heaving. Hector stared at his shaking hands. Antoine, the former correctional officer, stiffened in a way that must have given convicts nightmares.

"All of you saw this?" Arthur leaned against the memorial wall.

"Yeah," Kyle said, and the rest of them nodded.

"They said they were coming for us? Specifically?"

"No," Lucy said. "He said they would take the city and kill everyone not them. We know there are a few loners surviving out there, and probably some of the Eaters won't go along. But basically, it's them and us."

"Oh god," a woman moaned. "Oh god."

"What are we supposed to do against a hundred Eaters?"

"They have *fire*?"

"What about the kids? They won't harm the children, will they?"

"We can build walls," Hector said. "In the hotel."

"They'll vanish as soon as we leave them."

"So we don't leave," Hector said. "We guard them, round the clock. We hole up and we don't go anywhere."

"Yes!" A woman in a scarlet hoodie yelled. "Yes! We can move up to the upper floors. Barricade the stairs. Set up traps and weapons."

"Against Eaters?" An accountant-looking dude shook his head. "They're too fast, too strong."

"Won't matter if we do it right," Antoine said. "What we do is, we channel them. That's how it worked at Stateville. Felons might lose it in the yard, but we could always fall back. Narrow corridors where we get the drop—"

"And if we're at the top of the hotel, where does our food come from?" The accountant's face was turning red. "Where does our water come from?"

Madeleine said, "We have to run. All of us together. We'll be safe on the road. We could pack up our stuff and—"

Brody tuned out the yelling and turned to look at Claire. Her lips were set in a thin line, and he could see her brain spinning away, punching the obvious holes in these silly plans. It hit him in that moment that though these were good people, and though they'd existed in more danger than plenty of soldiers, they weren't warriors. They were just ordinary folks whose lives had been stolen from them. To their credit, they had adapted. Tried to make the best of the situation.

*Just like you had been about to.* For a moment, it had seemed he and Claire had a second chance. A way to make up for the monstrous unfairness of having met only just before death. They could be together here. Openly. Could build something like a life. Not the life they would have chosen; but as she'd said, not bad, either.

It had been a nice dream, and he was sad to let it go.

Claire said, "You or me?"

"How about both of us?"

She smiled, and leaned in. The kiss was brief but sweet.

Around them voices were piling on one another, making less and less sense. Hysteria, people shouting each other down. Brody caught Kyle's eye, mimed a whistle. The fireman cocked his head. Brody held the gaze until Kyle shrugged, and then put his hand to his mouth and ripped out another one of his ear splitters. Everyone froze.

"You're all missing the point." Brody rose. He stood calm and steady and looking from person to person, meeting eyes. "The echo has changed. The enemy has changed. We're not talking about groups of two or three."

"There are more than a hundred Eaters out there. They're working together." Claire stood beside him. "We are their food. If we run, they run faster. If we hide, they burn us without even bothering to fight. The echo has *changed.*"

"So what, then?" Hector asked.

"We break the rules," Brody said. "We go hunting. We take the fight to them."

His words were a boulder dropped in a pond. The reaction splashed out in a ripple. Most people shied away, cursed, shook their heads. A few, like Finn and some of the younger men, looked thoughtful.

"Those rules," Arthur said, "have kept us safe for two decades. They are the only reason we can trust each other."

"They're *not* the only reason we can trust each other," Brody said. "Look, yesterday, the Gospel According to Ray made perfect sense. It was simple and clear and it worked. Today it doesn't. If you never change tactics, you lose the moment the enemy changes theirs. And they have."

"I wouldn't mind a fight," Sonny said. "But how? We wouldn't stand a chance."

"He's right," Kyle said. "That's why we go out in big groups. Put ten of us to one of them, no problem. Wolf pack them, mob them, they'll lose. But in an open battle, they'd cream us."

"We can't win a fair fight," Brody agreed. "So let's not fight fair."

"We kill Simon Tucks," Claire said.

"You're still on your crusade." Arthur shook his head. "Still trying to do what an FBI agent would."

"All I'm trying to do," she said, "is survive. They aren't a family. They're following Tucks because he's stronger, because he can give them something. He dies, that all vanishes."

The words floated in the air, and in the minds of the other two hundred and seven people clustered in the park. Brody could see that they were reaching them.

"You make it sound simple," Kyle said. "But the dude's been laying out beatdowns on vamps. Powerful ones."

"Yeah," Brody said.

"He's got all their strength now, and he had plenty to begin with."

"Yeah."

"He made fire in a place where nothing burns."

"Yeah."

"So then how—"

"We don't have a choice," Claire said. "They're coming for us."

"The Eaters are faster and stronger," Brody followed on her flow. It felt like the rhythm of an interrogation, the two of them reading each other, setting each other up for the spike. "But we have something they don't. We trust each other. Look, the rules themselves are secondary to the fact that we are people who *want* to live by them. We want to be human. We trust each other. We've chosen community over personal power. That means that we can stand together, fight for each other. If we have to, we can sacrifice for each other. They can't. They won't.

"Look, I'll be honest. If we fight, we are going to lose people. But if we don't, we lose everyone." He paused, then angled his body, nodded his head, did everything short of point at the children. The tweens that had crept closer to eavesdrop. The little kids racing Matchbox cars down the hill. "Everyone."

Cheap persuasion psychology, textbook stuff, but it worked. Until that moment, people had been thinking about themselves. Now they felt the weight of responsibility.

For as fashionable as cynicism always was, the truth was that when it came to basic human responsibility, people rose to the challenge. Pretty much always. As many times as Hell had been created, history stood as indisputable proof that the mass of humanity was good. People built more than they burned, created more than they destroyed, not by a little but by a massive surplus. To know it, all you needed to remember was that we had started as chimpanzees—and then look around.

"I'm with you."

Brody turned, surprised. Two rows up and half a dozen people over, Emily Watkins stood. Cold wind off the river tugged at her hair. "I don't want to wait for them to come for us. Besides, he already killed me once. It's *my* turn." That brought chuckles, and Emily smiled. "I'm with them. Who else is?"

"A vote," Kyle called from his perch on the fountain. "All in favor?" He raised his hand. Emily followed suit, and Sonny, Lucy, Finn, DeAndre, a handful of others. For a moment, it looked like there was enough momentum. But with about twenty arms in the air, things stalled out. People were weighing it, talking to one another.

Looking at Arthur. The one who'd been here longest, who had known Ray personally. He caught the looks, stepped off the wall and cleared his throat.

"You all know how I feel about killing. It turns us into them. Even with the best of intentions."

*Shit.* Arthur wasn't in charge per se, but his opinion carried a lot of weight. The professor rubbed his hands, pale fingers knitting and parting.

"Our rules are simple. Pull your weight. And only kill in self-defense. Those two rules have allowed us to survive. They've allowed us to save countless new arrivals. More than that, they have let us be friends. Partners. Family. A life, in this death. I've always thought that those two rules *are* us."

It was going south, fast. Brody could feel people pulling away. He wanted to speak, but stopped himself. There was nothing he could say to turn this.

"But perhaps there's a more basic rule. Which is that we rise, or fall, together." Arthur inhaled, deeply. Sighed. And raised his hand.

In seconds, it was over. The vote wasn't unanimous, but it was close enough it didn't matter. Brody felt a flush of victory. It lasted precisely as long as it took for two hundred people to turn and place their existence in his hands.

*Right.*

His armpits went wet and his mouth dry. He took a moment to choose his words. "The Eaters are predators. That means they're opportunists. So"—he paused, looked around—"let's give them an opportunity."

# THIRTY-SIX

The carts were flatbeds on rickety castors, the kind used to load lumber. They'd found five of them in the Home Depot parking lot and lashed them together with chain. They were piled high with 2 x 4s under tarps, and rattled with every bump in the street. The noise bounced down the concrete canyon of buildings.

Brody and Sonny had their shoulders to the front cart. The combined load of five carts and all they carried had to be close to two tons, but with their hyped-up strength, they had no problem maneuvering it. Claire steered from the front, trying to avoid the worst of the potholes. *Even in the afterlife, Chicago has potholes,* Brody thought, and fought down a laugh.

He was worn thin. Yesterday he'd walked a thirty-mile patrol, followed by a midnight raid and a sleepless night scarred by screams. Then his speech this morning, and all that came after it—planning, debating, arguing. He'd hoped to snatch half an hour's snooze somewhere in there, but here he was, pushing a wagon train down a city street.

He wondered how much longer the strength he'd inherited from Raquel Adams would last. It already felt fainter, diminished in ways it was hard to quantify. He could still do impossible things, just . . . less. Like he'd been expending the excess power. It was draining away like a power meter in a video game.

*Jesus. Are you really reducing this to* Call of Duty?

Clearly, whatever strength he'd taken from Raquel, it didn't extend to preventing punch-drunk exhaustion.

The front wheel of the cart hit a crack, and the whole train shook, the metal creaking and bonging. In the silence of the echo, the sound would be carrying a mile, and he shot a glance at Claire. She nodded, her eyes as tired as his own.

There was something about the planning and operating under stress that put him right back in the Corps. He'd been trained as an officer at both OCS and TBS, and one of the central lessons was that combat rarely happened when you were well rested and ready. During written exams, instructors blared heavy metal and threw tennis balls at their heads. Surprise live-fire exercises were scheduled for the middle of the night. Everything was about fluidity and assault, about avoiding battle lines and strength-on-strength confrontation. "Turn the board around" was perhaps the holiest writ of Marine Corps strategy. See the situation from the enemy's perspective, and then strike at their weaknesses. Speed was a weapon. Aggression could provide a major advantage.

That was the reason he'd pushed for moving right away, despite everything. Sure, sleep would have been nice, and it was unlikely the Eaters would make their attack today. They were probably still ragged from the previous night. Brody hoped so. It would help, especially given—

"Uh-oh," Claire said, one hand above her eyes to shield them as she stared into the distance.

A tingle ran down Brody's legs. He straightened from the cart.

Half a mile back, a handful of figures stood in the center of the street. Hard to tell how many at this distance, but at least five, maybe more. Sonny had stopped pushing, his hands fingering the knives slung on his hips, his face drawn as if the skin had shrunk. Brody glanced around the street, a stretch of Harrison near the river. To the north was the old post office headquarters and central annex. They'd been abandoned for as long as he could remember, their rows of windows blank and black. The buildings were screened by a line of chain-link fences wrapped in plastic and held down by sandbags. The street was wide here, four lanes stretching to both horizons. Nowhere to run.

"Here they come," Sonny said.

"How many?" Claire's voice like a wire stretched too tight. "I can't tell."

The figures were moving now, made blurry by speed and haze off the concrete. "Six?"

"Look up," Sonny said.

The six on the street were matched by at least four more running along the tops of buildings. As Brody watched, one of the Eaters reached the end of a mid-rise and leapt off it, landing atop a parked bus, then dropping to the ground and moving before the impact sound even reached them. It was difficult to look directly at them, their speed so abnormal that it hurt the eyes.

"Ten." Sonny looked over at him. "Didn't expect ten."

Brody shrugged and picked up his sledgehammer. He took a deep breath, blew it out. His heart slammed against his rib cage. One of the Eaters wore an expensive black leather jacket and clutched a baseball bat. Brody remembered the sound of steel bars bending, a screech that plucked at his gut. He rolled his shoulders. "Think of that woman last night. Remember what they did to her."

"Will," Claire said. When he turned, he saw that she had the hatchet in her hand. She was pale and shaking—and smiling. "I love you."

There was time, just, to step over and put a hand behind her head and mash his lips to hers, and if he'd learned anything in the last week, it was that you never presumed there was more time coming. Better to take the good things when they came. For a second, two, there was nothing but her scent and the softness of her hair and the taste of her tongue.

Then footsteps pounding into pavement, and the smell of smoke and unwashed flesh. Brody turned.

There weren't ten after all. There were twelve.

They slowed to a walk. It wasn't caution. It was the strut of the schoolyard bully with buddies at his back; the showmanship of the date rapist unbuttoning his shirt. They twirled their weapons, smiling.

"Well, well," said the Baller. "Look at this. Heya, Sonny."

"Franklin."

Brody stared at Sonny. "You know him?"

"He used to be one of us."

"We were buds," the Baller—Franklin—said. "Until Sonny kicked me out of their luxury hotel."

"Wasn't me. We decided together. You claimed self-defense three times in a month."

"Funny. From here, it looks to me like you've had a meal yourself."

"Self-defense," Sonny said.

"You." The man who stepped out from behind Franklin was scarecrow thin and tweaker cheeked. He pointed his machete at Brody. "Bunny rabbit. You killed Raquel."

"Yeah. I did."

"She and I used to kick it. Of course, I'm not the only one been up in there. You've been inside her too, haven't you?"

Before he could stop himself, Brody had a flash memory of being Raquel in her dorm room bed, the boy pushing into him. The Scarecrow smiled as if he could see the thought. "Just take that memory and put my face on it." He turned to Franklin. "Last time, we let him go. You still feeling that?"

"Twelve on three?" Franklin smiled. "No."

"You got anything to add, bunny? Wanna beg?" The Scarecrow looked over at Claire. "Or introduce me to your friend?"

Brody said nothing, just adjusted his grip on the hammer, the handle sweaty in his palm.

"Guess we're going to do this. Alright." Franklin paused. "Hey Sonny, you want to come on over and join us? Let's let bygones be. We'll make a meal out of this one, and dessert out of her."

The biker looked at them, then at Claire and Brody. The moment had the clarity of a scene etched in glass, every line sharp. Brody could smell the smoke on the Eaters, the woodsy scent of the lumber, his own sweat. Sonny shook his head. "I'm on the right side now."

"Before you die," Brody said, "I want to say that I'm sorry about Raquel. She didn't give me much choice."

"Before we die?" The Scarecrow flashed his ruined teeth. "You going to take down twelve of us?"

"Me?" Brody lowered his hammer. "No."

Claire yelled, "Now!"

The tarps on all the carts flung back. Ten people sprang to their feet from between the stacks of lumber, raising bows and spears. At the same moment, the chain-link fence hiding the abandoned post office toppled over, collapsing with a crash to reveal two hundred men and women surging forward, Emily and Kyle and Lucy at the fore.

"What—"

There was a twang, and two feet of carbon-fiber arrow split Franklin's throat like it had grown from the center. A ribbon of blood dangled from the broadhead tip. Finn had another arrow strung before the man even fell to his knees.

189

Then chaos.

Emily charged, howling, glowing with energy, a length of steel pipe in her hand. With her came two hundred others, whooping and yelling, raging forward, a ragged, dirty mob fighting for themselves. Claire leapt onto the cart and hurled her hatchet, the edge gleaming as it spun end over end to slam into the Scarecrow's skull.

Curses and screams and the ringing of metal on metal, the meaty thump of landed blows.

The Eaters were surprised, but they had speed and strength. One of them had thrown a Bowie knife before Brody had even seen him draw it, the blade spinning end over end to thunk into the chest of a girl he didn't know. A worn man with cauliflower ears and a many-times-broken nose assumed a mixed martial arts stance, flipping one attacker over his shoulder, hurling another into the parked van hard enough to dent the side. Kyle tangled with a small woman whipping a length of chain around, the links smacking into his face, snapping it sideways, blood spraying out in an arc. He took the hit and plowed into her, slamming the handle of the axe into her stomach, and then Brody lost them in the rush of people.

They fought with reckless speed and the savagery of frightened people. Brody stood watching as Antoine and Madeleine and DeAndre together took down a woman with a knife in her hand and stunned look on her face, DeAndre driving her back with wide swings of a knife, Antoine's police baton lashing out to shatter her jaw and then her shoulder and then her skull.

He could feel each kill.

Not metaphorically. Viscerally. That same twist in the belly as before, a rolling gut clench like missing the last step on a staircase. The echo rocking and adjusting as power shifted. It was odd and disorienting, and yet fitting. Shouldn't the world shift with each death? Shouldn't we all feel each murder?

Lucy dueled with a big man swinging a length of iron pipe. Sparks flew where their weapons met. She was better than he was, but he was far stronger, and the fight could have gone either way until Hector charged in with a crowbar that shattered the Eater's knee. The man howled with pain. Lucy took two spinning steps and whipped the sword around in a flashing arc that cut off scream and head in the same move.

The battle was vicious, ugly, and brief. Only seconds after Claire had yelled, eleven of the Eaters were down. The last one hesitated, wild-eyed. Then she turned and sprinted away, legs blurring.

Brody said, "Finn."

The boy tracked her motion, his long leather duster swaying slightly, the red sunglasses reflecting back a bloody world. Another broadhead arrow was nocked to the string of the composite. The tip was a hollow triangle of wicked razors.

"Come on, come on, come on—"

Her speed was uncanny, impossible. One second she'd been there; the next she was fifty yards away. If she escaped, she'd warn the others about their tactics. The sniper would be more cautious. The whole plan could fall apart.

"Finn—"

*Twang.*

The arrow took her in the middle of her back. For a moment, her inertia made it look like she was still running.

Then it was over.

# THIRTY-SEVEN

"Okay people, let's not stand around with our respective genitalia in our hands." Kyle's face was a mess of blood with no wound. Brody had seen the woman's chain tear his cheek open, the angle such that it might have cost him an eye. But his face was smooth and unblemished. Around him, the world seemed slightly out of focus.

*New world, new rules.*

"Celebrate later," Kyle continued, "mourn later. Anyone with a wound that will keep you from fighting, beat it for home. Everyone who got a kill, onto the carts. The rest of you, police up your weapons and get ready to move." He paced like a drill sergeant, his axe in hand. "Now, people!"

Claire stood staring down at the body of the Scarecrow. The blade of her hatchet had struck his forehead square and slammed home, sinking two inches of black steel into his skull. The handle stuck out obscenely. There was very little blood.

"You okay?"

She turned to him, her expression naked. "His name was Lawrence."

Brody blew a breath. "Right."

"His mom was bipolar. He adored his dad, who was terrific—until he walked out on them. Moved to Albuquerque and mailed Lawrence presents he never opened."

"Yeah."

"First time he fooled around was with his cousin. They were twelve." A smile crossed her lips. "She went first, gave him a hand job, and when he finished they both thought maybe she'd hurt him, got so scared they quit.

"Booze. Weed. Mom's pills. Dropped out of school. He met a girl, Niala, and for a while they were okay. But he couldn't stop using, and she left. He overdosed in an abandoned row house, smoking crystal meth out of a light-bulb." She sighed. "I can still taste it. Like . . . chlorine. Chlorine and fog."

"I know what you're feeling." Brody thought about Raquel Adams, a woman who had hunted him, a woman he knew intimately, a woman he'd never met. "It's impossible to know someone that way and not love them a little bit. Even though he said he was going to rape you after he killed me."

"You know the worst thing?"

"Yes," Brody said. "The worst thing is that you feel great."

Her eyes widened, and she nodded slowly. "That's right."

"We had to do this."

"I know."

"It's not just killing twelve Eaters. It's taking that power for our side. That's why I didn't get in the fight."

"I know, Will." She planted a foot on Lawrence's chest, gripped the hatchet with both hands, and yanked it out of his skull. "I'm okay."

*Right. Forgot who you were dealing with there for a sec.*

Kyle was staring at his hands as he flexed them, a small smile on his face. He looked up as Brody approached. "Think we got their attention?"

"They'll be here soon. Keep the wagons together. Put the people who fed under the tarps. No reason the same trick won't work twice."

"Uh-huh."

"Don't go too fast. You want them to catch up. If you can time it on a bridge, or in a narrow street, that will even the odds some."

"I know."

"What we just fought wasn't the battle. It was to bait the trap. They're going to come hard this time."

The man grinned. "You just said come hard."

"Kyle—"

"Brody. Chill. We got it." Kyle put a hand on his shoulder. "Okay?"

"Okay." He looked back the way the Eaters had come. "DeAndre fast as he claims?"

"Kid's a rocket. And he got a kill there, like you asked. Lucy and Claire too. I was thinking though, what if Tucks is leading the pack?"

Brody shook his head. "Sniper, remember? He's not a lead-from-the-front kind of guy. Bet he never had a fight in his life."

"Yeah, but now he's the big boss."

"Not because he inspires them. It's dominance, not loyalty. Textbook stuff."

"Textbook," Kyle said. "Just to be clear, you're betting everything on an FBI psych profile. Of the gladiator of a dark god. In the afterlife."

"Yep."

"Okay." The jovial light faded from Kyle's expression, replaced by something grimmer. "Better be right about this, Brody. We'll buy you the time. But every second costs friends, so you better be right."

And there it was, the central truth he'd been trying to avoid. It was a hard rule of battle that victories were not free. Look at a chessboard. Even the most elegant of wins required sacrifice.

"I know," Brody said, and clapped his hand on the man's arm. "Go."

He left Kyle yelling orders, getting the wagon train rolling, a dozen men and women on either side to push it. The tarps had been replaced, the freshly fed hidden beneath them, including Finn. Leaving the archer with Kyle had been a tough call; there was the possibility that the kid could end the sniper with one good shot. But he was also the best hope of the others. He'd be able to help shape the battle, picking off Eaters as they came.

*Plus, he just got at least two, maybe three kills. Not sure we want to introduce him and Simon right now.*

Brody stood and watched the group move east. They were loud, the rattling carts and thumping lumber and the tromp of boots. All of them cast backward glances. They were flush with their victory, but fear lay just beneath it. He could smell it on them.

*Time to make sure you're not wasting their lives.*

Lucy had sheathed her sword and stood close to Sonny, her hands on his chest, their faces inches away, talking softly. Brody had a brief moment of wonder. Where else but here could those two have come together, a samurai soccer mom and a meth-running biker whose heart, it turned out, was in the right place.

DeAndre looked anxious and overenergized, one heel tapping so fast the leg blurred. Literally blurred; he glowed with stolen energy. That was part of the plan, but Brody wondered if it had been a wise one. Like the guy hadn't been through enough.

*Too late now.*

Claire was speaking to him, no doubt trying to keep him centered. It seemed to be working; as Brody approached, the kid broke into a blushing smile.

"Okay," he said. "We don't have time for speeches. You know what to do. It all depends on the five of us. We win, or everyone dies." He saw the impact of his words, let them sink in. Then he forced a broad grin. "So let's win, huh?"

# THIRTY-EIGHT

They came.

Like a tsunami slamming down a riverbed, all force and fury, pushing everything before it.

A hundred Eaters, maybe more. Sprinting faster than cars. Leaping atop obstacles without slowing down. Leaning into it, calves straining, fists pumping. Long hair streaming. Weapons in hand or slung over their shoulders, dirty steel firing glints of light. They raced, elbowed, goaded one another on. Some laughed. Some howled like wolves. There must be something in the blood, some primal joy in the hunt that burst free in that sound.

Some were faster than others, though all were faster than people should be, and the column stretched to a frayed line, no order or discipline. A race toward a feeding frenzy. Brody cringed to think of the people they'd sent ahead with the wagons. They'd be slaughtered. It had been one thing to take a group by surprise, an enfilade ambush that outnumbered their enemy ten to one. But this? Even if the others could find good ground, even with—

*Pack it away. You can't afford to worry about them.*

Though it took only seconds for the mob to pass, it felt much longer.

"He wasn't there," Claire whispered.

Brody nodded. That was what they'd expected, of course. In life, Simon Tucks had been a sniper, killing from a distance. Death had given him more power but, based on that speech last night, not made him any better with people. That he wouldn't be at the head of the column they'd expected. But they'd assumed he would still join the pursuit. What if they were wrong? What if he'd just loosed his fighters and stayed on his throne?

They could go to him. But it would take five, ten minutes. An awful lot of their friends could die in ten minutes.

"There." Claire jerked her chin.

Well behind his army of savages, Simon moved at an easy walk. His face was lit with a giddy energy, as if he were about to burst into laughter. Alongside him jogged six Eaters. Brody recognized the Dancing Woman and several others from last night's revels. They paced the sniper, but kept exchanging glances, turning wistful gazes ahead. Straining like dogs on a leash.

"Do you think DeAndre's up to it?"

Claire nodded. "I talked to him."

"I saw. What made him blush?"

"Told him I overheard Patricia saying how brave he was."

"Which one's she?"

"You know." She cupped her breasts.

Brody smiled. "When did you overhear her?"

"Didn't."

"Nice." He took a deep breath. "Can we do this?"

"Have to."

From some distance away, a shriek rang out. Then another, and then the clang of steel on steel, yells and shouts.

*It's started.* Brody's stomach pitched. People dying, he knew. Friends and enemies alike. He wondered if he would ever grow accustomed to feeling people leaving the world.

On the street below, the honor guard bristled, clearly eager to get in on the fun. But the sniper kept his pace.

"He's not going."

"He will."

Brody grit his teeth. The haft of the hammer was sticky in his grip. They'd presumed the sniper wouldn't be alone. That would have been too much to hope for. But for the plan to work, DeAndre had to do his thing. Brody wondered if the man had been pushed too far. A teenager murdered by cops and now following the plan of other cops.

*If he doesn't do his part, you'll have to attack anyway.*

Bad notion. They'd be outnumbered, and presumably the honor guard had been chosen for their strength. Not to mention Simon himself. *Still. No choice.*

He was starting to rise when Claire said, "Look."

Three stories below, DeAndre stepped calmly out of a van, giving every impression of having dodged a bullet. Staring after the Eaters that had passed, and wiping his hands on his pants. Brody could make out the cat-with-canary grin on his face.

Then DeAndre looked west toward the sniper and his companions and did a visible double take. His lips framed an *oh shit*. He spun and took off at a dead run. One minute standing still, the other a streak. Like the rabbit at a greyhound track.

With the same result. The Eaters around the sniper may have been an honor guard, but soldiers they were not. The sight of running prey was more than they could handle. Three of them took off immediately; the other three hesitated, torn between fear of their new prophet and hunger.

With a tolerant smile, Simon Tucks waved them on. They streaked away, leaving the sniper alone, and laughing.

*God bless you, D. May you and Patricia have much sex.*

He turned to Claire, saw she had her hatchet in hand. It had only been a few minutes since she'd killed the Scarecrow, and the evident flush of power brought her into hyper-focus. He could see the pale freckles on the hollow of her throat, the wisps of hair on her neck, the delicate crinkles at the corners of her eyes. She wasn't a classic bombshell, all pouting lips and big chest, meant to be captured in still frame. To appreciate Claire, you had to see her in motion. The clean posture, shoulders thrown back, the air of confidence. The fear she acknowledged and locked down.

He wondered what it would have been like to be together the normal way. To have jobs and a home and dinner together. To plan vacations and set alarm clocks and talk about books and bicker about things neither really cared about. He wondered if she wanted to be a mother, and thought that if she had, he would have liked that. Not yet, but in a couple of years.

"What?" She'd caught the intensity of his expression and mistaken it for something related to their plan. "What is it?"

*Everything. All the things.* "Just—I love you."

She flashed a smile. "Sweet boy. Move."

Below, the sniper had slowed to a walk. He was laughing to himself, a high-pitched giggle. *Dying didn't cure his crazy.*

Brody rose, stepped back, and ran for the edge of the roof.

There was a moment of purest panic, instinctive, intractable. Even as he planted a foot and pushed himself into the air, some part of him was wondering what the hell he was doing leaping off a five-story building.

Then gravity had him, legs whirling, arms pumping, the air rushing past, the ground hurtling up.

He landed hard, flexing his knees and letting momentum carry him into a roll, the hammer tucked in against his chest, his other hand scraping concrete, catching himself, then popping upward in front of the man who had killed him.

Simon Tucks looked harder, leaner, than the man on the fire escape a lifetime ago. The sagging face had been replaced by sharp cheekbones and burning eyes. He wore the same black clothes as the previous night. What looked like dried bones were slung on a leather cord around his neck.

Beside Brody, there was the sound of impact, Claire landing better than he had, her power fresh enough that she took it all in her knees without a roll. Then, behind Tucks, two more streaks fell from the sky. Lucy's katana rasped from the sheath. Sonny drew both his knives.

If the sniper was frightened, he hid it well. His gaze was cold and imperious, taking them each in and dismissing them. "A trick?"

"A trap," Brody replied. "Which you walked right into."

Simon smiled. "Do you have any idea who I am? Who I really am?" He fingered the necklace. "I am the gladiator of a dark—"

With a squishing sound, a curved metal tongue punched through his belly. A foot and a half of steel filmed with blood. The edge of the sword gleamed.

"Sorry," Lucy said, "heard that speech already."

Simon's smile didn't waver.

He grasped the blade in both hands and snapped it like a chopstick. Then he spun, lashing out with a backhand that caught Lucy full across the face, lifting her off her feet and sending her flying into the same van DeAndre had hidden in. The impact crumbled the steel and shattered glass. Her head cracked the mirror stem, and her body slumped slowly to the street.

Sonny's eyes flashed, and he leapt in slashing, weaving a tapestry of razor edges. The sniper juked and dodged. If Lucy's blow had wounded him, he wasn't showing it. Simon moved so quickly that Brody felt he was watching bad stop-motion animation, key frames flashing with nothing between them.

Brody joined the fight, trying to get behind the sniper, but the man kept moving, circling, pulling back, forcing them both to the front. Claire stood with her hatchet cocked, her eyes unblinking, waiting for a clear throw.

The biker was good, held both knives underhand and made controlled swings, feints and jabs, nothing that overbalanced him. Back and back he drove Simon, whose own hands stayed low, that was odd, why was he doing—

"Look out!"

Brody knew he was too late even as the biker lunged forward with a wicked swipe that opened clothing and flesh and muscle to the bare white of ribs. In the same moment, Simon twirled up the length of Lucy's broken sword he'd been keeping flat against his forearm, gripped the bare blade with bleeding hands, and drove the point into the underside of the biker's chin, fast and hard enough that the tip spiked through the top of his skull.

Sonny twitched, shivered, and fell. Even before he hit the ground, Brody felt the aching vertiginous tug of departure unspooling his belly.

Fear and frustration poleaxed Brody. How was Tucks doing this? He'd been stabbed through the stomach, had his chest opened wide, his hands split from gripping the bare edge of a razor-sharp sword.

*And none of it is even slowing him down. You're not hurting him.*

*Try harder.*

If he could get Tucks on the ground, the fight would be over. He could control the pace, rain down hammer blows, open him up to Claire. Brody charged, his shoulder down, bulling into the man.

It was like running full speed into a tree. The pain was explosive and unsubtle, his shoulder joint flirting with popping out of the socket. Brody gasped, spun, whirled the hammer in a brutal killing arc, twenty pounds of cold-forged steel backed by muscles that could do impossible things, a blow that would crack an engine block—

Until Simon Tucks caught it, barehanded, midair. Though his hands were coated in blood, the fingers were unscathed, and the wounds in his chest and belly had vanished. *Of course. He killed Sonny.* He was close enough that Brody could smell him, the reek of smoke and something else, a meaty scent like raw hamburger. Without letting go of the hammer, Tucks leaned in. "You cannot fight god."

His head lashed out, the center of his forehead connecting with Brody's nose. A sickening crack and an explosion of white light and the world blinked in and out as his balance went wobbly. Somewhere behind him Claire, yelling. Yelling for him to get down.

*Roger that.*

Brody went limp, dropped hard, the motion unintuitive in a fight, and enough to throw the sniper off balance. As he did, he heard the whir of Claire's hatchet, could imagine it spinning through the air. He looked up in time to see it slam into the base of the sniper's neck, just above the collarbone, the head buried deep.

An incredible throw, backed by superhuman force. It would have mangled the trapezius and scalene muscles and torn into the jugular. Death in seconds.

Simon Tucks paused. With a bemused expression, he reached up and plucked the hatchet from his neck. Flipped it end over end, caught it by the handle.

Then his arm snapped out, hurling the weapon hard enough that the blow caved in Claire's skull.

Brody screamed.

He was on his feet even as he felt the world shifting, rocking like a rowboat someone had just stepped out of. But the rowboat was all that was left of life and the someone stepping out was Claire and that just couldn't be, it simply could not fucking be.

Simon Tucks took his neck in both hands and lifted him into the air, choking off his breath at the same time. Brody kicked, punched, flailed, the blows powerful enough to dent metal.

Below him, unfazed by a lethal cut to his neck or the effort of holding two hundred pounds of flailing man in the air, Tucks smiled. "I told you. You cannot fight god."

Brody lashed out with a focused kick that snapped the man's head sidewise but didn't change his grin.

"Before you die again, know something." The pressure was hydraulic, unstoppable, like the blade of a garbage truck. "Your woman is in me now. I took her story. I understand her in ways you never could." That insane smile danced in the air. "How does it feel to know that?"

Brody wound his arms up around Simon's and pushed the elbows between them and flexed, but he couldn't bring enough force to bear. His head throbbed in frantic waves of pain, the world fading and flickering. Claire was dead, killed by the same man who had killed them both before, and he was about to follow her, and for a moment he dared to wonder if there was something else, some next step, some new valley, and if there was, he swore that he would find her there, he would chase her across the whole spectrum of existence if he had to. Again he kicked the sniper in the chin. He cupped his hands and smashed them on the ears to pop the drums, agony and disorientation, but Tucks just stood there and took it, took the pain and the damage like they were happening to someone else and Brody was getting wobbly, he was losing it, couldn't see, couldn't think, his hands finding the man's face and scratching, clawing, digging, everything spots and sparkles, thinking that if he could get to the eyes, maybe there was still hope, and he pressed forward, but Tucks just shook him like a rug, and Brody panic-grabbed with his hands, his fingers touching hair and skin and clothing, catching on something that snapped with a tug—

The sniper dropped him. Just opened his grip and let him fall.

Brody hit and crumpled in a pile, gasping, rubbing at his throat. The indrawn breath and rush of blood hurt even more than the denial of them had. Worse, he knew what came next. He was being toyed with. Soon came the duct tape, and the long, terrified wait, and the fire. At least Claire would be spared that.

It took all his strength to make himself sit up. He'd run, he'd regroup with the others—

Something was happening to Simon Tucks.

Brody squinted, not sure what he was seeing, not believing. The man was . . . melting.

There was no other word for it. The flesh of his face ran like warm wax. The sharp cheekbones slid away, forming into jowls. A second chin formed beneath the first. The blazing eyes faded. His body was shifting too, shrinking and swelling at the same time, losing height in trade for pudgy weight. The wound at his neck sprayed blood. Not the faint trickle that had been there before. Gushes. Geysers.

It was only then that Brody remembered the feeling of something tearing in his grasp. He still clutched it, something light and jagged with a hank of softness. Slowly, he opened his hand.

In the center of his palm lay the sniper's necklace. Three dirty lengths of finger bone held together by copper wire and suspended from leather.

Brody looked at it, then at Tucks, on his knees, shaking and sobbing and melting away. He was no longer the gladiator of a dark god. Now he was a pale man, droopy faced and weak chinned. His hands clenched the spurting wound at his neck, blood pulsing through the fingers.

What had happened, what protection or power the necklace had held, Brody didn't waste time considering. He just tucked the bones in his pocket and dragged himself to his feet. The hammer lay a few steps away, and he limped to it. Scooped it up.

He did not look at Claire's body. Not now.

On the ground, Simon was whimpering. "I'm sorry, I'm sorry, I'm so sorry. It wasn't me, you know that."

"Yeah," Brody said. "I guess I do."

Then he raised the hammer above his head and brought it down with all his strength.

# THIRTY-NINE

And found himself lying on the faded rug with its cracker crumbs and soda stains and dog hairs. *GI Joe* on TV, and next would come *Voltron*, then *Scooby-Doo*, then *Jem* which kinda sucked but made him feel funny, then the game shows. Mom was in the kitchen, smoking and talking on the phone, and by the time the game shows were over she'd be putting on bloody lipstick and telling him there were TV dinners in the freezer, and telling him not to watch too much tube as she walked out—

He'd built walls out of stones and tree bark and set good guys to defend them, Luke and Batman and Buck Rogers and Snake Eyes, who was supposed to be a bad guy but looked too cool in his ninja outfit. But the enemy had them surrounded, a troop of army men set atop a hill of sand, and a bunch of stones he pretended were Decepticons, and Monster Barbie, whom he'd found in the alley, the doll naked and chewed by something. The battle was about to begin when he heard laughter, and looked up to see Tommy and Eric and Paul not quite looking at him, and saying "baby" and "loser" and "fag." He hunched his shoulders and didn't listen, didn't listen, if you don't hear them maybe you aren't here—

Mom's bathroom is off-limits, but she's gone, and Brody sat naked and cross-legged on the floor, hand wrapped around a pair of her pantyhose, pantyhose wrapped around himself, as he stared at underwear ladies in her fashion magazines, not sure what he wanted but wanting it so badly, a yearning in his chest so powerful he can't believe they don't hear it, that the women don't crawl out of the magazine and wrap their arms around him and tell him—

Price gun in his hand, he applied stickers to can after can, *ka-thunk, ka-thunk, ka-thunk*, the fluorescents of the supermarket not quite flickering, headache behind his eyes. In the next aisle two kids from school were talking about college, how big the parties would be and where they'd live and how many girls they'd screw, and he tried to imagine himself doing that, going off to college, going off to life, moving forward. Tried to imagine himself like the people on TV, in a glamorous office or wearing a white hospital coat, and *ka-thunk, ka-thunk, ka-thunk—*

The sound of the house, the slump of the furniture and all the mirrors whispering. Still wearing the suit he bought yesterday, stiff and too short as he sat on the couch that was now his in the house that was now his and thought about how everyone had said Mom looked peaceful. But she hadn't, she'd looked like a mannequin, and he'd always thought mannequins look like they're trying to scream, and he imagined her in the box under all that dirt trying to scream—

Google had taught him to tie the noose. It was just for fun, something to do, not real. The soft double-braided rope felt good in his hands as he looped it, wound around and around. Comforting somehow, like his old Garfield stuffed animal, the orange and black faded to the same muddy brown, one eye lost. He'd loved that thing, slept with it every night until it vanished when he was ten. Mom said robbers must have broken in and stolen it but he knew she'd just taken it because she thought he was too old, and so he'd lay there at night feeling the hollow in the crook of his arm where Garfield used to be and not crying. Now he fell asleep with the soft rope of the noose in the same place, and dreamt of an angel. A radiant angel with the face of a boy, who sat on the bed beside him and whispered to him. Telling him stories. Telling him there was a plan. That he was important. He mattered. Together they would do wonderful things, and he would never be alone again—

The pudgy woman in blue scrubs is staring at her cell phone, unaware of the red crosshairs centered on the back of her head. The angel riding him, guiding him, telling him how to brace the rifle, how to breathe, how to squeeze the trigger. The blast so loud he jumped, and the nurse jumps too, before she falls over—

The FBI woman at his door is pretty, but she looks so tired, he wants to hold her and stroke her hair and tell her it will be okay. And then maybe tell her everything else. He wants to ask her to help him, to stop him. He thought she would be kind. She was asking about neighbors, but when he answered her, something changed in her face, the kindness blown out like a candle flame. Brody slammed the door and ran, whipped by fear, past all the wires the angel has taught him to string, trying to make it out the back. But she's fast, and the gun in her hand is pointed at him as she orders him to the ground, and it's clear she wants to hurt him. And then his angel is there, whispering that it's time to become an angel himself, and he reached for the detonator—

He stood on the sidewalk, a medium-busy stretch of the South Loop. Cars hummed by in both directions. A college kid with a preposterous beard eyed him. A pretty executive in high heels cut a wide berth. The coffee shop behind him smells amazing, rich and full. The street is loud, the hum of heating and electricity, the rattle of the distant El, the city's buzz. He wobbles, unsure on his feet.

"Hey." The man stood a careful distance away, but his eyes were kind. "Are you okay?"

Brody waited for the sniper to respond, for the memory to unfurl.

"Hey. Can you hear me?"

A moment passed.

"Buddy? Do you need help?"

Out of habit, Brody tried to shake his head.

His head shook.

*Huh?*

"Are you okay?"

The question was horrible and hilarious on about five different levels, but Brody didn't care. Testing, he tried to raise his hand. It moved reluctantly. He looked down, realized he still held the sledgehammer. It was heavy. Funny, it hadn't been heavy before. He opened his fingers and let it drop. The head knocked a divot out of the concrete.

The kind man stepped back nervously. He looked eerily normal: blazer and open-collared shirt, bifocals with wooden stems, a crisp shave.

"You . . ." Brody's voice came out rough, and he stopped, coughed. "You can hear me?"

"You're bleeding." The man raised his phone. "Do you need help?"

Brody looked down. Wet crimson was sprayed across his sweatshirt. He remembered the way Simon's throat had begun to spurt as he changed, remembered the impact that had rung up his arms when hammer met skull. Simon, who had said it wasn't his fault, and might have been telling the truth. Who was the boy angel, and how much influence had he exercised? Was it just whispers and promises, or had he actually controlled the man? If that was the case, Simon was a victim too. "It's not my blood."

A taxi leaned on the horn. In the distance, he could hear the *bing-bong* of the El, and the recorded voice saying, "Doors closing. 35th is next. Doors open on the . . ."

"Okay," the kind man said. He took several steps back, then turned around and hurried away. Brody ignored him.

He'd experienced Simon's original death. He'd seen Claire arrive, been chased by her, reached for the detonator that ultimately ended her life—just after she ended his. So why was he still in Simon's memory? It was like a buggy video game, and he was caught on a loading screen. The next level was supposed to start, but nothing did.

*Then maybe you're not playing.*

While he'd been living the sniper's story, he'd had no agency, no control. Just like with Raquel Adams, he had *been* Simon Tucks. He'd been able to experience only what Simon had as he played out a miserable hand from fate's tarot deck, a sad boy becoming a sad man.

But now he could move. He could speak and think. He could turn and see the coffee shop, and the people inside of it, the lights in the display cases, the smile of the barista as she passed a steaming cup. The building opposite, where he and Claire had waited on the roof, had been empty and dark. Now every window glowed with light. People in business casual moved down the hall, sat in cubicles typing at computers, stared out at the sky.

The sky. The clear blue sky.

Holy shit.

Brody stared at the sun until his eyes watered and his pupils burned. When he turned away, the afterimage of a perfect circle overlaid everything he saw.

Sounds. Car engines, humming power lines, distant sirens, cell phones, an airplane gaining altitude, the burble of conversation, a snatch of music from a passing Honda.

Smells of exhaust and cigarettes and fried food.

This wasn't the echo, and it wasn't Simon's memory. Nor was it a flash like he'd had in the park.

He was alive.

Brody buried his face in his hands and started laughing, a strange manic sound. Feeling scraped thin, like foil separated from the paper on a stick of gum. Delicate and very nearly torn. Was it just this morning that he'd told Claire he'd hit his limit of strange? What a difference a couple of hours—

Claire.

The memory ripped through him like lightning. Her eyes widening as the hatchet hurtled toward her with the force of a bullet. The wet crack of the blade shattering her skull. The slip-slide feeling of the world shifting as she—

Died.

Claire was dead. He'd lost her again.

Brody sunk to his knees. Some part of him seemed to be floating above, tethered like a balloon on a string. He watched himself hit the ground, heard his moan more than felt it. She was gone.

It seemed a desperately cruel joke. First he'd been dead and she was alive. Now it was reversed. The time they'd had together had been an illusion. Like heavenly bodies slingshotting around each other, drawing close only briefly before being hurled off into separate darknesses.

If he couldn't be with her, then what did it matter if he was alive?

The metallic smell of blood filled his nostrils. Gravel bit his knees. People walked by. Aware of him but choosing not to see. All of them hurrying to somewhere, from somewhere. Thinking of arguments and meetings, of things they should have said and things they wished they had done. Unaware of the invisible world stacked on this one. Clueless that they paced a battlefield.

He slumped in the middle of the sidewalk. Returned to a living world he had given up hope of. Separated from the woman he loved by ten feet and infinity.

Knowing that if he were to raise his head and look, he'd see only a bare patch of sidewalk where Claire McCoy's body lay.

# FORTY

Brody didn't know how long he lay there with his cheek against the dirty concrete and the feet of living people stepping around him. *Just another madman,* he thought to himself. *Like all the ones you've walked by.*

The blue light caught his attention first. A familiar hue, strobing off the ground.

The police were in a Chevy Tahoe, the light bar atop flashing. Both doors opened at the same time, and two uniformed cops clambered out. No doubt someone had called about the drunk in the middle of the sidewalk.

"Sir," the taller cop said, "are you okay?"

Before Brody could respond, the officer noticed something on the ground. The sledgehammer. Its head coated in gore.

*Uh-oh.*

The police looked at each other, then drew their weapons and spread apart, maintaining two direct lines of fire. The taller one said, "Sir, put your hands on your head. Do it now."

"Officers." He started to rise.

"Don't you move! Put your hands on your head. Do it now!"

Brody almost laughed. He entertained a brief fantasy of standing up and charging them, letting them gun him down.

*That won't get you to her. It'll just put you back in the echo.*

He did as they asked. Laced his hands and looked away as the cops moved to take him, one of them flanking and keeping his gun aimed while the other went behind him, pulled first one arm and then the other back, snapped cold metal cuffs around them.

The shorter cop said, "Look at his shirt."

"Jesus. Alright, on your feet. Let's go."

He didn't resist as they marched him to the Tahoe, opened the door, and guided him in. He didn't even try the inner handle. Out the window, one of the cops spoke into his radio while the other squatted to look at the hammer.

Ten minutes later, there were three more cars. Cops taping off the street. Evidence techs bagging the hammer. Searching for a blood trail. Noting the position of closed-circuit cameras.

All the things he'd once done.

The officers climbed in the squad car without a word. Brody stared out the window as the city scrolled past. Thronging with people hurrying to work, snapping pictures, hailing taxis, pushing strollers. His city, no longer gone strange, except to him. A bike messenger with a chain around her waist balanced on her pedals. Under the thousand bulbs of the Chicago Theatre marquee, a homeless man shook a Dunkin' Donuts cup.

None of them had any idea.

———

They took him to the 18th District. Patted him down, processed him, printed him, swabbed blood from his hands, bagged his sweatshirt. Marched him to an interview room, pushed him into the chair, cuffed him to the rail, and left. Idly, and without much interest, Brody noted they didn't take his personal effects or strip him; likely the detective wanted to play friendly at first.

He sat in the hum of fluorescents. His emotions were too big to fit mere words. Grief wasn't a big enough term. Neither was frustration, or rage. Numb sounded pleasant, but he couldn't get there.

She was dead.

When he'd arrived in the echo, all he'd wanted was a second chance. He'd gotten it. And lost, again.

He'd thought theirs was a love story. Turned out, it was a tragedy.

A tragedy with a dark sense of humor. How was he alive again? Claire had told him about standing over his corpse. She said the bomb had shredded him, made him very definitely closed-casket material. Yet here he sat without a scratch.

The notion of being whole in the echo hadn't bothered him—that was the afterlife, he didn't expect the rules to apply. But how did it work when he returned to life? Had his original body knit itself back together and magically teleported to the street corner? Perhaps he was a duplicate. He imagined exhuming himself, looking down at his own ruined self.

He wondered what the word "self" even meant, given the things he knew now. It was like that old riddle about replacing the handle of an axe, and later the head—when you were done, was it a new axe or the old one?

With a squeak, the door swung open. The man who came in wore a decent suit and an impeccable knot in his tie. He took his time stepping in, closing the door, walking around the table. Made theater of not looking up, staring instead at a folder in his hands. Brody wondered how many of these moves cops picked up from cop shows, a weird recursion of art imitating life imitating art imitating life . . .

After a long moment, he set it down on the table, pulled out his chair, and sat. "I'm Detective Kelly Gardner. Who are you?"

"I already told the officers who processed me."

"And now I'm asking."

"My name is Will Brody. I'm a special agent with the FBI."

"Any identification?"

"No."

"See, I have a problem with that," Gardner said. "You know what it is? It's not that you're pretending to be an FBI agent, although you should know that's a federal crime. But my problem is that you're pretending to be a *dead* FBI agent. A hero who died in the line, saving the life of a police officer."

Brody shrugged.

Gardner's eyes hardened. "You, my friend, are screwed. Your sweatshirt was covered with blood, bone fragments, and brain matter. The sledgehammer beside you was covered with blood, bone fragments, and brain matter. When we test them, they'll match. Your hands had blood on them, which means that you weren't wearing gloves. That means we'll find your fingerprints on the hammer. Are you following?"

"It's not complicated."

"No," Gardner said, "it's not. You are cooked. You're so cooked that I'm not even going to bother with good cop and bad cop. I'm not going to get you coffee and let you sit here for five hours until your bladder is bursting. Any state's attorney—I mean, the most pimple-faced, scrawny-bearded, soaked-behind-the-ears ASA—could slam-dunk you. Do you understand me?"

Brody did. He just couldn't make himself care. "Sure."

"Good. So make it easier on yourself. Where's the body?"

"Which body? Mine? Claire's? The guy I beat to death with a sledgehammer?"

The detective paused. He leaned back in his chair and crossed his legs. "Let's start with the guy you beat to death with a sledgehammer. Where's his body?"

Brody blew a breath, thinking about the question. "You know, I'm not sure." He paused. "Let's see. Lucy was still alive. So that should keep him there. But once she leaves, the echo will reset itself, and his body will vanish."

"I get it." Gardner smiled. "You ought to know, statistically speaking, trying for insanity is a bad choice. Almost nobody gets off on that."

"About a quarter of one percent," Brody said. "I told you, I'm an FBI agent."

"Look," Gardner said, "I'm trying to help you here."

Brody burst out laughing. On a certain level he sympathized with the detective, no doubt a decent guy confronted with what looked like a brutal murder and a psychopathic suspect. He just couldn't help himself, the sounds tumbling out manic, closer to hiccups than humor. When he finally got control, he said, "I'm sorry. It's just . . ." He rubbed at his eyes, packed the laughter away. "The woman I love is dead. Again. Second time in a week. Meanwhile, somehow I'm alive, and it means nothing to me. I've been arrested for murder and I honestly do not care. Last night I had to listen to a woman burning alive. How exactly do you intend to help me, Detective?"

Gardner paused. His mask of authority was slipping a little, and behind it was exasperation and anger. The cop studied him a moment. Then he collected himself and leaned forward, elbows on the table, palms together. A classic sincerity play. Brody had used it plenty of times himself. "Okay, Agent Brody—"

"Oh, nice touch, calling me by name."

"—obviously, you've been through a lot. I'm sorry if we got off on the wrong foot. I'm trying to understand what happened. Can you help me understand?"

"You want to understand."

"I just want the truth."

"The *truth*?" Something snapped in Brody, the vague screen of surreality giving way to the rage that tumbled in him. "You want the truth? Okay. The dead are all around you. When you eat breakfast or hug your son, we're there, in an echo of real life, fighting an invisible war. The corner where you picked me up was the site of a battle where I killed the gladiator of a dark god sent to organize the Eaters to feed on everyone in the echo." Brody paused. Smiled. "You feel better? How's the truth working out for you?"

Gardner sat back. A tiny smile on his lips. "Okay. You want to be an asshole, go ahead. I've been polite because I thought you might want to help yourself, but here's what's going to happen now. A couple of cops are going to strip you down. They're going to make you bend over and cough, and no law says the glove has to be lubed. Then you're going to put on the clothes you'll wear for the rest of your life, and I'm going to lock you in a cage. You, my friend, are doomed."

"No kidding," Brody said. "But I'm not alone. Wait until you get my fingerprints back. See how you sleep that night."

Before Gardner could respond, they were surprised by a sharp rap at the door. It wasn't the tentative knock of a detective who didn't want to disrupt his partner's flow. It was a sound intended to interrupt.

The man who stepped in wore formal blues and a captain's bars. His expression was at once angry and frightened, the look someone might wear while watching their dog being kicked. "Gardner."

The detective was on his feet. "Yes, sir."

"Get him out of here."

"I was about to. I'll move him to holding—"

"We're not charging him."

"What?"

"No charges. Let him go," the captain said, "and then lose his paperwork."

Brody's mouth fell open. What the hell was going on? Gardner seemed just as confused. "Sir, there's got to be a mistake. This guy claims to be—"

"There's no mistake, Detective, and I wasn't asking."

"But sir—"

"*Now.*"

Gardner stared. Slowly, he turned. It was the second time Brody had felt an urge to feel sorry for the detective. It wasn't just the disappearance of an easy win. It was that this case was beyond open and shut; it was slammed so hard the table might break. Yet here was the captain—not a sergeant, or lieutenant, but a captain, the executive officer of the whole district—coming down and telling Gardner to set a murder suspect free and then destroy the records of his presence.

Gardner pulled keys from his pocket, leaned over, and unlocked the cuffs. Anger radiated off him like heat. Brody stared back and forth. Rubbed absently at his wrist. Then shrugged and stood up. He walked to the door. "I can just . . . leave?"

"Yes," the captain said. He grit his teeth. "We apologize for any inconvenience."

Two minutes later, Brody pushed through the revolving door of the 18th District into a breathtaking autumn afternoon. A cluster of beat cops stood smoking, watching a woman in a short dress being tugged along by a Labrador. A line of tourists pedaled by on blue Divvy bikes. At the edge of the street, a black Lincoln Town Car was parked. Two burly men in dark sunglasses stood beside it.

*Ahh.*

They had the carriage of private security and the suits of GQ models. One of them opened the rear door. "Mr. Brody. This way, please."

Whoever had sent the limo had gotten him released. Clout to burn, but more than that, connection. He'd been in the station for an hour, two at most. For someone to learn of his arrest, find out where he was, and then pull the strings necessary to free him—especially given the evidence—well, it was an impressive display of power.

He didn't care. "No thanks."

The two bodyguards exchanged surprised looks. Then one of them opened his jacket to reveal the shoulder holster within. A ballsy gesture in front of a police station. "Now, Mr. Brody. Get in."

"Fuck off." Brody turned and started walking. The El was only about six blocks. He didn't have any money, but he could—

"It's not too late for Claire."

# FORTY-ONE

The limo smelled of leather, and the seats were very soft. There was a courtesy bottle of water. Tucked neatly in the seat pocket were copies of the *Tribune*, *The New York Times*, and *The Wall Street Journal*. The windows were tinted, and through them Brody could see the city roll by. The screen separating the front from the back was down.

"So," Brody said, "who do you guys work for?"

Neither man responded.

"What did you mean when you said it wasn't too late for Claire?"

Nothing.

"You're obviously private security, but I'm guessing former military. What, couldn't hack it?"

The driver pressed a button, and Brody heard a soft *thunk*. He didn't bother looking to see if there were locks he could reach. There wouldn't be, and anyway, he didn't plan on leaving until he got answers.

Obviously, Thing One and Thing Two here were taking him to meet someone. Equally obvious, it was someone powerful, someone with the influence to free a suspect that had arrived coated in blood. Brody couldn't even speculate what level of power that might be.

More important, though, was that they had known about Claire. Which was impossible. No one had known he and Claire were lovers. And the only people who knew she had died again were all dead themselves.

The drive took fifteen minutes, and Brody chewed over it the whole time, but was no closer to an answer when the limo glided to a stop. Thing Two got out, then opened the door for Brody. They were parked in front of a sleek silver high-rise with rounded edges like wind-filled sails and a spire that seemed to pierce the sky. Sunlight danced off a thousand feet of mirrors.

"This way, Mr. Brody."

"Whatever you say, chuckles."

The lobby was a study in modernist opulence, every surface gleaming. One in front, one behind, the guards led him to a bank of elevators. Brushed-nickel doors opened soundlessly. The swipe of a keycard, and the elevator began to rise. It took a long time to reach the destination. A soft voice with an English accent announced, "Penthouse level, 72nd floor."

The elevator opened directly into the room. The initial view was calculated to take a visitor's breath away, and succeeded, pale wood floors and high ceilings framing bright clean glass offering stunning views. The furniture was intricately baroque stuff that looked like it was straight from the seventeenth century. Without speaking, the men led him past the sitting room, through a professional-level kitchen—Sub-Zero and Wolf appliances, a rack of gleaming copper sauté pans, a block of Shun knives—and into a living room in the sky. It was broad and drenched in light. Through wall-to-wall windows Chicago reclined in all its hazy glory, almost lurid with excess.

Thing Two gestured him forward, and then the two men left without a word. Brody strolled to the window and stared out. Idly, he wondered how much a place like this cost. Fifteen million? Twenty? At this distance, nothing seemed real; the world was reduced to a play set.

"Welcome back, Mr. Brody."

He turned. A woman sat in a heavy chair of polished wood, the feet carved like lion's paws, the cushions tanned zebra hide. Her face was finely featured, and her hair was white, not the nicotine yellow of age but a vibrant snow. There was something about her eyes that made him very uncomfortable.

"Back?"

"To life," she said. "Everyone dies. Few return."

"Yeah, I'm real pleased about it. Who are you?"

"You may call me Isabella."

"Well Isabella, that is, without a doubt, the ugliest chair I've ever seen."

Her expression showed neither amusement nor irritation. She just kept looking at him with those weird eyes. Like a butcher examining a cow, seeing filets, rib eye, flank. "Are you always so rude?"

"Only when I'm being toyed with."

"You don't remember me."

Brody sighed. "Lady, the reason I'm here, the only reason, is that your guys dropped—"

"I visited your sleep."

Suddenly he did remember. In the echo, he'd had a series of crazy dreams, culminating in the prophetic one about Claire. But in the midst there had been a woman with white hair and ancient eyes, telling him truths too big to believe.

"You sent the dream. Telling me where to find her." Pieces continued to click into place. They'd wondered what it could mean, both of them having such vivid and tailored dreams. "And you sent one to her too, didn't you? Showing her the sniper."

Her nod was curt, a professor acknowledging that a pupil had reached the correct answer but unimpressed by how long it had taken.

"How did you do that? Why?"

"How isn't important," she said. "As for why, it was in my interest."

"What does that mean? Who *are* you?"

"Do you have it?"

Brody paused. *Do I have what?* Then it all started to come together. Not the whole picture, but the edges, like the corners in a puzzle.

Reaching into his pocket, he pulled out the sniper's necklace. The bones looked delicate, old and dry, the three phalanges wired together by shining loops of copper. By the size, it was the index finger of a woman, or a teenaged man. All this time, he'd been vaguely conscious of it. A sense of mass, like his pocket was stuffed with change, although the necklace actually weighed almost nothing. He spun his hand so that he was holding the leather with the finger bones swaying beneath.

Isabella extended a palm. "May I?"

Brody stepped toward her. She crackled like one of those Tesla plasma balls with the purple lightning. With some effort, he held his smile. "No."

Rage rolled across her face like a rogue wave in an otherwise smooth sea; calm, fury, calm again, as though the anger had never existed. Brody didn't flinch. "Tell me about Claire. What did you mean, it's not too late?"

"You of all people know that death is a relative term."

A tiny spark of hope kindled in him. Was it possible? Could she still be saved? "Who are you?"

She leaned back in her chair. "I am Isabella Maria Ravaschieri. The White Lady. She Who Hungers. The Scourge of Souls."

"Wow. Great nickname. I bet you never have to wait for a table." It probably wasn't a good idea to be so flip, but screw it. All he had right now was having nothing left to lose. May as well double down. "Can you bring Claire back?"

"Yes."

"How?"

"If I tell you, will you give me the totem?"

"Maybe."

Isabella rose. He had six inches and seventy pounds on her, and yet he retreated. He didn't plan to; he just did. "How much do you understand of what you have seen, Mr. Brody?"

"When I killed the man who carried this, I saw something." He ran his tongue over his lips. "A boy he thought was an angel."

She seemed amused. "That was Edmund. He is many things, but not an angel. We were lovers, once."

"A bit young for you, isn't he?"

The way her gaze snapped was almost audible. In that instant, he seemed to see two things in front of him. A handsome woman with white hair. And a beast with endless hunger, a huge, slavering thing made not of flesh and blood but of power and will and hatred. The visions overlapped. It took all he had not to retreat further.

"You would be wise to show more respect, Mr. Brody. You are speaking to a god."

He snorted a laugh. "Right. Well, Jesus Christ is a close personal friend."

If his joke bothered her, she didn't show it. Instead, she seemed thoughtful. "Jesus, yes. I was educated by nuns. Long ago, when I was a human girl. I learned the Bible, studied the verses, memorized the teachings of Christ. When I passed, I expected to find him there." She stared out the window. "But in the centuries I walked beyond the world, I never saw him."

Centuries? As megalomaniacs went, she was in a class by herself.

*Unless she's telling the truth.*

Killing in the echo filled you with power. It healed wounds and recharged vitality. Back in the Langham, Arthur had suggested it might even let someone live forever. Brody had taken that somewhat metaphorically, but now he considered it. Aging was essentially decay, the exhaustion of the body's ability to repair and renew itself. In the echo, that manifested as fading out, like Arthur was. But killing there could fix that.

In which case, all someone would need to do was kill again, and again, and again. Resetting the clock each time.

*She's an Eater,* he realized. If the term was even enough. *An Eater who sustained herself for centuries on the souls of others.* Again he felt an urge to move away, to step back. It was a primal, physical panic, like running out of air underwater.

He forced himself to stand still. If she was telling the truth, then she knew more about how life and death worked than anyone. And he needed to know it too. "Tell me about Edmund."

"I already did. In your sleep."

His dreams usually melted away as he opened his eyes, but now that he focused, he knew exactly what she meant. "I saw a boy on a broken ship. Alone. Eating and watching a sunset."

"The *Persephone.* In 1548, returning from America, the ship was caught in a hurricane. The masts snapped, the hull was breached, provisions and cargo washed away. When the storm finally passed, what remained was little more than a raft. There was nothing for he and his companions to do but drift and starve. But Edmund has a restless mind. He found a way to survive. For a while."

Brody was about to ask how, when he realized he already knew. He fought a shiver. Isabella smiled. "Yes. Edmund fed on men even before he died."

1548. A week ago, he would have laughed at every piece of the story, dismissed the whole thing as madness. Now he was surprised to register that he was barely surprised.

"For hundreds of years," Isabella continued, "he wandered, and he fed. He grew quite strong. And he realized, as we all did, that one could go further."

"'We all'?"

"The elders. The survivors. We who live for centuries. Eventually we all reach the same revelation. It's not enough to hunt the dead. There is a limit to their strength. But life? Life is the source of all. And so like the rest of us, Edmund began to cultivate crops."

"*Crops?* You're talking about people."

"Please." Her voice like chewing tinfoil. "Don't bore me with morality. How much time have you spent considering the immortal soul of your steak?" She showed her teeth. "It's all energy. The universe began in an explosion. Every element is forged in the heart of a star. There is nothing but energy. With enough energy, existence bends around you like the sea around a sailboat.

"I was born the second daughter of minor Spanish nobility in 1336. I learned courtesies and needlework and little else. But I transcended. I have walked the length and breadth of existence. I have watched the world fade with each step toward the abyss. I have stood on the plains of shadow, amidst the numberless hordes crawling toward nothingness.

"I have consumed the stories of great men and fools alike, and learned from both. When I met Edmund, I had already grown powerful. But he had new ideas."

Brody could see the plot of the story now. The shape of the puzzle filling in. All the pieces had been there, waiting. He'd just needed to free himself from notions of what couldn't be.

In the echo, the Eaters fought and killed for power. With each kill, they grew stronger. They could move faster, hit harder. But it was more than that. Food tasted better. The sky grew brighter. He'd felt the allure of that, the temptation. But he'd never extended it across a long enough timeline. Not weeks, or years.

Decades. Centuries.

Claire had compared it to heroin. He now realized she'd been wrong. The first hit of heroin was the best a user ever got. Every subsequent one was a pursuit of a lost moment. It was a downward spiral.

*Money is a better analogy.*

Every dollar a person owned made it easier to claim another. Every dollar increased their options. The journey from poverty to middle class was far more difficult than from middle to upper. And for those addicted to wealth as its own reward, there would never be enough. Until you were Donald Trump, or the Koch brothers, and would do anything, crush anyone for your own benefit.

"Instead of just killing," Brody said slowly, "he suggested guiding living people to do it for you." He remembered the boy angel whispering to Simon, promising him greatness, telling him he was important, part of a plan. "Sad, broken people. You turned them into murderers so you could feed on their victims."

"Oh yes." Her laugh scraped his spine. "But that isn't new. My kind has done that for thousands of years. Your tales of witches and demons, your psychopaths and serial killers, they have always been us. We have ridden the weak and the mad and fed on their victims. But Edmund saw greater potential. He realized that in this modern world, the souls were lesser than the fear."

"I . . . I don't understand."

"Every moment of true fear is a tiny death. Each moment a person surrenders to it, they lose something they will never recover. A wisp of energy into the universe. If our actions caused that fear, we absorb that energy. But it's meaningless, small almost beyond measure.

"That was Edmund's revelation. Even after five hundred years, Edmund was fascinated by the living world. He studied it. And he realized that in this era when all the planet is connected, any act could be multiplied.

"The energy of individual fear is tiny. But the blue whale is the largest animal alive, and feeds only on tiny krill. Not by ones and twos. By millions."

"My god." Brody leaned a hand against the window glass, suddenly afraid his legs might give. He'd heard the phrase "skin crawling" many times, but until that moment, he'd never properly understood it. His skin, his hair, his muscles, every part of him writhed and fought to be away from her. "The victims weren't the point at all."

"Riding one killer might yield dozens of souls. But if a monster could be shaped to terrify a city, or even a nation? The potential of terror is enormous."

*Claire was right all along.*

All the random, inexplicable brutalities. The school shooters and psychotic Uber drivers. The mothers who drowned their children. The serial killers with their duct tape and their butcher knives. The maniacs who fired round after round into crowded nightclubs, pausing only to reload. The atrocities for which there was no answer, no reason. The ones that made no sense.

How many bore the signature of these self-styled gods? These monsters who were nothing more than people run rampant, drunk on destruction.

Who had started as Eaters, and excelled at it. Who had literally built their power upon corpses, stacking bodies beneath them until they stood so high they thought they were divine.

Once, he had wished that there was a reason behind the horrors of the world. Not a plan, or a destiny, but just some logic. Some meaning that couldn't be grasped.

Now he grasped it.

Brody had a sudden, savage wish that the sniper's bomb had killed him properly. No echo, no second chance, no battles in the afterlife. Because all of it—all of it, not just those things, but his whole goddamn existence—had been meaningless.

He wanted to choke the life out of her. To wrap his hands around her thin neck and squeeze, feel the trachea collapsing and the flesh tearing. And knew with perfect certainty that he couldn't. The ancient crone radiated power. He could barely stand next to her, much less touch her.

"Why are you telling me all this? Are you bragging?"

The idea seemed to amuse her. "That would be like boasting to a cow. No. I'm offering you a deal. I will bring your woman back—for a price."

"The necklace. The, what did you call it? Totem."

"Yes."

"What is it?"

"That doesn't concern you."

"You're wrong," he said. "It concerns me. It concerns the hell out of me."

"I could take it from you," she said.

He shook his head. "I don't think so. If you could take it, you would have already. Taking is your first resort. So I'm assuming that for some reason you can't."

Her brows drew together, and her lips pulled back to reveal her teeth. The air around her seemed to thicken and scorch, wobbling like a heat mirage. "Perhaps. But I can wipe you from existence. As though you'd never been born."

Brody shrugged.

Isabella made a sound like a hiss, only deeper. A snarling whisper of menace and frustration. For a moment she looked like she was going to pounce on him. Not the slight woman in front of him, but the ravenous creature of darkness that lay behind and beneath and around her.

He stood his ground. It was easier now that he knew the truth.

She spun, stormed three steps away. Stood in front of the glass, peering down at the world below. After a long moment, she spoke. "I told you that everything was energy. Those of us who became gods, we guard our strength. We are not friends."

He laughed. "The Eaters, all over again. No trust, no faith."

"Trust is a weakness," she said. "Trust teaches you to turn your back on those who could destroy you. We feed upon your kind, but we will devour our own at the first opportunity." She sighed. "Do you have any idea how difficult it is to actively, continually distrust everyone, every moment? To do it for centuries?"

"I don't have to."

"Edmund and I complemented each other. So long as the benefit was greater, we each felt safe. And I suppose that over decades a certain fondness grew." Briefly, her voice warmed. But only briefly. "That was a mistake. Over time, I forgot that Edmund was not my friend."

"And he betrayed you."

"I escaped. But there was a cost. I had to flee the other realms. The valleys beyond the world. The only place I could be safe was where his power is weakest. I had to return to . . ." Her face wrinkled like she was tasting something foul. "Life."

Brody laughed.

"You find this amusing?"

"I do," he said. "I think it's hilarious. You got back what everyone else would want, but you didn't anymore. Because why be alive when you can be a soul-sucking demon."

"I told you Edmund has a restless mind," she said, continuing as if he hadn't spoken. "Your sniper is his newest notion. He would use the man to sow fear and pain here. But instead of discarding him, Edmund thought to use him in the echo. To imbue him with some of his own essence. To make him a leader, and unite the Eaters under him. Can you imagine the power? Every kill made would feed Edmund."

"I gathered that much," Brody said. "Tell me about the totem."

She sighed. "For Edmund's plan to succeed, the sniper would need to arrive in the echo with massive power. The kind it might take fifty years to accrue."

Brody pulled the necklace from his pocket, held it up in front of his eyes. The desiccated bones twisted slowly on the leather thong. "So this is a magic amulet, then? Wear it and gain superpowers?"

"The energy it contains is enormous, yes. But more important is that it is *Edmund's* power. It is connected to him. It is, in a very real way, part of him. That's how he benefits from every action."

"And you want it for revenge."

"I want it so that I can go home again." The words spoken so softly he could barely hear them. "You're right, I can't take it. Edmund understood the risk of putting so much of his power in the totem. It would be a target for all of us. So he wove his will in such a way that none of us, not the Aztec, not the Comanche, not me, can seize it. It has to be given."

"It wasn't given to me."

She scoffed. "You? A mortal? Edmund has preyed on you for five hundred years. It never occurred to him to fear that a mortal might take it. Especially not from his gladiator. That's why I . . ." She trailed off, but he could finish the sentence himself. *That's why she sent you and Claire dreams. To pit you against the sniper, in the hope that something like this might happen.*

"I cannot wield the totem. Edmund made its power poison to us. But so long as I possess it, he won't be able to strike at me without striking himself as well. I could leave this sad, foul place. Return where I belong." She turned. "In trade, I will save your woman."

Brody considered. Could she do it? With everything he'd learned, he imagined so. The echo he knew was only for people who died abruptly, with an abundance of what Arthur had called potential energy. But according to her there were other worlds, other echoes. What he'd seen was just one valley in a chain. If that was so, then it seemed reasonable that Claire had moved farther down the chain. "I understand."

"Good." She held out her hand, palm open. "Let me have the totem. Your woman's time is very short."

"No."

"No?" Disbelief and hatred warred on her features. "*No?*"

"I wouldn't help you if you were on fire." He tucked the bone back in his pocket. "Hell, I'd pour gasoline."

"Your woman walks the plains of shadow. The very end of existence, do you understand? The abyss from which there is no return. Without my help, she will truly die. Soon."

Brody shrugged. "I don't really know what that means. But I know Claire. She'd rather die than help you. And so would I."

"Mr. Brody." Her voice tinged with desperation. "There's more. Much more. I can make your woman more beautiful. More compliant. Lustier. I can give you wealth. Position. Long life." She gestured at her playpen in the sky. "Tell me your price and I will meet it."

He shook his head. "You really don't get it, do you? I guess being a predatory old witch for centuries will leave you out of touch." Brody stepped forward. "I don't want your help. I don't want you to change who I am, or the woman I love. In fact, the only thing I want from you, I'm already going to get. You gave it to me when you brought yourself back to life."

"I don't understand."

"I want you to die." Brody smiled, then started for the door. Over his shoulder, he said, "And her name is Claire."

# FORTY-TWO

He moved fast through the arch separating the living room from the kitchen. The appliances gleamed, not a speck of carbon to suggest they'd ever been used to cook. The knife block was lacquered wood. The hanging rack was laden with heavy copper pans. A crystal vase overflowed with hydrangeas. Without slowing down, he snagged the vase and a twelve-inch skillet and left the kitchen.

Thing One and Thing Two were in the sitting room, right where he'd expected them. Beyond them was the elevator.

Thing Two had a phone to his ear, no doubt receiving orders to stop Brody. Thing One stood at the entrance to the foyer, his coat unbuttoned and one hand already inside.

Brody tossed the vase underhanded, the crystal sparkling in the sunlight, flowers tumbling out. The bodyguard reacted well, sidestepping instead of trying to block the glass. It hit the wall and shattered in an explosion of water droplets and bright fragments. Before the first pieces reached the floor, Brody had crossed the ten feet, whipping the pan through the air in an edge-on blow. The man snapped up a forearm to block it. There was a crunch of metal on bone, and he staggered, his right hand still going for his pistol as Brody spun and brought the pan back the other way. There was none of the superhuman strength the echo had afforded, but plain old momentum worked just as well. Skillet met skull with a shivering *bong*. The guard's eyes went wobbly and he started to fall.

Brody grabbed him like they were dancing, one hand going inside the man's jacket. For a split second he fumbled, caught on the lining of the suit, then his fingers found the pistol in the shoulder holster. He yanked it free and dropped.

As he did, two gunblasts sounded from behind, achingly loud in the enclosed space. Bright red spots burst on Thing One's body. Brody rolled onto one shoulder and brought the gun up, disengaging the safety with his thumb. He lined up on Thing Two, aiming at center mass and pulling the trigger three times in rapid succession. A neat triangle of shots bloomed in Thing Two's chest. The gun fell, and the man followed it.

*Ah well.* Killing them hadn't been his goal, but he could live with it. He hoped they enjoyed the echo.

The gun was a Colt 1911, heavier than the Glock he'd carried, but there was no debating the stopping power of the .45-caliber rounds. For a moment, he considered stalking back the way he'd come. But he couldn't imagine killing Isabella would be as simple as pulling a trigger. Besides, there was no telling if she had other security. Speed and aggression had gotten him through once— oorah, Semper Fi—but there was no point pushing his luck.

He started for the elevator, then remembered the keycards. Brody used a foot to flip Thing One onto his back and dug for his wallet, brown leather worn into a mold of the cards within.

Twenty seconds later, he was in the elevator heading down, the pistol tucked behind his back. He could feel the heat of the barrel through his underwear. When the doors opened, he strolled calmly through the lobby, keeping his head low to minimize the chances his face was visible on the security cameras. Everything was calm. One disadvantage of living on the 72nd floor, he supposed—few neighbors to report gunfire.

Outside the climate-controlled lobby, a gorgeous fall day swirled, the sky burning blue. People walked in both directions like being alive was no big deal. Brody headed for Michigan Avenue and joined the throng.

The wallet held a driver's license, credit cards, private security credentials, and two hundred thirty-seven dollars in cash. He pocketed the money and dumped the wallet in a bin.

A smell caught him, a rich dark homey scent. A man carrying a cardboard tray pushed through a glass door on a brief wave of guitars and female vocals. Brody caught the handle and walked to the counter. There were a few people ahead of him: an executive type looking at her phone, two college students chattering, a mother cradling a zonked-out kid. They stood so calmly, so easily. Unafraid.

"Hi, welcome to Starbucks. Can I get something started for you?"

"A large Americano with an extra shot, please."

He paid and waited at the end of the counter. When his coffee arrived, he reached for it with something like reverence. The heat soaked through the paper cup to warm his hands. Brody added a bare splash of cream, raised it to his lips, and took a tentative sip.

God. He'd missed that.

He took a seat by the window and stared out at Chicago. Life streamed by around him as he sipped his coffee and watched and thought.

He was alive. The woman he loved was dead. The man responsible was five hundred years old. Brody knew more about the workings of the universe than he'd ever cared to. He hadn't just peeked behind the curtain, he'd yanked it aside, stepped back there and started fiddling with the controls.

*So now what?*

# FORTY-THREE

The keys were on the back of a fat drain pipe, held in place by duct tape. Right where he'd left them a year ago. Brody peeled them off and walked the two blocks back up Morgan. The trick to hiding house keys in the city was to stick them on somebody else's building. Needles in a needlestack.

A few days ago, on patrol in the echo, Brody had asked to swing by his home. He'd planned to go inside, had some vague notion of taking comfort from the place. But as their armed group had tromped through the dead neighborhood, reflections flashing in the glass of silent restaurants and empty stores, it had started to feel wrong. Did he want to feel his way through the dark halls to sit in his lifeless loft? What for? In the end, he'd settled for just standing on the sidewalk looking up at his windows.

Now a bus was beeping and hissing as the hydraulics lowered it to curb level. The air was filled with the smell of exhaust and the sound of distant construction. A group of guys in T-shirts and baseball caps passed, one of them walking backward, telling a story. Brody hesitated outside the front door, but only for a moment.

The building was a rehabbed packing plant, and the developers had left as much of the industrial chic as possible. The cement stairs were worn smooth and sloped in the center, the ceilings open to expose the floorboards of the rooms above. He climbed two flights, walked down the hall, and opened the door to 307.

Flipped the switches, and the lights came on. Magic.

The loft was the first home he'd ever owned, and he'd loved it with an intensity that surprised him, especially considering what he'd laid down to buy what was essentially a rectangle. The only separate room was the bath, partitioned off with drywall that looked out of place against the old brick. He shut the door and stood examining the place. The bookcases he'd built himself, the Murphy bed hidden behind curtains, the pressed tin panels he'd hung on the wall, the stack of bills on the counter; everything was the same. He supposed that would change soon. Change was what the world was about.

*Home sweet home.*

Brody set the gun on the coffee table, went to the bathroom, and turned the shower to max. He stood in the scalding water, leaning against the wall and thinking until his skin wrinkled and turned pink. Afterward he brushed his teeth and shaved, a week's worth of beard clinging to the side of the basin. He put on his favorite jeans and *In the Aeroplane Over the Sea*, opened a beer and flopped down on the couch, let his favorite album wash over him.

Idly, he picked up the Colt. It was familiar in his hand; the 1911 remained a common sidearm in the Corps, and he'd carried one for years before transitioning to a Beretta M9. This one was stainless steel with a textured grip patterned like wood.

The universe Isabella had presented was horrifying in every way. He was a realist, knew that the world was not a merciful place. Nature documentaries were far more existentially frightening than slasher films. But he'd never considered predation on this level. Self-proclaimed gods manufacturing atrocities to feed on the fear of the living? Only a deeply warped mind would dream of such a thing.

But that wasn't what he was focusing on. He'd always been good at compartmentalization, and in the shower he'd started packing away the distractions to focus on the most pertinent piece of information.

Claire was still out there.

She was dead, yes. Here and in the echo. But as Isabella had pointed out, death was relative. Claire had simply moved further down the chain of worlds—and she could be pulled back up. That wasn't speculation; all the proof he needed was to be sitting in his loft, warm from the shower, listening to music. Killing Simon and absorbing the energy Edmund had imbued him with had been enough to hurtle Brody back to life. Isabella had done it on will alone, when Edmund betrayed her. The boundary wasn't impregnable. It was just a matter of power.

Power like that in the creepy necklace in his pocket. The piece of Edmund's soul. In theory, he could use it to return her to life. All he had to do was cross back, journey to the plains of shadow, find Claire before she disappeared, and then use the soul of a five-hundred-year-old serial killer to bring them both back to life, all while avoiding the notice of the self-made gods that had stalked the afterlife for centuries. Simple.

Brody released the magazine from the pistol. Five rounds left after the three he'd fired.

Over the speakers, Jeff Mangum sang how dad would dream of all the different ways to die, each one a little more than he would dare to try. Brody swallowed cold beer. God it felt good to be alive. How had he ever taken it for granted?

This was a stolen moment. He knew that. He'd managed to claw himself back to the living world, yes. But not to his own life. To the world, he was dead. Soon someone would come and empty his loft, hire cleaners and painters and put the place up for sale. In a matter of weeks this would be someone else's home.

Generally he favored the truth as a strategy, but he couldn't see that working here. He was dead, his original body in a freezer drawer or a coffin. Not like he could just explain what had happened, either. It had been cruel to tell the detective the truth; the guy had only been doing his job, and Brody had set him up for some dark midnights.

Of course, there were people who wouldn't care about the reasons, so long as he was back. Mom and Dad, for example. He couldn't even imagine the pain they were in. He could reach out to them, tell them the truth. They'd be freaked out, sure, but also overjoyed. When it came down to it, what parent gave a shit about anything except that their child was alive?

He'd have to build a whole new life. No money; his bank accounts had probably already been frozen and credit cards canceled. His time with the FBI was over. Ditto the military or police or even being an EMT. There was no branch that wouldn't involve fingerprints.

Still. He was resourceful and he was smart. It wouldn't be that hard to build a new identity. New name, new ID. Go off-grid, not in some dramatic disaster-prepper fashion, but something low-key. Move to the islands, maybe.

Work in a dive shop, rent gear to tourists. Drink rum in the evening. Swim in the ocean, stare at the stars.

Stop reading the news. Shun stories of massacres and shootings. Avoid thinking of what came after.

Try to forget Claire.

Brody ejected the round from the pipe, then locked the slide and peered into the chamber. Slight wear told him that the weapon had been frequently fired; the cleanliness of the works and faint sheen of oil showed that it had been well maintained.

Claire was out in the darkness. If his understanding was correct, the echo they knew was just one in a chain. But that chain couldn't go on forever. Everything came from life, from the energy and passion of living people. Each step away from that was a step toward nothingness. She stood on the precipice, but she hadn't fallen yet.

"Yet" being the operative word. Isabella had said that Claire's time was short. He supposed she could have been lying, but it seemed out of character. She was too arrogant to bother. So how long did Claire have? Hours? Minutes? He had no idea. Nor did he have the first clue how to save her.

*That's not true. You do have the first clue. It's all the clues that come afterward that are the problem.*

Neutral Milk Hotel had reached the titular track, the least cryptic of the album. God, how this disc had blown his mind when he discovered it junior year. He'd listened to it over and over, puzzling over the references to heads in formaldehyde and Anne Frank, knowing that he loved it, that it touched something deep inside him, but not really sure what the hell it was about. Trying to solve it, like the music had been passed down from a higher power instead of made by human beings.

It had taken almost twenty years to figure it out. Every song was rooted in a desperate desire for a love that transcended. A love that wasn't about being with someone; it was about being them, melting into them. Losing yourself. The album at once yearned for that and acknowledged the fundamental childishness of the desire.

He knew the lyrics by heart, and laughed to notice the moment: *What a beautiful dream that could flash on the screen in a blink of an eye and be gone from me.*

Brody released the slide, picked up the magazine and slapped it home. Racked a round into the chamber. Lifted it fast and put the barrel in his mouth.

He didn't want to merge with Claire. He wanted to stand beside her. That meant gambling all that he was on a spin of the wheel in a game he barely understood, and which might be rigged.

Still. Better to die as Will Brody than live as someone else.

He squeezed the trigger.

# FORTY-FOUR

Everything whipped away like a hat snatched by the wind.

No pain, but impact. Force. Like he'd laid his head in front of a freight train. An explosion of intensity just beyond bearing.

Then it was gone, and so was the music and warmth and the light.

Brody tossed the gun. It clattered against something in the dark. His mouth tasted foul. Tentatively, he reached up to feel the back of his head. Just before his fingers made contact he imagined a jagged hole, wetness and sharp bone matter, and shivered. But all he felt was hair.

He waited for a moment, letting his eyes adjust. The blackness wasn't complete; faint grey light filtered in through the windows. Brody stood and walked to them.

The curtains had transformed into decaying rags, and the glass was cracked. Whole panes were missing, and the wind howled through. The view was and was not familiar. The buildings were in the right place. Shop windows were black mirrors, the neon dead. Nothing moved except debris stirred by the wind. Overhead, dense clouds of charcoal and green twisted and spun like water on the boil, so low he could imagine reaching them from the rooftop. Something like lightning tore across the sky, if lightning were pitch black and made the world darker instead of brighter. The rumble that followed sounded like heavy objects sliding slowly down stairs.

He was back. Sort of.

This wasn't the echo he had known. Brody had expected that; whatever existential physics drove the afterlife, the decision to kill himself would have an impact on his destination. He imagined the chain of worlds Isabella had described as a series of progressively tighter strainers through which souls were sifted. The more potential energy, the earlier they were caught. And just as in Arthur's example there was a difference between an old man riddled with cancer and a young girl hit by a train, there was a difference between a murdered FBI agent and a lover who knowingly ate his gun.

It took five minutes to make his way to the street. No lights, and the floors were untrustworthy. He kept a hand on the wall and moved slowly, the sound of his breath bouncing strangely around the dark hall. When he reached the entrance, the door was jammed, and he had to shoulder it open. It was freezing out on the street, the wind knifing between the buildings.

Another bolt of obsidian lightning split the clouds, and by its darkness he saw the skyline. The buildings were ravaged, windows shattered, walls torn apart, whole sections missing. Skeletal superstructures screeched in agony. A world of ruin like the wake of a bomb blast. The only hint of color was the tornado-green of the sky.

A girl was walking down the street toward him, holding her left arm in her right, staring at it, tracing it, like she couldn't believe what she was seeing. The wind whipped her hair into tangles. She was naked, her skin rippled with goose bumps. Brody held his hands low. "Hey."

She didn't look up, just kept tracing her arm and walking, as though operating on some lost instinct. Heading for a destination she'd already reached. The queasy lighting hollowed out her eyes. She padded past on bleeding feet, and he turned to watch her go. The last he saw before the darkness swallowed her was a flash of pale white flank as she turned a corner.

*Right. Well. Now what?*

He'd have been the first to admit that he'd acted rashly, without anything that counted as a plan. He'd just known that Claire needed help, and that time was running out. Now an acid spike of fear rose in him. What had he done? He'd thrown away his life. Left another corpse of himself where it was sure to be found, much to the pain and confusion of those he loved. All to land in a place that made the echo look pleasant.

*Well, you already leapt. So may as well look.*

Existence was a chain. Life at one end, vibrant and powerful; nothingness at the other. The echo he'd known had to be one of the first worlds, the valley closest to life. They would grow more grim with each step. So finding himself here proved the concept.

*So . . . it's a good thing.*

As with any lie a person tried to sell themselves, it was best not to linger on it, and Brody didn't. He was here for Claire, and her time was short. That was why he had eaten his gun. It was why he hadn't wasted time finding an anonymous place to do it. It was why he hadn't reached out to his parents to offer them comfort; what comfort could he offer when he knew what he was about to do? He was here for Claire, and her time was short.

If existence was a chain, she was at the end. What the old witch had called the plains of shadow. Brody had taken the first step when he'd left life behind. It was time to take the second.

He put a hand in his pocket and pulled out the necklace. As before, it was at once so light he could barely feel it and weighty enough it seemed like he shouldn't be able to lift it. He held it by the thong, looked at the spinning bones. If his hunch was right, that was Edmund's index finger. Three bones of a sailor who died five hundred years ago, after murdering and eating his shipmates.

Just looking at the thing made his lips curl and his palms sweat. In the living world, it had been a couple of dry sticks. Here it was different. It hummed with dangerous potential, like fireworks that hadn't exploded when lit. The idea of wearing it was as appealing as hanging a loop of warm intestines around his neck.

*Got a better idea?*

Brody raised the cord and put it on.

It was like grabbing both terminals of a car battery. A rush of energy so much so fast that it was hard to tell if it was pleasant or painful.

He thought he'd understood power in the echo. He'd seen people move too swiftly for the eye to follow, had watched them bend iron bars and leap off of buildings unscathed. He'd done some of those things himself.

Kid's stuff. Light beer. With the strength he had now he could crack the moon. He felt buoyed with light, remade by it, pumped full of radiance. The power itched and burned, tugged at him. It wanted to be used, to be spent, to run roughshod over everything like water released from a dam.

*Well, why not? Take a test-drive.*

Brody turned to the building opposite, a payday loans place, all dead neon and thick glass. He'd always hated it; it was ugly and garish, but more than that, he hated the clear metaphor of the place: petty servants of power behind bulletproof glass, the less fortunate queuing up to be taken advantage of.

He raised his hand. Visualized what he had in mind. Swung lazily at the air.

A wash of blistering force crackled across the street like a tornado. The building exploded, glass and brick raining out in ten thousand individual arcs each of which he could trace as the force of his will smashed forward, tearing down ropes and stanchions and smashing through the Plexi like a fire hose through a paper bag.

Brody closed his hand. The destruction froze. Chunks of debris hung motionless. He walked to a jagged chunk of glass, plucked it from the air. Examined the wicked edges, the portion of a decal from the sign. Dropped it to shatter, and the rest with it, the energy stripped from them, everything falling straight down.

*More.* He wanted more. To smash and burn for the sheer raucous pleasure of it. Brody imagined stampeding through the city, toppling skyscrapers with a wave, shaking out the streets like carpet, tossing El trains in the lake.

His laugh felt better than an orgasm. And why not? What he'd just done, the power that flowed through him, was miles beyond anything the Eaters were capable of. He was made of light, of crackling ionized energy. In this dark place, he shone like a sun. None of this pale world mattered. Nothing mattered.

*Nothing matters?*

What kind of thinking was that? He'd spent his whole life helping people, fighting for the side that built rather than the one that destroyed. Sure, everyone had the urge to smash something beautiful, but he'd never had trouble keeping it under control.

Then he remembered. The necklace wasn't just power. It was Edmund. He'd put on a piece of the monster.

*Not the monster. A monster. There are others.*

Isabella had said as much. It wasn't just her and Edmund; there were others. Old killers and gods of slaughter. Elder predators who had hunted for centuries. One-time humans who had grown so strong that merely feeding on the people in the echo wouldn't sustain them. Who preyed on the living world, orchestrating atrocities and horrors. Who sought power above all things.

*Power like you just flashed.*

Brody looked up, and knew fear.

What he was seeing couldn't be real. Everything was still there, the desolate street and the ruined building, the wind-whipped garbage under greygreen clouds. But there was something else too. A thing that couldn't exist. A presence his mind couldn't grasp, its shape changing and impossible. Massive as a moving mountain. Rows of teeth in ruined ranks. Around it the world warped like heat shimmers, and ruin ran behind it.

Something was coming, and it was hungry.

Sweat soaked his body, and his bowels ran riot. He'd faced death before, thought he understood the fear that accompanied that. But it wasn't death on the line here, it was something much bigger. Much worse. Death, entropy, decay, they were natural.

The beast that came for him now was something else. It promised not an end but a beginning, an anguish that would never stop, a blooming red flower of pain and evil scored by screams. It knew only hunger and offered only agony. It could not be reasoned with, could not be fought.

It blotted out the skyline, swallowed the clouds. It was at once a black hole that could tear the world apart and, somehow, a man on a horse, his lips pulled back, eyes wild as he whipped his frothing steed, the horse mad with a misery that would never end. Waves of power rolled in his wake, toppling buildings and tugging down the sky.

He tried to tell himself to fight, but how did you fight a mountain? There was nothing to do but wait to be devoured.

*That, and choose your last thoughts.*

Brody lowered his hands and closed his eyes and remembered the morning in her condo, their heads on the same pillow and eyes locked. Her hair flattened with sleep and her breath dank and her body warm and their future ahead.

The wind whipped at him, and he could hear the horse's hooves, its shrieks of mad pain. The air reeked of scorched metal. There was a heat against his chest, a sudden burning fierce as a brand. Brody stayed with Claire, the wrinkled white pillowcases, the sunlight flickering through the break in the curtains, the freckles spilled across her chest—

The world swayed like debris bobbing in the wake of a mighty ship. The shift in balance yanked him from his farewell fantasy, made him reach out a hand for a support that wasn't there, expecting to see his end inches away.

The thing had swerved and gone past.

The man-thing looked back at him with eyes that seemed to spark red, and in those eyes was a hatred and a promise. The rider beat his horse harder, cutting vicious lines in the animal's flanks, and then through some trick of the light seemed to vanish into the clouds.

*What the Christ?*

The totem. That searing feeling against his chest had been where it touched skin. Some kind of power feedback. Isabella had said as much, that Edmund had engineered it so that the others, his fellow monsters, could not take it. Edmund's will stood between him and the others.

The comfort that offered was terrifyingly small.

Brody collapsed. Hugged his knees. Took deep breaths, filled his lungs with whatever passed for air in this ruined world. When he opened his eyes again, the street was as it had been before the thing came. A dying world lit in hangover shades and haunted by wind.

He could change his mind. Isabella had brought herself back to life on will and power. The bones around his neck were those qualities made physical. He could be reborn.

But Claire was out there. And she didn't have a necklace to protect her from gods.

Brody forced himself to his feet. He had to reach her. Isabella had said Claire was at the end of the worlds, but he didn't know how to get there. In the few pants-fouling moments he'd spent here so far, he hadn't seen any signs saying PLAINS OF SHADOW, 2 MILES.

Still. He had the totem, Edmund's stolen power. The rest he'd just have to figure out. He had clues. Isabella had said she had walked the length of existence. That she had watched the world fade as she moved toward the abyss.

*Well, this place is certainly faded.*

He imagined a series of worlds nested like Russian dolls. Each smaller than the last. No, not smaller—lesser. Diminishing one at a time, until nothing remained. If he had the right idea, then Claire would be at the farthest end, the faintest place.

If this were a designed process, there would be a specific number of stages. But that didn't fit the afterlife he'd seen. There wasn't a neat order to it. There was no judgment, no shuffling of souls to a specific destiny. It seemed closer to physics than philosophy.

So maybe it was a matter of attenuation. The worlds fading the way light did. Not in a series of rigid steps, but over a slow gradation. Which meant the number of steps might be essentially infinite. You could always cut something in half.

Except. The elder, the beast that had come for him. Only seconds after Brody had flexed his new muscles, played with the power imbued in the totem, it had been rushing at him, mouth open. So it couldn't be about distance. Not unless the monster just happened to be around the corner.

Plus, each time Brody had died and been reborn, he'd landed in the same location. The world had changed, but not his position in it. All the metaphors he'd used to grapple with this—an echo, a chain, a series of valleys—suggested lateral distance. But that wasn't it.

*The worlds aren't in a row.*

*They're layers.*

*Life and death are stacked upon one another.*

Which meant that moving between them was about choosing the right layer. A matter of perception and problem-solving. He wished Claire were here. He'd never met anyone who could sort and analyze data so fluidly, who could find the signal no matter the noise.

*If Claire were here, you wouldn't be looking for the end of existence.*

Brody took another deep breath. He closed his eyes. Concentrated. Trying to imagine realities layered like a stack of transparencies, or old-school animation cells. Each almost the same as the one before. Changed only in vitality. He pictured them riffed out so that he could see not just the top, but the ones behind.

Brody opened his eyes.

Like putting on glasses in a 3D movie, everything snapped into a new kind of focus.

The street was still there, just as it had been. But at the same time, it had become only part of the whole. There were other places behind it, others in front. The two understandings occupied the same space at the same time, neither more or less true than the other.

*Hold on, baby. I'm coming.*

He focused on the farthest reality. The same street, only darker and more ruined. Shattered and shaken. A postcard of the apocalypse.

Then he went inside it.

———

Again.

Again.

Again.

The worlds blurred around him.

The sky lowered and loomed.

Buildings shook and shattered.

Reality flowed like candle wax.

———

Brody moved without taking steps. Chasing darkness. With each shift from one world to the next, things fell apart around him. A time-lapse of decay. Maggots feeding on the corpse of reality. Walls melted. Glass ran like water. The street was consumed by dirt.

People began to appear.

At first a few. Then more. With every shift he made, each step toward nothing, more people were on the street.

More people, and yet they were somehow less.

Fainter. Silent. Eyes blank as mannequins. Color and personality faded.

Each becoming like the other, the way entropy made all things the same.

At one point he stopped. Physically, if that word still had any meaning, he was in the same place he had been, but there was little to connect it. The buildings flickered. Hundreds of human forms milled aimlessly. They seemed only vaguely aware of each other, or of the world around them. In the dim light, features were difficult to distinguish. Out of curiosity, he crossed the street. The crowd of dead parted, their eyes fixing on him without menace or thought.

His building was still there, after a fashion. It was in ruin. Holes gaped in the walls. Tatters of fabric blew in the breeze. When he put his hand against the brick, the whole façade seemed to wobble. He had the sense that the faint reality it retained was only for him. Brody walked to the end of the building, stepped into what should have been the entrance. The hallway beyond was gone, fading into nothingness.

When he looked back, he saw that what had from the front looked like a wall actually only existed in two dimensions. Like the set in a play. A painted flat propped up by 1 x 4s. A ghost town with only the ghosts remaining.

And so many ghosts. The figures were barely human any longer. They were more like shades.

*This is the path the dead walk.*

Not the ones with what Arthur had called potential energy. The others. The people who had died more traditional deaths. Who had succumbed to old age, or illness. The ones with no excess of life force remaining. Somewhere on this gradient was where Arthur himself would arrive, when he faded away completely.

Somehow the realization didn't make him sad. Didn't fill him with melancholy. It was because, he realized, the dead themselves didn't seem troubled. Whatever they were, they were no longer aware. No longer really human.

They simply waited.

He returned to the street. He touched the totem around his neck. The physical manifestation of the lives and dreams and secret fears preyed upon by an ancient monster. Decades of hunted souls.

Brody kept moving. Darkness grew. At first he could see through it.

Then he couldn't.

———

When he had chosen the darkest worlds one after another, when he had gained confidence and speed, when he had learned to navigate between the stacked and fading layers of existence, he finally reached the last, faintest world. The plains of shadow.

Plains, because the city was gone. The buildings, the street, even the sky. Gone.

Shadow, for there was nothing but flat, featureless darkness.

All that remained were the dead.

Thousands of them. Tens of thousands. Shoulder to shoulder as far as he could see.

With each world, identity and form had been stripped away. The things around him had the shapes of men and women, boys and girls, but none of the traits that made them unique. They looked like a collection of shadows—formed, but featureless. Tallish, shortish, vague. Perhaps their faces would look different, but it was too dark to see their faces. There was no sun above, no looming clouds.

And yet he could see, because at the center of each shadow's chest hung a spark. Right where the heart should be. A tiny flicker like the flame of a failing lighter. He could see the light through what remained of their bodies.

An endless field of tiny sparks; a world lit only by the last miniscule hints of life. A tapestry of fading fireflies.

They moved without intent, and did not speak. They drifted slowly forward.

Brody tore his eyes from the multitudes to see what they walked toward. Nothing.

It was nothing. Not blackness. Not space. Nothing.

Pure and total nothingness. A black hole. An abyss. He could feel the pull of it, like gravity, like magnetism, like the hunger of matter for antimatter.

The end of all things.

As the faded people shuffled numbly forward, those nearest the nothing were swallowed by it. Like shadows entering a dark room, they simply vanished. The only trace of them was the tiny flicker of light in their chests, each of which floated free, drifting upward like sparks from a campfire, glowing briefly, wavering, rising, and then gone.

The plains of shadow.

It was beautiful.

Except that Claire was here.

She was one of these shades, these nearly empty vessels edging toward oblivion. The characteristics that had made her, that had distinguished her as unmistakably *her*, were gone. It was a nakedness of the soul. The little hopes and fears, the shameful secrets, the moments of triumph, all had been left behind.

How would he find her? The world had lost all feature, all topography. The hordes were numberless. He'd no more recognize her than he'd be able to identify her shadow. Here, she was nothing.

*No.*

No. He wouldn't allow it. Her death he could have survived. But he would not let her become nothing. She was Claire Goddamn McCoy. She had swept into his life like a hurricane, and nothing had been the same since.

Claire, who could command a room with grace and skill, a Glock on her hip and her mind throwing fireworks.

Claire, who had made love to him with such ferocity that they knocked pictures off her wall, who had tilted her head back and clenched her lip in her teeth as sweat gleamed in the hollow of her throat.

Claire, who had chewed him out for chasing after the sniper, all those lifetimes ago.

Claire, who had heaved herself atop a brick wall to watch dead children play soccer under a dead sky.

Claire, who had yearned for the Unabomber, and with him, a world that made sense, where bad things happened for a reason, evil and awful as it might be, but still logical.

Claire, brushing her teeth while she checked her e-mail.

Claire, telling him about working for months to help her father rebuild a sailboat he'd bought on a whim, a boat he didn't know how to sail yet. An eleven-year-old girl jammed behind a diesel engine with a ratchet in her hand.

Claire, doing yoga in morning sunlight.

Claire, ravaged and torn, adapting to the new reality of the echo in five minutes and moving on, when he himself had barely found space to take a breath.

Claire, with her always-cold feet and lousy morning breath. Her time fetish. Her empty fridge.

Claire, for whom he had put a gun in his mouth—

Something was happening.

Light. There was more light. He looked up, but there was no sun or moon or stars.

And yet there was light like breaking dawn.

It came from some distance, impossible to judge in a world without feature. Warm and orange and growing. Like a sun born in the darkness of a stellar nursery. Energy and radiance where there had been nothing.

A spark had begun to flare. A single spark in the chest of an anonymous shade. It was growing, the light he'd barely noticed a moment before now a spotlight, incandescent, breathtaking. Coming from one of the shades.

*No. Not just one of the shades.*

The one that had been her.

Brody started running, pushing through the figures around him. They offered no more resistance than crepe streamers, sliding and falling as he moved toward that light, toward the woman he loved.

She stood glowing on the plains of shadow. Whole and perfect, her skin flush with blood, her eyes bright and wet. She stood and saw him coming and she opened her arms.

He swept her up. Not a ghost, a living woman, heavy in his arms, full of life and possibility. Her cheeks were wet and her eyes were confused and she said, "Will?"

"It's me."

"I died."

"You keep doing that."

"It was different. Everything . . . went away. It was dark, and pieces of me kept falling." She shivered.

"It's over," he said. "You're back. We're together."

For the first time, she seemed to notice their surroundings. "What is this?"

"The end of the line." He took a shuddering breath. She'd been so close to that nothingness. To being gone forever. There was relief, but a shaky sort of panic too. It had only been the power of the totem around his neck, coupled with his memories of her, his desire, that had rekindled her. Brought her back to life like blowing on an ember. "You know how we thought there might be echoes after the one we saw?"

"They're so beautiful." Claire stared at the shapeless people all around her. "How did you get here? Did Simon kill you too?"

"No. I killed him. When I did, I came back to life."

"You . . . what?"

"I was alive again. The real world."

"Back to life?" She tore her eyes from the riot of sparks. "Then what are you doing here?"

"I came for you."

"You don't mean—Will, what did you do?"

"What I had to."

"Baby, please tell me that you didn't—"

"I was alive," he said. "And it was so sweet. Blue skies, people, music, hot showers. All the little miracles we took for granted our whole lives. But I realized something."

She waited.

"Life was sweet." He paused, smiled. "But I'd rather be dead, and with you."

For a moment she just stared at him, lips parted, eyes wide.

And then they were locked together, arms wrapped too tight for breath, faces buried in each other's hair, warm bodies pressed against one another as all around them the shades of the dead shuffled toward the abyss, the last flickers of their lives streaking like shooting stars, free and bright and perfect and gone.

# FORTY-FIVE

"Everything looks different now."

"No kidding."

"Not just this place. Everything. All of it."

"I knew what you meant."

"Think about it, Will. That was the end. We've seen the whole span, beginning to end. Life to nothingness. We know every step of it. Every fading footfall." She paused. "And still don't really know anything, do we?"

"That time you lost me."

"Well, we don't really know what happens. Not really. We know about the echoes, the way life fades out. We know that everyone who dies ends up somewhere on the spectrum, moving toward the plains of shadow. And we know that at the edge of that is the abyss, where the last bits of us flicker out. But what happens then? Maybe there's a Heaven after that, and a God. The real one, I mean. Maybe we just fade into nothingness. Maybe we're reborn, and start the whole cycle over."

"Maybe," he said, "we've had this conversation before. Maybe you and I have found each other, fought for each other, across a thousand lifetimes."

"Aww. That's cheesy. And sweet." She paused. "I wish we knew."

"One way to find out, I guess."

"I don't want to know that badly."

"You know what I want? A taco."

They sat in L'Patron, the restaurant where they'd first connected. An ordinary place made holy by an everyday act of communion, and coming here had been a pilgrimage of sorts. The joint looked much like last time, when

Brody had been mourning her. Stools and chairs pulled out, specials on the chalkboard, salsa bottles on the table. No doubt there were dozens of living people here right now, feasting on grilled steak in warm tortillas.

The journey back from the plains of shadow had been strangely lovely. Like rising from the depth of the ocean. Her fingers had laced with his, and they'd held hands as he'd shifted them through the worlds, the carpet of dancing fireflies fading behind them. There'd been a real sadness to leave their light. But each shift brought them new light, new reality. Brody had grown comfortable controlling their motion, and went fast, jumping stage to stage to stage, the world reassembling itself around them.

Pitch black gave way to grey light, and then eventually to color. The featureless surface beneath their feet developed texture, tone, became concrete. Bricks pieced together like LEGOs assembled by the invisible, knitting into walls. Shattered panes of glass flowed and smoothed and became whole. The sky started as a fog, then lifted to a poisonous cauldron swirling above their heads, then retreated further, slowing, softening, shifting to shades of silver and chrome. The effect was almost like a sunrise, and it was beautiful.

Finally, there were no more worlds to choose. Ahead Brody could sense the membrane separating death from life, and pushed against it. The totem grew warm against his chest as the sun burned through the clouds. He could see the living world flickering like a movie projected on smoke: cars and delivery trucks and a city bus moving where a moment before they had been still. Bright lights in the payday loan place, the real thing of course unaffected by Brody's fit of destruction. In front of them, not five feet away, a woman spoke rapid Spanish into a cell phone. She was facing them, and suddenly stopped talking. Cocked her head and squinted.

*She can see us. We're almost there.*

Against his chest, the finger bones went from warm to hot to searing. Brody grit his teeth and concentrated on the world, tried to seize details—music from an open window, the smell of exhaust, the bright autumn leaves on the scrawny trees—and weave a line to haul them back to life. The woman's mouth fell open. The cell phone fell from her fingers.

It wasn't going to be enough, Brody had realized. Their ride was drawing to an end. His will wasn't strong enough, and they'd spent too much of the totem's power. Perhaps if he'd let go of Claire's hand.

Instead, he'd stopped pushing, and with a wobbling snap, it all vanished, sun and traffic and staring woman. They'd stood in the abandoned street outside his loft, dazed, squinting. Back in the echo.

It didn't matter. Returning to life would have been nice, but he'd meant what he'd said. Gingerly, he poked at the flesh of his chest. It was tender and raw. Brody lifted the totem off his neck.

The change was as intense and sudden as plunging into freezing water. He gasped, swayed, would have collapsed if Claire hadn't caught him.

He'd gone from being filled with electricity and made of light to being just Will Brody. But there was more to it than the power differential. There was also a sudden feeling of absence. As though someone had been breathing over his shoulder, and now had vanished.

*Edmund.* Not his consciousness, but whatever fragment of him existed in the totem. Just as the bones had once been connected to his hand, Edmund remained connected to the necklace.

"Baby?" Claire stared at him, eyes wide. "You okay?"

"Watch that last step," he said. "It's a doozy."

She laughed, and braced herself under his shoulder. "Come on, old man. Let the dead chick help."

Back to the Langham Hotel, why not. The walk wasn't long, but it was oddly glorious. After having seen entropy in its purest form, having witnessed the decline of all things, even the echo looked magnificent. They stared at the high-rises and empty shops with the wide eyes of tourists.

"What in the risen fuck?" Kyle stood on the bridge, axe on his back, 7-Eleven sandwich in one hand. "Where the—you two are *dead*."

"We were. Also alive. Then dead, then deader, then deadest."

The man nodded slowly. Took a bite of his sub, chewed methodically. "Okay."

That evening, they all gathered on couches hauled out from the lobby, passing bottles of top-shelf liquor. The group was smaller, and the tone sadder.

Brody's plan to kill the sniper had been simple—an ambush to get the Eaters' attention, and then a holding action to buy his team time to kill Tucks. But that holding action had meant regular people facing off against Eaters.

In the end, it cost forty-three lives.

Madeleine, who knit scarves and left them to vanish.

Antoine, who had held the line even as they were overrun.

Sonny, and Lucy as well, who must have died from her injuries minutes later.

Emily Watkins, who had pretended to flee and in the process drew a dozen Eaters away from the main battle. No longer a victim—a martyr.

Arthur. The professor. In the end, he'd broken his own prohibition against killing. When two Eaters cleared the lines and made for the hotel, where the youngest children had been hidden, Arthur picked up a knife and hurled himself at them. He'd managed to kill one by surprise and badly wound the other before he died.

"The fight was grim," Kyle said. "We managed to make it to this narrow street in the financial district to channel them. Should've seen Finn climb up the outside of the building with his bow on his back. We got in a few good hits early, with the surprise and all. But they were swarming us inside a minute. Pushing cars as cover, throwing manhole covers. I think Hector died happy—got to star in a real-life superhero movie. It was ugly as a dick in a meat grinder when the whole world went suddenly wonky. You know how departures feel like a boat rocking? Well, when you killed the sniper, it felt like the boat capsized."

Instantly, the shaky truce between the Eaters had capsized as well. Some turned on each other, hungry to harvest more power. Some were killed as they faltered. Most fled.

"Days since have been hard," Kyle said. "Lot of wounded too—"

"Days?" Brody lowered the bourbon bottle. "That was this morning."

The gathered crowd exchanged glances. Kyle said, "Not so much, cochise. Try last week. Where you been?"

*Navigating between the planes of existence.* Put it that way, he supposed it wasn't the craziest thing in the world to imagine time got a little slippy.

Brody told them about the echoes that lay beyond this one leading to the plains of shadow. About the new breed of gods, elder humans who had taken the Eater ethos to its ultimate extreme. He wasn't sure he was doing them a kindness, but they deserved to know. And while Isabella and her kind were horrifying, the journey itself held no particular terror. There was no hell at the end of it. Just a forgetting and a fading and an end. There was nothing frightening about a fire dying.

They talked for hours. After their recent experiences, after learning of predation taken to its most extreme level, it felt wonderful to sit comfortably among a circle of humanity. Living people who breathed and laughed and farted. Who watched each other's backs, and fought to keep the darkness at bay. Not to end it—how could you end darkness?—but just to keep it from winning.

Eventually, people began peeling off. When he and Claire made to go, Kyle stopped them. "You gotta be tired. But if you're up for a climb, you might try the 12th floor."

"What's there?"

Kyle smiled. "Call it the bridal suite."

They'd laughed, started walking. Brody had snickered, "Bridal suite. After today. Right."

"I dunno. This afternoon I was nothing but a candle flame in the heart of a ghost." She shrugged. "Now that I've got a body again, seems crazy not to take advantage."

Their eyes met. That same sort of tangible snap that had happened the first time.

They made twelve flights in ninety seconds, and found that they both had plenty of energy after all.

That was two nights ago. The time since had been spent helping. Tending to the wounded, gathering supplies, watching the kids. Patrols were still going out, though they were smaller. A lot of Eaters had been killed, and a lot of Ray's Disciples had fed. And as Brody had hoped, as they'd all gambled, it hadn't turned them into monsters. Their trust and community ran deeper than simple rules. As a result, the echo was a quieter, safer place.

"For a while anyway," Kyle said. "Thing I'm wondering, can we use this time?"

It was an interesting notion, and Brody and Claire had been talking it out on their stroll to L'Patron.

There was a way to capitalize on the situation. A narrow path that kept to Ray's general principles while also expanding their territory. It would be risky—no way to limit themselves to simply self-defense—but if it could be pulled off, it would mean an echo that was far less terrifying.

"It would take real organization," Claire said. "Leadership. We'd have to set up outposts all over the city. Build outward from the Langham. Drive the Eaters away, and kill those that didn't go."

"That's risky."

"The addiction, yeah." She chewed a lock of hair. "Maybe if we planned it carefully. Made sure that no one killed more than once. That would still mean at least a hundred fewer Eaters. And a lot more newbies surviving."

"Doesn't seem that long ago we were the newbies," he said. "Still, even one kill would be too much for some people. Hard to taste that power once and then let it go."

"We'd have to set up safeguards. Some sort of a justice system. A way to judge who had gone too far."

"Build a new civilization in the afterlife."

"Yeah. It could be done. We could help do it."

Brody nodded. Pulled out the stool, his stool, and sat down. Claire took the other. For a moment they just looked at one another.

"You were trying to mess with me that day." Claire smiled. "Bringing me here."

"Maybe a little bit." He shrugged. "You took my job."

"*Your* job? Ha."

"Besides, you were messing with me too. That 'pick a place' test?"

She acknowledged it with a glance. "God those tacos were good."

"That look was good. Just before we left. Don't get many like that. Not in a whole lifetime." He paused. "Not more than ten, probably."

"Ten? Please. You never had anyone look at you like that before."

He reached out, took her little finger in his. Felt the warmth of her, the solidity. They'd lost and found each other so many times. He wanted to believe it would never happen again. He wanted to believe that it would happen over and over. He wanted to believe that they'd been lovers a thousand lifetimes over. Around them, the restaurant, the street, the city, the world, were gripped by stillness.

"He'll try again, won't he?"

"Edmund?" Brody nodded. "It's too good a notion for him. It might take a while, but he'll find another Simon Tucks. Someone to terrorize the living world, and to be his pawn in the echo. Whoever it is, every time they kill, every time their followers kill, it will trickle power upward. Edmund can just lean back and get fed."

"The afterlife as a pyramid scheme." Claire shook her head. "After all of this. After chasing Simon Tucks through life and death. We didn't really accomplish much."

"That's like saying there's no point in catching Ted Bundy because John Wayne Gacy also existed."

"Back when I was an FBI agent I would have agreed with you," she said. "But now we know different. Simon Tucks was a sad little man, but he wouldn't have, couldn't have done it himself. Edmund rode him like a horse. And from what Isabella said, the same was probably true of Bundy and Gacy."

"What I wonder," Brody said, "what if the same was true of Hitler?"

"Jesus."

He knew what they were doing. Their conversations tended to be icebergs, the part above the surface only a small piece of the whole.

On one hand, what they were not quite talking about was crazy. Ludicrous. Maybe even impossible.

On the other, how many atrocities had Edmund orchestrated? How much darkness had this dead man birthed into the living world?

"White blood cells," she said. "You once said that's what cops are. Something harmful gets in the body, our job is to take it out. And I said—"

"That you'd rather cure the disease. I remember."

"Well, Simon Tucks was a symptom. Edmund is the disease."

"Yeah, but . . ." Brody had a flash of the thing that had come for him after his suicide. A moving mountain with gaping jaws. An impossible predator that blotted out the sky. He shivered involuntarily. "Five hundred years he's been accruing power. Like, literally since the Middle Ages. I don't think he's even a man anymore."

"Sweet," she said. "So how do we kill him?"

He blew a breath. "Yeah."

They sat in silence for a moment. Brody found himself thinking about Isabella, in her fortress in the sky. Hundreds of years old, weakened by her battle with Edmund, and yet still so drenched in power it felt like he could have gotten a sunburn just by standing too close to her. She'd seen people as nothing but food. A resource to be harvested. Never mind that they had lives and dreams and children. To her, that had been beneath consideration. People had been beneath consideration.

"He won't be expecting us to come for him."

"Why not?"

"Edmund and the others like him don't think of themselves as us. They've been at the top of the food chain for centuries. And the top of the food chain isn't really in the food chain anymore."

"That's a Louis C.K. bit, isn't it?"

"Yeah," he acknowledged. "But he's right. Everyone talks about people as the top of the food chain, but really we're outside of it. We don't consider the creatures below us active threats."

"I don't know," she said. "Every time I go in the ocean, I think about sharks. I know it's stupid, but I do."

"That's because splashing around in the ocean, you aren't at the top of the food chain. But how often do you lock your condo door, crawl into bed, and worry about bears?"

"Never."

"So that's something."

"Maybe. Or maybe he won't think we're a threat because we're not."

"We've got the totem. It's part of him. I'm pretty sure it will let us find him. And maybe more."

"It's just a small piece of his power though, right? From what you've said about these elder things, they've raised paranoia to an art form. Would he have made it strong enough to destroy him?"

Brody shook his head. "No chance."

"So then how do we do it?"

"I don't know," he admitted. Paused. "Yet."

She smiled. "Like my dad and his sailboat."

"Yeah." He rubbed at his chin. Three-day scruff rubbed back. "I wish I'd known you then. Eleven years old and helping your dad fix a boat he didn't know how to sail."

"You probably wouldn't have liked me. I was skinny, had braces. Used big words. Finished my homework right after school. I didn't have a lot of friends."

"I'd have liked you."

Her pinkie squeezed his. She stared down at the battered wooden counter. "You know what I wish? I wish . . ."

"What?"

"I wish that someone else had gone into that church." She looked up, her lips twisted. "I know that would have meant more innocent people dying. But . . ." She shrugged. "We'd just gotten started."

He imagined it. The other path.

If he hadn't died, she wouldn't have dreamed the face of his killer, and she wouldn't have died either. Sooner or later, though, Simon Tucks would have been caught. He'd have screwed up, or imploded under the pressure, and they or someone like them would have caught him.

And a surprisingly short period of time later the city would have forgotten about being under siege. Life would have returned to normal.

By December he'd have left the FBI and bought her a ring.

He could see them, hand in hand, walking streets soft with snow and lit by Christmas lights. Speaking without words. Planning the life to come.

Music on the stereo while they painted a new place, her elbow streaked with blue.

Lazy weekend mornings, something braising in the oven, the couch their universe, constellations of novels and the Sunday *New York Times*.

Her promotions, his new job. Working late and waiting up for one another. Living room passion and midnight feasts.

Seasons and haircuts and presidents changing. Discussions and decisions.

Making love to make a child, the intensity that must bring, the way their eyes would be locked in wonder at this thing they were doing.

The surreal swelling of her belly, skin straining like it might tear, the bump of a tiny foot moving beneath.

Playgrounds and patched knees. Midnight emergency room visits. Cartoon-themed birthday parties with sheet cake and balloons. The ache of standing over a single bed, watching a child sleep, knowing that someday that child would have a life of their own, that they would leave and never truly return.

Dinner parties and crying jags, terrorist attacks and sitcom marathons.

Lonely 3:00 a.m. insomnia.

Parents dying. Coming face-to-face with the relentless rhythm of life, how the children their grandparents had watched sleep were now gone. How one day their child would think the same of them.

Grey creeping into hair, pounds thickening around the waistlines. Politics and fights, couch sleeping, making up. High school graduation and college-bound boxes. Earlier bedtimes and questions about meaning. Thanksgivings and Christmases and holding each other in the night while storms raged outside.

Perhaps someday a sailboat rebuilt together, and a cruise that never ended.

All of it spent as normal people, unaware that the world they saw was only a layer in a larger whole. The brightest layer, the base of all that came after, but just a fragment nonetheless. Existence wasn't a painting, one clear vision laid over clean canvas. It was a palimpsest, meaning layered over meaning, each forever changing the shades and tone of original intent.

"We don't have to," she said.

Brody blinked. "What?"

"We'd be safe here. And we could do a lot of good."

"Do you want to stay?"

She twisted a lock of hair, slipped the coil between her lips. "Do you?"

Hell yes. He'd already made the choice between being alive without her and dead together. Doing what they were not quite talking about risked everything they had managed to salvage. If it was even possible.

*Really? You're going to let dying a couple of times keep you from being yourself?*

There was a chance to end a monster. They had the totem, and they had each other. That combination might be the greatest threat Edmund had faced in five centuries.

True, he was only one of a host of monsters. But he was their monster. They couldn't end predation, but maybe they could end a predator. It was like cancer. You never beat cancer—you just beat it back. But that could make all the difference. Who knew how many people they might save, how much horror it might prevent.

"If you had known you might die if you visited Simon Tucks," he said slowly, "would you have?"

"If I'd known, I'd have brought a SWAT team." She shrugged ruefully. "But that's not what you're asking. What about you? Would you have gone into the church, if you'd known there was a chance you wouldn't make it out?"

"Yes."

"Why?"

"Because there was a chance to save people too."

She nodded. "Exactly."

"Okay," he said. "Let's go kill a god."

# FORTY-SIX

One more night.

They'd talked longer, pacing the restaurant, kicking around notions. It was Claire who broke it, of course. Claire who figured out the answer, or at least the best answer they'd been able to think of so far. By that point they were amped up, and tempted to just go, to hold hands and step off the precipice. But they agreed it was better to be well rested.

"Besides," Brody said. "There's something we should do first."

"What?" She'd cocked her head, looking at his face. Her smile had bloomed slow and sweet. "Oh."

By unspoken agreement, they'd walked back to the hotel slowly. Not talking much, just looking around. The afternoon was cool, and a fog had risen, cloaking the world in mystery. Every step revealed something they couldn't see a moment before. The smooth curve of a Jaguar's bumper. A nameless skyscraper cutting a perfect line into the clouds, marble façade slick with condensation. The gentle sway of a dead traffic light, function stripped away, hanging like a necklace over Michigan Avenue. The fractal pattern of gum ground into the pavement and trod black. The wind-whipped ripples on the dark river, flowing endlessly into one another.

*So beautiful,* Brody thought. *How come I never saw how very beautiful it all is?*

After so much abandoned silence, crossing the bridge to the hotel felt like entering a party. People talked and laughed. Kids sat on car hoods and tossed a tennis ball idly back and forth. Finn fired arrow after arrow into a leather chair, his speed and power dizzying. DeAndre was talking to a pretty blonde girl who kept fixing her hair and touching his arm. Patricia, Brody assumed, and smiled.

Kyle opened the case of beer at his feet and tossed one to each of them.

The simplest thing in the world, and the most precious. People coming together to help one another. Strangers forming a family. Brody and Claire each took one end of a lobby couch and hauled it outside to join the party.

Later, in the suite on the 12th floor, they pulled the curtains to let the city darkness flood in. The room was magnificent, white marble and soft fabrics, silver vases with autumn leaves arranged in them. Brody thought about the living people who had moved through the room today. The maids fluffing pillows and refilling decanters of scotch and bourbon and brandy. The wealthy guests, investment bankers or rock stars, who had plunked down thousands of dollars for a night in the sky. He could imagine them tapping at the grand piano, or naked and eating strawberries, soaking in the steaming tub. Were they happy? Or were they, like so many people, bothered by tiny gripes and silly frustrations?

To learn the true value of something, all you had to do was lose it.

Brody poured drinks in crystal tumblers. They'd stopped by the pool first, the closest thing to a bath, and he could smell the chlorine on his hands when he sipped his drink. He found Claire at the window, brushing damp hair and staring out at the night. The city spilled out around them in a hypnotic geometry of darkness.

"They can't be right," she said as she took the glass. "Isabella and Edmund and the others. It can't just be about energy. I understand that's part of it, I felt that. But when I killed that Eater, Lawrence, I didn't just get his strength. I got his story too."

"So?"

"Well, if it was just energy transference, just a flow of power from vessel to vessel, then why would their lives come too?"

"Maybe that's just how it works. A side effect."

Claire shook her head. "We're not just energy. We're people. Everyone, good and bad. There's something ineffable and perfect and indestructible that makes us who we are. That survives even when we die. Lawrence is dead but I remember his life. He lives inside me. Like Raquel inside of you."

"You talking about a soul?"

"I don't know." She shrugged. "Maybe that's just the best word we have to describe something we don't understand."

"Maybe." He sipped his bourbon. Caramel-colored warmth filled him, warmed him from the inside out. Down below, he could just make out figures lounging on couches, leaning against walls. Shadows not quite swallowed by the darkness. "I've been thinking about something you said. When you first got here. You said that entropy always increases, but that it didn't happen like flipping a switch."

Claire nodded.

"Thing is," he said, "it doesn't always increase. Okay, fine, eventually everyone dies, and the stars burn out, and everything just drifts forever."

"That's what entropy means, babe."

"Yeah, but my point is that it may win in the long run, but it doesn't *always* increase. Sometimes it's losing. Sometimes we, people, are winning. When we're building cities and making love and writing poems. Sometimes *life* is winning. And that's worth something. Even if it won't change the ending." He finished his bourbon with a swallow. "So screw entropy."

Claire turned, set her tumbler down on a nearby table. In the dark of the room, she was a silhouette in a white bathrobe, her features barely visible. Slowly, she untied the sash of her robe. With a shrug, she let it drop from her shoulders. Beneath it, she wore nothing at all, her body a symphony in curves and shadows. She said, "I've got a better idea."

There was no wall-rattling passion, no pictures knocked loose or broken glass. This was the other kind of love. They took their time. Lounged beneath covers thick as a cloud. Shivering a little in the cold. Tasting of bourbon and chlorine. Eyes locked in the darkness. She pulled his lip into her mouth and sucked on it gently. He ran a hand down her arm, savoring the softness of her skin, tracing the muscles beneath.

They made a feast of each other. Building up heat in the bed, their communion pushing away the cold. Touches and nips and growing pinches. Her breath hot in his ear. Her body firm and soft atop him, the weight of her, the feeling of her breathing, the beat of her heart. Savoring and teasing and soaking.

Even when they finally slid together, they did it slow, a fraction of an inch at a time. Trying to feel every moment. To record it like fire against the darkness. The searing heat of her. The catch of her breath. Her fingers in his mouth. His hands cupping her, filled with her. His tongue capturing the sweat between her breasts. Her hair draping them both like a curtain to screen out the universe. The way they had always both preferred it, the two of them alone together and everything else forgotten.

It was sex, and it was making love, and it was a choir, and a prayer. It was the only church he would ever need.

When they were finally done, when she'd pointed her toes and clenched her legs so hard the muscles trembled and shut her eyes and moaned and told him not to stop, never to stop; when he had spread his hands around the hinges of her thighs and pushed himself into her heat again and again, until he couldn't tell where he ended and she began; when the song built between them, resonating back and forth, a glissando of slippery intensity; when she had screeched through closed teeth and he had groaned with his head thrown back; when they had collapsed, slick with sweat, hands trembling and breath coming hard, and held each other; when they were finally done, only then did Brody let himself admit what he'd held at bay throughout, the idea that both of them thought this might be the last time.

They lay spooning, pulses gradually slowing. Bodies connected, his nose in her hair. Soon her breath grew steady, a gentle rhythm like the tide, and he knew she was asleep.

Softly, not wanting to wake her, he put his lips to her ear, and spoke.

He told her she was right. That for all they knew, they still knew nothing. That for all they knew, there were still worlds after this one, eternities that followed the abyss.

And he told her that if they died tomorrow, he would follow her across them.

He would chase her through existence if that's what it took.

# FORTY-SEVEN

The hatchet smashed into her skull. There was a lightning strike of agony and the urge to scream and then she was jerked away. The world retreating from all directions at once like she'd been strapped to a rocket. Then the perspective shifted and she wasn't flying, she was falling, plummeting into darkness, and as she fell pieces of herself kept shearing away, and each time they did she felt calmer, simpler, more at peace—

Claire's head jerked off her pillow. Still in darkness, but not the same. She could see a little, the shape of a table and windows and a faint light. Her heart thumped so hard it made her dizzy.

A dream. It had just been—well, not a dream. A memory. Her second death.

She took a breath, then another, then remembered to do it yoga style, in through the nose, out through the mouth. The rhythm of it calmed her, brought things under control.

The hotel. They were in the hotel. In bed. She turned, saw Brody on his back, eyes shut and mouth open. A faint guttural snore rose from his throat. He did that sometimes, nights they'd been up too late or had too much to drink. There had been a time when she imagined how it might be decades hence, whether she might one day lie awake imagining smothering him with a pillow.

Through the windows, the sky was only barely touched by what passed for dawn here. Something like five in the morning. Claire glanced at her wrist, remembered that the Rolex was gone, vanished into . . . wherever things went. Gone like she had been.

She considered lying back down, knew it was pointless. Sighed and rolled her legs out of bed. Stumbled to the bathroom, peed in the dark, then took a long swallow from a bottle of water.

*pieces shearing away, all the things that make you you*

The shiver shook her whole body, a quick involuntary tremble. The kind people used to say meant someone had walked over your grave. A funny, nonsensical expression, she'd always thought, until she got to the echo and realized that the dead were all around the living. That every moment of her life—dancing at her sister's wedding, reading a book, taking a bath—had been shared with the dead. She thought of Brody trying to bring them all the way back to life. That poor woman at the bus stop. One minute everything was normal, a phone call on a sunny fall day, and the next, two people were materializing in front of her. How confused and frightened she must have been. Would it change the course of her whole life? Or would she bury it, write it off as a vivid daydream? Strange to imagine the ways moments like that must have shaped the world, instants when the line between life and death smeared enough to glimpse what lay beyond.

The living room was broad and opulent, pale silver light falling across luxurious fabrics. Claire ran through sun salutations, then a plank sequence, side, down, side, back again, holding each pose until her arms shook. Her muscles warmed and her body limbered, but the visions of falling kept looping in her head.

*You may as well admit it. You're frightened.*

*No. You're terrified.*

It wasn't an easy thing to acknowledge, even to herself. Normally she could compartmentalize her fear. But this was primal, too raw and huge to cram into a box.

It wasn't the dying itself. That had been strangely easy. With each piece of her that went away, she'd grown increasingly calm, placid, until she was just a nameless selfless shadow approaching the abyss.

That was the scary part. Alzheimer's was far more terrifying than death.

Out the windows, the brightening sky revealed the world, the city sprawling out in all directions. Mist rose from the river. The sentry on the bridge jogged in place. Claire wanted coffee so badly she thought she could smell it brewing.

In the bedroom, Brody had rolled to one side, his arm flung across her pillow. She stood and watched him sleep. There was something childlike in it, his tousled hair and splayed limbs.

The necklace lay on the nightstand.

Claire padded softly across the room. There was a sensation that she was watching herself walk there. She bent at the waist to examine it. Three yellowed bones, wired together with bits of patinated copper. She wasn't a forensic specialist, but she'd spent enough time looking at bones to guess it was an index finger, most likely of the right hand. The base of the largest was chipped, suggesting the cut had not been clean.

*He hacked off his own finger to make a weapon to equip a serial killer to burn innocent people alive.*

*That's the kind of will and evil you're facing.*

Gingerly, she poked it. The bones felt normal enough, smooth and without temperature. Claire picked the necklace up by the leather strap, and held it in front of her face. The totem spun gently. Somehow it was light and heavy at the same time.

For her, Brody had put a gun in his mouth and pulled the trigger. Then he'd put on this evil thing and used its power to dive into the abyss after her. To snatch her hand as she fell and pull her back to herself.

It was such a crude and ugly trinket. The primitive jewelry of a shaman in some forgotten time, blood magic out of a myth. Brody had been able to feel Edmund when he wore it. *We weren't chatting or anything,* he'd said. *But it felt like my head was more crowded. It's not a bank account he deposited power in. It's him. A piece, but still him.*

That belief—that the totem wasn't jewelry, it was Edmund himself—was central to their plan.

If one could call what they had a plan.

Claire had a sudden urge to leave the suite, run down the stairs, and throw the necklace in the river. Without it, they wouldn't have the option of going after Edmund. There would be no choice but to stay. To spend the rest of their days together, instead of risking everything on a desperate maneuver.

How would he react if she did? He might be happy about it. Maybe not initially, but with time, and in his heart.

Or he might look at her with disgust. It could be a wound that grew infected, festering and poisoning the only thing that mattered to her.

"Hey."

Claire jumped, almost dropped the necklace. Will hadn't moved, but his eyes were open and looking at her. She had the guilty rush of a kid caught tucking a candy bar down her pants. He could sense what she'd been considering. He was judging her for it.

Then he smiled.

In that moment, Claire realized that the thought of her acting that way would never occur to him. To Will Brody, she was better than that.

———

To his surprise, Brody had slept like diving into a dark lake. No dreams, no sense of himself at all, just a deep and consuming absence. Once, he'd imagined that was what death must be like.

When he opened his eyes, he saw Claire standing nearby, examining the totem. "Hey," he said.

She jumped, and an expression flickered across her face that he couldn't parse. Then it was gone, and she smiled. "Hey yourself."

Brody rose and stretched. Brushed his teeth and ate a granola bar and got dressed. They'd made a few stops on the walk home yesterday, and he poured out the contents of his pack. Good knives, a hammer, a throwing hatchet like a tomahawk. An aluminum baseball bat strapped to the outside. He remembered the moving mountain, razor teethed and mad. The notion of fighting Edmund with these seemed ridiculous.

Claire hefted the hatchet, spinning it so the edge caught the light. "Are we crazy?"

"Probably," he said, and grinned. He strapped the longest knife to his belt, tucked another in his boot. "Edmund won't be expecting it. The element of surprise has turned worse odds."

"What do we tell the others?"

He paused. "Let's not."

"Nothing at all?"

"They can't help. No point in worrying them."

"They'll worry if we just vanish."

"Yeah, but . . ."

"You'd rather no one tried to talk you out of it, because they might be able to."

"Yes," he said, and met her eyes. It was a naked look, no attempt to hide the fear he felt, the dread.

"Okay," she said. "Well, it doesn't matter. We'll be back soon enough, we can tell them then."

She said it matter-of-factly, like they were running an errand instead of risking a desperate plan against an enemy they barely understood. Like she wasn't even afraid. Like she believed in the version of him that wasn't either.

*Maybe that's what love is. Believing in the best version of your partner, so they have the courage to believe it themselves.*

"It's a good plan," he said.

"I know. I made it."

He snorted a laugh. The tension and fear blew away. They had a job to do, and they would do it together. "Ready?"

She looked around the room like she was taking stock. The lush space they could never have afforded, the bed they'd made love in, the windows and the cloudy morning. Nodded.

"Hand me the totem, then."

"No."

He'd been reaching for it, and her response froze his hand awkwardly in mid-gesture. "What do you mean?"

"I'll wear it," she said.

"Like hell you will. It's too dangerous, there's no way I'm going to let you—"

"Let me?" Her eyes flashed. "Are you kidding?"

"I didn't mean—"

"Shut up." Claire stepped forward, squaring off with him. "When I was gone and you'd been reborn, you didn't hesitate. Even though you're likelier to attend a square dance than commit suicide, you put a gun in your mouth. You came for me when I had forgotten what it even meant to be me. So if you think that I'm going to stand behind you like the cheerleader in a horror flick, you're out of your mind. We're doing this together. And it's my turn to take the risk. Do you get me, Agent Brody?"

"Claire . . ."

"Do you get me?"

"Yes, ma'am." They stared at each other from inches apart. Then he smiled. "I should probably tell you. Before I came to help I took a really long shower and had a beer."

"Is that right?" She pursed her lips. "Some hero you are."

He stretched his arms up and out, shook out his muscles. Picked up the baseball bat. "Probably better anyway."

"Why?"

"The way it works, the way you sort worlds and everything, you're a natural for it." He paused and smiled. "You know why?"

"Because I'm anal?"

"Because you're anal."

# FORTY-EIGHT

"The trick is not to think of it as moving."

It was early yet, and not many people were up. A woman sat reading *The New York Times*. DeAndre and Patricia lay on a couch, her sleeping body covering him like a blanket. DeAndre had been awake, stroking her hair, and when Brody had winked at him, the teenager had managed to look at once sheepish and triumphant. The never-ending poker game at the sentry station continued, but no one questioned them as they walked past.

They stood on the other side of the river, a block from the Langham. Across the river stood the Marina Towers, what everyone called the corncob buildings. Brody flashed on an old Steve McQueen movie, a car chase that culminated in the King of Cool sending the bad guy's Pontiac hurtling off the building to plummet seventeen floors into the river. The water looked cold in the morning light.

Claire said, "What do you mean, not moving?"

"When we died, we woke up where we had been, right? That's because all the worlds, from life on up, are layers. Once you put that thing on, you'll have the power to shift us between them."

"So I just concentrate on one?"

"The trickiest part was making myself imagine it that way. Once I did, I could see a bunch of layers at the same time. Like a stack of photographs." He paused. "You know, maybe I should—"

Claire flashed him a look that could have cut steel, then pulled the necklace from her pocket. "What's it feel like?"

"Getting electrocuted."

"Thanks for that."

He shrugged.

With a rueful expression, she lifted the knotted leather cord over her head.

The world tilted. Brody snatched for the railing. It was the same stomach-seizing vertigo of a new arrival, only a hundred times stronger. Claire was rigid, her arms out and head thrown back, lips peeled back from her teeth. Every muscle of her body seemed to be clenching at the same time. Across the bridge, the sentries had come alert, clutching weapons and leaping to their feet. In the hotel, curtains were yanked aside, revealing startled faces.

Slowly, slowly, she relaxed. "Oh my god."

"You alright?"

She nodded uncertainly. Held out a hand, and he took it, their fingers lacing. Her grip was strong, the skin rough.

"Okay," he said. "Now try to—"

With a rippling sensation, everything changed. They stood in the same spot, but the world had shifted around them. The clouds were low and black. Wind knifed down the street. The buildings looked worn and battered, as if abandoned to twenty years of rain. Much of the glass was broken. All the people were gone.

"... do that," he said. He looked around. "Jesus. You jumped us further on your first try than I was doing by the end."

"This is amazing," she said. "I've been waiting for this my whole life."

"Okay, that's creepy."

"You know what I mean. It's thought made reality. I can see so many things overlapping." She turned to him. "Can you?"

"No."

"What if you touch the totem?"

He tried it. There was a tingle like static electricity, but nothing compared to the energy that had filled and buoyed him. "No. Built for one, apparently."

Claire moved her jaw side to side, rubbed at the joint. She looked around. "No one came. None of the elders."

"Traveling doesn't do it. The one I saw came after I'd messed around, blown up that building. I think the energy caught his attention. Like striking a match in a dark room." Brody stepped away, glanced around. There was a barge on the river, a flatbed piled with gravel. "You'll need to get the hang of it. Try to tip that over."

When he turned back, he saw that she wasn't looking where he'd pointed.

Her eyes were closed and her hands were out, palm up. A halogen smear of light bloomed in each, spinning energy that was hard to focus on.

"Claire?"

The orbs of light in her hands were like miniature suns, twisting with heat. He couldn't look at them, and he couldn't look away.

"Claire?"

With a cry, she opened her eyes and flung her arms forward. White streaks blurred across the river, missiles bright as noon, casting everything into weird relief. The orbs slammed into the corncob buildings with a sound like artillery firing.

The explosions started at the bottom, a blast of fire that drove concrete and metal in front of it. Another and another and another followed quickly, each higher, rings of flame and smoke chasing each other up sixty stories. The buildings trembled, listing slightly, and then the balconies began to fold inward. Thick smoke rushed outward in billows. There was a roar, and the scream of metal bent to breaking, and then buildings began to collapse. First one and then the other, a hypnotic inward and downward fall, each floor hammering into the one beneath it. The ground trampolined, and the river erupted as five-ton chunks of concrete smashed into it. A cloud of dust raced toward them.

Brody tore his eyes away to stare at Claire. She was smiling. "What?"

"So much for starting slow."

"We wanted to call the sharks, right?"

Yesterday, pacing the restaurant, he'd described the creature he'd seen, the elder. How massive and impossibly powerful it was. How he'd felt like a man in an ocean churning with sharks.

"That's it," she'd said. "That's how we beat him."

"I don't know. From what Isabella said, they're constantly circling each other, never letting down their guard. But I don't think they fight much. Any battle would leave them prey for another."

"And sharks don't usually attack one another . . . unless one is bleeding. Then the others will tear it apart."

It had hit him like a slap. "We don't have to beat him. We just have to lure the others nearby—"

"And make Edmund bleed."

The first step was simple enough. The second they'd have to figure out. Hopefully with the benefit of surprise, and by using his own power against him, they could wound him enough. Spill blood in the existential water, so that other predators finished the job. Then escape in the midst of the feeding frenzy.

It had sounded good. But now his hands shook and his armpits swamped up.

Because it had worked. They were coming.

Seeing one had been bad enough. A man turned monster, an embodiment of raw predatory power. Brody's mind had struggled to even perceive the thing, to focus on it, seeing at one moment a moving mountain with gaping jaws, and in another a savage rider beating his horse past death. As the thing had moved, the world had fallen to ruin behind it, a streak of smoking devastation that swallowed the clouds.

Now, as Brody looked around, he didn't see one.

He saw a dozen.

From every direction they came. Rings of teeth and bleeding gums, hurtling balls of black force. The whole city trembled as they tore through it, buildings canting and streets erupting. The air reeked of scorched metal and burning chemicals. It sounded like an earthquake, like tectonic plates of rock grinding and shearing.

Claire wore a look of pure animal joy. She seemed lifted up by light, swept up in power. She yelled, "It's working!" her voice barely audible.

The beasts were coming. Converging on them from all directions. Tearing this fragile echo apart.

Then something occurred to him. An obvious flaw they should have thought of. "We have to go. Now!"

She turned, confusion in her eyes. "What's the rush? You said the totem kept you safe. That they couldn't harm the person . . ." Suddenly she got it. "Oh. Oh no."

Claire thrust out her hand, and he grabbed it. With her other hand she gripped the totem. She closed her eyes.

Blasts of concussive sound buffeted them from all directions. The world shuddered. Brody squeezed her hand, whirled around. They were coming, these devourers of souls and destroyers of worlds. The river vibrated like a tuning fork. Clouds swirled and sucked inward, tornadoes touching down in every direction. Something black and shifting slammed through the State Street drawbridge, snapping it like a screen door torn off the hinges. The barge he'd seen lifted from the water and spun over their heads like a thrown playing card. He could see the thick algae on the bottom, and the massive anchor trailing a lash of spray. It careened into the high-rise behind them, which began to lean, the upper stories tearing away in a rain of stone. He couldn't hear he couldn't breathe he couldn't move and there was death coming from every direction—

"*Claire!*"

# FORTY-NINE

She had been made of light and fire. When the Marina Towers collapsed the way she'd imagined, a controlled demolition and a rain of stone, she had been filled with a physical joy of such intensity it was almost painful.

Now, as other, older beasts swept in, she realized how small she was. Whatever power Edmund had put in the totem, it was only a fraction of himself.

The ones coming were his equals.

And while she might be protected, they'd tear Brody apart.

She snatched up his hand, wet against her palm, and closed her eyes. Around her, the world was shaken like a rat in a tiger's mouth. She tightened her other hand against the finger bones, smooth and warm.

When Brody had come for her, he had been heading for the last, darkest place. The plains of shadow. But that wouldn't work for them, wouldn't protect them. And it wasn't their goal, anyway.

They had spilled blood in the water and summoned the sharks. Now they had to bring them to Edmund.

*This is not jewelry.*

*It is not a magic necklace.*

*It is* Edmund. *His finger, sawn off by his own will. His power.*

The world bounced and shook. She heard Brody shout her name, but didn't dare open her eyes. Not yet.

*The trick is not to think of it as moving.*

They weren't looking for a place.

They were looking for a man. A man who had become an idea that bent the world around him. She concentrated on the totem. Felt a presence in her mind, like something peering over her shoulder. Grasped at it, focused on it, and on the bones in her hand. The roaring grew louder, her ears ringing, dust whipping her skin like sandpaper.

"Claire, now!"

She focused all her will on the totem. Let it take the wheel while she put a foot on the gas.

Ahead of her she could sense something, a cyclone of furious light and a million rabid mouths racing at them, yards then feet then inches away and she screamed and pushed—

And everything went silent.

She opened her eyes.

The city was gone. The river. The buildings. The funnel clouds and monsters.

Brody gasped and panted and gripped her hand so hard her joints ached.

They were . . . somewhere else.

A room, of sorts, only without walls or ceiling or boundaries. A platform floating in nothing. Around them empty space hung with shining stars. Infinite and twinkling, every constellation in the night sky.

There was a bed, an antique four-poster baroquely carved and draped with silks. In the bed lay an attractive older woman with hair of purest white. Her eyes were closed and her chest rose and fell. Kneeling on the bed beside her was a teenaged boy with long hair. His hands were poised above her throat, as though about to strangle her.

Brody said, "Are you okay?"

She turned to him. "Are you?"

He nodded. All around was silence, and the twinkling of stars. "This . . . is not Chicago." Then his eyes fixed on the woman. "Isabella."

"Who?" Then she remembered. The elder Will had met. The one who had offered to trade her life for the totem. "Then is that—"

Brody nodded. "Edmund. I saw him in the dream Isabella sent me, and again when I killed Simon Tucks."

"It can't be this easy."

"*Easy?*"

"No, listen. I did what I did before, what you did, when we traveled. But instead of looking for an echo, I focused on the totem. I let it drive. So this is . . ." She shrugged.

Brody nodded slowly. "This is the moment before he betrayed her. They were lovers, partners, for a long time. Decades. Then he turned on her."

A ripping crack like a lightning strike. Claire whirled.

Behind them, a shape her mind couldn't process blotted out the stars. Moving. Coming for them.

Another lash of sound, and then another presence, and another.

"It's working," Brody said. "They're following us. But how do we make him bleed? Should I just . . ." He hefted the baseball bat.

"No," she said. "This isn't him. There's more."

"More?"

A wind whipped up, a wind that came from no place but the stars. Cold and mean. Claire said, "Like how when you came for me, you kept going until there weren't any more worlds. There's more."

He nodded, looked around. "Then maybe we should . . ."

But she was already concentrating.

The stars blinked out. The bed hung in nothingness, two ancient predators in the sky. Again she matched her desire to the totem's identity.

They were back in the world. Outdoors. The air was soupy and vegetal with the smell of growing things. There was a river, but not the Chicago River. This one was wide and brown. They were on the outskirts of a city of ornate low buildings. Whitewash and cast-iron railings, thick trees draped with Spanish moss.

A ghostly woman knelt in the water. She was pale and translucent, the world visible through her. Her face was dirty and her cheeks were stained with tears and she held something under the river's surface.

Beside her stood Edmund. He was smiling. A good-looking teenager, a little thin but strong, smiling like he'd gotten the birthday present he'd been dreaming of. In his arms he held a baby.

"This looks like New Orleans." Brody turned a slow circle without releasing her hand. "Sort of."

"A long time ago, I think." Claire stared at Edmund. He was breathing, but not moving. Like a figure in a tableau, or an actor playing freeze.

Brody walked over to them, peered into the water. For a moment he stared, confused, and then he recoiled, one hand clutched to his mouth.

"What is it?"

"She's . . . the woman . . . she's drowning a . . ." He looked at Edmund, at the baby in his hands, face twisted up in a silent squall. "He must have ridden her like he rode Simon, and convinced her to drown her son."

"These aren't echoes," Claire said. "They're memories. The moments that made him."

The river began to ripple and shake. Brody said, "They're coming. Keep going."

Claire had gotten the hang of it now. It was a matter of at once relaxing and concentrating. Like yoga, remaining calm while also engaging her muscles. She provided the impetus, and the totem provided the destination.

Without moving, they went through place after place. Around them the world changed as they journeyed deeper into Edmund's self. Each place a memory, some vital component of his being.

Each a nightmare.

An African American man, six feet tall and muscular. His back a mass of gore, like he had been whipped to death. Edmund held him in the air by his throat. At his feet, indolent as if recently fed, lay a lion, a huge male with a full mane.

Next they stood on a plateau dotted with twisted trees. They were squat, ugly things, all bent in one direction as if by wind that never ceased. A Native American in full war regalia sat atop a horse. The man's face was lean and hard, painted with streaks of grease. His eyes sparked red, and Edmund recoiled from him, hands up. He looked frightened.

Then came a primitive village of thatched huts, domes that stood beneath a clouded sky. In the doorway of one of the huts lay a man's body, a knife in his chest. Thirty feet away a woman was pinned to the ground. Her head was tipped back in pain. Edmund lay astride her, his legs scissoring hers open.

Claire couldn't take her eyes off the woman's face.

She was staring sideways. Looking at the dead man, Claire realized. Her husband? If so, Edmund had killed him and then raped her in sight of his corpse.

It was one thing to know, intellectually, that he was a monster. She'd had more than enough motivation to hate Edmund just based on Simon Tucks.

The innocent lives stolen, nurses and cab drivers and marketing executives. A young girl shot in front of her father. And then the damage Tucks had done in the echo, the woman burned alive, the forty-three good people who had died buying them time to kill him.

It wasn't that moving through Edmund's memories made her hate him more. It was that it gave her a fuller context. The wide-angle lens to just how much damage he had done. The savagery and horror he had spread across the centuries.

The ground began to tremble. Brody said, "They're still with us."

She forced herself to look away. Took a deep breath. Let it out, took another.

For the first time, though, shifting didn't come easily. The process was the same, and she could sense the destination ahead of her. But as she pushed for it, something pushed back. Before, it had been like stepping through curtains. This time it was a wall.

*It's the last one,* she realized. Beyond this was Edmund himself. The real one, not the avatars of his memories.

The totem grew hot in her hand. Her animal brain screamed to let go, but instead she gripped tighter and looked at the woman on the ground. Violated near the body of her husband. Had she prayed for help? Had she screamed to the universe, begging for someone, anyone, to kill this monster?

*I'm sorry we were too late to save you. But we can avenge you.*

*Do you hear me, Edmund? We're coming to end you.*

There was a sudden yielding, and a sensation of falling. She staggered.

Heat lashed her skin. Claire squinted against brilliant light. Cobalt blue and burning white.

Blue sky, and white sun.

*My god. The sun.*

Claire stared upward, let the light warm her face. She'd almost forgotten what blue looked like. The sky was perfect, unmarred horizon to horizon. The world bobbed around them.

It was the ocean.

They stood on the deck of an old wooden ship. It had been badly damaged, the masts just jagged splinters, the rigging in tatters. The ship heeled drunkenly. Though much of it was underwater, it didn't seem to be sinking. Water lapped at the side, soft and susurrant.

Beyond there was nothing but blue. The feverish sky and the chilling navy of deep ocean. Waves slid and rolled, making the ship bob and surf. Sunlight—sunlight!—sparkled like diamonds on the crests.

In each previous reality they'd visited, they'd arrived near Edmund. Spectators at a grotesque tableau. This was the last place, she could feel it.

But they were alone. Marooned on a broken ship in the middle of an ocean under a blast furnace sky.

"I know where we are," Brody said.

# FIFTY

*A broken ship on an endless ocean. A boy, chewing smoked meat.*

"Edmund was a sailor," Brody said, "on a ship called *Persephone*. There was a storm. When they ran out of food, they ate the dead. When they ran out of bodies, Edmund started killing."

He knelt down, touched the wooden deck. The boards were smooth and tightly fitted. His shadow was drawn in sharp relief. The sun made everything so real. Somehow the fact that the echo existed in clouds and shadow had kept it from ever feeling whole. "I wonder if it drove him mad, or if he already was when he got on the boat."

Claire said, "Where is he?"

Brody straightened, looked around. The ship was low in the water, the aft section dipping under the waves. "You're sure this is the last memory?"

"Never done this before." Claire shrugged. "Yeah, I'm pretty sure."

Brody understood what she meant. He'd used the totem himself, knew that like everything else here, it came without instructions. But Claire had picked it up far faster than he had, and with far greater effect. If she said they were at the end, that's where they were.

Yet Edmund was nowhere to be seen, and their plan, sketchy as it was, depended on finding him. They had to face him. Was he hiding, somehow? Perhaps he'd sensed them coming, and chosen not to fight.

*No. Frightened people hide. Five-hundred-year-old apex predators do not. He should be waiting right here . . .*

Wait a minute. "Maybe we've been thinking of it wrong. We've been picturing finding Edmund. But maybe he's beyond 'where.'"

"Explain."

"Think about it. Where are we? One version of me is in a coffin. Another is on the couch in my loft with the back of my head blown off. And yet here we are, standing on the deck of a ship." Brody watched a seagull drift on thermals. "'Where' is starting to seem like a bit of a meaningless concept."

"I see your point." Claire sucked her lip between her teeth. The sun beat down. "We've been moving through his memories, formative experiences made physical. This is the end of that chain. But it's basically the first memory. The primary one. For all intents, Edmund was born on this ship. The handful of years he was alive don't mean anything. This is where he became what he is." She paused. "I don't think we're in the echo. I think we're in Edmund."

*Jesus.* It was a hideous idea, but it fit. On the way here, they'd been too busy running to think. But she was right. When he journeyed to the plains of shadow, he'd stayed in the same physical location. The world had faded around him, but he hadn't moved. But with each shift here, they'd been to different places. On the banks of the Mississippi. On a wind-blasted tundra, facing a man whose eyes glowed red. Even in an impossible room hanging in the sky. "The totem *is* Edmund, part of him, at least. So when we followed it, it brought us into . . . what? His psyche?"

"Maybe," Claire said. "The elders are all about power and will, right? Maybe after hundreds of years of living that way, their will becomes their world. They live inside it."

Brody thought of the monstrous shapes that had pursued them, the moving mountains and many-mouthed hurricanes. Predators that traversed worlds and toppled buildings in their wake. "I guess it was silly to imagine him chilling with his feet up. Okay. We came looking for Edmund. And we found him. This is his heart." He tapped the baseball bat against the deck of the ship. "So then all we have to do—"

Claire grinned savagely. "Is tear this world apart."

# FIFTY-ONE

She had never been a plate thrower. Never punched a mirror, or hurled a glass at the wall.

In fact, before today, Claire couldn't remember a moment that she had consciously smashed something. It just wasn't her nature. The closest she could think of was the private joy she'd always felt on snowy days, when she would come upon a parking lot or a playground covered in pure and unbroken white. How there had been a delight in stomping across it, feeling the crust snap beneath her feet, the flurry of snow as she kicked. It was the chance to destroy something beautiful without any guilt.

But blowing up the Marina Towers had been fun.

It had happened just how she'd imagined. She'd pictured a video of a skyscraper in a controlled demolition. How charges had been set throughout the building, impeccably timed, mathematically calculated. How floor after floor had blown, the backbone of the building shattered so precisely that the thing collapsed in on itself. Countless tons of cement seeming to hang for a moment before succumbing to gravity. The flash of light and the roar of force and the flashing billows of smoke.

She'd pictured that, held it center of her mind's eye, then conjured pure energy in her palms and unleashed it. It had been a rush unlike anything she'd ever known. A joy like the fraction of a second before orgasm when she knew it was about to happen.

*Yes. But it nearly killed Will.*

He'd been unprotected. The totem that had shielded her had left him standing alone.

"It's okay," he said, as if reading her mind. "Do it."

Could she? Could she sacrifice this man like a chess piece, just to win? Of course not.

But on the heels of that thought came another. Everywhere else, the totem had been an extension of Edmund's strength. It had drawn on the energy he had collected. Something she could tap into across a distance.

If they were right, then there was no distance now.

"Try something," she said. "Hold the totem again."

"We tried that—"

"We tried it out there. Now we're in Edmund's heart. This is where his power comes from."

Brody shrugged. Stepped forward and put a hand to her chest to cover the necklace.

They both gasped.

She flashed on last night, the way the two of them had made love slowly. Teasing, easing, moving so gently that it was hard to tell where one began and the other ended. It was like that, but instead of their bodies, it was their minds. Their spirits, or souls, whatever name one wanted to put to it.

It was them. The essence of them. Not her, not him. Them.

It had often felt, even back when they were alive, like the connection they shared was deeper than just attraction and conversation. Deeper than like minds. It had felt like they had known each other for years. For lifetimes.

*And maybe,* she thought, *we have.*

They stared at one another, adrift on a broken ship in the imagination of a beast. Locked in communication—communion—unlike any she'd dreamed of. She could feel his strength flow into her. Feel him put his back to her burden. Together, what couldn't they do?

"Do it," he said. "Just like with the buildings. A controlled demolition. Snap his spine and bring him down."

Claire took a deep breath, and remembered.

Remembered every victim of the sniper, nurses and cab drivers and parents. Living human beings reduced to data in her files. She could picture their autopsy photos, rattle off every birthday.

Remembered standing over the torn body of Will Brody on a metal table. Remembered a woman whose name she'd never known screaming as she burned in the heart of an inferno. Remembered a slave whipped to death three hundred years ago, reborn only to die again. Remembered a woman pinned to the ground and raped while the body of her husband lay feet away.

She remembered it all, every face, every horror. Focused on them, felt them. Channeled them, imagining a beam of white light tearing the heavens. Imagining blue sky shredding and peeling, the seas boiling, the world collapsing in on itself. Tumbling down just like the Marina Towers.

When she had it, when she could see it in every detail, she set it free.

It lashed out, perfect and sharp, a brilliant beam hurtling upward like a spotlight. Crackling with electricity and smelling of rain. Ten feet across and built of blameless fury. Like a spear that punctured the sky.

*We're coming for you, Edmund.*

———

It was the most intimate thing he'd ever experienced.

Standing in front of her, his hand pressed to her chest, to the necklace of bones but also to the warm flesh below. He could feel her strength, taste her rage. He could see what she was planning as clearly as if it was him visualizing it, and as she did, he poured all he could into it. A tub of melting ice cream on dirty concrete. A rainbow sun born in a dark church. Simon lifting Claire up by her hair. Brody on his knees in the real world, knowing her body lay invisible just feet away. The taste of a gun in his mouth. All the things that should never be allowed to happen. The horrors for which there were no adequate explanations.

When the spear of light launched outward, the whole world jumped. A shriek rose from everywhere and nowhere at once, directionless, eternal, brutal as a mouthful of broken glass. He was every tiny mortal who had stared in wondering horror at things larger than themselves. A primitive hunter fleeing a snarling forest fire. A man on a beach watching the tsunami sweep in. A child outside Hiroshima seeing a mushroom cloud blossom.

Because the sky
was looking
at them.
And it was angry.

His skin tightened and every hair stood at attention in a moment of claustrophobic terror. They were alone on a shattered boat in an endless ocean that only existed in the mind of a monster. And they had woken him.

Storm clouds coalesced from nowhere. Thick and roiling, blotting out the blue. A sudden gale tugged at his clothing and whipped the waves, gentle swells turning grey and mean, tipped in white.

The spear of light tore into the heavens, into Edmund, opening a wound, a hole that spread outward, shoving the clouds aside. The edges of the hole rippled with light, expanding, consuming what they touched. Behind the sky was nothing.

Not blackness. Nothing.

*It's working.*

Brody could feel Edmund's shock, his rage. He thrashed like a beast in a pool, and around them the world reflected it. The ship began to roll with the waves. The wind carried spray.

And a dozen feet away, where the ship met the sea, something thrust out of the water.

A hand, gripping the wooden planking. And then another.

Something was pulling itself out of the deep.

———

Claire was the last straining lift of a long set of weights. The split-second tension of an almost car crash. She was force and potential. The more she used the power, the more she understood it. It was the collected promise of thousands of lives. It was pure creation, raw force that she could focus however she wished. She could have used it to build worlds, to shape cities.

She used it to kill its master.

Where the beam hit the sky, the abyss opened in an expanding circle. First it was the width of the spear, but quickly it was devouring the sky, feeding on it, spreading to cover half of the heavens.

And between sky and nothing, she could see motion. Predatory ripples and the flash of teeth. The others like Edmund. The elders. Beasts that cared nothing for life or love or one another.

That cared only for hunger. That had come to feed on one of their own.

It was working.

Until Brody let go of her.

——

Brody stared at the hands on the edge of the deck. Feeling the shiver of lifting a rock and seeing the squirming life beneath, the blind and crawling things that do not know daylight.

A dead man pulled himself out of the ocean.

His skin hung in ribbons. Seaweed stuck to a scalp grown patchy and rotten. The rags he wore were old and faded. His face was a horror of fish-eaten flesh.

The corpse hauled itself aboard. Its empty eye sockets turned to face them.

Behind it, more hands rose. Dozens. Hundreds. Creatures pulling themselves from the depth of Edmund's psyche. The souls that he had taken across the centuries. The stories he had consumed. Some part of them lived inside him now—and they obeyed.

Brody looked at Claire. She was rigid, every muscle and thought engaged in attack. He could feel her savage concentration. She was focusing on every horror they had seen, every atrocity Edmund was responsible for, and directing all of it back at him. A blast of righteous ferocity driven like a wedge to split the sky.

In the abyss above he could see the others circling. Probing at the edges of the hole, making the clouds ripple like claws scraping canvas. The elders were almost in. When they slithered into Edmund's secret heart, they would tear him apart.

But they weren't in yet. And if those dead things reached Claire, it would all be for nothing. Maybe they could hurt her, maybe not, but at the very least they would distract her, split her focus.

Brody let go of the totem and hefted the baseball bat.

Four quick steps across the pitching deck brought him in range of the dead sailor. It had no eyes, but it swiveled to face him nonetheless, hissing and lunging.

Brody swung, and the bat met the thing's skull with shattering force. He didn't wait, just spun and swung the other direction, this time into the dead thing's chest, feeling ribs crack like kindling. It toppled into the sea with a splash.

Others took its place.

Brody tuned out everything else. Tuned out the rolling seas and the hole in the sky. There was nothing but the fight. Nothing but the baseball bat in his hand and the muscles of his body. Striking, dodging, shoving. Weaving patterns of whistling aluminum.

A spin, a plant, a swing. The crack of bone, the spatter of blood and seawater. A woman missing half of her head lunged at him. Her fingernails, ragged and filthy, tore into his cheek. He head-butted her backward, then swung. The force of his blow lifted her off her feet.

Panting, he took a moment to look around.

Corpses rose on every side. Skeletal hands gripped every edge of the boat. Hundreds of dead. The souls Edmund had taken into himself across centuries.

And beyond them, the sea was churned to froth with others.

———

She wanted to yell to him, to scream, to tell him to return to the safety of the totem. But it took all of her energy to maintain the attack. All she could do was watch, out of the periphery of her consciousness, as he faced the horrors Edmund had dragged up from the deep.

Brody took one down with ease, then a second. A vicious blow knocked a third into two that came behind it.

The corpses were slow and weak, almost hesitant. As though unwilling, or imperfectly understood. Despite their numbers, Brody was managing to hold them back.

*Then why would Edmund send them?*

The answer was obvious. She felt it coming. There was the reek of ozone, but it wasn't that. She could sense it. Knew that the corpses were a distraction to separate them, and to mask the real attack. There was no time to think, to weigh consequences.

As lightning ripped downward, Claire flung herself in front of Brody.

The death meant for him instead lashed her.

A billion volts of electricity. Her body rang like a steel plate hit by a bullet. The totem crackled against her chest, searing so hot that her flesh blackened and peeled. Conscious thought scattered like papers in a hurricane. There was nothing but pain. She hung in a state of perfect agony like a martyr of old. Pure white wiped away the world. Her fingers seized and joints sparked and lips spasmed.

But the scream came from something else.

# FIFTY-TWO

A rip of thunder knocked Brody off his feet. He was swept up in white. Lived inside the pure brilliance of the lightning.

There was a scream Brody could sense more than hear. Sandpaper stroking a bare nerve.

Then it was gone, the electricity and the scream and the blinding white.

The dead men and the circling monsters.

The ship, and the sky, and the sea.

Brody was in a white room. He blinked, tried to focus. The walls were white, the floor polished hardwood.

"Will?"

He whirled. Claire stood on the other side of a low coffee table. There was a comfortable-looking couch behind her, grey fabric with yellow throw pillows. Above it was an open window. Trees swayed in the breeze, their leaves whispering.

"What happened?"

"I don't know," Claire said. "He was trying to separate us. Get you away from the totem."

"The lightning," Brody said. "I felt it hit you. Hit us."

"I tried to block it," she said. She stared around the living room. "Where are we?"

"I don't know." The room was airy and bright. He didn't recognize it, but he liked it. There was a fireplace framed in painted bricks, and candles along a side table. An abstract painting on one wall, a riot of colors. Sunlight through the windowpane caught dust motes dancing in the air. "Maybe the lightning killed us. All the way this time."

"I don't think so," Claire said. "I think maybe he sent us somewhere. Sidelined us."

Brody squeezed the handle of the baseball bat, glad to still have it. He felt like a man about to wake from a dream, that sense that he was in two places at once, and believing in both of them. "Let's see if we can find him."

Claire nodded. Her fingers were on the totem, rubbing it gently. Brody led the way, bat at the ready.

A sliding glass door was open to a small but pleasant backyard. There was a patio set and a barbecue grill. A hammock slung between two trees. The ground was carpeted in red and yellow, and a neighbor must have been burning leaves, filling the air with a campfire scent.

The kitchen was bright and clean. A breakfast nook was tucked in the corner, the booth alive with dancing sunlight. A large cutting board covered one counter, and the gas stove had six burners. The pantry was a cluttered, homey chaos of canned goods and baking supplies. Brody opened a cabinet, saw glasses and stemware. In another, he found pans stacked up. He pulled out a heavy cast-iron skillet. It was beautifully seasoned, the bottom glistening and a faint smell of oil to it. "It's like whoever lives here just stepped out."

"This doesn't seem like Edmund."

"No."

The dining room was warm and inviting. A farmhouse table glowed with polish. Brody ran his fingers along it as he passed, tracing the cool texture. One entire wall was given over to floor-to-ceiling bookshelves, thousands of hardcovers and paperbacks. The opposite wall was covered in framed photos, neatly arranged. Brody looked at them, did a double take. "Hey."

The pictures were of them.

Claire in a café, smiling over a coffee mug, the steam rising.

Brody and his father bent over the chessboard, a bottle of bourbon beside them, cigars in their hands.

He and Claire on a beach somewhere, the shot obviously a selfie. He had two-day scruff and a tan. She wore an electric-blue bikini and an indolent, sun-stoned smile.

Claire at some sort of press event or award ceremony, shaking hands with the director of the FBI.

Brody in bed, apparently asleep in a tangle of white sheets, his hair mussed and sunlight spilling in.

Photos that had never been taken, in moments they'd never lived.

Claire moved down the row of pictures, leaning in to study them. "Oh. Oh god."

"What?"

She drew a shuddering breath and turned to him. Pointed at a frame. He strode over to see.

It was a picture of her, looking pale and exhausted. Her hair matted with sweat. Lying in a hospital bed.

With a newborn baby on her chest.

Brody gripped the baseball bat until his bones ached.

The next picture was him holding up a baby girl in a purple onesie. He had her at arm's length and must have been spinning her. The grin on his face didn't look like the one he saw in the mirror. It was wider and purer and lit with emotion he could only imagine.

This was the life they might have had.

The life they'd only begun to dream about. This home was like the one they might have made together. These were the books they might have read in bed. That was the kitchen he could have cooked in.

This was the little girl they never got a chance to meet.

The offer was clear enough.

*And to earn it, all we have to do is ignore the things we know he's done. Just look the other way and let evil get back to business.*

They stared at each other. A gaze beyond words.

Then Claire turned and started walking, and he followed. There were stairs in the front hallway. She started up them slowly. Moving as though she were walking toward a cliff. The wooden stairs creaked beneath their weight. A familiar, cozy sound.

At the top, Claire paused. Looked in each direction. Steeled herself, and chose the hard one.

The room was flooded with sunlight. The walls were painted seafoam green, all except one, which was covered in chalkboard paint covered in scribbles, doodles and smiley faces and the alphabet. The ceiling was peaked and airy. There was a white dresser, and a bin of stuffed animals.

In the center of the room, in a beam of light, was the crib.

Nothing elaborate, no brand names or intricate woodwork. Just a bright wooden crib. A mobile of paper birds spun above it. In the crib lay a small purple cloth with the head of a hippo on it. A lovey.

Claire sobbed, once. A chest-deep sound.

"I thought we should talk," said a voice from behind them.

## FIFTY-THREE

Brody whirled, raising the baseball bat.

Standing in the doorway was a teenaged boy. His hair fell to his shoulders in waves. His face was slightly androgynous, his cheeks soft and beardless. He looked something like a Caravaggio angel—except for the missing finger on his right hand.

"You fucker," Brody said. "You evil fucker."

Edmund cocked his head. "Why? Isn't this everything you've ever wanted?"

"You can't think we'll take it," Claire said through clenched teeth.

"I really think you should," Edmund said. He strolled into the room, sat in a rocking chair in the corner. "It's the best you'll get."

"No," Brody said. "Killing you is the best we'll get."

Edmund smiled. "You think I'm offering this because I'm frightened."

"You should be," Claire said. "We're winning."

"No," the boy said, with a soft laugh. "No, you're not. It was a noble effort, but there's no chance of success."

"Then why try to buy us off?"

"While you hold my totem, I can't simply destroy you," Edmund said. "But I can fight this battle for as long as it takes, while you're here on borrowed strength. Eventually, I'll wear you down. However, it will cost me a great deal of energy. Energy I collected over a long time. Far simpler to just give you what you want. It's what your contemporaries would call a cost-benefit analysis."

Brody wanted to argue. Wanted to beat his chest and rage.

Because Edmund was right.

Their best chance of winning relied on surprise. They had no power here. The only weapon they had belonged to their enemy. When they'd first attacked him, it had seemed like there was hope. But as soon as the dead had begun to pull themselves from the sea, Brody had known it was over. They were insurgents in an enemy's stronghold, and now that the moment of surprise was past, they were wildly outgunned.

He'd kept fighting because that's what there was to do. Not because he thought they would win.

As if reading his thoughts, Edmund said, "The damage you've done isn't nearly enough to tempt the others to risk facing me. You are in my world. I make the rules. You cannot hide beneath the protection my totem affords while using its power to attack me. And without that protection, I'll wipe you from existence." Edmund smiled beatifically. "Why not spare yourselves?"

"Take the bribe, you mean." Claire shook her head. "Even if we were willing, do you think we could live with ourselves afterward? What you've built here is a fantasy. Knowing the price would poison it."

"I can remove the memories of your time here. All of this will seem like a dream. As if you never died at all."

Was it possible? Brody supposed so. Isabella had made bolder offers. He imagined it for a moment. Not only returning to life, but forgetting all they'd learned. Going back to the happy ignorance of the living. Worrying about bills and sex, instead of dark gods that arranged atrocities. Forgetting the long fade to the plains of shadow, and not discovering it until they were walking it properly.

"Don't let pride compel you." Edmund leaned forward. "If you continue to fight, I will annihilate you. And your sacrifice will mean nothing."

Brody imagined stepping forward, swinging the bat at this smug monster's head. Shattering his skull and painting the wall with his blood. Impossible, he knew. Edmund would never make himself vulnerable in that way. The boy in the chair wasn't really him.

Edmund was the world. The sea and the sky and the ship. The army of the dead. This house, manifested out of nothing, and perfectly tailored to them.

How could they fight that kind of power?

"What would you know," Claire said softly, "about sacrifice?"

"A great deal." Edmund smiled.

"That's taking," she said. "Sacrifice is giving. It's me stepping in front of the lightning."

Brody remembered the flash of blinding white. The roar of electricity. What an incredible thing she had done. No hesitation, no faltering. She'd simply thrown herself between him and death. He remembered the scream—

Wait. That scream.

It hadn't been Claire. He'd felt it, not heard it. It had been a visceral thing. It had been the world screaming. Edmund screaming.

*Of course. He summoned the lightning bolt to kill you. It never occurred to him that Claire would put herself between it and you.*

The Eater mentality, all over again. Just like with Isabella. No trust, no faith. No belief in anything. No love you would die for.

No love you would die for.

The very concept was foreign to Edmund. For five hundred years he'd practiced nothing but predation. The notion of willing sacrifice was completely foreign. Valuing something more highly than his own survival simply wouldn't occur to him. It was a blind spot in his mind.

And a blind spot could be exploited.

What had he said? *You cannot hide beneath the protection my totem affords while using its power to attack me.*

Maybe there was a way to win after all.

Brody felt a smile creeping onto his face. He had to find a way to communicate the idea to Claire. He looked over at her, trying to put it in his eyes, ready to mouth—

And saw that she was already there. She'd worked it out before he had. Of course. That was why she'd said the thing about the lightning. It had been a cue to get them on the same page. And now that he'd caught up with her, she was waiting to see if he was game. Knowing the path, but unwilling to make the decision for him. They would do it together or not at all.

*I love you, Claire McCoy.*

Brody said, "Okay."

Edmund smiled. "Excellent." He stood, stepped forward, one hand out.

Claire grabbed the necklace of bones and jerked hard. The leather thong snapped. "Find me in the next life?"

Brody nodded. "Nothing could stop me."

She smiled. Without taking her eyes from his, she flipped the totem across the room.

The necklace arced slow, a tail of leather unfurling behind.

Brody cocked the bat and unwound with all he had.

A clean, smooth motion.

The metal bat caught the bones square.

They didn't break.

They exploded.

And the world tore open.

The house flickered and vanished. They were back on the boat, the *Persephone* bobbing in a wild sea. But there were no dead men this time. And this time, they weren't alone.

Edmund stood at the prow of the ship. Still a teenager, but no longer a Caravaggio angel. His hair was greasy. His arms were thin. His delicate lips were wide in a shriek, a howl like a thousand hurricanes as he stared upward—where a jagged rent split the sky from horizon to horizon.

Nightmares piled through it. Beings of pure force and hunger. So massive that they could barely be conceived, much less comprehended. So powerful they could not be withstood.

It was like watching an avalanche, all sense of scale swept away. A rushing wave of black energy, rolling, tumbling, spinning. Sweeping everything before it. Moving at impossible speeds. A wall that grew ever closer, a defined edge beyond which there was nothing but destruction.

It slammed into Edmund. It bore him up and tore him apart. Hungry shadow mouths with vicious teeth. The wail that rose wasn't a sound or a taste or a feeling. It was all of them at once. A shriek of pure panic. Of disbelief and horror.

It was five hundred years of predation being ripped apart by its own kind.

The avalanche didn't even slow.

Brody dropped the bat and turned to Claire. They locked hands and locked eyes. Two lovers in the path of destruction they could not avoid. A path they'd chosen willingly. Together until the very last moment. Unsure what came next.

But facing it together.

Just before everything went away, they smiled.

*I have been here before,*
*But when or how I cannot tell:*
*I know the grass beyond the door,*
*The sweet keen smell,*
*The sighing sound, the lights around the shore.*

*You have been mine before,—*
*How long ago I may not know:*
*But just when at that swallow's soar*
*Your neck turn'd so,*
*Some veil did fall,—I knew it all of yore.*

*Has this been thus before?*
*And shall not thus time's eddying flight*
*Still with our lives our love restore*
*In death's despite,*
*And day and night yield one delight once more?*

*—Dante Gabriel Rossetti*

# FIFTY-FOUR

The sign had come down the week before.

He'd been up in the tree, working on the fort, when a woman arrived in a grey car. The trunk had opened, and she'd gone to the sign stuck in the front lawn and started wiggling it. A few minutes later, she'd freed it from the ground and put it in her trunk. Then she'd driven away.

He'd gone back to work. At this point, the fort was pretty simple, just a couple of 2 x 4s between the broadest limbs. He'd put a lot of thought into it, though, and knew what he wanted to do. First, finish the platform. Then build a spy spot in the very upper boughs, probably just like a shelf nailed in the crook of them. The tree was big, and swayed with the breeze, and he figured the spy spot would be a lot of fun to sit in, like surfing the wind. Maybe add some ropes too, big thick ones like jungle vines, for swinging between the branches or sliding to the ground.

Unfortunately, all of these plans required stuff he didn't have. He'd raided all the scrap lumber in the garage. Dad had said he'd take him to the hardware store when he had the money, but it would take a long time on his allowance.

So for now all he could do was sit on the 2 x 4s, which is what he was doing, reading a fantasy novel, when he heard a rumbling sound. A big yellow truck turned the corner and rolled down their block. It pulled up to the house across the street, and men climbed down, began opening the side doors and extending a ramp from the back. A minute later, a regular car pulled into the driveway, and a family climbed out.

He watched for a few minutes. Then tucked the book into the waistband of his Levi's and climbed down.

In the house, Mom was in the kitchen, NPR on in the background. "Hey kiddo. Want a sandwich?"

"No thanks." He pulled himself up on a stool. "New neighbors are here."

"Oh yeah?" She mashed tuna fish and mayonnaise together. "Any kids?"

"Girls."

"Your age?"

He shrugged. "One of them, I guess."

Mom smiled. The radio story changed to the sniper. Normally he thought the news was pretty boring, but he liked hearing about that. It was the ten-year anniversary, and they'd been talking about it a lot.

It was scary in an interesting way. Partly because Mom and Dad had a story about it. Mom had told him a million times, how most of the gas stations had been wrapped in tarps, but how she'd had to pull into one that wasn't because her car was empty. How Dad had come over and offered to pump the gas for her. How they'd started talking, sitting on the floorboards of her car, and how she'd known right then that they were going to fall in love and get married.

It was interesting trying to picture the city like that, all turned upside down. Sometimes walking to Sean's house he pretended that the sniper was still out there. Aiming at him. It gave him a shiver like the horror movies Sean's mom let them watch.

"Mom, can I please have some money?"

She laughed. "What for?"

"I need to buy wood for the fort."

"What about your allowance?"

"It's gonna take forever."

"Patience is good for the soul," she said. "Builds character."

"But I'm *bored*."

"Toughsky poopsky," she said. "Why don't you go across the street and introduce yourself?"

"I told you, they're girls."

"So? Girls don't bite."

"They don't play anything fun, though."

Mom looked up from her sandwich. "Kid. You're bothering me. Go make a friend. That's an order."

"Fine," he said, and jumped off the stool.

The men were busy unloading the truck. It was packed full. Weird seeing all that stuff that was normally in a house stacked on top of itself in a truck. He stood and watched the men work.

"Hello."

The voice came from behind him, and he jumped. It was the older girl. She was skinny, her arms thin inside a T-shirt with an enormous cartoon mouth on it, the tongue sticking out. "Hi," he said.

"You live here?"

"There." He pointed over his shoulder. He thought he should say something else, but wasn't sure what. "Cool shirt."

"You like the Stones?"

"What?"

"A lot of people say *Sticky Fingers* is the best, but I prefer *Let It Bleed*." She wore braces, and spoke in that lips-covering way girls with braces did. He had no idea what she was talking about. "Were you up in the tree?"

"Yeah," he said. "I'm building a fort."

"Cool."

"I don't have much yet. Wanna see?" He led the way across the street. At the base of the tree, he pointed up. "It's just the frame now."

"Can we go up?"

He looked at her, then back at the frame, fifteen feet off the ground. "Well, I don't have a ladder yet—"

She was hanging from the lowest branch and swinging her legs. It took two tries, but then she got a foot over and pulled herself up. She rose slowly, her legs shaking as she eased up the trunk to grab the next branch.

Huh.

He followed, the bark rough against his palms. By the time he'd reached the frame, she was already sitting on one of the boards, her legs kicking. "This is really cool."

"It will be. This is going to be a big platform. I want to put on a roof too, so I can come up here in the rain. But I need more wood."

She cocked her head as if thinking. "I'm pretty sure we have some."

"Really?"

"In the old house, anyway. I could ask my dad if we can have it."

He noticed the "we," wasn't sure how he felt about it. He'd planned to build the tree house himself. *But she climbed up here on her own. And you could start building right away.* "That'd be awesome."

A gust of wind kicked up. They both gripped 2 x 4s as the tree swayed. He loved the feeling, the gentle rock, the shush of the leaves, the way the breeze tingled on his skin. It always made him grin. When he looked at her, he was surprised to see she was smiling too, not seeming scared at all.

"Honey?" It was the mom from across the street, standing on the porch with her hands cupped around her mouth. "Where are you?"

"Oops," the girl said. "Gotta go." She lowered herself to the next branch, then hung from it and dropped five or six feet to the ground. "Coming!" She started across the lawn.

"Hey," he said. "Wait."

She turned.

"What's your name?"

The girl smiled, revealing her braces. "Claire. What's yours?"

# ACKNOWLEDGMENTS

This one was a beast.

In one form or another, in napkin scraps and dream fragments, I've been haunted by *Afterlife* for almost a decade. It has changed shape a thousand times, spent months hiding from me only to tug at my shirttails when I tried to turn away. Without a lot of talented help, this book would not exist, and I am deeply grateful to all who lent a hand.

Very few agents get down in the mud and help wrestle an idea, but Shane Salerno did, starting with naming the damn thing before I'd written a word. Thanks for the passion, the support, and the tireless acumen, brother—chess, not checkers. Thanks also to Jon Cassir and Matt Snyder of CAA; a tougher trifecta you'd be hard pressed to find.

My editor Alison Dasho is also my friend Alison Dasho, and it's honestly hard to say for which I'm more delighted. She's been a guiding voice in my work for eight books, and I hope will be for all to come. Love you, FF.

The entire team at Thomas and Mercer is exceptional, and it's a privilege to publish with them. Special thanks to Jeff Belle, Mikyla Bruder, Gracie Doyle, Jacque Ben-Zekry, Laura Costantino, Shasti O'Leary Soudant, Oisin O'Malley, Chrissy Wiley, Laura Barrett, Gabrielle Guarnero, and Sarah Shaw.

Over last-second weekends and hours-long phone calls, through the days good and bad, via decadent dinners and inadvisable bar tabs, my friends Sean Chercover and Blake Crouch have had my back every minute. Perhaps someday one of them will write something worth reading.

Thanks to Michael Cook for terrific notes and much needed distraction and especially for being Uncle Michael.

Librarians and booksellers and teachers everywhere—you're undersung heroes in the only war that matters. Keep fighting.

Thanks to my mother and father and brother, for loving me so completely, and for raising me to believe that both stories and people matter.

My wife G.G. is my person and my partner, my luck and my love. For you baby. Twenty years is just the start of always.

Jossie, daughter and fellow dreamer, when you're old enough to read this book, I hope you don't wonder what was wrong with your old man. But I'm certain that you will know then, as you do now, that I love you more than the universe.

Finally, as I said on the first page—I get to do what I love because of you, dear reader. I am so grateful. Thank you.

# READER GROUP QUESTIONS FOR MARCUS SAKEY'S *AFTERLIFE*

1. Do you believe that the universe created/described by the author is ultimately hopeful or bleak? Why?

2. Would you take comfort in the idea that your loved ones may be physically near you, but existing in the echo?

3. What parallels do you see between the echo and the living world?

4. At the edge of the abyss, in the deepest level of the echo, we see the last sparks of life from all the shuffling husks of people rise up and disappear. What do you think happens to them? Do they flicker out entirely? Are they reborn? Sent to judgment? Where do they go?

5. Did you see a message of unity in these pages, or a message of individualism?

6. The theme of sacrifice is woven throughout the narrative. At key points, characters willingly make sacrifices—who, and to what end? What does this tell us about their moral centers?

7. What purpose does "living" someone's story serve, when a

character kills in the echo? Could it be a kind of cosmic check/ balance system, to discourage killing for energy?

8. How did Brody and Claire's relationship contribute to the ultimate resolution? Could either of them have succeeded alone against the gods in the echo?

9. Do you get the sense that Brody and Claire have done this all before, and will do it all again? What about their connection allows them to come together time and again in the living world?

10. The Disciples of Ray build a community in the echo, and care for one another. They actively seek new arrivals to offer them protection. But we never meet Ray—she's faded before Brody arrives in the echo. Why do you think Sakey kept her off the page, when her influence is such an important part of the echo?

11. Was Edmund born evil, or could he have become someone else, if shown kindness before his death?

12. The gods of the afterlife shown here are really people, just grown enormously powerful. Do you believe that still leaves room for a true god, a divinity? If so, why would that god create or permit the echo?

13. Can "good" gods exist in the echo, or is the system of taking energy mutually exclusive with benevolence? If "good" gods cannot exist, is there a check on the evil ones?

14. If the echo were real, where do you think the best places would be? What about the worst?

15. If you found yourself in the echo, what would you do? What kind of life would you make for yourself there?

16. Who was your favorite character, and why?

17. The desire to uncover and understand a motivation for heinous acts is one of the themes at the heart of this novel. In fact, the question "Why?" is central to human existence. Do you look to literature to help answer that question for you? What other books, movies, or stories have given you glimpses into the "why"s essential to our humanity?

# ABOUT THE AUTHOR

*PHOTOGRAPH BY JAY FRANCO*

Marcus Sakey's books have sold more than a million copies and been translated into dozens of languages. He lives in Chicago with his wife and daughter.

For more information, visit MarcusSakey.com.